I0691517

So many of you have been waiting for the journey to continue...The time has come...Take a stroll through the New World...and stay awhile.

The Book of Joe

The Fall of The Realm

Table of Contents

Chapter 1

  Soaring. The nonexistent wind hits my face with alarming speed and threatens to tear the dark, golden robes from my body. I see His Earth as my cloudy skies as the ceiling to The Abyss, my new home, is only a few miles high. I soar as a caged Eagle; As close as I can to the jagged rocks without colliding with them. It should be a crime, to give someone wings, and hold them absent from the sky. I soar as long as I can on every single phantom day, my New World meditation, with music filling my soul. The music of my sweet Sasha is forever playing in my heart. I listen to her singing almost every minute of every day here in this New Hell, known as The Abyss. Since her first day with me, her beautiful voice has filled my halls.

  I turn over on my back, soaring as I did during my last embrace with her in the New World, and watch as the rocks speed past. I feel weightless, as if an invisible ocean is holding me and readies itself to throw me into the stones that pass me so violently.

  I wish for the sky, to use my true wings again.

  A phantom pain shoots through the arch of my left wing as I find myself suddenly spinning towards my kingdoms floor.

  Should of been watching out for those rocks, you moron.

  I regain my senses in time to recover my glide as my wing shoots strange sensations all the while. I'm the ruler of the The Abyss, and yet I still feel some sort of pain, and will do so as long as I hold onto the Human element inside me.

A blessing.

Bringing myself to a glide, I land next to a pillar of stone that stands miles high, one of hundreds of millions that run throughout my home. The Abyss was a giant place before I inherited it, stretching the distance of eternity. It was the darkest place in existence before I took over and was consumed by a void of darkness. It now stands well lit, with small lights glowing along the sides of the pillars running all the way to the false clouds above. It was the only concession I asked for. I lived my mortal life in the darkness. I want my soul to always be in the light. I'd yet to explore it all freely, only going to the populations of lost souls needing guidance. I'd found every soul in The Abyss, a remarkable feat in and of itself. I've only seen a fraction of this dark world, but felt no need to rush in my exploration when I have an eternity to do so.

Then again, I've only been King for seventy one days.

"You okay, Cuz?"

His steps are always quietly behind me, as an assassins steps should be. There is only two sets of Servant wings in The Abyss, with me possessing one. The other belongs to the Servant known as Robert, or Big, as so many of us have come to know him. He is the only Servant in The Realm or in The Abyss to dress his crown with a black Cowboy hat, with the sides turned high, and a crucifix adorning the front of it. He's the darkest Servant filled with the most light, a truly fierce warrior on loan from The Creator. He protects me while I work, always lurking behind or alongside me as my shadow does.

I turn to greet the giant of a Servant. He stands tall with dark skin accompanying long, dark hair that's offset by his white robes. His eyes are soft and kind, as well as reserved, hiding a killer instinct just below the surface. He is a blessing to me in more ways than one, sharing connections with me from afar. He's laid back for being one that so many have labeled as a 'Bad Ass'.

"I'm good, Brother."

I stretch my wings far and hear the crack in my injured left arch as the bone pops back into place. *Thank goodness for hollow bones.* "Ouch! That didn't sound too good."

He touches my injured wing with his soft hands, caressing the marks from my moment of interrupted solitude. The light inside him warms me and melts the pain away.

"Aaaah man...That feels so much better...Thanks, Big."

He chuckles at me as he pulls his hand away while his eyes betray the smart remark to come.

"You can't fly with the Crows yet, Cuz."

I giggle to myself and nod in a reluctant agreement.

"Yeah...Tell me about it...but the day is coming."

I look at him with the curious eyes of a student while he stands a teacher who withholds the secrets I'm eager to learn.

"Yeah, Cuz...It is, along with the day you won't feel pain anymore."

Turning my gaze to the false ground in front of me, I close my wicked eyes.

I need to feel her. I need to speak to her and hear her voice.

"Joe."

I open my eyes and raise them to see him smiling his kind grin that turns his eyes into dark, quarter moons.

"What's up, Big?"

"Before you run off and play Lover Boy, I need to tell you something...There's news from The New World."

The first news since he came to me to tell me he would be the bearer of news as well as my Guardian. I feel the excitement rising in me, wanting to hear good news.

"Good or bad?"

"Both," he shoots sternly.

Of course there's bad news.

"Start with the bad."

He begins a frantic pace in front of me while the information he holds begins eating him up. He was never short for words, and his lack of them now make me doubtful of the excitement I was just feeling.

"He's raised a hundred thousand and counting. The odds are still on our side, but won't be for much longer."

The Necromancer in the stars, the self proclaimed New Fallen One, has been rounding up the souls of evil men and turning them into nightmares, a new monster of a new sort. A hundred thousand in seventy one days is a feat that stands truly remarkable.

"How do they stand in comparison to their predecessors?"

His gaze becomes as hardened as the pillars surrounding us.

"Fierce."

The 'demons' of the Old Abyss were ancient and lumbering. The 'demons' of the New World, created by the Necromancer, are young and fresh and more lively than the first 'demons' to walk His Earth. It wasn't until I took my throne that I learned the creatures we labeled as demons were actually called 'The Damned'. This new menace being created have been labeled as 'The Cursed', due to them being cursed into existence. My mind immediately falls to those I left behind.

"Any news on my family? I need to know they're safe," I demand with sharpened eyes while fighting the anxiety that slowly rises in my chest.

"They're good, Cousin, don't worry. The Cursed are about fifteen hundred miles from where they are now. Plenty of distance. Also, The Cursed aren't roaming. They're amassing an army, staying together in a tight unit. Only a few dozen have strayed."

He pauses in his words to take a knee in front of me.

"The New World is filled with bad men believing *he's* the next coming. They line the roads for miles, looking for him. They give themselves over to him and he rebirths them into atrocities. He remains elusive, despite a road leading to him...No one has been able to find him."

I find this news troubling. After all that the world has been through, there's still people who refuse to believe what they saw with their own eyes.

It's not like the people of the New World are clueless.

"How in the world can people still follow the Necromancer blindly when they know The Creator above is real?"

His mouth forms a tight frown as he shakes his head in disagreement.

"Because, they're still people...they're not perfect. You know that," he says as he pauses to swat my arm, "we were men once."

A lifetime ago, it seems.

"Lines for miles...but can't be found...Do you think he may be hidden underground?"

He shrugs his shoulders as he gives reply while sporting a bewildered mask as his new face.

8

"Possibly."

"Do me a favor?" I begin, "stand up, Robert. I know it's a 'respect' thing, but it still weirds me out, Cousin. You don't *ever* have to kneel to me...It's just fucking weird."

He rises up chuckling and towers above me, reminding me that he's the most intimidating Servant in any realm.

"You ready for the good news, Cuz?"

I exhale sharply, as good news has become a thing of the past.

"Sure."

He reaches out and places his large hand on my shoulder.

"We have to prepare. We'll be heading to the New World soon."

Clouds, Earth, wind and water, the Sun.

I feel the excitement return at the prospect of flying again.

"When do we leave?"

I don't want to waste a single moment and it can be heard in my breath, no doubt.

"Whenever you're ready, Cuz."

"I'm ready. Let's head back and suit up, grab whatever you may need to take with you."

He releases his hold on me and basks in a new confusion.

"You're not going to tell Sasha the news?"

He's referring to me closing my eyes and sending my soul to her, the way of the old ways of communicating. From what I was told, I'm capable of doing amazing things, if only I can touch my new, immortal soul.

"Not yet. I'd rather tell her in person."

"You know you can do so much more than that...don't you? Joe, you can do anything. You have the most powerful soul, other than The Creator...You just gotta learn to use it."

I look at him with determination in my eyes and a voice filled with hope.

"I will someday...I'm trying."

He pats me on the shoulder and steps back a pace, readying for take off.

Today is the day I beat him.

"C'mon, Robert...I'll race you there."

I smile at him with the hope of a challenge. He chuckles softly at me, shaking his head in disagreement.

"I've had my wings longer than you have, Cuz...I'll always beat you."

Sharp laughter escapes me as I slap his arm playfully.

"Bro, I'm the New Ruler of The Abyss...Get ready to eat my flames."

We smile at each other before we thrust our wings violently, sending us racing towards my home and creating a scorching fire on the ground behind us. I'd never wanted for fire to be a part of my kingdom, but it was something I needed to get used to.

It comes with the territory.

****

With my home in sight, I rush past Robert and take the lead, yet it's only temporary.

"Not today, Cuz!"

With a thrust of his wings he soars past me, racing

ahead and claiming victory as we make it to the base of my nightmares, the giant Kingdom of The Abyss. It resembles a medieval castle, only red and white stones compose it's walls with windows overlooking a view of nothing.

We land and are greeted by several souls waiting outside its doors. It's the people of the Old World, the same to suffer under The Tyrant. They embrace me as their new King, a loving man who is tasked with being their master, and shower me with affection. I hate the fact that I still have a job to do after a mortal lifetime of work, but cannot deny that I love it so.

He told me I was the only choice and that my soul had been forged for this destiny.

I embrace them all, knowing everyone by name, reassuring them that their time for wings would be near. They all touch mine one by one, all fourteen of them, and say praises for The Creator Above. I join them in the praise, telling them of how I stood a man once and defeated the 'Fallen Beast' with only the strength of Him to guide me. It brings them comfort to see it from my point of view. The Creator could work miracles, even through the most ordinary of souls. He would allow them their wings.

I need to find my love.

"Hey Robert, you think you could take over?"

He stands as a true Servant and the only other in my kingdom to offer the warmth of The Creator. He's been the only other who stood in my place while I shared moments with Sasha.

12

"Go find her...Give her the news," he says as a wily grin overtakes his face.

I shake his hand and offer my gratitude as we walk past each other.

"Thanks, Brother."

"Anytime, Cuz."

My kingdom, my home, stands as a nightmarish skyscraper before me. I make my way to the enormous double doors as they crack their seal and creak open, opening to a large empty room where a throne sits in the center. No ordinary throne, it's dull in color and forged with the bones of evil men. I hate it, but even less so as Sasha sits perfectly perched in the center of it.

She looks so angelic in the white and green robes she chose, playing dress up as much a part of her new life as the old one. Her eyes never lost their blue, only growing deeper in the death she was spared from. She gives me a slice of her beauty in the form of her radiant smile and rises slowly as I approach. I stop a dozen feet from her and offer her the smile only she can create.

"Hello, My Sweet Sasha."

She begins her slow stride towards me as her own smile blossoms with every step closer to me.

"Hello...My handsome King."

We embrace and share the same love we did as mortals

by holding each other and letting our faces join as one. Our forbidden kiss and love affair is the only thing we have left from our past life.

I hold her closely, pressing her into me as she lovingly puts her arms around my neck, and I find her mouth so warm and inviting. I savor our kiss, the moment as wonderful as the first time, so long ago when I learned to love this woman. We share our moment a while longer before my soul allows my hands to let her go.

She pulls back and stares into my new eyes, which are now so green and vivid. Her blue eyes reflect my new color.

"I love you, Baby."

I brush her cheek with my thumb, tracing the lines of her beautiful sleeping smile.

"I love you too, My Sweet Sasha."

She slowly flashes the smile that saved my world and created a king.

"I've got news," I spill quickly.

She tilts her head in the flirty little manner I love so much.

"Good or bad?"

I laugh at her as I pull her back into me and feel her body so slender and perfect, and find she truly has the body of a Goddess.

"My mind and yours stand as one, my Soul of Souls," I say as I kiss her head, "as well as our heart...that's exactly what I asked Robert when he said he had news."

"I'll always know your heart, Baby."

I lean back and look into her eyes and find them as blue as the bluest oceans.

"Can I ask you something? When we were alive, it seemed like you could read my thoughts sometimes...Could you?"

She laughs a surprised laughter as her face is suddenly animated.

"I didn't need to read your thoughts to know what you were thinking...Your eyes would say it all."

"It seems like you knew, somehow...When we didn't talk...it was as if we spoke with our eyes."

She brings her face to mine and kisses me softly, causing me to melt into her.

"We were speaking with our souls, my Soul Mate," she whispers.

I feel her loving energy surrounding me, as it has a presence unlike any other. I hold her close once again as I whisper in her ear.

"Tonight's the night."

There is no day and night in The Abyss and I hope my cryptic words give her a hint of our travels to the New World. We hadn't made love since she came to The Abyss, something I'm not prepared to do in this place. I promised her we would again when we returned to the New World.

"Yeah right...Don't tease me, asshole."

I laugh at her and her never-ending lust for me.

She doesn't get it.

"Really, tonight is the night I take you back into my arms and make love to you once again."

She glares at me with evil intentions as her eyes become small, blue daggers.

"There isn't even a fucking night in this place, and you said..."

She brings her face closer to mine slowly as she reads my eyes. Her smile returns in full force.

She gets it now.

"We're going back home?!"

I look at her with mischief while breathing life into an old game.

"Maybe."

"Don't play with me, asshole! Are we?"

"Possibly."

She sighs and shakes her head while rolling her glowing eyes.

"Are you trying to piss me off?"

"Definitely."

She erupts in her sweet laughter as we fall into each others arms one again.

"I can't wait to see everyone again. It seems like it's been a lifetime ago," she confesses through her excitement.

"You've been with me in The Abyss for thirty-three days, today included."

She looks at me with a curious mask as her eyes morph into blue, full moons.

"How do you know how many days it's been?"

"It's just something I know. I was the New Ruler for thirty-eight days when you came to me. I don't know how I know the day count, I just do. I guess it's my Human element that keeps track. I died seventy-one days ago."

Her lovely face paints a picture of horror as her memories force her to relive my death.

"That was the worst thing I've ever fucking seen...watching you die."

Her eyes fight the emotions that now claw their way through the seas I swim in.

"It was necessary. I was supposed to die that day...I'm sorry you had to see it...I'm sorry I wasn't there for *your* day."

Her mouth forms a tight, little line that barely resembles the smile I crave.

"Don't forget, I never died...I was about to...and He saved me. I didn't have to go through the horror of dying."

I give her a heartfelt, playful smile in return.

"I'm so thankful to The Creator that you didn't."

We share a small embrace of our lips. It's a quiet moment that stands one of many that we managed to capture during our time together. It seems that her smallest affections move me the most.

"So...*Why* exactly are we going back? I know something happened, and it can't be good if *we're* going."

I take a false breath and deliver the bad news.

"He raised an army...The Necromancer...He has a new breed of demon he created...They call them 'The Cursed'...and so far he's at a hundred thousand strong."

She places her hand on my hip and squeezes lightly.

"You'll need your sword," she says while looking up at me with her sweet eyes.

"You'll need yours too, Sasha...The New World needs a couple of bad motherfuckers."

****

The dusk approaches in the New World as the seven remaining prepare their feast in the store, sitting at their dinner table, in the place they called home for the past two months. They turned it into a shrine of sorts to honor their fallen friends. They rarely went home anymore, instead choosing the comforts of a world that no longer existed. A world with a friend named Joe, and his beloved Sasha.

"I miss Joe," Greg speaks to the air, even though there are six souls surrounding him.

"I think we all do, Greg," Carmen replies.

John chuckles to himself while setting the plates as everyone else wallows in their misery. Greg turns to him as a look of offense crosses his young features.

19

"What?"

"Nothing, Friend...I was just thinking of how we all miss the Devil."

He bellows his big laughter and everyone joins as John suddenly becomes the life of the party.

In his usual fashion, Danny brings down the mood.

"You guys remember what he told us on his last days? He told us we would have to spread the word about what happened...So far, we haven't seen anyone else but us...and those three guys that killed Sasha."

"She's not dead, Danny," Amy J. coos softly.

"Well she's not here, Amy," Danny retaliates.

"God saved her," she continues, "so she didn't have to die. He can save us all, Honey."

Dannys' face becomes a portrait of concern as he leans in.

"My point is," Danny continues sounding annoyed, "you think we're gonna get in trouble?"

They look at each other with the hopes that the other has good news to shed on the subject.

"I don't think we'll be in trouble. Joe wasn't a bad man, he's not a bad...Devil? Didn't he call himself 'The Fallen One'?" Amy K. sits confused by her own words, but she continues anyway.

"What *is* Joe? Who is he? Do we still call him that or do we refer to him as...you know?"

Greg stands suddenly and sends his chair screeching backwards behind him.

"HE'S OUR BROTHER!"

The silence is deafening and as thick as snow and just as heavy. No one looks at Greg while his chest heaves in a rapid race with his thoughts.

"I'm sorry, Amy K., it's just that...He's our brother...He isn't evil...we shouldn't think of him as...the Devil."

"I'm sorry, I didn't mean it like that...I know you miss him an awful lot."

He seizes the sobs in his skinny chest, but the tears flow and betray him. He misses his big brother and it hurts him to live out his days *without* his best friend by his side.

"It's okay, Honey," Amy J. says softly, "we all miss him so terribly much...Him *and* Sasha. But we know that they are both in a better place...It's so sad that they can't be together...but, he's safe where he's at and Sasha is safe in...Heaven? The Realm? Whatever they call it, they're both safe, Honey."

He wipes the tears away as John approaches him and places an arm around his shoulder.

"That has to be the worst part of all this," Greg says through the lump in his throat, " Joe loved Sasha so much and didn't want anything else but to spend his life with her. They were together for what? Exactly *one day*?..How fucked up is that?"

Greg was always the one to hold a grudge and could never let anything go.

"You know what, Friend? Do you remember how happy he was on that last day? Him and his gal made it count...He left this world a happy man."

John wraps his arms around him and hugs him tight.

"Don't worry, Friend...I promise you he's happy."

"He's in The Abyss, John...Alone...How happy could he be?" Danny offers his take and tries to be positive for his brother.

"Don't forget he's the one running The Abyss," he pauses to look around the table, "he can have anything he wants. That doesn't sound *too* bad to me."

"Not everything," Greg says softly.

"I pray they find each other again someday," Amy J. adds as her face begins fighting the tears.

Will stands up as his towering figure eclipses Carmen and brushes aside the golden mane that now hangs past his ears.

"This is gonna sound really stupid, but...can we say our dinner blessing to Joe?"

John turns to Will and reminds him of the words I spoke to them before leaving this world.

"He said we are The Creators children, not his...and we could never pray to him. He said the best thing we could hope for in the next life is to see His Gates. Joe isn't evil, but he *is* The Fallen One...it's a calling he was destined to answer. He's a good man, one of the best, and I understand why he was chosen...only a Servant could lead the way...but he remains the New Ruler of The Abyss."

He gives Will a frown as he shakes his head.

"I'm sorry, Friend, but Joe said himself *not* to do that."

Will returns to his seat, but sorrow moves him in slow motion. Carmen leans over and puts her arm around his waist and cuddles her big, simple bear.

Greg quickly sets his sights back on John.

"The New Ruler of The Abyss...Does that sound like being happy?"

"Friend, has it ever occurred to you that maybe I miss that man just as much as you do? He was my friend, as well as yours. I pray he's happy, Greg. I pray to The Creator every night to take good care of our friend, to take care of Sasha, and to one day give them a pass to see each other somehow. I pray for

Joes happiness. Believe me, Friend...I pray. I want nothing more than to believe our friend is happy."

Greg swallows the knot in his throat before speaking.

"I'm sorry, Bro...I know he loved you, John. We should all pray he's happy."

"I'm sure wherever he is, he's doing just fine, Friend."

****

"You know what to do, Brother."

Robert turns his head slightly, glancing at me from the corner of his eyes from under his black hat. The sight in front of us holds our attention.

"I got you, Cuz. When you come back, you'll be greeted by reformed warriors...forged to defend the Realms, yours and His."

I don't turn towards him as he addresses me, as I can only watching the souls in front of me.

"Not too shabby," I say to myself.

He chuckles as he watches the ground moving in front of us, given motion by the gathering of souls in my Abysmal front lawn.

"It's a good start, Cuz. These are the ones with the most potential...Mistakes are almost paid and ready for wings...The best of your twisted lot."

I chuckle to myself and pat him on the back. It's comforting to know so many will be able to stand beside us.

We stand on my balcony, one of hundreds, with ours being the equivalent of a 'Penthouse'. The Abyss shakes with the movement of two hundred and fifty thousand souls, all eager to learn and fight alongside their new king. I look down at their faces, men and women of all ages and creeds, and see the future Servants that will be at my side for the confrontation to come. I raise my hands to them as the clamor settles down.

"May The Creator of all stand with you!"

My voice shakes the very ground as if thunder lies within it.

"And also with you!"

They add their own thunder, a quarter of a million souls united in one voice.

"The moment is coming...the time when I will need you, when The Creator himself, will need you...You can rise up with me to the New World and possibly the very Realm, if you but give your soul to The Creator and wage war against His enemies. I am the Ruler of The Abyss. I give my soul to Him to use as He deems fit."

I point out into the crowd, running my finger over so many faces and memorize every single one, down to their eye color.

"You!...Can be my vengeful hands and fight for Him. You!...Can redeem yourselves in His Eyes. You!...Can become the Servants I believe you to be. Train hard in the time to come...When we rise up to the Earth to meet our foes...We will show them that The True Abyss came with us!"

A deafening cheer shakes the world to its core as the fires of The Abyss are stoked in unity. They will be fierce Servants, ready to claim the lives of The Cursed for the very Creator who sent them away. Such is the power of love.

Robert laughs as he turns to me and playfully tags my arm.

"That was one Hell of a speech, Cousin!"

I smile, feeling rejuvenated as Sasha comes up beside me and squeezes me tight.

"He's a smooth talker...It's how he stole my heart," she confesses while cracking a smile.

Robert glances at her with his smile already a permanent fixture on his face.

"I've known him a long time. He's always been a smooth-ass talker," he informs her.

"I fall in love with his words every day. I can get lost in his voice."

Robert looks at me and chuckles again.

"You're blessed, Cuz...I can't say it enough."

I turn and wrap my arms around Sasha and pull her close to me.

"You don't have to tell me that, Brother. I feel blessed."

He turns to the crowd and finds them in a frenzy for combat.

"Give me a little time with them," he turns back to me, "and you'll come back to an army worthy of The Realm."

Mimicking a Human characteristic I no longer need, I draw in a deep breath.

"Give me an army worthy of The Realm, but capable of bringing the Old Hell with them."

His face comes to life as his body fills with adrenaline. He offers a bump of his fist and finds me accepting his offer.

"Ha! Right on, Cuz!"

As he turns to face the crowd, Sasha hugs me tight and whispers in a seductive voice only my ears can hear.

"Tonight...You'll be in Heaven...when I bring the Hell."

I lift her up and hold her face close to mine and reciprocate my own secret words.

"Let's find us a shower, and knock the fucking walls down."

She squeals as the memories come rushing back to her and her small laugh begins filling my ear.

"Let's find the house we were going to live in, Baby...then knock those fucking walls down...I need you inside me."

I place my hand on her firm backside and squeeze it gently while my mouth begins caressing her neck. She shivers as she feels the desire in my hands once again while small moans pass her lips. I allow my lips to glide lightly over her skin before I end the tease and set her to her feet.

Robert's still here, fool.

I turn to him and find that he's still watching the crowd, yet feel the need to apologize anyway.

"Sorry, Brother...I lost myself in a moment."

"No need to apologize. Get ready to go, the both of you. Your kingdom is in good hands."

He finds my eyes and offers a reassuring nod before turning from me and pacing towards his new duties.

"I've got a lot of work to do."

Sasha jumps on me the moment he disappears from sight and my hands suddenly find all the parts of her body I so missed. I let my hands roam everywhere, giving the most attention to the place she wants me most. She still has her earthly body and mine stands its' reflection. I feel lust as much as she does, and find it a comfort that the urges came along with my new vessel.

She reaches down between us and guides her hand to her favorite part of me, grasping a handful and moaning between the soft laughter that escapes her lips.

"You're still the King."

I kiss her on her neck and allow my tongue to follow the slender curve of it to her collarbone.

"Tonight, I'll make you my Dirty Little Queen."

She laughs as she pushes me back a bit before her smoldering blue eyes become lively and playful.

"Keep the animal caged for now. I really want to see everyone as soon as we get up there," she assures while placing her hand on my chest, "we'll have our time."

She sounds like me and my voice is starting to reflect hers.

"We fucking better...Mmmmph! The fucking things I'm gonna *do to you*," I growl through clenched

29

teeth.

She laughs at the beast within me who's only born in her sexual presence.

"We will, Baby...I'm gonna fuck you silly."

There's my girl.

We share a laugh and embrace for another session of soulful kisses. I'm careful to keep the beast in its' cage.

****

"He said he would come back to us, Honey."

Greg looks at Amy J. as they all sit around the lantern in the old store while reading passages from The Book of Joe.

"I know he did...I wish we knew *when* is all."

"I can wait for that day," Danny begins, "cause he said when he comes back, we would all have to play a part in the next chapter of the *whole fucking world*. That sounds like a lot of fucking work. Won't be much 'down time' when he comes back."

Gregs' voice becomes soft as he glances at Danny.

"Our whole life is *down time* right now, Bro. When he comes back, we'll have a purpose. We'll get to hang out with Joe again."

"I miss his crazy ass too," Carmen joins in, "you know, he really had a way of making you feel good, making you happy to be alive and keep trying even though it seemed hopeless."

"Working with souls...That's what he did," John voices as he revisits the memory of our last supper.

They sit quietly and as calm as the night around them. It lasts for a fleeting moment as Amy K. breaks the silence.

"What do you think Sasha's doing in Heaven? Oh wait, The Realm, as they called it. I'm not sure I'm ever gonna get used to calling it that...Anyways, you think she still wallows in her misery, missing Joe? If so, that sounds like a terrible eternity. The Realm is supposed to be about happiness, right?"

Will finally joins the discussion, asking what should be the most obvious question.

"How are you all so sure she went to The Realm? Yeah, The Creator saved her, but that doesn't mean he took her in...He could of sent her to Joe."

They all wear the same stunned look. The thought never crossed their minds and suddenly, it's Will that takes the mantel of genius, for once.

Greg begins to laugh softly while his smile replaces his

ever-loitering frown.

"If He gave Sasha a choice..."

"There would have been *no* choice," Danny finishes for him.

Carmen giggles quietly, looking like a tiny mouse next to her giant of a husband.

"I can see that girl tearing away the ground with her bare hands to get to Joe, hahaaa!"

They all share a small laughter until it's interrupted by a small thud that resonates from the back room, known as my old office. On cue, they stand and pick up the weapons resting beside their chairs. Their steel hasn't left their side since the night they met The Serpent.

John motions to Greg and Danny to follow him as his bamboo cane flashes its' shiny silver.

"Wait," Greg whispers.

Everyone focuses on his face as his voice begins trembling though his words.

"Remember what Joe said about reading nature and following the signs?...I have a feeling this is what he was talking about."

John cocks his head confused and his brow wears the same expression.

"If there isn't anything back there," Greg continues, "we find the source of the noise...What if The Creator is giving us a sign right now?"

"Honey, there's something in the store...and I don't think it's Gods work," Amy J. says while raising her Katana slightly and sharpening her eyes for battle.

"I think Greg may be right," Will says, causing all to focus their attention on him.

"I have a feeling too...We were just talking about Joe and Sasha...Maybe The Creator knows how miserable we are and he wants to cheer us up."

Danny rubs his swords together in anticipation of battle. His swords, under his guidance, have become a deadly duo, as I promised him they would be.

"Fuck all that. I'm not standing here talking about finding shapes in clouds and shit when there might be a fucking monster in here. Let's go."

He makes his way from the table and the guys follow, except for Will. He protects the ladies and wouldn't dare leave his lovers side.

They move as fast and deadly as they were taught to be, keeping their weapons pointed to the ground, creating the illusion of a centipede with sharpened metal legs. The lanterns in the room give the faintest glow all the way to the office door, giving them just enough sight to see an empty hallway.

John gazes at everyone and nods his head to give them

the command to charge into war.

They rush to the door as if their feet are wrapped in cotton, with their steps never landing or making a sound. The office is deadly silent inside, calming their nerves as they rise up from their crouched positions. Lessons of the past taught them well. The Damned were never this quiet. Danny retreats to the group and retrieves a lantern to aid in their inspection.

John opens the door slowly as my office sits as it always had, a scattered mess of pens and CDs resting on a small desk. They walk in quietly before Greg raises his arms and pauses all movement.

He begins to whisper with desperation in his voice.

"God...Creator....Whoever you might be...If you left us a sign...Please, let us see it."

****

"Damn, Baby...You look so fucking hot."

I giggle as I look at Sasha, standing so radiant in her black and blue war robes I created just for her. A thicker material designed for combat, it hangs perfectly on her body, along with her Long sword that hangs from her waist. I continue to fumble with my breastplate clumsily, as if I'm some sort of medieval Squire and not the leader of The Abyss. Black and shining with a small Moon in the center, it's a bit more flashy than I had hoped for. Sasha had it made, just for me, and teased that she wanted me to look as good as she saw me.

"Why did you pick the Moon, Sasha? Don't get me wrong, I love it...I'm just curious."

"Well," she begins while running a hand across the small emblem, "If The Creator represents the light, and the Sun...You should represent the night...and the Moon is the ruler of the night sky...You're my Moon, Baby...That's just how I see you."

Backing up, I look her up and down and want nothing more than to tell her how I see her beauty. If I'm the Moon in her world, she is definitely the Stars I swim in.

"Sasha, you look..."

The room around me vanishes and leaves me alone in a darkness that seems to have no top or bottom. I'm incased inside some sort of void, yet I can hear Sashas' voice in the distance.

"Joe? Baby, what's happening?!"

"It's okay, Sasha!...I'm okay!"

I feel phantom hands touching my face, small and delicate, and know that she's holding my face. It's a strange sensation, to be disconnected from my physical body.

"Something's wrong...They need me...Look down."

"What?"

"Not you, Sasha...Look down!"

I feel her arms wrap around my waist and she begins squeezing me. I can feel the fear that has consumed her in her grasp.

A hollow ring fills my ears and grows into a maddening screech. I feel their hopelessness, followed by them feeling lost and confused, unknowing of what to do.

I can feel Greg...It's really you, Little Brother.

I point my face high to the darkness overhead and pray I'm not hidden too far into its' depths. I let out a roar that seems to shake the very world.

"LOOOOK DOOOOWWWNNNN!"

****

Looking around the office, they pause and stare at each other in disbelief.

"Did you guys hear that?"

Greg's eyes are almost as large as his head while John slowly nods his head in agreement.

"Look down...Someone just whispered to...*look down*."

Their eyes fall to the floor and begin searching the scattered mess of pens that litter the ground around them. Confusion sets in Dannys mind as he realizes they have no clue

36

what their searching for.

"What are we supposed to be looking for?"

"I have no idea, Friend. Joe never explained that part. I guess we find what made the noise?"

Greg raises his pointed finger to the highest point of the back wall where a perfect, invisible square resides among the dust. He follows his finger down to the small painting resting on the ground in front of them.

"*That's* what made the noise."

They walk over and examine the painting. A small Moon sits over a set of trees and casts its' light over the treetops. It's a simple painting of a simple Moon, leaving Danny as confused as ever.

"What does it mean?"

"It's not the painting itself, Friend...We need to look around the area too, I believe."

Gregs' voice becomes a whisper as he points at the painting on the ground.

"No...we don't. Look under the frame."

A series of scratch papers blanket the ground under the painting, as my handwriting peeks up at the three faces above. Greg reaches down and lifts the painting before passing it to Danny. He retrieves my notes and breathes life into the first words.

"We won't give up, we will not rest...until we've passed Your Final Test."

"We may fall short but never fall, until the day You need us all."

"We'll survive the horrors, Your ruined Sun....when the Moon rises, we'll be joined as one."

"My soul may plummet, but you'll know I'm saved...on the day I speak to you..."

Greg drops the notes and gasps before wailing in agony. Danny and John look at each other with a renewed horror, brought about from my words stopping Gregs heart. Danny reaches down and fetches my notes. He shoots John a look of wonder as he finishes the last line.

"From beyond the grave."

****

A deafening crack as loud as a lightning strike rings in my ears as the Underworld comes back to me to find Sasha squeezing the afterlife out of my immortal soul.

"Sasha...I'm here."

She releases me and grabs my face while panic tightens her delicate features.

"What the fuck happened just now?"

38

Tell her.

"I'm not really sure."

She glares at me and reminds me that the ghost of the Evil Sasha is always lurking about.

She knows you're lying.

"Baby...Look at me...I love you...What the fuck just happened?"

I smile at her and step back, proving I'm the worst Prince of Lies to ever be.

"The Creator told me I have an extraordinary soul, capable of doing great things. I don't know how to do anything though, other than talk to you. Robert said I needed to learn how to use it...I didn't try to do it just now, but I felt the entire group. They're all so sad...They miss us...I was surrounded by darkness...I couldn't see anything. I could hear you, but nothing else. I felt them though...and the first thought to come to my mind was..."

"Look down...You were screaming it," she finishes with wide, blue eyes.

"I think...I think they may have heard me."

"The whole fucking planet just heard you. The whole place shook and your eyes turned solid black, like you were empty."

I had a hunch I looked scary, judging by the panic in her voice.

39

"I'm sorry, Love. I didn't try to do it...Maybe they needed me so bad I somehow felt them. Maybe I was relaying a message...I have no idea why I said that."

She holds me close once again and I feel her body trembling against mine. She will not lose her King again.

"You've always had a powerful soul, even back when we were human. It's always shone in your eyes."

The same story everywhere I go.

"I hope I was strong enough for them to hear my voice."

"If you weren't, it doesn't matter, Baby...We'll see them later."

They need us.

"No, My Soul, we're going to see them right now."

Grabbing her hand, I turn towards the door and lead her to our destiny.

****

"It was Joes voice...I'm sure of it."

Everyone sits around the table as Greg finishes the tale of our otherworldly encounter that leaves mouths hanging and eyebrows raising.

"What if it was a ghost?" Carmen asks.

"Joe said there weren't *any* ghosts left in the world," Danny answers.

Greg retakes his seat before repeating himself like a scratched record.

"It was Joe."

"I have to agree with Greg. It sounded an awful lot like Joe," John adds.

Amy K. wears her worrisome painted face and shakes her head, unable to grasp that they heard a voice from beyond.

"How is that possible?"

John turns his attention to her and places a hand on hers.

"I have no idea, Ma'am. We've found a lot of things are possible in this New World... ...things unheard of...I think Greg is right on this one...it was Joe."

Greg sits back in his chair and releases a relieved gasp.

"It was Joe...We love you, Bro!"

He screams towards the sky above, forgetting that the entrance to The Abyss sits somewhere below his feet. They all share a quiet laugh before Greg jumps from his seat as an epiphany explodes across his face.

"From beyond the grave! From beyond the grave! We need to go to Joes' grave!"

Everyone sits startled by his new request and look at each other to see they share the same sentiment.

"Right now?" Danny asks.

"When the Moon rises, we'll be joined as one," Greg states.

He looks at everyone with hope in his eyes, wanting more than ever to see his brother. John nods his head slowly and rises from his seat.

"We can go, Friend, just the two of us."

"Screw that! I'm going!" Carmen shrieks.

"Fuck it, let's all go," Danny adds.

They glance at each other and study their faces before nodding in agreement. Amy K. voices the elephant in the room.

"What if he's not there?"

Greg looks at her and smiles his childish grin.

"Then we make our peace with our Bro, and let him do his thing....and try to move on."

They all rise slowly and retrieve their weapons while looking at each other with sorrow. They won't be wearing the expression for long.

****

The ceiling of The Abyss stands over us as I take my lover into my arms and hold her in an empty wasteland around a mile from my kingdom. Robert stands a few feet away and takes his usual position as a Guardian coach to The Fallen One.

"Remember Cuz, the New World is *your* domain. You can control it as you wish, once you get there."

"So...I can just part my hands and the Earth will split open?"

He chuckles as he takes a step back.

"If that's how you want to do it, you can. Don't forget though; You're not on Earth anymore. The entrance to the Abyss is underground, but not The Abyss itself. The Realm isn't in the clouds any more than The Abyss is underground...Only the entrances lie there. Wait until you're there before you try parting any dirt with your hands, Crazy."

He chuckles and salutes me before turning and walking away from us. We watch him for a moment as his giant body sways and animates his giant robes. I return my gaze to Sasha and peer into the blue eyes that will always hold my attention. She smiles at me and holds me tighter as her flawless face begins making my dead heart race.

"We going for a ride?"

She smiles wider than ever, remembering our last embrace in the Sunlight.

"Hold on tight."

She buries her face in my chest as I raise a fist towards the jagged rocks above. I tense up as my wings spread wide, ready to catch the air and send us home. I thrust hard, catapulting us into the air and straight towards the stones and ground we call our clouds.

The world around me shatters as my fist makes an impact and sends stones and dirt falling all around us. My knuckles prove as sharp as my blade, cutting through the ground with alarming efficiency. I hear Sasha squealing with excitement, along with the sounds of ruin that I create.

Hang on guys, we're coming.

****

They hold hands around the only known entrance to The Abyss; The crater where it all began and ended, yet it's now sealed and full of dirt. The place where The Serpent came to the New World is also my grave. The Creator sealed the ground around me when I stepped into the pit and made sure no evil would ever step through again. I remember everyones face when I took my leap of faith and could feel the sorrow spread out amongst the group. I remember smiling at them as I winked, a gesture of positive energy while I fell to a very negative place. I remember their prayers from that day. It's the same ones they're giving breath to now.

"All praise be to You, the true and only Creator...Amen," they finish.

They release their hold and allow their arms to fall flatly to their sides while looking at each other and holding their collective breath. In her usual fashion, Amy K. breaks the silence.

"Did it work?"

"Prayer always works, Honey," her sister informs her, "but the answer comes in its own time."

"So we wait then?"

They all glance at Greg as his heart stands the most wounded among them.

"What do you wanna do, Partner?" John asks, sensing the overwhelming disappointment in him.

"I guess...we go home...if that's okay with everyone."

"Sure, Greg...Let's head back home," Will says softly.

They all huddle together and begin the trek back to the store that stood as a home to me. They make it a short distance before the ground shakes suddenly, pausing them in their tracks. It stops as quickly as it starts, but leaves a small rumble vibrating their feet.

Greg whispers loudly enough to address them all.

"It's Joe."

Chapter 2

It happens so quickly I barely see it, but feel it as we pass through it. Through all the rocks and dirt, we pass through the portal that leads back into the New World. Whatever grounds we were in before was not of the Earth, and it leaves me wondering on what world exactly The Abyss inhabits.

That flash. That's what Robert was talking about.

"The Realm isn't in the clouds any more than The Abyss is underground...Only the entrances lie there."

She screams between fits of laughter as we tear the Earth apart and my laugh joins hers. I shred through it with ease and am surprised to find my body is so much stronger than it's ever been. I feel my soul burning with Light, and not the Hellish fires I would expect. I truly feel like an unstoppable force.

The Earth becomes soft and I feel the ground becoming moist, assuring me we're almost to the surface of the New World.

Almost there.

"Here we go, Baby! Wooooo!"

I laugh at her outburst before joining in the excitement with her. The ground explodes as fresh air once again graces my face and I continue our ascent with a thrust of my wings, sending us high into the true clouds that we missed so much. Sasha clings to her Dark Servant and continues giggling before realizing we're hanging in the air. Still wearing the smile of my dreams, she looks at me and pushes the hair from my face.

Kiss her you fool.

I draw her lips close to mine and hold her in my arms on His World once again as our souls become as much alive as our hands. I hold her face and enjoy the soft comforts, running my hands through her brown hair while she wraps her legs around my waist. We hold each other in the bright moonlight, so far above the New World. This first moment back on Earth will be ours.

We drift down following the trail of dust our grand entrance created, with smoke and dust consuming the world around the new path to The Abyss. Even through all the haze, I get the feeling that we're being studied by curious eyes, but can feel the love and wonderment they all exude.

Our Earthly family is here.

We make it to the ground at the very edge of the new crater as my love stands by my side and squeezes my hand. Even through the haze I can see her eyes, the only eyes capable of loving me, so soft and blue. She stands my loving Sasha and I remind her of it so.

"I love you, Sasha...I'm so thankful I have an eternity with you."

"I love you too, Baby...To the end of fucking time."

We coo softly together like true Lovebirds as we exit the edge of the miniature dust storm my wings unleashed to find seven sets of mesmerized eyes. We stand quietly facing each other, my Dark Queen and I standing opposite the seven people we survived with in the New World. Their energy more otherworldly than my own, their hearts beat in unison. In this moment I realize I can smell their souls, the same talent I had when I stood mortal and picked up on Sashas. I step forward the same moment Greg does and we begin a slow march to a reunion he craves more than the air he breathes.

I look at him as if I'm experiencing a dream come true. He looks at me as if I'm a dream.

"Hey, Bro...I missed you, Little Brother."

He cracks the huge grin I'd hoped for and it's accompanied by a tranquil gaze.

"Is this real?...It's really you, isn't it, Bro?...I can't believe you're here."

"Well, you better believe it," Sasha says as she joins me.

Greg and I lunge forward in the same instant and lock ourselves into a deathly hug while screaming to the Heavens with tears stinging our eyes.

My family is whole again.

They surround us screaming in joy as the hugs and kisses abound. Their faces are a blur as they pull Sasha and I in all directions to offer their long lost affections. The girls want to talk to Sasha and the guys stand equally full of questions and wonder as the world spins with love. I'm lost to it all, not knowing which question to answer first. Danny throws his stubby hands in the air and halts the madness.

"Everyone shut the fuck up!"

We all stand shocked as we meet Dannys' gaze.

"I wanna talk to King Salami."

We laugh together again, a sound once heard long ago in the New World, and it would be the first of many. As Fate would always have it, we don't have a lot of time, but enough time to enjoy ourselves before our work begins.

"I've missed all you guys so much!" I scream in excitement. They all laugh as they echo the same sentiments.

"What's your...home like?" Amy K. asks in a shy voice.

"It's as hot as Hell, Amy," Sasha responds before bursting with laughter.

We join her before I give the details about the home I call The Abyss; The same place they call 'The True Hell'.

"When I arrived, it was all smoke and fire in every direction, with pillars of flames stretching miles high. Basically, it's what we were taught what Hell would be like. As soon as my feet touched the ground, the flames extinguished, revealing a kingdom so big I've yet to explore it all. I have a home with Sasha...It's this big ass, dark castle that we've filled with light. The Abyss was dark and unforgiving before it became mine. It now stands a well-lit, barren wasteland, with vast amounts of nothing stretching in all directions. Only sad people remain, tolling under the weight of their own misery...until they've earned their wings."

"Earn their wings?"

Amy K. stands intrigued, remembering the first time she saw a Servant and labeled him an Angel.

"Yes," I say to her and nod, "earn their wings. When they pay for all the bad they did, I give them wings and send them home. All of The Creators creations belong in The Realm...except for me, of course."

They all stand quietly in awe as the revelation of my new home startles their souls. Carmen is the first to speak.

"So...You and Sasha *finally* got your home together...I'm so happy for you two!"

Will stands with his own question he asked earlier in the evening.

"Hey Sasha, how did you get to The Abyss?

I love hearing this story.

"When I was saved, He pulled me up into the light. I felt so sad knowing I wasn't able to follow Joe. When I reached the end of the light, I was in a small room alone. His voice was all around me. He gave me a choice. He said I could rest in The Realm, or I could follow Joe to The Abyss for all of eternity. There would be no coming back to The Realm, He made me aware of that. When I agreed it's what I truly wanted, a young man entered the room, along with a petite, beautiful woman. It was Joes wife and son. She handed me a letter to give to him before she hugged me and told me to take care of him. His son told me to tell him how proud he was of his father. We had a lengthy conversation about Joe and what it was like for her to love him, and how hard it was for her to leave him. We bonded the only way two women can who love the same man...We became friends in that moment. She wished me well and they left the room. He commanded me to close my eyes and when I opened them...I was standing in front of Joe."

The ladies begin to weep as the guys do their best impression of tough guys, fighting to hide the happy tears.

"Damn, that's beautiful," Danny begins before turning to me, "what went through your mind when you saw her?"

My turn to tell the story she loves.

"I was walking in the emptiness, a barren field full of pillars as far as the eye could see. I was missing Sasha, thinking about her every minute we were apart. The ground shook slightly before a vicious lightning bolt hit the ground in front of me...and there she stood...eyes closed with a smile on her face. I looked up at the ground above me and whispered..."

She turns to me and smiles as she finishes the story.

"My heart is mine again."

Tears fall down my face as I relive the moment my loving Sasha was returned to me. We embrace as we share the kiss we did on that day, so long ago.

"That's so wonderful. We all prayed The Creator would let you be together," Amy J., confesses.

I release my new hold on Sasha and meet Gregs stare.

Did it work?

"Hey, Bro...Look down."

I crack a small smile as he points at me while his eyes shoot wide open.

"I KNEW IT WAS YOU, BRO!!!"

He jumps forward in my arms while laughing to the moon above. All of our laughter reaches sky high as the shock and awe of our conversation from beyond the grave moves us all to utter amazement.

"How did you do that?!" Greg asks in a loud breath.

"I really don't know...I can do a lot of great things, but haven't figured out *how* to do them."

"His eyes turned black as fuck and he screamed so loud it shook the world. It was scary at first, but afterwards, I had never felt so turned on by him," Sasha finishes while placing her arms around my waist and swaying her body into mine.

"You screamed? We heard your voice as a whisper while..." John begins, before I cut him off.

"Wow, just a whisper?" I interrupt confused, with my eyes no doubt screaming the emotion.

"Yes, Friend, just a whisper," John concludes.

"Shit, he screamed so loud I thought the walls were gonna fall down around us."

Sasha turns her blue gems to me as they fill with

excitement.

"You're voice made it all the way from The Abyss."

"Yeah," I quietly agree, "in the form of a whisper."

She senses the disappointment in me and runs her slender hand through my hair before resting it on my cheek.

"Baby...You *are* powerful. The most powerful person I've ever met," she pauses to place both her hands on my cheeks while staring deeply into my eyes, " Your voice traveled all the way from another dimension...Think about that."

I pull her into me and kiss the top of her head and allow her soul to fill my senses the way water fills a glass.

"You're right, My Love...I just wish I was able to do more."

"You will in time, Baby," she consoles and wraps her arm around me to constricts me once again. Greg pats me playfully on the arm while smiling from ear to ear.

"You hungry, Bro? It's almost time for dinner."

Sasha and I both turn to him with small, tight smiles.

"We don't eat, Greg," Sasha informs him.

"You...don't eat?"

"No, Brother," I begin, "we also don't sleep or need to breathe."

"Whaaat?"

He stands completely dumbfounded with his dark eyes suddenly bright and wide and full of questions.

"We're immortal, Greg. We still have bodies of flesh and bone...but we are both eternal now. Sasha never died, but her human need for nourishment did. The only human urge we still share with you guys is...well...you can figure it out."

At least I hope we still can.

He smirks at me as a drunken Frat boy would.

Of course he was wondering. Always a kid.

"But, I won't pass up the pleasures of all your company. It's the reason we're here tonight."

Danny grabs my shoulder and turns me towards him.

 "You're not here to put us to work?"

They all hold their breath as their hearts freeze in their chests while waiting for a reply.

"Not yet. *Right now* is all about you guys. We needed to see you."

"Something tells me there is a workload coming though, isn't there?" John asks firmly.

I turn to John to answer his stern words with softer

ones.

"Yes Sir...A workload indeed."

I look at them all with smiling eyes, in the hope of alleviating their concerns.

"But, not today...not soon, either. There is work to be done on my part before your work begins. I'm not sure how much time we have for our visit. I know we need to make the most of it and enjoy our time together...Let's head to the store, I'm curious to see my old home." Greg nods to me as he steps aside and waves his arms in an inviting gesture.

"Lead the way, Bro."

I smile as I take Sashas hand in mine.

"I'd be happy to, Little Brother."

****

The glass stands absent with plywood taking its place as the door to my old home is now unrecognizable. The Damned shattered the glass the night we layed waste to six of them and I finished the job of destroying it in my panic to catch Sasha.

This is no doubt Johns' handy work.

I push the door open to a familiar sight, the store of old not changing much. Sasha walks beside me as we lead the group, with all of them watching for our reaction. We pace over to the table, half setup and left with haste to meet our arrival. Sasha and I remove our swords and lean them against a nearby chair.

They have very little food.

"What was on the menu tonight?"

Amy J. marches forward quickly and eager to explain the cuisine as she inspects it.

Always the passionate cook.

"Well, I didn't have much to work with, *but,* I had a few fresh carrots from the garden," she pauses and turns to me, "which started growing, by the way, the week you left, Honey, and also some canned corn..."

"Hold up!" I startle her with my abrupt words."You guys are still eating corn?"

I place my hand on my forehead in disbelief. I had grown to hate corn by the time I no longer needed it.

I have to do something.

"There isn't much else to eat, Honey, but we get by just fine, don't we?" She says while glancing at the group.

I take a phantom breath and ruffle my wings as I walk up to the table and grab an empty plate, placing it perfectly

56

centered in front of me. I grab the largest bowl and place it face down slowly over the plate, covering it completely.

Our encounter was brief, but I clearly remember His words.

"When you were My creation, you always tested your mind. You were right, but, you were also confused. You didn't realize you were testing your soul as well. If the soul believes something and the mind cannot see otherwise, the soul makes it real. You've always known this. It is how you will become a True Ruler, when you touch your new, immortal soul."

"You guys want a Steak and Lobster entree? Or burgers? Or...well, anything?"

Something stirs deep within my chest, almost like an unholy adrenaline. It gives me confidence, knowing some sort of magic lays just beneath the surface and waits for me to tap into it. I smile wide as I look at their faces, knowing they're about to eat better than they have in months.

I can do it.

"Place your orders."

Danny raises his hand as if he were in a schoolroom, trying his best to get his short arm over Gregs' shoulder.

"I'll take a Steak dinner!"

I can do it.

"Coming right up, Brother."

I set my focus on the small, blue dome in front of me as I wrap my fingers around the bowl. I feel the heat pass from my fingertips and a small vibration emitting from them. My gaze burns a hole through the bowl as I see a vision of wonder underneath it.

There's a big-ass juicy steak under this bowl.

Darkness creeps into my vision and leaves the world darkening by the second. My hands begin to tense up and burn.

Cooked medium rare and seasoned to perfection.

The darkness rushes in, leaving my sight now absent. I hear them gasp in shock and can only image they're seeing the black, hollow eyes I possess, the same ones that Sasha saw when I spoke to them from beyond.

Dinner is served.

A moan escapes me as my eyes return to their radiant green and my vision returns to the world again. They surround me now, watching with childish eyes, needing to know if their magician pulled off his feat.

"Come and get it."

I lift the bowl slowly and am greeted by an empty plate.

What the fuck?

The sound of the air escaping the bowl breaks the silence as a dome-shaped steak falls to the plate, sending its wonderful aroma around the room. Staring at the hunk of meat in front of me, I feel like a deer caught in the headlights.

That thing has gotta weigh forty ounces.

"No fucking way!" Danny screams as he snatches a fork off the table.

Cheers fill the air along with the scent of Dannys dinner, but abruptly halts when they turn to placing their orders.

"Hang on! Joe! Can I get some Steak Fries too?"

Done.

I grab the bowl and place it over another plate before lifting it up seconds later to reveal a mountain of golden fries.

I didn't even try that time...that was easy.

"Fuck yeah! Wooo!"

I burst out laughing at Danny and his newfound happiness, a comical sight, as he rushes away quickly and leaves a trail of fries behind him.

There's more mouths to feed.

"Alright...who's next?"

John raises his hand while stepping forward and quickly makes his request.

"I'll take that Lobster, Friend, and maybe a Steak too, if that's not asking too much."

"Coming right up, Sir."

I walk a step over to the next empty plate and place the bowl over it. I fight the darkening sensations in my vision to keep from traumatizing them any further.

Steak and Lobster, with a few twists of Lemon.

My hands burst with heat immediately and it becomes almost effortless.

Like riding a bike.

Lifting my hands quickly, I'm greeted by the desired entree, a meaty steak and a plump Lobster complete with the Lemon twists.

"Praise be to The Creator! Thank you, Friend!"

He grabs his plate and fights his way through the group to the chair at the end of the table.

He'll eat like a King because of me.

Amy K. rushes before me while giving voice to her requests. I giggle as she elbows her way past Greg and Will without letting them get a word in.

"Can I have some Fried Chicken? The white meat, and also some Mashed Potatoes with extra Butter and, its sounds silly but, Corn on the Cob? Oooh! And Dinner Rolls!"

I chuckle at her as she stands with her small hands

against her chest, still adorned in crucifixes, with her mouth pressed tight as if she's fighting off additional requests.

"Anything you want, Amy K.."

I arrange three plates in front of me as I drop the bowl over the first and lift if quickly revealing her chicken, all white meat, as she requested. I follow suit with the next two plates, completing the requested meal.

"Oh my goodness! Thank you, Joe!"

She gives me a hug as she whispers through her pre-meal prayers, readying to dive into her food.
"No problem Amy K., just happy to bring happiness."

Sasha steps forward with her eyes giving away their own request. Her soft voice fills my head.

"Don't forget about us. We need to hurry the fuck up....I need you...bad."

I smile at her and shoot a quick wink.

"I'll move it along."

I give her a half smirk-half smile while cocking my head with my own flirty grin. It dawns on me that I can talk to her however I want in our own private internal dialogue, meaning I can speak to her exactly how she likes me to.

"I'm sooo gonna fucking tear you apart."

Her laughter fills my head as she gazes lovingly into my

eyes and bites her bottom lip.

"I'll believe it when I see it...Better bring 'the animal'."

"Okay! Let's make this quick with the rest of you! You guys need to have dinner. Line up, single file. Tell me what you want."

Greg laughs and humorously gazes at me as he steps forward.

He knows why I'm rushing.

"Bro, beggars can't be choosers."

He turns to Will, Carmen and Amy J., as his eyes make a pitiful attempt to tell a story. They look at him with stares of confusion as his eyes dance inside his head. He begins mouthing silent words and cocks his head towards me and Sasha. Their faces light up immediately as they slowly nod in agreement.

Well, that was smooth.

He returns his gaze to mine as a coy smile spreads across his face.

"Steak dinners for the rest of us, and a few sides of Steak Fries, Bro."

I smile at him with gratitude painted across my face. Feeling a magic I've never felt, I decide to test the boundaries just a little bit more.

I should try something else.

I focus on his squinted eyes, falling to the dark center of them and deliver thoughts that are heavy with sincere praise and an uncomfortable truth.

"Greg...If you can hear me...Thank you, Little Brother...I love you...We just need to get laid."

He bursts out laughing, indicating my thoughts made it into his brilliant mind. He calms himself as he takes his own shot in the dark and his voice quickly fills my head.

"You're welcome, Bro. Have fun tonight."

I smirk in reply and bow my head to him.

It worked...we just exchanged our thoughts.

"A few more Steak dinners on the way...Give me a little room."

They stand back as I make my way around the table arranging the plates. The need to hold Sasha again forces my hands to be quick. The thought of being with her sends waves of excitement through my mid-section, making me feel as a first-time lover again. I make my way to the first plate and grab the bowl.

A surge of kinetic energy bolts through my body and I feel like a battery that has been overcharged tenfold. I place the bowl over the plate and raise it seconds later revealing the long lost cuisine they requested. I repeat the process in a blur, moving quickly until all plates are overflowing with a new delicious bounty.

I need to be with her.

"Done! Enjoy dinner! We're going for a walk!" I exclaim as I toss the bowl to the floor beside me and turn from them without another word.

Sasha joins me on cue, grasping my hand as she shouts her farewells while heading towards the door. I hear laughter filling the room as the door swings closed behind us.

****

We'll never make it.

Only a dozen yards from the stores exit, we find ourselves groping and kissing madly with her hands all over the places she missed the most. My hands keep the pace with hers, roaming from her breasts to her firm backside to the place of all my desires end. I lift her up and caress her sweetest of spots softly and it causes shivers to race throughout her body and forces soft moans to escape from her chest.

We're not gonna make it.

She fumbles as she tries to untie the breastplate straps from my shoulders. I drop her to her feet and grab it and rip it in half, tearing it from my body as if it were a Tee shirt and not hardened Steel. It clangs to the ground next to me as I pull her back into me and kiss her with a passionate purpose.

Fuck trying to make it, I gotta have her right now.

64

I talk through the lustful kisses as I can't pull my face away.

"Sasha...I need you...Right fucking now."

I shove her back a step and reach for her robes in the same instance. She grabs my hands quickly before they can turn her black and blue war robes into mystical rags.

"I love this robe."

She releases my hands and slips the robes off her delicate shoulders to expose her inviting breasts, which call out to me in the soft moonlight. I feel my body shake with an otherworldly desire.

"Joe, hey Cousin..."

"Fuck!" My face says it all.

What a time to get a phone call.

"Is it Robert?"

"Yes."

"Well put him on hold!" She commands, "He'll understand!"

"I can't! Something might be wrong...also...I need to ask him something."

I close my eyes, inviting the darkness, and send my

questioning soul to The Abyss.

"What's wrong, Brother?"

"Sorry to bother you, Cuz, I just wanted to tell you that things are moving along swiftly. Give me three days with them and they'll be ready."

"Sounds good...Hey, Big...I have a question, Brother...Can we still be intimate and it be okay?"

His loud, deep laughter fills my inquiring mind.

"Umm...sure...if you want to."

"Will it offend The Creator?"

"Cuz...You stand as the Ruler of The Abyss, whether you want to accept it or not. As long as it's okay with you...I think the rest is history."

Good enough for me.

"Okay bye bye then," I blurt out before sending him away. His laughter roars in my head as I tune him out and open my eager eyes.

"Is everything okay, Baby?"

My eyes fall to the vision of her perfect breasts. Somehow, I forgot she undressed her upper half.
"Yep."

I slam her body into my own as I wrap my arms around

her.

Walking takes too long.

"Hold on."

I thrust my wings and float us up into the air while turning in the direction of our destination. With a single flap of my wings, we shoot towards the forbidden playground that is our Earthly home. Slicing through the air with a renewed, lustful energy, we move as if we're ready to knock the whole house down.

We would by the end of it.

* *

The door flies off the hinges as I kick it with a mighty blow while holding my seductive Sasha in my arms. She giggles as I race up the dusty, blue marble stairs that match her dreamy eyes.

"I gotta fucking have you right fucking now!" I growl.

"Don't threaten me with a good time!"

She squeals as I race towards the door to the Master Bedroom, mumbling on about how I'm going to ravage her. I focus on the door and swing it open with only my gaze, never slowing a step as we make it to the bed we once shared. I delicately toss her on it before I begin removing what's left of my armor.

She kneels on the bed as she finishes removing the rest of her robes, exposing her naked body to me once again. She laughs softly and seductively as her hands move over her own body, bringing me to life. I'm mesmerized by her perfect curves and soft features, as every part of her is completely perfect. My gaze falls between her legs to the wet joys I've missed so much. Removing the last of my steel clothing, I approach the bed and stand as nude as her and just as ready.

"I have to make love to you right now, Sasha," I confess through deep, false breaths.

"No...Not today, Baby," she says while gazing upon me with sharp, blue talons.

She reaches forward and grabs my face, pulling me to her before we kiss softly. She releases her hold on me and gazes into my eyes while a fire begins burning in hers.

"Today, I want you to fuck me."

I growl as a beast as I lift her up and slam ourselves down hard onto the bed. My body stays close to hers as I fall on top of her, kissing her neck and guiding myself inside of her. I slam my hips against hers and begin pounding hard and without mercy.

She screams in passion as she clamps her legs around me. It's a feeling missed by us both, made abundantly clear by the way we clasp onto one another. Her claws rake my shoulders and chest as I continue my aggressive stance, taking her as roughly as she requested. She finds my mouth between her screams to kiss me hard and with a lost passion that proves she missed our lovemaking as much as I did. I roam from her mouth to her breasts to every inch in-between, allowing my hands to play with all the parts of her sexually energized body. It takes no time at all for her legs to begin trembling and giving a hint of the passionate pleasure to come.

I relive the memory as I let my hand drift down between us to her sweet spot, which is now burning hot to the slightest touch. I move my hand in unison with my body, setting her up for the explosive orgasm inside her that I would stroke to life. I pound her hard as she squeals and screams underneath my heaving body, while her talons begin scratching my arms and digging into my shoulders once more. The bed breaks off from its corner posts and falls to the floor, crashing down hard, as I continue giving my sweet lover the aggression she desires. I move my body harder and faster, causing her screams to turn from beautiful yells to sharp gasps. She digs her nails into my lower back as she voices a deafening scream from the orgasm her body releases inside her. I slow my hips to a slow crawl, letting her recover her senses and enjoy the lustful moment as much as I am.

She opens her eyes and glares at me with a fresh command upon her gaze and her lips.

"Don't you dare fucking stop."

I rise up on my knees as I flip her body over and place her on her hands and knees. I enter her from behind, holding on to her slender shoulders as my hips start pounding against her sweet backside. She thrusts backwards into me with every stroke, threatening to take me just as roughly. She begins to scream in delight when my hands find her hips and begin pulling her into me faster and harder than humanly possible. The bed begins to slide across the floor with every stroke as the rest of its' corpse is scattered around us. I grunt and growl as I give her all of me and cause her screams to turn into lustful groans.

She's coming again, harder than the first time.

She pitches forward on the bed and I fall with her, still inside her and still thrusting as hard as she commanded me. She screams in ecstasy as her whole body begins quaking while sharp breaths escape her between the yells of passion. Her gorgeous, blue eyes become wild and glance back to greet me from just over her shoulder. She turns over and shoves me back with her feet, following me as I step off the bed.

She places her hands firmly on my chest and shoves me backwards hard as she plants her feet with every step. We travel halfway across the room before I crash viciously into the wall. The sheet rock and wood crunch behind me and give way to our mad passion. She places her hands on the back of my neck and lifts herself up onto me to straddle me against the broken wall. She reaches down and returns me to the place I love the most.

Her bucking begins with her body up against mine as I hold on to her legs. I hold her up for her to continue her forbidden lap dance. She moans and moves faster and causes my body to tense from the tables being turned. She pounds herself against me as the wall continues to crumble behind me until I feel the wood unable to hold up against our immortal passion anymore. She begins her beautiful song of ecstasy again as the wall suddenly collapses, sending us into the next bedroom. She lands on me and never misses a stride. Holding her firmly in place, I rise up and place her back against a new wall while kissing her madly all the while. Her loud voice returns to her as I continue my loving assault on her sweetest of areas. I shove myself into her with force, kissing her with the lips of her lost lover as she pulls me into her even harder. I willingly oblige and pound her as hard as I can, causing her screams to fill the air alongside the crunch of the wall behind her.

Don't hurt her!

I freeze and look at her face to find her beautiful mouth hanging open as she calms her moans.

"Are you okay?

She looks at me with a burning, red passion just behind her fierce, blue eyes.

"Knock the fucking walls down."

Give her what she wants.

My lips quickly return to hers as I begin hammering her through the wall again. She moans loudly as the wall begins to crumble from the force of my thrusts and my hips never slowing as I take what belongs to me. I look to the ceiling as I drive home full force, with every new thrust bringing the wall closer to ruin.

"Don't fucking stop! Fuck! Oh Fuck!"

She clings to me and bites down hard into my shoulder as the orgasms of her fantasies shake her once again. She yells into my ear as her loving talons again rake my body. She jumps around in my arms, pulling on my long, brown hair, while finally being unable to take anymore. The pulsing around my manhood forces me to finally yield to the moment and my orgasm joins hers. With a final thrust of my hips, the second wall gives way as we crumble along with it, falling through into the hallway.

I lay on her with my wings stretched out to protect her from the collapsing wall as we fight for breath we no longer need. The joys of the physical body remain, and our heavy, false

71

breathing remains a part of the lust. It feels strange to draw breath into my body, but it seems that I won't survive without it.

She catches her false breath and begins to laugh softly as the adrenaline of our lovemaking leaves her immortal veins. I join her as we lay under my wings as charmed lovers, laughing at the notion that we literally knocked down the walls. I raise my wings up forcefully, sending chunks of wood and wall airborne, to prove that we made good on our lustful promise.

It wouldn't be the last time I would have to dust off my feathers.

****

My legs feel weak as we walk out the front entrance, hand in hand. Both of us now fully dressed, we still manage to be covered in dust and rubble. She squeezes my hand and it causes my gaze to return to hers.

Her eyes reflect the glow of the blue moonlight as her head tilts while wearing her lovers mask. She radiates elegance and love as well as power and sex appeal, with her long, brown hair shining and hanging delicately past her shoulders. She wears her robes like a Goddess who's commanded them to make her the most desirable creature in my existence. She is my Sasha; My Dark Queen, who happens to be so full of light, that she forever holds me captive with her irresistible soul.

"Sasha, you look so beautiful...It hurts my heart to look at you...Your beauty is without an equal...I can't believe you're mine."

I feel my eyes churning with sorrow.

"I can't believe I almost lost you."

She clings to me as the green does the grass, and her arms morph into a small, straightjacket that ensnares me.

"You could of never lost me. The moment I met your true heart...I knew I would love you forever."

She looks at me with her eyes widening slightly as she whispers softly.

"I'll never fucking leave your side."

We pause in our talk and share a moonlit kiss under a clear sky. It seems that the stars can only shine half as bright as her loving eyes.

"You better not...or I'll burn you with Hellfire."

She laughs and playfully slaps my face for my jest, but loving that I'm a Joker at heart. It was the very thing that endeared me to her first, in a cave in another life.

"You would never hurt me! You asshole!"

I chuckle at her as I touch her delicate face and pull her close to me with my free hand.

"Never."

The sound of steps approaching catches our

attention and sends my hand reaching for my absent sword on instinct.

We left them in the store.

The steps grow louder as I take my stand in front of Sasha, shrugging my shoulders and shielding her with my wings. She shrinks behind me, but I remember the wild woman who beheaded The Damned and know she's protecting me more than hiding from anything.

> *I'm the King of The Abyss. With Sasha beside me, nothing can defeat me.*

> Soft voices fill the air before Dannys' unmistakable, shrill laughter pierces the night.

> *It's just our family.*

I relax and lower my wings as Sasha retakes her rightful place at my side. She giggles and smiles softly as she delicately dusts my shoulder off and sends paint chips falling from my hair.

> *We're both so filthy.*

They appear in our vision while holding lanterns and rush to us with their eyes wide with questions.

> "Joe! What happened?" Greg asks loudly as he stands holding my torn breastplate.

> "We're okay, Brother...Just had a little wardrobe malfunction is all."

Sasha giggles next to me as our secrets are revealed in her small laughter.

"Oh...OHHH!...Shit, my bad, Bro."

He hands me the two pieces of black steel and I chuckle as I retrieve my torn armor. I hold both pieces together while focusing my aim. I bring them apart and back together quickly, causing the metal to return to its' original form with a loud clash.

"Damn, Bro!" Greg exclaims, "That was cool!"

I laugh in agreement before shaking my head and releasing a false breath.

"I have no idea what I'm capable of...I'll try to do something else in the coming days."

Get the hint Greg.

"Man, I wish I could do..." His eyes lose focus for the briefest of seconds before widening.

"You're staying tonight?"

I nod my head and grin as a fool as I pull Sasha close to me again.

"And the next two nights as well, as far as I know."

He lifts his skinny fist to the sky as a smile explodes across his face.

"Hell yeah! Bro! There's a lot of stuff I wanna talk about and..." He pauses as his eyes focus through the dim light on the rubble we're both covered with.

"Why are you...how..." He can't find the words to ask about the filth we're covered in. Sasha comes to his aid.

"Take a walk through our house tomorrow and see for yourself."

We both begin laughing as the vision of immortal passion plays out in his head. His brow arches high and his cheesy smile returns to his face.

"Damn, Bro...You really are *King Salami*."

"Ahh shit, man, not you too."

"I told you," Danny adds.

We begin laughing in the quiet night as Dannys joke becomes new by being voiced by someone else. The moment is cut short by the sound of glass shattering loudly down the dark street. Silence follows quickly as we dare not move or breath. Glancing around, I find their faces gripped in a terror that greets my own panicked gaze.

Big said there were no Cursed nearby...So, what is it?

"Baby," my love whispers, "we don't have our swords."

I scan the hips of everyone in the darkness and find that they are all absent their steel.

I don't need a sword.

"It's okay. I'm going to have a look. The rest of you stay here."

"No way, Bro...We're still with you. We all go."

"Greg's right, Friend...We're coming with our brother."

They stand as warriors absent any means of combat, yet, they're ready to follow me to doom. I nod in respect as I raise a single finger to my lips before motioning for them to follow me. They turn off their lanterns as I turn and walk away, but hear my group following me closely in the darkness.

****

The night is heavy with an energy I've roamed through before; A surge of current created with hate. I felt it when I entered The Abyss for the first time. The residual energy of The Evil One, it was his own deadly calling card.

I round the building and take the street leading to my old home; The place of my Humanly misery. A fire burns in the road and I can see a figure making his way back and forth in the glow of it. He paces with anxiety while being ready to meet the creator of his torment, who happens to be the foul-smelling one he tracked here.

The one they call Joe.

I raise my arms up and my wings follow in kind, pausing the steps of those behind me. I turn to them in the pale light as my eyes begin to glow with the green essence of my immortal soul.

"Everyone...Wait here. No heroics...Just please stay put."

Silence in return confirms our unspoken agreement. I look at Sasha with softer eyes as I send her my thoughts.

"Something doesn't feel right. Stay and protect them. If something goes wrong...Get Robert."

Her eyes reflect the loving, blue night sky above us.

"You got this, Baby. Tear the fucker to pieces and come back to me."

We embrace for a small kiss before I turn and head towards the meeting of a New Beast in the New World. My steps fall lightly while my wings tense as if ready for flight, but my hands remain ready for combat. The figure grows in the firelight with every step closer.

He smells...different.

He remains unaware as I draw closer and am now only fifty feet away and cloaked in darkness. I prepare to speak when he turns his back to me and shrugs his shoulders, causing the light to illuminate a terrible pair of wings that are long and crafted in a leathery skin that resembles human flesh. He gags and lurches before turning to greet me approaching out of the darkness of the night.

To my surprise, he stands in only a pair of jeans. His balding head, with only a few strands of hair remaining, reflects the fire. His pupils are nothing more than small, burning red embers surrounded by a pitch black emptiness. He lowers his stance as if preparing to attack and his small, red coals begin pulsing as if on fire.

A mad hissing begins as he stretches out his arms wide and stomps his foot in an attempt to command fear. It only causes me to smile at him.

He used to be Human.

"Hello...Who might you be?"

He lowers his arms and begins sniffing the air around him, but my aroma brings disgust as he begins waving a clawed hand in front of his face. A dark, unforgiving voice greets me in return.

"The Fool of Mercy..The Beast massster...The one who rules the Old Lands...This is who you are...Is it not?"

I nod my head to him and my gaze never wavers.

"I stand the Ruler of The Abyss, as The Creator has deemed it."

He pitches forward in a hysterical laughter with a voice as raspy and as empty as The Abyss I preside over.

"*You?*...This cannot be true...You're too weak."

I stretch my wings fast and hard, creating a loud swosh that pounds the air violently before bringing them to rest again.

79

"I'm stronger than you are."

He chuckles through another raspy, slithering hiss, and sounds more like a serpent.

"He said you were sssmart...A real thinker...Someone who would be better ssserving him than fighting against him...You don't have to die, Beast massster...This is the message I bring."

A new fool preaching the old ways. More lies.

"I serve The Creator...The One in The Realm...The One that has given me the strength to tear you limb from limb with only my hands if I choose...Answer a few questions for me and I may have mercy on your soul."

He stands taller now, stretching his own filthy wings against the fires behind him and casting a frightening shadow across the town. His face turns to that of a snarling dog, with his small, pointed teeth now barely visible.

"You ssserve only to die...You cannot win this war coming for you...Not even with the help of The Realm."

I've heard this nonsense before and let it fall on deaf ears. I continue as if he didn't speak.

"First question...Where is your master?"

The raspy laughter cuts through the air once more as his head twitches and shakes, but he keeps his eyes firmly on mine.

"I only have one answer for you...Fool of Mercy...Yes."

"Yes...What?" I question him.

He stands and grins wide to fully reveal a row of sharpened teeth.

"Yesss...You will die. You will not defeat the Army of The New World...Your false Creator will fall from The Realm...My massster will pull you from the Earth...He'll crusssh you both as he joins The Realm *and* The Abyss with the New World...to make a perfect world."

He wants to rule over every domain.

"It begins with me. No harm will come to The Realms...His, or mine...I stand as His shield, along with an army of my own...I have one request...Answer one question."

His eyes narrow as his horrendous smile turns into a clever grin.

"Just one...Fool of Mercy...before I end you."

I smile at him in return and nod in agreement.

"Very well...When I *kill* you...Where will your soul go? To The Realm? To The Abyss? Or do you return to *your* creator?"

My eyes come to life and begin glowing the radiant green that I was blessed with for my afterlife. A few seconds later, I'm bewildered by the green fires that begin to envelope my hands.

How did that happen?

His brow raises high as he steps back. I focus my eyes on his, digging deep to his tormented soul. Panic strikes his frightening features as I sift through his tortured mind.

He'll return to his maker.

I smile wide as I find the answer to my question.

"Tell him I'm coming for him."

His wings shoot up quickly before swinging down and sending his body rising up faster than any winged creature I'd ever witnessed.

He's got a fast take off.

My phantom heart races and urges me to take action. With a thrust of my wings, I spring into the sky and follow his invisible trail while my body cuts through the cool night air. I see him traveling fast and heading upwards towards the gathering clouds. He intends to lose me, and his alarming speed promises that he has just the tool to do so.

He's really fast.

I pump my wings hard, shooting breath out of me as if I'm a mad horse, and begin closing the distance quickly. He looks over his shoulder and sees me, his unwanted traveling companion, as I draw near. He thrusts hard again, sending his body racing away as if a rocket and not a Cursed Human.

DON'T LOSE HIM! DO SOMETHING!

My hands burst with heat beside me, reminding me that I still have tricks up my sleeve that I've yet to discover.

I can do anything.

I scream loud as I swing my hand forward and send the energy of an otherworldly power straight from my palm. A green bolt of fire tethers from my hand and a long, terrible lasso finds the monsters' leg. He screams in agony as the fiery light burns his soul.

He's not going anywhere, but don't take any risks.

I cut the night air in a straight arrow to him as my 'tether of demon misery' holds true.

The burning tether dissipates as I grab him by the shoulders and allow my fingertips to pierce his flesh, digging deep and hooking thebones with myfingers. Heshrieks again as I pull himcloseand stareinto the red coals that are surrounded by his darkened eyes.

"I know you'll see him tonight."

He moans in agony as I begin to crush his bones while the small pops and snaps accompany the misery in his voice. He calms himself enough to mutter a single sentence.

"We'll be back before the Sun rises."

I growl through clenched teeth and pull him closer still.

"No need...TELL HIM I'M COMING TO FUCK HIM UP!"

I roar in a Godly voice and shake the world as I bring my hands apart. The sound of bones and cartilage separating fill the air as I tear him in half and send a web of rotten innards to the Earth below. His throaty gurgle hangs in the silence as his new, dark blood drains from what's left of him. Both halves of his body tremble from demonic nerves firing off for the last time.

I release my hold on him and watch both ruined pieces fall from the night sky and travel to the fires below me, which has become a small light in the darkness of the night.

Watching the ruined beast fall, I'm haunted by his words.

Before the Sun rises.

****

The ground shakes as my feet plant firmly from my mile-high dive and sends a cloud of dust rushing away from me. The tremors travel as thunder throughout the silent, unmoving New World. The group stands nearby with their lanterns now back on as they were examining the torn halves of The Cursed before I made my descent. His body lays in ruins and is a beautiful sight to my glowing eyes.

He was so damn fast...and there's a hundred thousand more.

"Everyone gather around! Quickly!"

They look at me startled as if I stand a nightmarish clown. I feel the Cursed blood that creates the face-paint

84

dripping from my cheeks.

"Now!"

They rush to me at the sound of my commanding voice and Sasha approaches me with panic as she quickly examines me for wounds.

"I'm fine, Love, but none of us are going to be for long."

Her eyes widen with the same fear I hadn't seen since the Old World.

"What's going on, Baby?"

I take her hand and squeeze it tight as I look at the seven faces of fear that greet my hardened gaze.

"This is a New Beast...a demon born of the New World...They're called 'The Cursed'. There's a hundred thousand of them about fifteen hundred miles from here. I've never seen a creature like this. He was Human once, that much I know. He tracked me here...He's a Scout for his master...Do you all remember the man in the stars?"

They look around at each other confused before John enlightens them.

"The man with the staff...The mystery man."

I nod my head slowly in the pale moonlight.

"He isn't a mystery anymore."

85

He swallows hard knowing this new threat must be great if it's bringing worry to The Fallen One himself.

"He was the right hand of The Evil One...A powerful Necromancer who promised to raise the beast if he fell to my sword. When I emerged victorious, he broke his promise...He wanted to step up and claim the throne for himself, only The Abyss wasn't his intended target. He fled The Abyss in the final moments, before it collapsed with the death of The Serpent. He's the only 'Damned' left from the Old Abyss, before I took it over."

Will steps forward and speaks quietly while pointing a shaky finger at the fallen corpse.

"Where did that one come from?"

I let the words spill out quickly, feeling a sense of urgency.

"The Necromancer is creating The Cursed out of men. They must willingly give their soul to him and he somehow turns them into these beasts. They follow him, believing him to be the New Ruler."

"There's lots of other people left?" Carmen asks. I find her gaze and explain quickly.

"Millions. There are millions of people left in the New World. The job you were given, spreading the word about what happened, is no longer your job. The Cursed," I point at the lifeless half closest to me, "shares the same methods of communication as The Damned of the Old World. Before I killed him, he said he would return with more...before the Sun rises."

"You said this Necromancers' target wasn't The Abyss. Is he trying to take over the Earth?" John asks abruptly.

"He wants The Abyss, the New World, and The Realm itself...He wants to combine them all."

I feel Sasha gripping my hand as if I might somehow fly away without her.

"We need to prepare for war. We don't have long. Let's head in and gather our steel, along with any other weapons we can find."

John stands firm with the sharp gaze of a warrior.

"We're with you, Friend. We'll slaughter these beasts like the ones that came before them."

I meet his gaze with a fierce one of my own.

"These are *nothing* like the ones that came before them...This is a whole new monster."

****

"Everyone keep preparing. Gather anything we can use to defend our position."

They scramble about in the lanterns soft and inviting light while ignoring the panic in the air that hangs about. I turn to Sasha and see a desperate fear in her eyes as she silently swings her sword, readying to deal death with it once again.

"I have to contact Robert and let him know what's happening."

She stops mid-swing and takes to my loving arms, squeezing me as tight as she did when we both stood as mortals.

"Okay...I love you, Baby."

I kiss her head sweetly and whisper softly.

"I love you too, my Soul of Souls."

She steps back and resumes battling her invisible foe. I watch her swing her sword so gracefully and deadly as the world around me vanishes in an instant and leaves me in the dark again.

"Robert? Brother! Can you hear me?"

"I'm here, Cuz. How's it going up there?"

"Not good, my Brother. We encountered The Cursed, just one demon of the Necromancer. He tracked me to our location. I robbed him of his life, but he spoke of returning with a group before the Sun rises. He's coming with reinforcements. It's just me, Sasha and the rest of my family."

"Your army isn't ready yet, Cuz. They need a lot more time."

"How long?"

"It's hard to say. You and Sasha have only been gone a

few minutes in our world. Remember that time moves differently on different planes, Cuz. A day up there might only be a couple hours over here."

"Shit..." I pause and sit with my thoughts for a moment, searching my mind for an answer.

"Cuz?"

"Yes, Robert?"

"What do you think about the new breed? Ugly, right?"

"Ugly and deadly, Robert. We needed a few more races before I came up here. They're really fast in flight."

"They can fly?...The first of The Cursed didn't have wings."

"This new breed of Cursed possess talents unlike The Damned, although they share a few characteristics. They communicate the same and their souls return to their creator when vanquished. He reincarnates them into other men, recycling the souls and making them stronger. Bro...They're faster and stronger than The Damned...and stronger than Servants as well."

Silence answers my words and leaves a hollow ring in my mind.

"Big?"

"Sorry, Cuz, I was on another call. I let Him know what's going on."

89

"You put me on hold?"

"Hahaa! Sorry, Cousin, I had to."

"Well fuck, put us on a three-way call or something!"

"He's already back to work. He's sending you a gift for your people, along with someone to help you get through the night."

"Thank Him for me. All praise to our Creator, Brother."

"Amen, Cuz, I'll see you soon."

The world rushes back into a living color and I find the group standing wide-eyed and shaking as leaves in a thunderstorm. They stand in front of me, no doubt watching my long distance call.

"Bro, you looked fucking crazy just now! What the fuck was that?!"

"Told ya, Greg," Sasha replies with a small laugh.

"There's no time guys. We can talk about it another

time. Grab your weapons, we're leaving." My words

shake them like giant grasping hands.

"Where are we going?" Amy J. asks, her voice

trembling.

"To meet a Servant who brings us a gift. We have to hurry."

****

We make it to the entrance where Sasha and I returned to His Earth and find the hole dark and eerily quiet. No screams of misery will ever rise from The Abyss again, as long as I rule it.

"Baby, why are we here?"

She stands with a quiet fear living inside her as her lovely features return to the frightened woman of old that I died protecting. I take her hand in mine to ease her worry.

"I..."

Why did I come here?"

I don't know...I felt like this is where we're supposed to be."

"This is the way to our home...There are no Servants down there, other than Robert. The Creator is sending a gift for us...so why are we *here*?"

I stand in silence for the briefest of moments before a sound is heard rising from the pit. It's the sound of air traveling at a fever pitch from the path to The Abyss itself.

"Everyone stand back!"

They rush back a few paces and draw their weapons, eager to face battle.

"There will be no need for those...That's my house down there...There will be no horrors rising from it, ever again."

The screeching sound comes to a halt in the same manner a tea pot does when removed from the scorching heat.

A large figure floats up out of the pit as his wings move him gracefully while he drifts to the ground in front of us. He stands holding a large wool bag over his shoulder as his soft eyes meet mine from under his Cowboy hat.

"Hey, Cuz."

"Robert? What are you doing here, Brother?"

"I'm here to help you guys for the night."

He steps closer to me as I meet him with steps of my own, embracing for a hug before my mind shoots with questions.

"Who's watching The Abyss right now?"

"He sent a few Servants to keep watch over it so I could fulfill my duties. I was tasked with guiding you and protecting you, before any other job."

He turns his attentions to the group, who are all dwarfed by his giant frame. They stand frozen and appear as surprised statues.

"You guys must be Joes' Earthly family I keep hearing about. I'm Robert, but you can call me Big."

Danny approaches him and has to stretch his neck back as far as it can go to meet his eyes.

"No shit."

Robert laughs as he puts a hand on Dannys shoulder.

"It's nice to meet you, Danny. I have something for you...for all of you." Robert turns his attention to me with a small request upon his face.

"A little light, Cuz, if you don't mind."

I stand quietly as I contemplate how to create light.

How did I make that fire earlier?

I bring my hands together slowly, but only a few sparks shoot from my touching fingertips.

"Go to a place of desperation, Cuz...Go to that moment that you *have* to make something happen...It's the easiest way to release it."

Standing quietly still, I think of the moment I was losing Sasha as a mortal man, the morning we woke up together and I kissed her as she tried to walk away from me forever. It was one of my most desperate moments.

My hands come to life with fire as soft, green flames rise from my palms. I reach down to the Earth and place both palms close together before swiping them across the ground and release a long, green flame from my touch. The world around us becomes bright and well lit.

Robert smiles as he nods and reassures me the way any good coach would do.

"You got it now, Cuz...You just gotta learn how to tap into it."

He directs his gaze at the bag in front of him. He opens it up quickly and the glint of steel begins peeking out. He lifts the bag as a new array of weaponry falls from it, a whole selection of beautiful white and silver instruments of doom. He lifts two swords from the stack and hands them to Danny.

"These are for you."

They glow in the green firelight while reflecting the color against the white handles and slick silver. They're as light as feathers, yet as terribly sharp as Eagle talons. Small inscriptions line the blade, the same writing on every new gift from The Creator.

"Wow...These are beautiful...What does the writing say?"

Robert smiles as he begins to explain.

"The writings aren't for you. They were written by the Servants who crafted the blades, to bring torment to The Cursed of the world. If offers their souls a last chance to end up in one of the True Kingdoms, rather than being resurrected by

The Necromancer."

I can see confusion in Danny as he looks over his new weapons.

"What happens if they don't take the offer?"

"Your guess is as good as mine," he answers him.

They all make their way over one-by-one and retrieve the mirror images of their own worn weapons as awe circulates throughout the group. There are seven new sets of warriors weapons, as Sasha and I already have our own.

"Bro, I love this machete! Wooo!"

Greg spins as he slices the air with his new deadly plaything, while his boyish charm returns to him.

Robert laughs as he raises his hands and I see the black polish shining on his fingernails, complimenting his black hat.

He always has been the only Servant with his own style.

"Easy, Little Brother. The blade has been sharpened to a deadly edge."

He retrieves the machete from Greg with one hand and with the other takes the old one from his side. He brings the blades together as a chef would, rubbing the sharpened edges together. He swipes the new blade against the old and barely makes an effort as it moves through the old blade effortlessly. The ruined steel falls to the ground in front of Greg.

"Holy shit!"

Robert bellows his big laughter as he hands Greg the otherworldly machete that was crafted to carve through the hordes of The Cursed that now walk the New World.

I step forward with a sense of urgency in my voice.

"Guys, we can admire our weapons later. We need to get back and fortify our position...We're going to lure them into the store."

Robert turns to me with his eyes wide for the very first time since he came to me.

"You sure you want to take this fight indoors?"

"They can't fly with a ceiling over their heads. Their biggest advantage will be stripped from them."

"We won't be able to fly either, Cuz...Something to think about."

I draw my sword and point it at the group as they all stand lined up with their weapons thirsty for blood.

"We won't need to...and besides...I have *you*, Robert."

Chapter 3

The silence of the past two hours is finally broken by the flapping of wings as dawns first light is approaching fast. I see them in the distance from my seat on the sidewalk in front of the store, small bird-like images in the distance betraying the horror that truly is. I remain seated as the figures grow into monstrosities to reveal a dozen in all. They approach lazily and land in the street in front of me.

Calmly, I remain seated.

A familiar face greets me from the crowd as The Cursed I placed in his grave only hours ago makes his way to the front of the pack. He grins wide as he approaches eagerly to reveal his reincarnation.

Still, I remain seated.

"Fool of Mercccy...I told you I would return."

I smile from my seat on the ground, just a dozen feet from him.

"The first truth you've probably spoken in your new life."

He begins to walk towards me with his stance lowering for battle. I bring my hands up to my sides, palms up, and release the green fire I'm fast becoming fond of. He pauses in his steps as I rise from my seat slowly with my hands still burning bright.

"I'll make you a deal," I begin, as my hands return to their normal state, "I'll face you now, one on one, and if you win...I'll serve your master...Turns out, you were right...I don't have to die."

He suddenly finds intrigue in our conversation and calms the anger in him as he speaks.

"And if you win?"

"Your ugly friends can take me captive...and I'll meet your master regardless."

"Then what is the purpose of a contessst?" He hisses.

I walk towards him while drawing my sword and it causes him to flinch slightly.

"To let you have the revenge I know you seek...and to be honest...I wasn't done whipping your ass...you scared, little twat."

His grin turns into a malicious mask and his sharp teeth start grinding in anger.

They're falling for it.

"Agreed."

I walk backwards a few paces as he turns towards his fellow Cursed and nods at them.

They're going to rush me. I gotta be quick.

He turns to me and spreads his wings and hisses while the morning glow makes his eyes burn brighter than they appeared in the night sky.

My eyes turn dark as I give a command I haven't spoken since the Old World.

"Come at me."

He charges forward with his claws slashing the air, hissing as if he was a mad snake, and the distance between us shortens at an alarming pace. Against my better judgement, I don't move a muscle.

They're fast on their feet too.

He pauses a foot away and stands in front of me while raising a terrible claw to the air. In the same moment I reach forward and grab his throat, yanking up fast and violently and tearing his head from his beast-like neck and sending a spray of blood into the dawn air. I drive a straight kick to his chest and send his headless body flying backwards to the ground. The rest of The Cursed hiss and lower their stance.

They're fixing to charge.

I toss the head to their feet as I walk backwards towards the door. It lands and rolls past them as they begin skulking toward me.

"The rest of you bitches can come get some."

I turn and push my steps hard as the flapping of wings

screams behind me. I hear them on my heels as I run into the store.

****

A low, humming ring fills my ears. I leap as my wings twist to spin me mid-flight, turning me to the beast about to cling to my back. The world becomes a blur of color, causing the dimly lit store to seem more of a nightmare than a reality. The world spins as if it was a Merry-go-round of horror as a face only inches away greets me and reveals itself to be more monster than man. He appears to be the only thing not moving in the blend of the New World.

My sword makes its way upwards between us and the blade finds the soft spot behind his chin, traveling through and piercing the crown of his head before it protrudes through with a sickening pop. I grab him while still in the air and shove him back, tearing off his bottom jaw, and sending him crashing into the next two about to lunge at me. My aim is spot on, sending them to their backs. The remaining eight pause to regroup at the entrance of the store.

I float to the ground and begin walking backwards once again. They walk forward, and so far, everything is going as according to the plan.

Just a little more.

"You're a dead man...Fool."

"I died a long time ago, yet, I'm still here," I tease.

100

I pause in my steps and give them a false opportunity that they happily seize upon.

I roar as if the King of the Jungle and not the True Ruler of The Abyss as my blade explodes with fire, burning as bright as my eyes and just as unforgiving. My voice masks the steps behind them and my burning vengeance holds their attention. They never hear or see the silent assassins I trained as a mortal man.

Blades pierce their backs in unison and the gasps of The Cursed begin filling the air. Robert appears behind one as he brings his hands together around its head and creates a crunch almost as loud as the plea for mercy that preceded it.

They stand as deadly as the day I left them. Nine down, one left.

I motion my arm quickly at the last Cursed and my deadly tether returns as a whip. It finds his throat and forces him to his knees.

"Everyone hold!"

The room becomes silent, with only the sounds of The Cursed choking in front of me echoing throughout the store. He calms himself as I stand before him and flick my wrist, causing my fiery leash to loosen enough to give him a voice.

"This changes nothing...We'll be back with more."

"Did he get my message?"

The hissing chuckle of this new breed fills my ears again.

"He...he ssstands...most eager to kill you."

"Then why doesn't he come himself?"

The serpent hisses again while struggling to find my eyes through the pain I'm inflicting.

"He will...when the time comesss...he brings...an army...capable of crussshing all worlds...but today...we'll be back."

They won't stop until they've killed us all.

I return my sword to my side, but feel my anger taking a hold on my emotions. My tether dissipates as I grab his head with both hands and attempt to do my best impression of Robert moments before.

"Don't keep us waiting."

His scream is high in pitch as my hands slowly make their deadly clap. My palms facing each other, I take my time bringing them together, applying pressure slowly and steadily, and relish the bending of his skull and its fracturing every few seconds. The sounds pop the way a guitar string sounds when plucked, and his eyes bulge as the screams get louder. A sinister part of me yearns to make all of The Cursed suffer.

"REMIND HIM THAT I'M STILL COMING TO FUCK HIM UP!"

My hands join suddenly and his head explodes between them, sending a wave of Cursed blood and brains all over me. I shake my head from side to side to cast off the evil paste. Sasha runs to me as she tends to do, always forgetting that I now stand as the most fearsome soul in The Abyss.

"Are you okay, My Love?" She asks as her hands search me for wounds.

"I'm good. Are you okay? Are any of you hurt?"

I glance at them quickly as they clean their swords of the foul blood that stains them. Every last one of them appears calm.

They're good. It wasn't their first Rodeo.

Sasha wraps her arms around my waist and brings me back to the world. I wipe my face clean before delivering a small peck on her lips.

"Just the fleeting moments of your touch always move my soul to a better place...I love you, My Queen."

She giggles softly as she pulls the bloody gore from my hair and tosses it aside.

"Always just so fucking romantic."

Her eyes glow as full moons while her slender features bring me back under her spell. She is the Queen of All Things Beautiful.

"Hey Cuz!"

Robert stands at the front entrance while peeking out. He turns to me with his fierce, black eyes now burning with hate.

"There's more coming."

I gaze into Sashas' blue panicked dreams and hate to see her eyes so full of anxiety.

"Stay here with the others. I got this."

"Fuck that! I don't think so!"

"Sasha, please, just listen to me...I got this."

She stands quiet before finally nodding her head slowly, while her eyes return to the scary storms of old. I'm reminded of the powerful woman she can conjure if she wished.

"I'll be watching for you, Baby. If you need any help, I'll be there, killing those motherfuckers for even thinking about hurting you."

I pull her close and kiss her with purpose, in case it's our last kiss in this world. Her lips are as soft as clouds and her touch ignites a fire inside me.

I'll burn this fucking world to the ground before I let anyone harm you.

I let our lips part and take a final few seconds to stare at her. Her slender cheeks puff as she forms a smile, while her vivid blue eyes become alive once more.

She knows how much I love her.

"Everyone, listen closely," I begin while turning to the group, "stay here in the store and don't make a noise. Robert will stay and protect you...I have to do this alone."

"We're with you, Friend. Don't ever forget that," John reminds me.

"I won't, Sir, but right now, please just stay put. I can handle this."

I turn and march towards the door and find Robert standing ready to join me.

"Stay here and protect them, Brother...in case this doesn't go well."

He scoffs at me and giggles as he waves a hand as if shooing away a fly.

"You're immortal, Cuz, they can't kill you... Bring the true death to those abominations."

On instinct I feel the handle of my sword.

"You can count on it."

****

The morning Sun is beautiful and lively, shedding rays across the town. They splash against my face as I close my eyes and direct it to the sky above.

I've doubted you in the past...But this one is for you.

I open my eyes to the sight of twenty new Cursed clouding the sky and filling my vision, their balding heads and grotesque skin reflecting the gorgeous Sun. Their dark eyes pulse a hellish red, and their wings becoming almost transparent in the light. They land down the street close to the Shower Shack I used as a mortal man. One by one, they quiet their hissing voices and focus on me, The Fallen One who rules The Abyss.

Drawing my sword from my side, I focus on the symbols emblazoned across my blade. They stand a reminder that nothing in this New World is impossible. A forbidden love placed me where I am today; a reminder that a light will always follow the darkness. I'm the most powerful creature to walk in the New World. It's time I learn how to embrace it.

This is my world.

I begin a jog towards the creatures of nightmares.

This is my time.

They begin to scramble in my direction, low to the ground, ready to pounce on the fool that invites his own doom.

That's my family in the store..They're dead if I fail.

I thrust my wings and shoot through the air towards the beasts that would meet my blade. I drift down a few small feet in front of the closest one and spin my body, bringing my blade up like a home run hitter. It catches his torso just right, tearing him from his lower right side to his left shoulder, and sends his body falling in two before me.

Let the madness begin.

106

Time slows as the hissing fills my ears. My sword moves quickly, slicing through the slowed version of the world. I bring my sword from side to side, swinging wildly while snarling like one of the monsters, as my blade tears through their flesh. One falls decapitated while I impale the next, kicking him off my blade in time to tear another in half from the waist. I twirl on my feet, spinning in my deadly Ballet, with the next two falling decapitated from the spinning death I create.

They've had enough. They lunge onto my body and their teeth begin tearing into my flesh. They bite and hiss while trying like the Devil of old to kill The Fallen One in front of them. I drop my sword to grab the one clinging to my chest as another falls upon my back and begins biting at my neck. Oddly, I feel no pain.

Like magnets, they attach to me and their weighted hate brings me to my knees. I feel them Dog-pile me as I fall to all fours before the sharpened razors they call teeth start biting into my shoulders, neck and arms. The force of their demonic bodies pushes me to the ground in their frenzy. I feel them pinning my legs to the Earth as they make a final attempt to keep me grounded.

Alright. Fuck this.

The fires begin to burn inside me slowly before igniting in the same manner as gasoline thrown on a match. My flesh comes to life, sending a wave of pale green fire in all directions. I roar as I leap to my feet and send burning bodies flying every which way. They scream as I regain my footing, burning from a Godly fire that my new, dark soul created. I watch as they rise and fall one by one, reaching to the sky as if He would save them.

Not this time. This time, you belong to me.

The last one falls to the Earth as I walk over and raise my hand in front of him and cause the fires to evaporate as quickly as I created them. He lays smoldering and smoking as he twitches with fading life for the final time as I place my foot across his throat. I'll have words with him before I send him back to his master.

"How many more of you must I send back to him before he realizes he wont fucking win? How many more of you are on the way?"

He grasps my foot as I begin to apply pressure.

"Answer me."

He wriggles and I begin to smell the awful aroma of his burning flesh. It pities me to keep him suffering, but I need answers that only he can provide. He remains silent, other than a few gasps for air.

"Have it your way."

I raise my foot up and hold it over his face. I bring it up quickly, preparing to stomp his head into the ground as he raises his hands to shield himself.

"Wait! Please!"

I pause in my movement and slowly set my foot back to the ground.

"Something to say?"

The hissing voice of a serpent is replaced by a wounded soul as small sobs begin to escape him.

"Please don't kill me...Please."

I kneel down next to him while he covers his face and rolls from me as the agony of some strange pain begins leaving him.

"I wasn't a bad man...before...They made me this way."

Be careful with this one...It could be more lies.

"*Who* made you this way?"

He whines on the ground while keeping his back to me and his face buried in his claws.

"A man with a staff...He did it."

"You have to give your soul to him willingly in order to be reborn as The Cursed...You asked for this Fate."

He calms his whining down to a small whimper before rolling towards me and slightly uncovering his eyes.

"Not all of us...Some of us changed our minds. I changed my mind. I have a family in The Realm...I wanted to see them again, so I said no...A lot of us did...He forced us to do it."

If this is true, I'm about to murder an innocent man.

"How is he changing them?"

He lowers his claws completely to greet me with his terrifying face and his eyes now carry a desperate plea within them.

"They held us down, the others he made, and he walked over to us one by one and stabbed us with his staff. That's when it happens. After he stabbed me, I felt a thick fire course through my body, almost like some kind of lava, moving slow and burning me inside. I felt my wings grow and my heart...changing...I felt really...mad...worse than I ever have before."

His staff holds the power. He's filling them with hate.

"The staff he uses...What makes it unique? Do you remember?"

He nods his head quickly in agreement.

"There's a small stone on the bottom. It's a bright red, but looks like an ordinary rock, only it's sharp, with a point on the end of it. It looks like a small spearhead."

"Did you see his face?"

"Yes, I did. He looks like a twisted man...Half monster...Half man...His eyes are black and empty..." he pauses and whispers the secret he uncovered, "I heard him say he has no soul."

He's telling the truth...He's innocent.

"What did you do in your final moments before he

turned you?"

His mouth turns into a hanging frown as he begins crying.

"I prayed...I prayed for whatever God is out there to save me...but He left me to die...I was a good man...I prayed He would remember me."

I feel his heartache in this moment. He isn't Cursed, at least not by his own actions. He feels he was forced to take this path and I have to agree with him. He's just confused as to *which* hand it was that forced him.

"What was your name...before?"

He slows his crying and returns his gaze to my own.

"Sam."

I smile down at him and place a hand on his scorched, melted shoulder.

"Hello Sam, my name is Joe. I was a regular guy when the Old World ended...I learned that everything really does happen for a reason, Sam. The Creator left me behind to defeat The Fallen One that we knew as Satan. I became the new Ruler of The Abyss. I thought He was being unfair with the path I was put on...I didn't feel that I was deserving of such a cruel fate. I learned after my death, right before my rebirth, that it was always my destiny to suffer in order to become who I am. He prepared me for it."

Squeezing his shoulder gently, I nod my head and let him know that his path was meant to intertwine with mine."The Creator didn't save you...because he needed you like this in order to deliver the words you just spoke...Without them, I would stand a little less wiser."

He earned his mercy.

"Sam...I'm going to do something for you now...Rise to your knees."

There is still a mortal life in him.

I rise from my knees and stand before him as he kneels down at my feet. The group approaches behind me and silently watches the spectacle in front of them.

"I'm lucky to find you in my company, Sam."

I hold his right shoulder firmly with my left hand before striking him with my right palm on his chest, and complete the ritual I had performed so many times to give lost souls their wings.

I'm taking your wings.

He screams in agony and begins swiping his claws at the air around him.

The hate is leaving him.

My eyes glow bright as I steal the very essence that he's infected with. I feel it enter my body and dissipate almost instantly. He wails like an infant and begins convulsing as his wings begin to shrivel. I wrap my wings around us both and whisper silent requests to The Creator and he joins me with a torn, ragged voice. The lightning hits with the force that a

112

terrible bolt should, the energy shocking us both, as it travels from The Realm. He flinches under my wings and I feel his body transforming under my feathers. I hear the others scream for the briefest of seconds from the surprise lightning bolt we've been struck by. I also hear a voice in the crash not belonging to anyone standing amongst us.

Unwrapping my wings, I'm greeted by a small, chubby man with pale skin and messy brown hair. Giggling to myself, I smile wide as he smiles back.

"Welcome to the New World, Brother."

Turning to greet my family, I place my arm around his shoulder.

"Everyone...meet Sam."

****

"You were...a demon?"

Amy K. sits quietly along with the rest of us, perched inside the store, and plays her million questions with the newest member of our family.

"Yes Ma'am...I believe I was called a 'Cursed'...I didn't wanna die and when they caught us they offered us the chance to live forever if we'd give up our souls. When I changed my mind is when they forced me to do it."

"Did it hurt to become a Cursed?"

"Yes Ma'am...but it hurt worse when Joe took the bad stuff outta me."

They both direct their gaze in my direction as Amy K. sets her sites on me.

"Did it hurt when you took it, Joe?"

"No, not at all...I felt it enter me and vanish. My soul has been blessed by The Creator. It's now full of His light, or whatever it is that makes Him so good...When the bolt hit us...He spoke to me. He told me that true evil couldn't exist in me, and that I was doing the right thing."

I shift the focus of my gaze to Sam alone.

"You can still go to The Realm and be with your family. The day you die, which could be years from now, will be the day you see them again. Continue to be a good person, Sam...I think it's the only way."

"I will, Joe...Thank you for my life, Sir."

I scoff lightly at his praise and wave my hand in a dismissive manner while we exchange small smiles between us.

"Ehh, don't thank *me*, Sam. It wouldn't have been possible without The Creators help...and you're very welcome."

I look around the room at everyone and see the energy around them dimming from the result of a sleepless night. For an immortal being, I feel foolish for looking over the very important fact that they still need sleep.

"Guys, get some rest. Go ahead and sleep for a few hours. Sasha and I can watch over you while you do."

I observe their movements and see that they are slowed by the weary night. Will and Carmen head for a corner to cuddle up while Greg, Danny and John lay where they sit. The two Amys make their beds next to the Dinner table. They all move as if ancient, and I find it strange that I've forgotten the feeling of what it was to have a tired, mortal body. I never feel tired or restless, only my new dark mind does. Sam lays alone between two aisles, as he feels that he's not yet a part of the family.

Robert approaches me as his towering figure shakes the floor under me with every step.

"Cuz...Why don't you two go off and have a day together...for as long as you can."

Another moment to be alone with Sasha.

"You're going to watch them?"

"Of course...I won't leave them until you return."

I glance at Sasha and see a small, devilish smile creeping across her face.

"It could be a while, Brother."

I tilt my head slightly and wrinkle my brow, hoping he gets the meaning. He smiles wide and looks away while chuckling softly to himself.

"They're going to sleep for a while, so there's no point

in rushing back...Take the whole day."

He turns to me as a Jokers' mask takes the place of his hardened features.

"Go put some more holes in the walls, you filthy animals."

Sasha and I erupt in laughter while the sound stirs everyone from their bed. They all look at us while I apologize.

"Sorry, guys. Get some rest."

Greg shoots me a thumbs up and mutters, "Have fun, Bro," before rolling over to begin his pursuit of dreams.

"We will. Sleep well...You have the *Best of the Best* watching over you...Be blessed, everyone."

A murmur of blessings greets us as they return to their comfort. I make sure they're settled back in before locking eyes with Robert and questioning him.

"How did you know?"

He begins laughing softly, yet carefully as to not disturb the others.

"You two got so loud that we could here you all the way to The Abyss."

I feel my facial features change as quickly as Sashas, into shock and disbelief. Sasha steals the words from my mouth.

"Whaaaat...the fuck? Are you serious? How is that even possible?"

"Joe has the second-most powerful soul in existence. He can be everywhere and nowhere in the same moment, projecting his souls voice to all corners of the universe."

He looks at me while wearing his Teachers hat once again.

"You have almost unlimited power, Cuz. You have to learn how to control it. When you two were making love, your soul was truly free in those moments. Your voice was everywhere, strongest at your home...it came through *booming* like an intercom."

I take a false breath and feel stunned as Sasha once again becomes the thief of my words.

"You mean all of The Abyss heard us fucking?"

He gasps in laughter, chuckling as softly as he can."Yeah, but only for a few seconds. We heard you telling him to knock the walls down and then...Well, you know the rest."

"If Joe has the second most powerful soul, how did you hear *my* voice?" She asks. Her eyes have now become wide and filled with panic.

"You're a part of his soul now."

I'm warmed by the thought of Sasha being a part of my Immortal Being, but stand completely mortified knowing that I played audible porn for millions of souls to hear.

What if my voice went...everywhere?

"Big...My voice didn't travel...to The Realm, did it?"

"No. Only The Abyss."

The shock still grips me and I know my lower jaw is somewhere around my feet.

"Don't worry...Everyone was happy for the both of you."

I smirk and look at Sasha while giggling to myself.

"Well...Did it at least *sound good*?"

We all laugh quietly as his dark features begin to turn a dark shade of red.

"No comment, Cousin."

"Well," Sasha begins, "at least Danny will be happy when he finds out that he was right about you and you *really are* a Porn Star."

Robert laughs and punches my arm playfully before turning away and tucking his wings close to his back. I turn to Sasha in time to catch her jumping into my arms. We share a lustful kiss as our bodies begin to burn with anticipation. I enjoy her a moment longer before pulling her away.

"Let's go, My Queen...I can't wait another second."

Her eyes become dreamy and her smile seductive as

118

she pulls me close and whispers to me with the voice of a Temptress.

"I have a surprise for you."

This could be interesting.

"Do you now?"

She giggles and bites her bottom lip while releasing me a bit before looking down at the floor between us.

"I do," she says softly while meeting my eyes again, "head over to our house," she pauses to close the distance between us and brushes her lips against mine, "and I'll meet you there."

"Hold on," I begin, feeling alerted, "I'm not leaving your side."

Her eyes become sharp, blue talons as they lock onto my gaze while she whispers intensely.

"You're going to do what your Queen commands. Do you hear me?"

She places her hand on my breastplate and pulls my face only centimeters from hers.

"You'll do what I say...*When* I say...For as long as I fucking want...and you'll do so without questioning me."

This could be very interesting.

"Sasha, I don't..."

She grasps my body tightly and the intensity in her eyes brings my lips to a halt.

"Go now...Your Queen commands it."

She pushes me back a step and gives me a fierce smile before turning away and heading to the front door. She walks past Robert and gives him a high-five, leaving him looking stunned and comical. He looks at me with confusion on his face as he raises his hands up in a questioning manner.

I laugh softly and shrug my shoulders, as I'm just as stunned as he is.

What are you up to?

****

My armor sits tucked into the corner of our bedroom while our bed resembles a broken carriage. The holes in the walls tell of the immortal love that took place within them. I pace continuously, careful to avoid glancing out the window. I don't want to ruin the surprise that Sasha has in store for me.

What is she doing?

I continue with my mad dash to nowhere, walking from wall to wall while my mind races.

She's up to something...I know it's good...but what?

The creaking of a door opening draws my attention and pauses my steps. I freeze and listen as small clicks fill the air before I realize I'm hearing the sound of High heels shoes on the hard floor. The door closes softly before the silence takes over.

She's here.

I feel frantic for some reason as the sound of the clicks up the stairs becomes a countdown. I look around the room for a place to sit or lay or prop myself against, but our room is in shambles. The clicks grow louder and fill me with an excited, yet anxious energy.

She's at the top of the staircase.

I scan the room for anything that hasn't already been smashed to pieces. A single stool sits in a lonely corner of the bedroom in the only square feet our previous passion didn't invade. I rush to it and grab it quickly, hurrying back to the center of the room before placing it down. I sit in time to hear the sound of her lovely feet reach the door.

It creaks open slowly and a vision of Sasha I've never seen greets me with smoldering eyes. Her newly dyed red hair acts as an endless wave of flames and falls perfectly on the dark, black Trench Coat she holds shut with both hands. Black pantyhose hug her sleek legs, peeking from the bottom of her coat, just above the black High heels she wears. She cracks a smile as she steps forward a few paces into the room. She pauses a few feet from me, giggling softly as she shimmies her

121

delicate shoulders, enticing me with the gift of her flesh.

I begin to rise with a fire burning inside me.

"Sit."

I fall back into place as my Queen commands.

She slowly opens the coat to reveal a vision of heart-stopping beauty as her slender body is wrapped in a delicate, black transparent Lingerie set. Soft lace caresses her body in the places I long to touch. It leaves nothing to the imagination, but makes me dream of what's underneath. I see her perfect breasts through the bra that holds them and her panties are equally transparent. She lets the trench coat drift off her shoulders and fall to the floor, along with my bottom jaw. She spins slowly and seductively, giving me a complete view of the surprise she dreamed up for me. The view of her from behind brings me to life and the urge to jump out of my seat becomes overwhelming. She picks up on my carnal urge and spins around to command me.

"Nope...You stay put."

She approaches me and brings her leg up slowly and places her foot on my thigh. My phantom heart begins racing as I begin fighting the urge to touch the lustful beauty in front of me.

"You don't move...*or* touch me...until I fucking say so."

"Sasha...You're fucking killing me right now."

She giggles and retrieves her slender foot, placing it

back to the floor as she brushes her legs up against mine while her pantyhose scream for my hands. With one hand, she grabs a handful of my hair and grinds the air in front of my eyes before releasing it and stepping back a pace. She places her finger to her bottom lip and hooks it softly.

"Awww Baby," she begins shyly, "am I not worth," she pauses to pull one side of her bra down with her free hand, "dying for?"

Her eyes meet mine and seem bluer than ever when surrounded by her fiery, red mane. She slowly completes her seductive removal of her bra as I stare on in disbelief. I feel myself becoming the animal she desires as she allows her hands to roam over her body. Hooking her panties with her thumbs, she pulls them down a few inches to reveal my biggest desire before allowing them to snap up and hide away my visual pleasure. I tense hard in my chair while my breathing becomes Beast-like. She begins to giggle again, knowing the torture she's inflicting upon me.

"Sasha I can't take this shit anymore!" I blurt out quickly, almost blending the words into one.

She laughs wildly as she spins around, giving me her backside again. Her blue eyes look back and lock onto mine just over her slender shoulder, and I can see her smile is hidden just behind it. She giggles seductively as she bends slightly and places her hands on her thighs and allows them to slide slowly all the way to her ankles. The view she presents to me now drives me completely mad.

I'm in a dream, I have to be. This is a fantasy.

"Sasha...You're worth dying for...just fucking kill me

already, Baby."

She pops up and turns around while laughing playfully and revealing that this new putty in her hands is entertaining her. She approaches me once again and places her legs on both sides of mine, threatening to straddle me. She takes my face in her hands and directs my eyes to her now commanding gaze.

"Your Queen commands you to close the door."

I don't even have to look at it to swing it shut.

****

The evening sun warms my body as I lay out on the front lawn with my wings spread out across the grass and covered in rubble, with Sasha curled up on my chest. We moved our lovemaking to the front yard after the East Wing of the house collapsed from our mad passion. It lays in ruins now, with half the house sagging into a pile of wood and steel. I can't recall how we ended up in the grass when only visions of her beautiful face and violent love dance in my mind. The sounds of her screams were louder than the houses screams of submission, as the world of lust and sex and destroyed walls and floors had become our only home for the day. It's a world I wish I could forever live in.

"Baby."

I direct my gaze from the clouds to her loving eyes.

"Yes, My Love?"

124

Her eyes are so blue and true. I love them...I love her.

"We need to do that again before we go home."

I begin to chuckle to myself, with my heaving chest bobbing her head up and down.

"Well...We still have the West Wing of the house."

I stroke her new, beautiful red hair away from her eyes and admire her slender features as they compliment her new color. Her cheeks rise up as she smiles.

"After this one, we'll find another house...I love having you inside me."

"I love to be there, Sasha...I wish I could spend my timeless existence making love to you."

"We really would fuck like Wild Rabbits."

I laugh to the sky as her foul language always makes me smile. It seems so odd, even after all this time knowing her, to hear such a beautiful creature possess a Sailors mouth.

"He took her savagely in the grass and ravaged her like the Wild rabbit he was, screwing her as hard as his little, furry, Bunny body would allow..."

She erupts in laughter as she props herself up and smacks my chest playfully.

"Shut the fuck up! Don't you dare ruin your beautiful words repeating the shit that comes out of my mouth."

125

"I've got a big carrot for you, the Wild Bunny confessed while..."

"Your Queen commands you to shut the fuck up! Now!"

She falls on me as we both laugh before she wraps her arms around my neck as I put my arms around her waist.

It feels so wonderful to be in love.

The aroma of her soul fills my senses while the warmth in my heart grows like a wildfire. She makes herself comfortable again on my chest and begins to sing our song, and I find her voice soft and spellbinding. I lay my head back and close my eyes while feeling the warmth from the sun and Sashas love, both feelings that should be lost to a Dark King.

Thank You. You really have blessed me.

"Baby."

"Yes, My Love?"

"Nothing...I just wanted to hear you call me 'your love' is all."

She nuzzles her face into my chest and sighs and I can feel her smiling face pressed against me.

I love her curses...She loves my words.

"You're my life now, Sasha...You'll always be my world...I'll always be your Moon...You'll always be my girl...With loving lips you command me...With eager ears I listen...You're the Queen of my life...And serving you is my mission...You stole my heart with eyes so blue...but you captured my soul...by being you."

I feel her crawling up my chest and moving her face to mine. I close my eyes and direct my face towards her and await the enchanting touch of her lips. It never comes and causes me to open my eyes to find her staring at my face with her silly smirk.

"I fucking love you, Joe."

I laugh softly as I stroke her hair and take a false breath.

"I fucking love you too, Sasha."

She chuckles at my use of her favorite word so I decide to run with it.

"Fucking words can never fucking describe the fucking way I fucking feel about you, you fucking fucker."

She erupts in laughter and falls back to my chest as her voice fills the air. She begins to snort, unable to catch her false breath or find her voice. Her laughter is my sweet music, the sounds I would remember throughout our battle stricken night that is on its' way. She finally finds her voice after what seems an eternity.

""It's so funny to hear you talk to me like that...Oh God, I fucking love it.

She returns to her giggles and I join her, but the moment is fleeting. I suddenly realize we're both still naked to the world around us.

"We need to find our clothes. I feel naked without my sword."

"You are naked," she replies before reaching down and grabbing her favorite part of me, "and you have your sword."

I look at her and meet her seductive eyes that now burn as bright as her new hair.

We don't have time.

"Later, My Love...after the group is assembled."

"I still have my Teddy."

We can make time.

"Then what are we waiting for?"

We jump to our feet and begin our race up the steps. The front door is sagging in its frame, with the weight of the collapsed house now too much for it. I motion my hand forward in front of the door and send it creaking open. The beautiful blue stairs have disappeared on the right wing, as the ceiling has somehow collapsed onto it.

"I'll grab my Teddy and we can go."

This won't do.

"You don't need it. You're sexy without it. Let's grab my armor and your clothes. We're going someplace else."

"Where to?"

"We need a shower."

"Baby, we don't need to take showers. This shit just falls right off of us," she says while brushing away the remains of our house that cling to my feathers.

She doesn't get it.

I reach down and grab a handful of my own and allow my fingers to begin stroking the warmth they are now holding.

She gasps and shows surprise in her eyes as I repeat myself.

"We need a shower."

****

She screams loudly, as the sensations have become too much for even her immortal body. We climax in the same instant while water pours over us as the Shower Shack has become our latest playground. I'm behind her and catch her as she pitches forward, before I pull her slowly up towards me. I hold her against my body as I kiss the back of her neck and let my hands roam across her chest while she comes down from the orgasmic high our lovemaking placed her on. We were careful not to damage the Shower Shack. Only a single stall wall fell from our passion, creating a project for John to take up later. She continues breathing heavy as I whisper in her ear.

"Next time..."

"Our house," she finishes.

She turns on shaky legs to meet my gaze.

"I know, Baby, it was hard being...restrained...I don't want to mess up everyones showers, but at the same time," she leans in close as her eyes beg with new requests, "I want you to *fucking take me*."

"Should we head back now?"

"Still trying to kill me?" She asks as she giggles with surprise, "I'm already dead!"

I drift towards her and kiss her softly as my hands run through her now brown hair, now that the temporary dye has all washed away. She knows my lustful thoughts and is once again the voice of reason.

"We really should check on the others, Baby. We'll make time before we go back home."

"I know we will, My Love," I admit, though feeling a bit disappointed, "Let's get dressed and go."

I run my fingers through her hair and suppress the small smile being caused from the memory of her red locks. She notices me reminiscing and moves to remedy my newfound sadness.

"You want me to dye it permanently? I will. I saw how much it turned you on. You *really* like me as a Redhead."

"Ain't gonna lie, it was *fucking hot*."

She giggles again and runs her finger down my chest as her eyes fall to her favorite plaything.

"I love turning you on."

With her mood shifting quickly, she lifts her head up to mine as her eyes grow wide.

"Hey! Why don't you try and turn my hair red for me? You can do anything. Give it a shot," she says as she reaches for my hand, "I trust you."

The thought of using my powers on her terrifies me, as I still don't know the full extent of them.

"I don't know, Sasha, I don't..."

She interrupts me playfully by throwing her slender arms up.

"Yeah yeah, you don't want to hurt your Queen, blah blah BLAH!"

I laugh as I take her hands in mine and lift them to kiss the back of them. We stand and smile like fools as her eyes reassure me that she trusts me with her life, much less her hair.

"You're not going to hurt me, Baby," she assures, "I mean it...I trust you."

I can do it.

I focus my gaze on her lovely blue jewels and fall deep into them. I feel something stirring in my chest and feel a rush throughout my body a moment later.

"Don't move, My Queen."

I bring my hands up to her forehead, palms down, and stop at her hairline. I let my hands feel the sensations of kinetic energy surge through my veins and feel the heat ending at my fingertips. I stroke my hands back in a smooth motion, running all the way down to the end of her beautiful mane. She gasps as she feels the sensations of her color changing like Autumn leaves.

Her fiery red locks have returned, and I immediately find myself turned on again. She pulls her hair forward into her view before squealing in excitement.

"Holy fuck! I love it, Baby!"

"Not as much as me, apparently," I confess before directing my gaze down and letting hers follow. She sees my lustful reaction to her hair and laughs before taking a swipe at it.

"Wait until we get to our house! Put it away, your Queen commands it."

"Okaaaay," I whine playfully, "as my Queen commands."

"Hey," she begins, "Your Queen is gonna rock your world later, I promise. I'm gonna make your fucking toes curl," she pauses to take another swipe while giggling, "just now right now!"

Ecstatic, she returns her attention to her hair and

inspects every wave of her new locks. The sight of her in red continues making my blood rise and my strength disappear, proving that she truly is my forever weakness. It's a vision I would keep burned into my memory for the battle to come; Her beautiful face surrounded by a living nightmare of flesh and wings.

My God, you're so beautiful. I can stare at you for an eternity.

She turns her attention to me with hearts in her eyes as her hair falls from her fingers.

"Awww, Baby, thank you. That's so sweet."

"What is?"

Her brow wrinkles as her squinty eyes look at me with curiosity.

"You just said that I was beautiful and that you could stare at me for an eternity. Not out loud, but you sent it to me."

I'm confused as to how she heard my innermost thoughts without me projecting them to her.

"I didn't mean to say it to you...I just thought it...and I mean it."

She brings her hands to my face and cups my cheeks and begins staring deep into the pit of my endless soul.

"Robert's right. You're so strong, Baby. Your soul has so much power in it, almost too much to keep in your body. You *have* to learn how to control it...You'll be unstoppable once you do."

I smile as I reach up to my face and take her hands in mine before placing them over my stilled heart.

"I'll learn it all eventually...It's not easy to will your mind and soul to do something."

"You learned how to communicate without words pretty easy. Now you've done it without trying. You're getting stronger by the day."

She returns her hands to my cheeks and finds my eyes with her own.

"And I believe in you."

I chuckle softly before allowing my lips to deliver a small kiss. I feel a renewed life coursing through me, just knowing I have such a wonderful woman to call my own. She makes me weak with her body, but stronger than I've ever been with her love and devotion. Behind every man may indeed be a great woman, but *beside* every King, you'll only find a Queen as strong as the one who now holds me.

"I love you, Sasha...I can't say it enough."

She grins as she puts her arms around my waist and binds herself to me.

"You fucking better...I love you too, Joe."

We allow our faces to come together for one more silent moment to capture, her soft nude body radiating heat and warming mine all the way down to my soul. We savor the seconds as if they are the last we possess, enjoying the eternal touch of our love. I lift her up and kiss her as if it would be the last time, and find my soul hungry for her deafening screams. She puts her arms around my neck and goes with the moment...but only for a moment.

"Baby," she begins as she pulls her face away, "we need to get back to the others."

She's right, as usual...I hope she didn't hear that.

Her laughter catches me by surprise and signals confirmation that she did.

"You heard that too, didn't you?"

"Yes. I. Did!" she sings in a victorious tone.

She becomes playful as I set her to her feet and she smacks her hands against my chest.

"I can hear your thoughts! You're screwed, buddy! And you know I'm right...as usual."

She smiles at me as her mischievous eyes return to her. I grab her arm and spin her around, bringing my other hand quickly to her backside and returning the playful pat and it causes her to shriek in surprise.

"Don't let it go to your head!" I command.

She turns to me with her mouth hanging open in a wide smile.

"Or I'll have to remind you who's the King."

"Oh yeah," she questions defensively while her eyes grow wide, "I'm your Queen and you will obey *my* commands. You're *my* bitch, so don't get it twisted," she finishes while trying to hold her laughter. I stand smiling and silent as I try to hold my own laughter, causing her to carry on.

"Oh, what are you gonna do about it? Huh?"

"Why don't *you* try and hear my fucking thoughts," I say smoothly, "and find out how I'm going to punish you."

Her blue eyes become seductive and intrusive as she prys at my thoughts. I don't have to send her any messages as she gets the answer from the smoldering look I give her from my lustful soul.

"Ooooh...Baby...I love it when you get like this."

She brings her hands to my waist as we both finally break and begin laughing at our own bullshit.

"We still don't have time, Baby...I'm sorry."

I wrap my arms around her slender body and give her a reassuring smile.

"It's okay, Sasha. I can wait. We *really do* need to get back."

"We have an eternity to make love," she reminds me.

"Thank the fucking stars it's an eternity."

136

Leaning forward, she plants a small tender kiss on my chest over my beatless heart.

"Let's get moving, Baby."

****

The dusk hour approaches and threatens to turn the world to darkness as we retrace our path into the store. The room is well lit from the glow of the lanterns with the group sitting quietly around the Dinner table, only hardened steel has replaced the dinnerware. They get familiar with their new weapons as Robert stands in the corner and watches. With Sams' small figure sitting next to him, it makes his giant figure appear even bigger. I look on as well before turning to Sasha, who's also preparing for the carnage.

"Be safe tonight, My Soul. I'll be at your side."

She looks at me with the coy smile I love so much.

"Those motherfuckers are going down. I don't know what you're so worried about."

I smirk and release a hushed giggle.

"I know you're a badass, Sasha, but be careful nonetheless. We still don't know the extent of *their* powers."

"They don't know the extent of *yours*, My Loving King."

I reach down and take her hands in mine and hold them

137

close to my chest.

"Nor yours, My Beautiful Queen," I confess before taking her into my arms again.

Robert drifts from the corner with Sam by his side, and the duo appear comical. It almost looks like the opening of some comedic sitcom as they couldn't be more different.

Here comes Bobby the Bulldog with his tiny, Terrier friend!

I feel Sasha snicker against my chest, confirming she heard my unspoken jest towards them.

"Hey Cuz, we need to talk."

"What's up, Big?"

"Our new friend here has never seen battle as a Human. I'm thinking we leave him hidden somewhere while we take care of business."

I set my gaze on Sams small, finicky face.

"Is that okay with you?"

He looks down at his feet as he shuffles them while his mind races towards nowhere.

"I would *like* to help...I just don't think I could be much use right now."

"Sam."

138

His eyes find mine as I read his petrified thoughts.

"It's okay to be afraid. I have a powerful soul, but I'm *always* in fear...It's okay."

His energy becomes erratic as panic begins to grow inside him.

"How can *you* be afraid? You killed twenty of those things by yourself!"

"I'm afraid for my family. The Cursed can't hurt me, but they can still hurt everyone else in this room, minus Robert and Sasha. You're now a brother, Sam. I don't want you going into a war if you're not ready. I trained with everyone in my mortal life, passing my knowledge of swordplay to them. They are warriors of The Creator, ready to give their lives for His cause. I know you *want* to help. I'd worry a little less if you had proper training first...Have you ever held a sword?"

"Yes, but I never used one before."

I step back a few paces from him and wrap my wings around my body, shielding me from the world. My body trembles as I imagine a sword in my hands and the fires of my soul brings the steel to life. I feel the familiar touch of a handle forming in my hands. I release myself from my feathered cocoon to reveal a dark and terrible sword, with a black, ivory handle joining a crimson, steel blade. I pass the sword to Robert as everyone gazes in awe.

"Do your thing, Brother."

He doesn't offer his hand in return, but he does offer a soft gaze in its' place.

139

"I can't, Cuz."

"Why not?"

"You forged it, technically, in the fires of The Abyss. A Servant can't bless it."

I feel offended for some reason, but shake the notion off quickly as I know Roberts' loving heart.

"Are you saying this is an *evil* sword?"

"No, Cousin, not at all."

I focus my gaze on his dark eyes and try to get a read on him.

"Then what's the problem?"

He steps up to me and places a hand on my shoulder.

"Not The Creator or Servants can bless something that comes from The Abyss. It's not a personal thing, or a bad thing, in your case, Cuz. The Creator is light and you are the darkness," he says, coining words that Sasha had said to me, "something forged in The Realm can only be held by holy hands, and a Servant can't touch something forged in The Abyss."

I look to him with fresh questions running rampant.

"I rule The Abyss...My sword is from The Realm."

"Given to you before you became the rightful ruler. You were only a Fallen Servant for your first three days. In your case, it doesn't matter. Your sword was crafted for you alone...The same way you crafted Sams just now. It was created out of necessity. Your sword was blessed by His light. It can do amazing things. The one you made for Sam can be blessed by you alone."

"To do terrible things," I say and finish his thought.

I look at the terrible, dark blade in my hands a spin the handle in my palm.

It's a beautiful piece...I'll make it deadly.

I close my eyes and let my mind drift to a dark place, the only place I could ever feel true anger anymore. I imagine the man who shares my face. The man who tortured my Sweet Angel. The man Sasha called her husband, who happens to be the same man responsible for almost killing her loving soul.

I'll meet my reflection one day, even if I have to pull him out of The fucking Realm myself.

A hearty roar escapes my throat as the blade comes to life in my hands, bursting into an emerald fire. They leap back a few paces as the blade begins to emit a hollow scream, with the fire growing with the sound. I hush myself as quickly as I began, the fire dispersing immediately and revealing a red blade encrusted with silver Moons. It appears glossy as if covered with blood and emits a beautiful glow in the soft light of the lanterns. It feels weightless, which is an odd feeling considering its size.

I pass the blade off to Sam and see his eyes fill with wonder and appreciation of his new gift.

"Oh my God...It's beautiful."

Unable to see anything other than his new blade, it's obvious he's completely awestruck.

"Put it to good use one day."

He returns his soft, brown gaze to mine with fresh questions swirling in his mind.

"Can it do anything?"

That's...a good question. What the hell can it do?

"I'm not sure, to be honest with you."

Looking confused, he tilts his head and questions me further.

"Um, you just *made it*...How can you not know?"

"I'm still learning the extent of my powers, Sam. I put a part of me into it...I'm sure it can do *something*...I just have no idea what that is exactly," I reply while looking as confused as he does.

He steps back a few paces and begins to get a feel for his new harbinger of death. He takes his stance and swings it a few times and surprises me, as his form isn't bad for such a small, chubby man. He pauses briefly as he has an epiphany sprint through his head and it shows on his face. His eyes become alive while his voice becomes a small, booming thunder.

"Fire!"

The blade erupts in its emerald glow and the flames cut the air around it. A wave of awe passes among the group as bright eyes and new questions rise with the flames. The excitement of it all breathes life into a new examination of their own blades.

The fire halts and Sams display is greeted with cheers before the group sets their sights on the only two Servants in the room; The one on loan and The Fallen One. The questions spread as quickly as a wildfire that threatens to consume me. I glance at Robert to see him meeting the same Fate as the two Amys bombard him to extract knowledge. We all have a lot to learn still, it seems.

Even me.

"Guys! One at a time," I say as I set my gaze on Robert.

"What can the blades from The Realm do?"

He takes a deep breath out of necessity as the words coming are sure to be heavy with insight. He addresses my question towards the group as they all look on while holding their relics.

"They can cut through the strongest metals and stones with ease. The Cursed cannot withstand their power...when properly harnessed."

He stops and glances at all the faces glued to his. A few, long seconds follow before everyone realizes he won't continue.

That's it?

Amy K. beats me to solving the riddle.

"Could you be a little more specific? Can they burst with fire too?"

"No."

"Can they do anything else?"

"Yes."

"Just not fire?"

"No."

It looks like Robert just joined our little game of one liners.

"What do you mean...properly harnessed? They can hold power?"

"Yes."

"What kind of power?"

"Unmatched."

Like a curious cat who always catches her mouse, Amy

K. refuses to give up.

"How do I make it work? And please be specific, I can bug you all day."

He begins to chuckle as he glances at me. He remembers the stories I told him about our curious, little Amy K., always needing to be informed.

"Amy K., the blade you have, all your blades, contain the ability to release The Creators light upon The Cursed. The good you have in your heart translates over to the power of your blades."

Greg rises and joins the discussion as his lips begin bursting with his own questions.

"So you're saying that the more love we have in our hearts, the stronger the weapons will be?"

"That's exactly right, Greg."

"We're fucking good then, Bro. I love these guys and would die for them. Any one of them, even Danny."

"Gee thanks," Danny says as he cracks his crooked smile and turns to Greg to flip him the middle finger and blow a kiss. Robert cracks a small smile at their jests before answering.

"Then it sounds like your weapons already harnessed the power...Try it out."

The room becomes as silent as a graveyard as Greg walks to a clearing next to the door and releases his machete from his waist. He holds the blade and examines it closely while his eyes study the blade as if he's looking for some sort of hidden switch in its carvings. He turns the blade over and over while his mind tries to unlock the secret that now consumes him.

C'mon, Little Brother...You've always been such a smart kid.

The blade continues turning in his palms, as do the gears in his mind. He appears to be growing impatient.

The answer is simple, Little Brother...Stop thinking so hard.

He glances at me as if he heard my thoughts and it makes me wonder if my mind has betrayed me and broadcast itself live once again. He smirks and laughs under his breath, ready to give up when it finally reveals itself. He exhales sharply and smiles.

He looks at the group and addresses them softly.

"If The Creator is the opposite of Joe...and Joe represents the darkness...then it can only be..."

Everyone leans in on instinct, trying to absorb the scene in front of us, until Greg whispers loudly and changes the scenery around us.

"Light."

146

His blade explodes with light and creates a wave of white and yellow beams that paint the room around us. The entire store becomes illuminated and resembles a false Realm created on Earth with the light forged in The Realm itself. A collection of cheers fills the air at Gregs' new discovery. Greg begins howling to the sky as he twirls his new, bright blade and fights an invisible foe. The group follows suit until the glow in the room becomes deafening as the light of seven sets of charged weapons invades every corner. Sasha makes her way over to me and leans in close to my ear.

"Do you think our swords can do that? Mine came with me from The Realm."

The thought hadn't crossed my mind at all. We had ours the longest and, not once, did we ever consider the possibility.

How could we have not known?

"I don't know, My Love," I reply as I shoot her a sly grin, "Let's find out."

We take a step back from each other and draw our death instruments. She smiles at me in the glow of the otherworldly light and appears as a Warrior Sprite, appearing so beautiful and deadly in the same instant. I show my own beaming smile and wink at her.

"Let's see what ours can do, Sasha. Ladies first, My Love."

She nods and focuses on the steel in her hands before breathing life into her command.

147

"Light."

Her sword comes to life and reflects the seven before it and illuminates her surprised face.

"Oh fuck yeah! Look, Baby!"

She swings her sword in imaginary combat and beheads a phantom enemy, while the light emitting from it is a bright and frightening Baby Blue.

It matches her eyes on a sunny day.

I admire the scene in front of me a moment longer. I watch all of my family and my Warrior Queen engaged in the pursuit of knowledge while honing their skills to a deadly degree. I break away from it and bring my sword into my view while reminding myself that the bright blade is a reflection of my soul inside my dark body. The blade calls to me, as the crosses Sasha engraved remind me where all power comes from, regardless of what symbol or label is placed on it. My sword is Holy, no matter how unholy my hands may be labeled, and will only forever shine with The Creators light, and not the fires that once consumed The Abyss. I close my eyes and wrap my fingers around the handle in the same manner that a constrictor kills its prey.

"Light."

A silent burst of radiant green energy explodes from the blade and sends everyone to their backs, including Robert. I stumble back a step before finding my footing and observing that my sword is now calm and smoking. A small line along the sharpened edge glows with white fire and appears hotter than the fires of the Old Abyss. I pull my blade close as my eyes search the scorched metal for damages. That wasn't the light show everyone else received as my own display resulted in a fiery dud. I pray silently it wasn't at the cost of my sword. I turn to the group as they rise from their backs in confusion as they're unaware of the misfortune I just unleashed. Robert meets my gaze and I see his eyes holding answers to my riddles.

I don't know what the fuck happened just now, but he does.

I walk over a few small steps and pull Sasha to her feet. She meets my stare with one of her own, reflecting my thoughts as well as my face. Her blue eyes always appear so wild when she feels fear. She stands my mirror image in needing to know what took place. We share a mind, and may as well share a body as we both turn to Robert.

"What the hell was that?" I ask sharply.

He approaches me while dusting off his now stained white robes and pauses a few feet from me. He shrugs his shoulders and pops his neck as if preparing for a war of steel and not a waterfall of words. He smiles at my bewildered eyes and chuckles softly to himself.

"Seriously, what the hell happened just now? I *know* you know, Robert."

He swings his head back, black hat and all his long, dark locks, and bellows to the sky. He continues his laughter as Sasha and I exchange glances of shock and worry. I take her hand in mine and squeeze it tight, and exposing my worry through my panicked grip. She squeezes mine briefly and smiles at me, and

149

her small, beautiful Crescent Moon calms my immortal nerves.

Whatever that was couldn't have been bad...I hope.

Robert finally finishes his long winded laughter and meets my worrisome gaze. He lifts his hands up in front of him as if to stop my phantom charge and his eyebrows arch high and his face becomes lively. He chuckles a bit more before finally addressing me.

"Cuz, it's okay. You don't need to be worried about that...It happens."

My Warrior Queen steals my words before I can voice them.

"You make it sound like he blew his load too quick or something."

The laughter reignites in him as he speaks.

"In a sense, he did."

He turns his eyes to mine while still giggling.

"Cousin...You have so much power in you. Sometimes when the spirit is too strong, as in your case, you expend too much energy at once, making it uncontrollable. Cuz...*You gotta get control over it.* Too many of those misfires and the soul cannot revitalize properly. You'll become weak. Your sword is the vessel in which you can channel the energy. Let it trickle out of you into the sword...Try to avoid the Tsunami. You stand more powerful than all but The Creator. It's not going to be easy to do...but I know you can do it."

150

I take his words in slowly as I nod in agreement.

I know I can do this.

The sounds of splintered wood and twisted metal screams throughout the air as the doors of our sanctuary cries out in submission. We all stand frozen in surprise as The Cursed hurl themselves against the door. There will be no time to learn my new skills, as these monsters are making sure of it. I shoot my wings out and shield the group behind me while Robert follows my lead, and the both of us stand our ground to protect the mortals in our presence. We're both aware that if we fall, they will swiftly follow if such a thing comes to pass.

"Everyone prepare for battle! Have no fear of these cowards who turned from The Realm. Let us shine down our light upon the ugly sons of bitches and show them *who the fuck they're messing with!*"

The roars are loud behind my feathered shield as the clashing of steel and promises of death lift to the ceiling. They taunt The Cursed who fight to enter our store, while preparing to make our last stand in this world. Sasha rallies them on, screaming her curses of screwing The Cursed with three feet of steel, inviting them all to participate in her orgy of death and terrorized monsters. She has no wings, but may be the most powerful presence among us. I'm happy it's her to take the reigns and keep our family motivated. The sound of the door falling to the ground reminds me that my work lies ahead.

I charge forward while Robert takes my place and assumes the mantle of their shield as I begin my assault on the first to make it within my reach. He screams loud and terrible as he swipes his talons at my face and misses by a hair before I bring my blade up from my waist and impale him quickly. I feel the blade slice his heart in two and pray he didn't stand as Sam, as an innocent who was forced to be evil. I think about Sasha and everyone else behind me and, feeling a strange hate rising in me, care a little less about them being innocent.

They came to kill my family. There will be no mercy shown tonight.

I kick him off my blade violently and spin my body to regain momentum. I let my sword drift to my right hand and bring it across my field of view to the sight of three heads becoming airborne. My left hand follows the trail and emits an emerald flame to scorch the wave behind them. I hold my hand forward while crying out for battle and let the fires pour out of me until a pile of burning Cursed flesh fills the newly created entrance. The taunts of The Cursed behind the burning bodies sound to be too many in number. I can hear the screams of dozens, if not hundreds, of tortured voices. The fallen Cursed now burn upon the fallen door, but the blockade is sure to last only moments. I hear the screams of my family and turn to see a part of the ceiling at the back of the store collapsing, a small section, yet big enough for a Cursed to make his way in. A few feet away, another piece of the ceiling mimics the first and crumbles to the floor. The Cursed, slashing through the mound of burned flesh behind me, regain my attention as their brothers begin to fall through the holes above like tormented rain.

There's too many. Move quickly.

The sound of Johns voice is deafening as he bellows a war cry and follows it with swift commands. He stands as their leader now and takes the reigns in my absence. They look to him for guidance they way they used to look at me and await instructions of who should meet their blades.

"Back to back!"

They fall into formation, a circle of eyes and steel pointed in all directions, as The Cursed begin their charge to end them. They stand deadly accurate in their thrusts, impaling The Cursed and severing limbs and heads with ease. The two Amys stand side-by-side, the deadliest of sisters, while Carmen and Will match their enthusiasm for the death of enemies. Danny and Greg complete the ensemble while Robert and Sasha take on the strays. They steal life as quickly as it falls through the ceiling.

They're good. Don't lose focus.

I set my undivided attention to the newly created entrance in front of me and see a grotesque tunnel carved by The Cursed through the flesh of their fallen brothers. The first to enter stands taller than the rest and is unnaturally tall for a former Human. He appears as a living Grim Reaper, minus the robes, but with all the presence of a real death dealer, with his naked body only dressed by his hanging, thinning hair. He gazes down at me with hollow black eyes that hold smoldering coals as I stare up at all eight feet of him.

He has no wings. This was no Human before death.

He roars in a raspy voice as his clawed fingers shoot forward and wrap around my neck.
Dropping my sword, I grab his arm at the wrist with my right hand and place my left on his elbow and begin pushing it in the direction nature didn't intend it to bend. It snaps off while the tearing cartilage and cracking bones fill my ears. I pry the fingers off my neck and toss it aside as his other hand finds my throat and lifts me into the air with ease. He squeezes tight, constricting the airway I no longer use, before pulling my face

close to his. He smiles as he begins his attempt to break my neck.

Nothing happens as he gives it his all while I crack a smile of my own.

I shoot my hands towards his throat and mimic his attempts a moment before, only finding success where he found failure. I wrap all my fingers around his neck and waste no time applying pressure and feel his neck collapsing between my palms. I jerk my hands upwards towards the sky and feel the cold blood shower my face as his head tears from his body with little resistance. I drop from his claw to the Earth in front of his still standing headless body and kick it with a violent force, sending it into the wave of Cursed advancing through the entrance. I use his head as a fastball sent straight out of The Abyss to complete my assault. I glance back at my people, still fighting like Servants and winning like Gods, and see The Cursed piling up around them as they fight a disciplined battle. The sight of their calm faces eases my worries.

I retrieve my sword quickly and start a mad slash directed at the entrance. My blade travels with speed and efficiency as it does its job with the screams of Cursed and severed limbs becoming the end result. I start to pick them apart, one by one, destroying each with single slashes. The ground becomes littered around me as wings and heads and arms decorate the floor. The screams of The Cursed awaiting entry are still plentiful in number. Their voices are as sharp as their talons as they force themselves into the awaiting death known as my blade. Hot phantom breaths shoot from me as the fight rises in me. I feel the terror of The Abyss about to be unleashed *by* me.

A hollow ring fills my ears as the world around me

quickly vanishes into a deep darkness.

Again, what a time to get a phone call.

****

The darkness surrounds me as the ringing subsides in my hearing. Looking down, I find my feet standing on a shadowy floor. It appears to be a never-ending, pitch black void in all directions.

"Hello?"

The silence returns my greeting as my words echo down an invisible tunnel.

"Could you make this quick?...THIS IS KIND OF A BAD TIME!"

My inquiry rings throughout the emptiness and confirms to be the only sound in this void.

"The answer is in your hands. Remember what Robert told you."

"Who are you? Are you the Creator?! Is it you? I have questions!"

I feel my heart alive and racing once again as the Human

element of discovery creates a frenzy in my immortal body. The Creator, The One and Only, is finally reaching out to me since the first time I heard his voice on my Death Day. It must be urgent if *this* was the most opportune moment.

"I know you do...There is no time for that now...You can summon them...Remember Roberts words."

The darkness begins a slow transformation back into the light as the gray becomes more alive with every second.

"Wait! Please!"

"In time."

****

The world returns in an instant and the moment in front of me is painted by the sight of Cursed pouring into the entrance. I glance back and see my family faltering, as Sasha and Robert are now engaged with twenty or more. The circle of death created by my family is beginning to shrink as the number of tortured souls begins to grow and swarm them. I feel the heat rising in me, as the fires of desperation begin to warm me from within. My hands begin to burn as if dipped in the hottest fires. I glance down to see my sword emitting a small glow.

The answer is in my hands...Roberts words...My sword.

Taking the handle in both hands, I point the tip of the blade to the ground and lift it to the air. I focus my energy and the burning of my soul into the very blade. My body shudders as the emerald fires of The Abyss begin dancing on my skin, the brilliant green replacing the Old Abyss' traditional orange. I take all the hate of the world and all the suffering I took from the souls seeking wings and channel it into the palms of my hands. The blade erupts in green flames and reflects the fires of my new soul.

Summon them.

I scream to the Celestial bodies above as I slam my blade into the floor and call upon the forces of The Abyss. The ground quakes and The Cursed shake while my family pauses and looks on in confusion. The store around us becomes alive and lit with small, green flames leaping from the ground at random and it appears to be a fire containing its own mind.

It contains its own limbs at least.

Hands and arms belonging to the tortured souls under my wings begin to sprout from the flames and reach for The Cursed of the New World. They grasp them violently and pull them down before pulling them apart, leaving arms and wings and heads scattered about. They pull them into the flames in droves, taking as many alive as possible and destroying those who resist. Such was my command, to spare the souls who stand as Sam.

We will not murder innocents if we don't have to.

They scream from fright, unable to take the emotions they do their best to bestow upon others. I look out the entrance and see the same fires consuming The Cursed outside the building at a rapid pace. My family stands frozen in awe at the sight their eyes are showing them. They can't take their eyes off of the small ponds of green flames that give birth to

157

hands and arms. The masses of monsters inside the store begins to dwindle to a resisting few and we watch in silence as the last of them are torn to pieces. Sasha makes her way through the mess of death and approaches me quickly and grasps me tightly. She still appears so beautiful, even with her arms and robes slick with the black bloods of putrid evil. I grab a hold of her hand and head towards the entrance with Robert and my family following quickly behind.

This isn't over.

Chapter 4

The flames continue consuming the last of The Cursed as we make our way out the front entrance to meet the crisp air of a cold night. The light is dimming and making the world around us invisible, even for the New Ruler of The Abyss. Sasha holds my hand tight and squeezes it twice, drawing my gaze to hers. She speaks to me with our shared soul.

"Baby...This isn't over yet. I can feel them close by."

I give her a look of reassurance in the darkness.

"I know...We have to prepare for a long night...and maybe a long day as well."

"They'll never make it that long. They're still Human. They get tired."

"Then you have to protect them, Sasha. When the time comes, you have to leave my side and protect them."

Her brow creases with worry and uneasy anxiety at the thought of breaking her promise to me.

"I won't leave your side...Don't even ask."

"I'm not asking you to leave my side...I'm asking you to protect the family we love so much. Protect our brothers and sisters, My Love. I have to protect us all, starting with you...I love you, My Queen."

We find each others arms and cling to one another as if we've forgotten how to let go.

"We don't have a lot of time to get ready, Cuz...They're coming back," Robert reminds me.

"Fuck," Danny begins, "I'm so fucking thirsty! I'd kill all those bastards myself if it meant getting a beer!" He exclaims rather annoyingly as he turns to Sasha.

"By the way...Is your hair red now or am I fucking tripping?"

She grabs a handful of her hair off of her shoulders and squeezes the black blood from it.

"It *used* to be red...I'll explain later."

He looks at it with his bottom lip forcing itself up while his sweaty brow wrinkles as if studying her.

"Well...I can tell it *used* to look nice."

"Guys! Focus," Greg interrupts, "Joe, how much longer are we gonna do this? How many more are coming? It's just...I'm tired as fuck, Bro. I don't think I could do that again."

"I don't know, Greg, I wish I did. I'll do my best to hold them back for as long as I can."

"Joe," Amy J. begins, "I can't see anything out here, Honey. Can you do that thing with your hands and make some light for us?"

160

The night around us seems alive, and we can feel a pulse of energy hidden in the darkness. The world seems quiet, but this New World has taught us to be ever mindful of the peace and quiet. The worst is always hidden in the silent shadows, waiting for our guards to fall. It makes Amy J. and the others uneasy, as well as my dead heart.

"Sure...Stand back."

I raise my hands slightly above my head and begin to feel the sting of fire being created in my palms before Robert halts my movements with deadly speed. He grasps my wrists as the flames are coming to life and sends them back into my palms.

"Cuz!...You can't. It'll be a beacon to them, bringing them in droves," he pauses to point to my family, "they won't survive another wave."

I lower my hands and I see their faces in the dark and watch while their eyes study my own. Carmen and Will resemble ghosts, yet not in appearance, but in presence. They seem to be drifting in the wind, floating above the ground. Thirst overwhelms Danny while John tries desperately to catch his breath, as Greg and the Amys do their best impersonations of him. It becomes painfully obvious that they don't have the strength to withstand another assault.

Something's missing...Someone.

"Guys...Where's Sam?"

They glance at the shadowy figures next to them until they all realize the newest addition to the family is missing.

161

"Where did he go? I thought he was with you guys," I question them.

"He was there when the fight began," Greg informs me, "but I lost track of him, Bro...when the shit hit the fan."

The sound of the faintest, false wind seizes my attention. The winds of the New World seem different from the silent swishing that now fills my ears.

"Everyone be quiet."

I bring my palms together in front of my chest and feel my hands burning to life to create a small sphere of fire. I bring my hands apart slowly and watch as it grows, while the world around us begins to come into focus. The group stands silent as I perform the act Robert forbade and create enough light to see the streets around us. My dead nerves are on edge, made more so by the swishing of the false winds now growing louder. I lift my hands towards the sky and bring them apart suddenly, forcing the sphere to explode with light and illuminate the sky around us.

The flash reveals the creators of the false breeze, as hundreds of The Cursed hang in the air only a few dozen feet above us.

"GET INSIDE!!!"

They sprint towards the store as fast as rabbits, but not nearly fast enough. The threat of winged death above screeches in the air as they begin their charge towards my family. I scream in kind as I hurl my hands forward and create a fiery green dome over my family, leaving The Cursed to disintegrate as water does when poured over a stone. My family cowers beneath their blazing roof as The Cursed refuse to cease. They hurl themselves at the dome in the hope of weakening it...and it's working.

Focus...Get them out of here.

I charge forward to the dome with my wings tucked closely and prepare to join my family. A single Cursed drops from the sky and interrupts my concentration. The dome, roughly twenty feet in diameter, begins to dim as I stop for the briefest of seconds to tear the monster in half. I move fast and efficiently, grasping both shoulders with angry hands and pulling apart until I possess two mangled halves. I hear Sasha screaming as she exits the dome and charges towards me with her eyes blazing as bright as her soul. She hurls her sword past my head and impales another of the giant Grim Reapers who managed to slip behind me. Her sword finds his face in the same moment that his claws find my throat, and I feel the long talons piercing deep. I feel the jagged edges tearing my flesh away as he falls to the Earth behind me with pieces of my flesh in his hand.

I'm immortal...How the fuck?...Just focus.

I throw my hands forward again and bring the dome back to life as Sasha runs past me and retrieves her sword. They refuse to stop, these Kamikazes of the Necromancer, willingly dying knowing they'll be reborn shortly afterwards and will be stronger and more deranged. The fall as demonic rain, a typhoon of evil intentions all directed at those I love the most. Sasha joins my side and begins slaughtering the ones who would otherwise take me by surprise.

"Sasha! You all have to get out of here! There's too many!"

She slashes away, taking the crowns of The Cursed and keeping me undisturbed.

"Fuck that, Baby! I'm not leaving you!" She screams her beautiful war cries as she decapitates another.

"You have to go...Protect them. I'll find you again, My Love."

She brings her sword down violently on the shoulder of a Cursed and splits him to his stomach, before a dead tangle of guts spills out as she kicks him off of her blade.

"I won't fucking go so don't even ask!"

She engages the next one as the fires of the dome start to dim.

"Sasha! They're all going to die! I can't save them! Go! Please! I'm begging you!"

"I WON'T LEAVE YOU!!!"

She sends another crown to the Earth as the blood starts pooling around us, along with a fresh offering of torn limbs. Desperation sets in, and I feel the sinking in my chest where my heart used to be.

"Sasha, I love you! I'll find you again! I PROMISE YOU, MY LOVE!"

She sends a single slash upwards and tears another in half before turning to address me in the midst of the chaos.

"You fucking better."

She charges forward into the dome as Robert corrals them all under his wings. She makes it in and turns for the briefest of moments to lock eyes with me. Our souls begin to speak.

"I love you, Joe. Please come back to me, Baby."

I feel the sting of tears threatening my vision as my heart replies.

"You're my soul now. A man cannot live without a soul...Not even an immortal dead man like me."

Her eyes reflect mine as the tears flow as she forces her body backwards into the haven of Roberts' wings. She dips her head slightly and disappears behind angelic feathers. Like a Mother Hen, he shields them with his wings. Like the children of spiders, they cling to him and secure their hold. He commands them to grab a hold of arms, legs, robes, just anything. He glances at me from under the folds of his black hat and nods his head.

He's ready to save them.

"Go for it, Brother," I mutter to myself, yet I know he hears me.

He brings his wings up and slams them down violently into the Earth, ejecting them into the air, as the dome of fire explodes and sends a wave of sparks and flames in all directions. The Cursed fly past me as the energy rushes past and carries them with it, and they become the ugliest of debris in our little storm of death. My family rises into the air as I fall to

165

my knees and I see Sasha watching me fall before her. I see the panic grip her face as Robert clings to her and reminds her I'm immortal, yet her flailing arms and legs show me that she's refusing to listen.

"It's okay, Sasha. Go...Be safe, My Soul...I love you."

"Baby no! Please get up! Fly to me dammit! Pleeaassee!"

"I love you, Sasha."

"Joe, get up Goddamn it! Please, Baby please!"

"I love you, Sasha..."

The darkness rushes in as I fall to my back and watch them float to the darkest Heavens in the night sky. The portrait is ruined by the sight of balding heads and glowing eyes entering my vision, as the living nightmares make themselves known before my world fades to black. My body hurts for the first time in my new existence. It doesn't hurt long as I fall into unconsciousness.

****

"He warned you."

I feel the darkness taking on a life of its' own and some sort of energy recharging my spent, eternal soul. My head feels groggy and my vision limited, but I know the Being hiding in the shadows is awaiting my reply.

"Who warned me?"

166

It's all I can manage to ask as my voice barely forms the words.

"Robert warned you that you could become weak...You didn't listen."

"I had to expend all my energy...They were going to die."

"And what's so bad about death? They would have been in The Realm...Isn't that the end result you want for them?"

It dawns on me in this moment that I'm talking to The Big Guy Himself.

"My Creator...Have I failed you?"

"No...You failed no one but yourself. You must control it. You are immortal, but there are limits. You can still rip yourself apart if you're not careful. I know you, Joe...After all, I created you. You have the strength in you to change the world around you if you would but get a grasp on it. I cannot help you do this. I can only help guide you on your way and hope you find the path. You cannot fall...or we all fall. It's time for you to go back...You're ready."

There would be no time to beg for a moment to press for answers. The darkness vanishes as if I blinked my eternal eyes and the world now surrounding me is familiar. I'm on the floor in the store. The Dinner table lies on its side as they rummage around it, these winged rats of the New World. They sniff through the plates and bowls and silverware and even taste them with long, serpent tongues complete with long forks. They don't notice I've rejoined the world of the nonliving, watching them go through the belongings and dinnerware of my family. My armor lies in the wreckage around them. They continue their forage and speak amongst themselves in the hissing tongues I'm beginning to hate.

"He touched thisss too," the balding Cursed says to his brother.

The Cursed takes the bowl I used to create the bounty for my family and hands it to another one, only this one stands with a complete mane. His hair has yet to thin, giving away his age. He's a fresh Cursed, newly born from a human. The new Cursed takes the bowl and begins holding it to his face while smelling and licking and drooling all at once. He lets out soft murmurs as he enjoys whatever pleasure he seems to be getting from it. The long, bony face of another Cursed enters my view as he crouches next to me and sets his eyes burning upon mine and examines my face.

"Ssstrange...Isn't it?" He asks with a small smile.

I blink the grogginess out of my eyes and try to focus on this talking nightmare.

"No...It's repulsive."

He silently laughs in a whisper as his crescent smile grows frighteningly large.

"We're showing our new brother how to feed...Off of *you*." "If you're going to eat that bowl...I hope you fucking choke on it."

He giggles and hisses in the same breath.

"Your energy is all over this place, so thick it's like

walking through sssand...It's delicious."

I let out a small laugh while continuing to bring my eyes into focus.

"*Please* tell me I taste like Chicken."

I laugh loud as he looks at me with a hateful glare. The fact that I refuse to take him seriously begins to dig under his rotten skin. He grabs me by my shoulders and lifts me into a sitting position. I feel my hands bound behind me as he kneels in front of me. He tilts his head from side-to-side, trying his best to understand the man in front of him. He appears completely puzzled by the small laughter I continue to voice. In his mind, I must seem more deranged than he is.

"Why do you laugh, you fool?"

I feel my head swimming less and less by the second as the burning in my soul slowly returns to me.

"Because...in a few minutes...I'm going to feel a lot better...Then, I'm going to kill all of you stupid motherfuckers."

My demeanor turning serious causes the silence to take over the air around us. He leans forward and places his frightening mask next to mine.

"You won't be alive in a few minutes. My Lord is coming to take your sssoul," he says as he lays a hand on my shoulder and places his face only a hair away from mine, "and it's going to hurt...A lot."

He lets his long, slithering tongue slip past his lips and onto my cheek. He moves it down to my chin before licking

169

slowly upwards all the way to my forehead. He chuckles slightly as he does it, feeling some sort of perverse ecstacy from my energy. He pauses his tongue on my forehead for a few more savory seconds before retracting it.

"You're going to regret that," I warn as he smiles wide and chuckles.

The Necromancer is coming...I need strength.

"I pray that your words are true...I'll gonna kill your fucking Lord too."

He laughs loud and stands up before me and brings his foot to my face with alarming speed as his heel smashes into my right eye. The stars appear as falling snow and a surprising pain shoots across my head. The sensations of pain shocks me to my core. I'm immortal...I'm not supposed to feel any pain.

Please...Wake my soul in time.

****

"Where are we going?" Amy J. asks before her sister can breathe life into the question. Her sisters habit of asking questions is beginning to rub off on her.

They soar through the clouds in the night, one immortal and seven humans clinging to a Servant for dear life. Roberts wings thrust them through the sky with ease, an easy task for a Servant, especially one of Roberts stature. They don't call him 'Big' for nothing.

170

"We're going to The Gates," Robert replies.

"We're going to The Realm?" Danny asks.

"Yes. I'm going to fly as high as I can and then drop you. After you die, I'll meet you at The Gates," Robert says.

"What the fuck, man?!"

Robert glances down at Danny as he hangs from his leg.

"Joe said you guys like to joke around...Just trying to lighten the mood a little."

"Well, maybe you can tell another joke," Greg begins, "that doesn't involve dropping us to our deaths!"

Robert bellows a huge laugh while continuing to focus on his flight. He flaps his wings harder and faster and sends the wind rushing past them and stinging their faces. Only Sasha and Robert don't flinch.

"We're going to The Gates. There's someone there waiting for us. They have a gift for you all."

"What is it? Do you know what it is?" Carmen asks out of her curiosity.

"I really don't know, Carmen...but, you'll know soon enough. We're almost there."

He glances down at them and speaks quickly with a sharp tongue.

"When I tell you, close your eyes and don't open them! I mean it!"

He picks up more speed and begins to grunt as he turns his flight straight up towards the highest clouds.

"Get ready...Close your eyes!"

He waits a second for everyone to follow his command before he thrusts his wings a final time, as a brilliant light appears through the clouds that seem closest to the stars. They shoot up into the awaiting light as the path to The Realm lies before them. The light flashes brighter than the brightest stars as they enter the clouds and disappears instantaneously, along with the rising Servant and his new family. They make it to The Gates, but arrive just a little too late.

****

The laughter is loud as The Cursed scream around me and play with my wings. They lunge forward and bite and claw them and make The Fallen One their new, personal chew toy. They hiss and flap their wings as they taunt me, kicking me in the face and chest, and laugh when I grimace in pain from upon me knees. It brings them joy to deliver misery to The Fallen King, as it allows them to feel as they defeated a God and now stand as such. Every blow and bite brings with it the growth of the rising fires in my soul. I feel an anger only The Fallen One is capable of feeling, and very soon, they would feel it too.

"Get up...You pathetic bitch!" He screams as he kicks me in the chest.

172

I fall to my side and begin to feel the energy changing around me. I feel some sort of cruel presence inside me that bathes in hate and yearns to make itself known. My body starts burning on the inside and I realize that my own growing hate is what is fueling my energy. It's almost intoxicating and ignites me like an ember coal. If I am to regain my strength, I'm going to have to feed on whatever energy is around.

Including hate.

"Is that all?...My God, you kick like a little girl...Were you a little girl before he changed you? You should be wearing a fucking bow in your nappy hair...You weak cunt."

I giggle at him from the ground while laying on my side with my hands still bound. He walks up and raises his hands into the air to halt the screeches around him. The silence sets in as he falls to his knees and lifts me back into a sitting position.

"We're going to feed on your sssoul. He's coming to take it for usss. When you die, we'll eat your body as well. I think I'll have a wing...to sssee if you taste like Chicken...What do you have to say to that?"

I let out a small giggle before replying and looking into his eyes.

"I have this buddy...He can be an asshole sometimes...He used to call me King Salami in my old life...Why don't you start down there?...Choke on it while you're at it."

He stands up and silently gazes down upon me as I look up to greet his dark eyes. I smile at him once again and my jest is met in kind as he delivers another kick across my temple. It hurts, but I notice this time, it hurts a little less.

I'm getting angry...Use the energy.

****

The clouds are as soft as Goose Feather pillows and sink with every step as the group walks behind Robert. They're surrounded by a light haze as they walk through a forest of clouds, and make their way towards the glow in front of them that's just hidden behind the mists. The excitement is running through them the way wild animals run through the crisp, morning air; They feel alive and afraid in the same moment.

"Hey, Sasha...Do you remember passing through The Gates?" Amy K. asks.

"I never made it to The Gates," she says before turning her attention to Robert, "Big, what the fuck are we doing here? We should be helping Joe!"

She walks behind him quickly and as he answers without pausing.

"We can't help Joe. He doesn't need help. Your family needs help."

"Joe's my love! My whole life! He loves you like a brother!"

He pauses his steps and quickly turns to her.

"We can't help Joe without the means to do so. That's why we're here. This will be a quick trip, Sasha," he pauses and leans in close to her face and continues on softly, "we're not

174

supposed to be here."

They all feel their hearts stop in unison at the thought that they aren't welcome in The Realm.

"What do you mean *we're not supposed to be here?*" Sasha retorts sharply.

"He doesn't have knowledge of us being here. We're here without permission. I love Joe very much, Sasha...I'm risking my wings for him, along with a few other Servants and a couple of other people."

He leans forward and speaks sharply from a wounded heart.

"I love my Cuz, and I always will...I'll die for Joe as quickly as I would die for Him."

The silence is as thick as the clouds around them and the tension even thicker. Amy K. comes to the rescue with her endless supply of questions.

"Why do you always call him that?...*Cuz*...If you don't mind me asking."

His gaze finds hers as he replies, "Joe was my cousin when we were living, so I always called him *Cuz* when we would see each other...you know," he points his fingers at her, 'Hey Cuz'!"

Will steps forward with his own silly question.

"You're Joes' cousin? You knew him before the world ended?"

Roberts gaze turns comical as he replies, "Well...yeah...He *was* my cousin."

"Back on topic, Friend," John chimes in, "Why aren't we allowed to be here? Who's helping us? Who would risk their eternal lives for Joe, other than you?"

"Let's just say there's a lot of good people in The Realm that would risk their soul for The Fallen One...A lot of people loved Joe before they parted from his old life...We're gonna go meet a few."

He leads again and they follow behind and it doesn't take long for them to approach a thicket of fog, a wall of clouds concealing them from the world of The Realm. He commands them to follow with a nod of his head and they walk through the fog and into an open field that stands before the entrance to The Realm.

A small Gate standing only a dozen feet high greets them about fifty yards ahead. They all freeze in their tracks as Danny speaks to the air in front of him.

"This...Is The Gates to The Realm? It's not that big."

Sasha approaches Robert and stares up at his towering face.

"Sorry I snapped at you before, Robert...It's just..."

"Think nothing of it," he says as he waves his hand, "I know how much you love Joe. I can't fault you for that."

"Robert...What's going on? These aren't The Gates...Where are we?"

He stands and gazes forward and doesn't meet her questioning eyes.

"These are gates *into* The Realm...The Gates *of* The Realm aren't the only entrance. This one is never used...These are more like a back door to the place."

He points forward and utters one small, hushed word.

"Look."

They focus their eyes through the remaining small mist and see the figures of a young man and a woman entering the gates. The duo pause briefly and look directly at the group hidden in the misty shadows. They don't acknowledge them, only glancing and walking away with two larger figures trailing behind them. The sight of wings on the larger two is noticeable, even from so far away through the mist.

"Let's go, and be quick."

They move like a silent mist along the clouded ground and make their way to the small gate. Twenty yards before they arrive, they come across a large chest sitting in solitude and know it's their intended target. Robert lifts up the chest with one hand and turns quickly back in the direction they came from. They follow him in the same manner that ducklings chase their mother and try their best to keep up. They complete their mad dash and head back through the safety of the fog that acts as their shield from the dirty, little secret they try and hide from The Creator. Robert sets the chest down gently and tears off the large gold lock that secures their cargo. He cracks the seal and opens the trunk of secrets to reveal several sets of golden armor, complete sets of protection from head to toe. Symbols adorn every piece on every plate, complete with strange words written by Servants, and blessed by His hands. This armor is reserved for only The Creators mightiest Servants, the few he chooses personally to lead his Legions. A single page letter hides in the corner of the box with only a few lines written. Robert fetches it while everyone stands distracted and quickly places it in his robes.

From Joes old family to his new family.

Take care of him and each other.

Give him this letter when you see him.

We love you, Babe. We're proud of you.

****

He kicks me violently, this giant Grim Reaper of a Cursed, and laughs all the while. I laugh along with him like a madman while feeling the anger beginning to take a hold of my immortal body. I feel my strength returning by the second. He leans down to my bruised body and slaps me with the back of his clawed hand.

That hurt...but not so bad...Keep laughing at him.

"If you're gonna keep up this foreplay...You're gonna have to buy me a drink soon, you ugly bitch. HAHAHAAA!"

He grunts as he puts his all into another thrust of his foot, digging it deep into my ribs. I laugh again and keep my taunts flowing.

That hurt a lot less.

"Two drinks...maybe three...You're really fucking ugly."

He howls as he stomps my chest and kicks my head.

Think of Sashas husband...How he hurt her...

He leans down and slams a clawed fist into my jaw with evil intentions.

That didn't hurt at all.

I bring my hands apart and tear the bindings with ease and scramble to my feet. Panic overtakes him and causes him to foolishly lunge onto me in attempt to ground me, only his body seems to be as light as feathers.

I'm me again.

I roar like only The Fallen One can and grab him by his throat and begin squeezing. His eyes begin to bulge while his tongue falls from his mouth as he flails about, before I grab his tongue with my free hand and rip it from his mouth. He wails in pain as I pull him close to me and stare into his eyes.

"I meant it when I said that you were gonna regret that."

Tossing his tongue aside, I place both of my hands on his shoulders and bring my hands apart violently. He tears in two and falls to the ground, just as the others are beginning to make their charge. My body ignites in a bright fire and sheds the greenest flames I've yet to produce. The anger in me is overwhelming now.

I burn with green fire from head to toe and thrust my wings out suddenly and with force. A wave of fire surrounds me in all directions and travels with the force of a typhoon. The world around me suddenly fills with fallen Cursed as they burn and scream as they meet a true hate, the angry hand of The Creator, who is also known as The Fallen One. My wrath isn't yet complete. I charge to the nearest Cursed and lift his burning body from the ground and tear him in half as if a piece of paper and not a spawn of the New World Monstrosities. I take the one next to him and part his head from his shoulders without hesitation. I take the severed head and slam it down onto the head of another Cursed and watch as they both disintegrate. I turn around to see one of the fiery nightmares charging with his hands stretched out to me and his eyes revealing how he years to kill me. I raise my hand up and watch as he explodes and am bathed in a shower of limbs and blood.

Kill them all.

Roaring as The King of The Abyss, my wrath will be known. I raise my burning hands up in front of me and watch as every Cursed in the store rises as if on strings and have become my puppet show of death. I scream, knowing my family is gone and Sasha is once again lost to me. My soul is brimming with a hate I've never experienced. I bring my hands together and watch as The Cursed come together in the same manner and cause a train wreck of flesh colliding in the center of the room above me. They implode and a fresh rain of Cursed blood showers me. I feel the anger rising still, an emotion not necessary, now that every Cursed in the room is now vanquished. Yet, I still feel angry...I feel hate.

I feel him.

Now coated in black blood, I turn to the entrance of the store and see a figure in the doorway. He wears a hood to mask his eyes, but I can see his chin, long and slender, with a small Goatee hanging from it. His smile is small and twisted, and it's the only glimpse of the deformed face he doesn't hide under his hood. A long, purple robe hangs from his frame and resembles that of royalty. Only he is no royal blood. He is no Creator. He is no Human. He is the one who wants to rule the world, The Realm, and my Abyss as a false God-King. He points his staff forward with unnaturally long slender hands while his bent smile grows by the second. He whispers to himself and waits for a secret doom to befall me.

It never comes.

I scream with hate in my voice and violence in my eyes as I charge forward and throw my hands in front of me and send a massive wave of emerald fire in his direction. It stretches to the ceiling and hits the wall of the store in full force and causes the building to yield to the power of my green torch. It explodes outwards toward the awaiting night, along with everything in its path.

Roasted that motherfucker like a marshmallow.

181

I stand for half a moment, breathing deep, but not air. I'm surviving on the very energy of my own hate. My hands shake and my muscles seize up violently, as the power of The Abyss' fury stands unparalleled. I know in this moment what if feels like to stand as a God as my body trembles with otherworldly power. I stand without surprise that the power of pure hate is intoxicating, and that the Necromancer would fuel himself with such energy. It feels like a wonderful drug...and it scares me more than anything I've yet to encounter in any life. It's not me, nor will it become me.

I walk forward with my hands still shaking and my head twitching while my soul ignites within me. The front of the store lies in ruins, and the entire wall is now spread out over the dark street. Fires burn their gleaming green here and there, creating small lights scattered about the ground. There is no sign of the Necromancer, as his body is absent the carnage. Other than bits and pieces of stone, nothing else remains. I allow my eyes to adjust to the world around me, my hearing and sight now my only means of survival. I begin to make my way out onto the street and pray for some sign that the Necromancer has left this world. Of all the places my eyes roamed on the street, they should have been looking up.

The steel web falls upon me and quickly proves to be a metal unlike any other. The power of The Abyss subsides in me as the net pulls me to the Earth while a strange paralysis overtakes my now weak body. I collapse to my back and feel my wings begin to burn as the netting causes pain to the touch. My arms and legs fail me as the strength is drawn from them and I finally fall motionless, my body once again dead to me, with only my eyes alive. The stars betray him, revealing him in the shadows of the night air as his long frame and slender wings blacken them from the sky.

He has wings.

He drifts to the ground in front of me and leaves only a few feet between us. He places his feet softly on the Earth and draws his wings close as he once again owns his small, twisted smile.

That's why there was no trail to him.

He begins to walk to me with the Staff of Nightmares in his hand and it takes only a moment to reach me. He stands silent as we lock eyes and exchange hateful glares.

"Hello, Joe."

****

"This is never going to fit me...I'm a Plus Size Lady, Honey," Amy J. informs Robert as she stands before him with a handful of blessed steel.

"Just try it on before you say it isn't going to fit. You may be surprised," he instructs.

"Honey, I'm telling you now...it's not going to fit. I'm a big girl."

"Hey Robert," Greg interrupts, "What do all these writings mean?" He stands while studying a breastplate that was crafted from some unknown, golden steel .

"They're hexes written by the most spiritual Servants

that The Creator has, intended to be worn by the fiercest warriors. They keep the wearer safe from all evil hands and crafts. They will, in a sense, make you immortal to The Cursed. The hexes will destroy any Cursed that touches them."

Danny shimmies his belly into the breastplate as John pulls it closed on his left side.

"I got mine to fit," Danny declares.

"Well, I know better than to try it," Amy J. states flatly.

"Amy, just try it on. I'm telling you, you may be surprised," Robert concludes again with a smile

and a wink of his now kind eyes.

She stands as a child who lost an argument and looks to her feet while slowly nodding her head. She pulls the breastplate over her head and places it on her chest, holding it against her with both hands. Amy K., already fully dressed, stands beside her and begins to pull the leather straps together. The plate begins to stretch and mold around Amy J. without ever losing it's true form, instead growing to fit her body. The front and back plates come together and fit perfectly as if it was made for her.

"Oh my goodness, Honey, how in the world did that just happen?"

Robert laughs quietly to himself as the guys continue to dress into their new death attire.

"These suits of armor are one-size-fits-all. They will form to the body of the person wearing it."

184

"I do thank The Creator for that, Friend," John says as he places his greaves on his shins.

"Don't do so yet, at least...not out loud," Robert replies with a small chuckle.

"Hey Big," Carmen begins, "what's gonna happen if The Creator catches us out here with all his personal goodies?"

He turns to her with the look of a man who knows personally all too well what would happen if The Creator discovered their thievery. He glances towards the fog where they entered while his eyes are unable to hide the panic he feels. He looks at everyone in the group with fear in his eyes.

"I'm not sure...but let's not wait around to find out."

A trumpet sounding in the distance makes everyone jump in place as the horns audible voice is powerful and carries a bone-shaking sonic boom.

Danny walks slowly towards the sound and the clouds they entered as he speaks silently to himself.

"Something tells me we're about to find out."

****

"Does it hurt yet?"

He kneels next to my head and leans close, this cat

185

playing with the new mouse he's captured. He's really enjoying the lust of the kill.

"Not at all...Not nearly as much as it'll hurt when I take your head from your fucking shoulders."

He shakes his head slowly, yet his hood keeps his eyes hidden.

"So much hate in you...The Old One was wise to want to contain you and make you his own. You could have been a fine addition to his army...but, not to mine. Don't worry...It's going to hurt worse than anything The Creator or The Old One could of ever done to you...It's going to be an honor taking your soul."

"Do it then...Go on...Pussy."

"It's almost time," he informs me as he reaches down and places his long fingers around a web of the net.

He's going to kill me..I can't die.

"This material is amazing...A metal not found anywhere in the world...Do you know where it came from?" He asks as he pushes the netting around my face down to the ground, causing it to dig deeper into my flesh. I let out a small grunt, trying my best to conceal the true pain.

"I'll take your silence as a no. This metal was crafted by The Old One. With the fires of His Abyss, he smoldered it down into its liquid state and formed a few tools with it, a few...playthings...you could say. It's his writing that graces the metal...The same writings that now draw your soul out of your body. The metal itself...well...The Creator has a habit of trusting

186

too many people. It was his own people that stole this metal and gave it to The Old One. This net," he pauses as he touches the metal webbing once again, "is made from metal that graced The Creators own skin...It's how I'm going to give you your final death."

He rises slowly to his feet as I fall slowly from this world once again. I'm powerless, with the energy of a God no longer present in my body. I feel as if I'm just a weak Human once more, just an insect in the presence of a very evil child. He places his staff over my shoulder and slowly begins the descent of the Red Rock of Doom that's securely in place on the bottom of the staff. He places the jagged point on the exposed flesh of my shoulder and threatens to penetrate my skin.

"This," he says as he pushes the rocky blade into my flesh, "is just the beginning."

The pain is instant and my body contorts to the pull created by the evil rock. My body begins to freeze from the inside, a feeling lost to the King of The Abyss. I feel it all leaving me...The life bestowed upon me...The love hidden in the depths of my heart...I feel it all fade away...

"Fire!"

The sound of a burning blade cuts the night air as the culprit finds itself upon the shoulder of the Necromancer. He screams and falls to his knees as he's bathed in surprise. He scrambles away a few feet before turning to meet the newest member of my family, Sam, the former Cursed who was turned into a monstrosity by the creature cowering before him. He stands with a blade of fire, his small stature now the size of a skyscraper, and glows with the hate of vengeance. He will have his revenge upon the one who threatened to keep him from his family forever.

"Surprised to see me? I'm glad to see you!"

He charges forward at the false man he wishes to kill with the fires in his eyes reflecting his blade. The Necromancer rolls forward to me and places his hand on the net before jumping back to avoid Sams steel. The net yanks off and with it, the Necromancer. He jumps to the sky as Sam swings wildly at him and rushes off into the darkness. I hear his wings in the distance, the small sounds emitting from every thrust growing quieter until lost to me.

Sam rushes to my side and collapses next to his former hero. He gazes into my face and has the look of a child who just lost a pet. He lifts my head off the ground and studies my almost lifeless eyes. I see his face. The face of my brother. The face of my Savior. He watches me form a small smile with the last remaining energy I have left in me. He returns it in kind tenfold.

"I thought you were dead, Joe."

"I could say the same thing about you, Sam...I thank The Creator that you're not."

****

The sound is deafening and the group has become delirious. They stagger to-and-fro and seem to be heading nowhere. Robert screams commands as loud as he possibly can, but they fall on deaf ears. Everyone covers their ears and begins walking as drunk souls as the clouds around them have become

188

their tavern. He motions for them to follow while still commanding silent screams, his arms gesturing towards the path. They stagger forward, the most well dressed group of misfits The Creator has ever commanded to be hunted.

They run, their steps as silent as their panicked voices, as the trumpet grows louder. Sasha screams and falls to the clouded ground while covering her ears. Robert reaches down and picks her up with one arm and continues his dash to escape. He glances behind and sees them keeping pace while a small trickle of blood escapes their noses, one-by-one. The sound of The Realms' alarm is enough to kill a living soul.

They make it out of the clouded forest and into a clearing, a field of low hanging fog that hugs the ground tightly. The sirens continue to grow as the trumpet continues screaming for the discovery of intruders. The blare masks the sounds of the Servants on the hunt behind them. It matters not, to the Servant known as Robert. He can feel their presence closing in, and he can't allow them to see his face.

One-by-one, he motions them to grab on. They sprint into his massive robes in a panic, ready to escape the beautiful Realm that just became a torturous Abyss. They grab on and hide their faces in his robes, hoping it will shield the misery of the unbearable horn. He feels the Servants close...too close.

He lifts his right foot off the ground a few inches and slams it down into the clouds under his feet. The sky falls beneath them and a hole appears and reveals a dark sky. They fall through as he screams for the group to hold on for their mortal lives and turns his body into a nosedive. He can't allow the Servants to see anything, not even his wings.

They rush forward into the night sky, the clouds

shrinking behind them as they lay distance between themselves and their would-be captors. He glances back and sees the escape rout closing up with no signs of any Servants catching a glimpse. He cannot take a chance. He must not take a chance. He continues his nosedive and begins to flap his wings and their speed picks up dramatically. The Amys begin to scream as John does his best to comfort them, yet the rate of their movement is frightening, even for a Servant.

"Slow down, Bro! Please! You're gonna fucking kill us!" Greg pleas as they hang upside down.

"Not until I know we're safe!"

A flash fills the world around them as they pass through the hidden portal back to the Earth. It's so brief that they barely register its' existence, but they feel it nonetheless. They continue their descent into madness as the world begins to appear before them and see the dark ground approaching fast.

"There's the fucking ground, now slow down!" Greg begs again.

He shoots his wings out and they catch the air as a parachute would. They lurch into the air before beginning a slow fall towards the awaiting dark Earth with Robert guiding their descent. They make it to the ground, and the moment of Roberts feet making contact becomes the same moment they fall from him lifelessly. Exhaustion and wear has set in for all.

"Do you," Greg fumbles, unable to catch his breath, "think...they saw us?"

Robert stands and gazes straight up at the clouds they just escaped from.

"They didn't," he answers in a hushed voice, never breaking his ten thousand yard stare.

Will rises up slowly and helps Carmen to her feet as they all follow suit with the metallic sounds of their new armor filling the air. He addresses Robert in a voice dripping with hope.

"Are you sure? How do you know for sure?"

He fixes his black Cowboy hat and the jeweled Crucifix shines in the soft starlight. He extends his wings out and ruffles the feathers before folding them neatly along his back. He adjusts his robes to their original folds, yet during all these little activities he makes sure to peek at the sky between chores. Will grows restless at not receiving an answer.

"Robert...Did you hear me? How do you know they didn't see us?"

Robert turns to him with relief in his voice.

"We would've all met our final deaths by now."

"Big," Sasha whispers from her knees, her immortal body feeling the strain as much as the mortals surrounding her, "we need to help Joe...I'm going to reach out to him."

She rises slowly to her feet and takes a few deep, false breaths, and prepares her mind and soul and not her body. She closes her sad blue eyes, the pain in them almost more unbearable than the whiplash they just received from their descent. Her eyelids flutter as a Butterflies wings would in a storm, threatening to open up to the world around her. A soft gasp escapes her as her eyes shoot open with fear and desperation crawling from them.

"Oh no! Robert! Robert!!! I can't find Joe! Please! I can't find Joe!"

She collapses to her knees as the memory of her eternal future husband being overtaken by Cursed invades her thoughts and plummets them into oblivion. She screams softly into her hands as the ladies rush to her side and hold her close while the pain of losing her beloved Immortal Love tears her soul into a million pieces. Pain and sadness overtake Robert as he closes his eyes from the world and sends out his own soul. It takes only a second for him to return to the group.

He kneels next to Sasha as she keeps her face hidden in her hands and cloaked by her red hair.

"He's alive, Sasha...He's in bad shape, I can't communicate with him, but he's alive...I promise you he is."

She pulls her Angelic face from her hands to meet his stare.

"Are you sure? Tell me you're sure! Tell me you know for a fact that he's still alive!" She screams into the air before returning her face to the safety of her palms.

"I can feel him, Sasha...His life force. He's...weak...somehow, but I know he's still in this world. We need to find him."

"Where do we begin," John asks, "do we even know where we are?"

They glance around to a dark world in the middle of a small city, several hundred miles from where they left this world to sneak into The Realm. They remain clueless as to just how far they stand from my now broken body.

"I can feel Joe...I just can't talk to him...We follow the energy and we'll find him. We'll start at the first light. We need to find a place to lay your heads tonight...You all need to get some rest."

Sasha looks up from her hands and directs her face towards the sky.

"Please let him be okay...Don't punish me by taking him again."

* *

"What do you think, Sam?"

He examines the showers hanging overhead and turns the small lever next to the head before the water begins pouring from the dry fixture. He jumps back and giggles softly before reaching up and turning off the water. I sit in the corner with my broken body, my broken wings, my torn soul, and watch as he relishes in the thought of a shower as I reapply my armor.

My breastplate feels heavier than I remember.

"I didn't think I would ever see a working shower again in this world."

I chuckle softly to myself.

"Those were my thoughts exactly, the first time Greg showed me. Take a shower, Brother. I don't know how much use I'll be right now, but I'll keep watch."

He walks from the showers over to me and sits next to me, a small grunt escaping this small man as he plops on the floor. He takes a deep breath and sighs while his mind begins to wander. He seems lost to the world and living inside his own mind.

"I'm good, Joe...I'm too scared to take my hands off this sword."

He chuckles nervously as he spins the handle in his hand and makes the blade dance a deadly

twirl.

"Sam...Where did you go when the battle started? We lost you in the chaos."

He leans back into the wall and places his head against it, staring at the air as he answers me.

"When they came in...I got real scared. I ran and hid in an office in the back of the store. I felt like a coward," he hangs his head down and stares at the floor, "here you guys are, fighting like real warriors and I'm hiding like a little kid. I just don't have it in me...I'm not a brave man."

He shakes his head slowly as his own words sink in as if someone else had breathed life into them. I see small tears appearing on his cheeks and the sadness in him reflecting in his soft, brown eyes.

194

"You remember Will? The big blonde guy that looks like he was born on a surfboard?"

He chuckles softly and nods in agreement.

"He stood a coward once. He was afraid of fighting, as big as he is, and spoke similar words to me months ago. I showed him how to fight, and then I showed him what to fight for. He loves his wife, Carmen, and I made him realize a strong man was the only thing that stood between Carmen and death. You just need a purpose, Sam. You need something to drive you to be a killer. I can see in you...and I don't see a killer. However...I *do see* a survivor. You'll learn to fight and one day will have a true purpose to fight for."

He lifts the blade to his face and studies it closely before turning his attention to my own blade. He compares the blades and smiles to himself as a small epiphany lights his mind.

"I already found a purpose."

He points to the Moons on his crimson blade and creates a trail with his finger to my own steel. He points out the symbols on my blade while his eyes appear trance-like in the dark.

"You found a good one, Sam...It's the only real purpose any of us have left anymore. I guess the only thing left is to learn to be a fighter."

He spins the blade again and the red steel appears as dark as the night in our dim lit room while the stars do their best to be our lanterns.

"I don't want to be a fighter...I want to be a killer...for

Him...To see my family again..."

I reach over and place my hand on his shoulder.

"You will be...and you'll see them again."

He nods his head slowly in the darkness.

"Sam...I need to try and contact Sasha and the others. I have no idea where Robert took them."

"Um, okay...Should I leave the room?"

"No...Just...don't freak out."

I close my eyes and begin to focus on the darkness and send my soul...nowhere.

What the fuck is going on?

I concentrate harder and the darkness I've become accustomed to never arrives. The world around me remains in place as I find my mind unable to do anything. I stand confused and begin my search of an answer that eludes me. I try thrice, the silence never coming and the darkness remaining stubborn and hidden from my sight. I feel my head begin to hurt and my chest tighten as my false breathing picks up. The line to my loved ones will remain silenced by the weak attempts I can only muster as the energy of the Abysmal King is no longer alive in my body. I stand the weakest of Immortals...if I'm even Immortal anymore. I open my eyes to the sight of a panicked brother.

"Joe?"

196

"Yes, Sam?" I reply as I meet his worried gaze.

"What's wrong? I can see that something is wrong."

I shake my head, "I don't have the strength to reach out to them...I've lost my abilities...I've lost our family...I can't feel them."

Sadness overtakes me in the form of a vicious knife that pierces my soul. I feel the hopelessness return to me as when I lost Sasha the first time in my mortal life, on the night she tried to kill me. The agony is unbearable, but thankfully, fleeting when the sound of feet planting firmly in front of the door startles us. Sam and I both jump on cue.

"Joe," Sam whispers as the shadows mask his worried face, "what was that?"

I feel my body weak and without the will to lift my sword.

"I don't know."

He stands up, his legs beginning to carry him to the door as my hand shoots out and grasps the leg of his jeans firmly.

"Sam...Don't."

I see his face turn to me in the darkness of the shadows.

"It could be Robert and the others," he whispers softly.

I shake my head in disagreement, "It's not."

He returns to my side and crouches low, listening to the sounds of the scavenger outside our front door. He smells us, without a doubt, and searches the area where the scent ends. He paces back and forth in front of the door, his raspy hiss and fluttering, leathery wings giving away his presence. The sound of his misery can be heard in his voice as he speaks to himself. He mumbles about nothing and everything and speaks enough for Sam to recognize the voice he hears.

"Joe," his soft voice whispers, "I know that one...He was forced *against his will*." "There's nothing I can do about it now. Stay quiet." "He's not evil...He was a normal guy, like me. He was confused and..."

The door crashes open, the sound like an artillery shell splitting the silence. He stands in the dark, his wings stretched as far as his unholy limbs allow it, and glares at us with red beads of hate. He steps forward as I draw my sword from my sitting position, yet my wings hold me up more than my will. Sam draws his sword as well and breathes life into the key word, setting his blade ablaze. The room lights up in the soft green firelight, showing us both the monster that sniffed out our trail. They stand locked as Cobras with their eyes waiting for the slightest detection of movement to unleash a deadly venom. The creature steps towards Sam slowly, as if time suddenly slowed this wicked vision in front of me.

"Stop! I know you! Do you remember me?...We were in line together when he changed us!"

The Cursed hisses and twitches his balding head while taking another small step.

"It's me! Sam! I tried to help you when he changed us! I'm the one who tried to fight them off of you! Sam! My name is Sam!"

The monster pauses as his head tilts in a confused manner while his soul relives a memory.

"Ssssam?"

"Yes! Sam!"

His face shifts from a nightmare to that of a crying child.

"Ssssam...Run...I'm gonna kill you," he confesses through the soft weeps now rising through his slender neck.

"You don't have to! Look at me...I'm Human again. You can still be changed," Sam informs him while holding his free hand up in a calming posture, "just take it easy."

His head begins to twitch and his chest bucks as he does his false regurgitation and dry heave. It's the nervous tick of the New World Cursed, caused by the burning of their souls in their bodies.

"How...how?"

Sam points to me as I sit almost lifeless on the floor.

"He can change you...just as soon as he's strong enough. You don't have to die as a monster. Remember you told me you had a little girl? She would want to see her Daddy again, I'm sure."

His head jerks and twitches violently, forcing him to break eye contact and stare at the sky for a brief moment while his muscles spasm out of control.

"Rebecca...Becky."

The twitching begins to grow more violent in its dark nature.

"That's right! And your name is Ralph. I remember your name. You have a name, and a daughter...just take it easy, Ralph."

He covers his face with his new monstrous hands and screams as if his heart was taken from him. He lifts his face from them and reveals the nightmare reincarnated.

"Nooo! I ssserve the master!"

"The Creator is the master! Please, Ralph! Remember your daughter!"

"Fuck you and her! Fuck my life! Fuck my family and all the ressst of them! Fuck you Sssam! Fuck you!"

Screams of death escape him as he lunges at Sam with his hands reaching for Sams' throat. The hum of my blade is quiet as it leaves my hand, the four feet of holy steel usurping the last of my reserve energy to attack. It flies by Sam in a flash and impales the New World Cursed known as Ralph, the father of Rebecca and now, the soul withering on my blade. It hit the mark perfectly, as bits of black heart litter the end of the blade protruding from his back. He falls over on his side and gags on his own blood as it travels up his throat. Sam drops to his knees and grabs the monsters' head and lifts it slightly as the blood begins pooling in his mouth and cascading down the side of his face. He glances at Sam with eyes of sorrow.

"I'm sorry, Sam...I couldn't help it."

"It's okay, Ralph, I know...The hate inside is too much...I'm sorry too."

He hacks and spits a black rope of blood a yard in length as sickening gurgles travel through the thick ooze. Sam turns his head to me with tears falling from his cheeks. His eyes give away his request.

"I can't, Sam. I don't have the strength."

"Could you at least try? Please, Joe...He was a good man."

Creator, give me the strength.

I climb to my feet and make my way to the sad sight of a man and his former Cursed comrade clinging to the hope of a miracle.

Creator, give me strength.

I hit my knees next to him with my wings heaving behind me and feeling heavy and bring my hands together in front of me. I feel no heat as I focus my mind.

Please...give me strength.

The Cursed hacks again while a wave of blood resembling tar spreads across the floor. I feel a small spark of

201

heat, but barely enough to do anything.

I have no strength.

A familiar voice fills my head.

"You've always had the strength inside you."

My hands burst to light and I slam my right hand into his chest, with it being more of a hook to the body than a shot of faith. He screams through the blood and contorts his body back and forth while his Cursed wings crumble from his back. The light around him begins to glow, only it's His light and not my emerald flames and spreads like a small wildfire. The light I use to give Fallen Souls their wings still shines in my unholy soul. I've always drawn my strength from Him, as the light of The Creator was always brighter than the fires of the former Abyss. His evil body reacts in accordance and twists his limbs from the shock of otherworldly power. The hate in him forces him to scream one last evil plea before he goes limp. Flames burst from him and swallow him whole as the blanket of green flames causes Sam to scurry away. He remains in flames for several more moments before the fire subsides around him, revealing a young man with long, slender wings. My sword lies next to him and is no longer a part of his body.

"Ralph? Are you alive?" Sam whispers a few feet away. The question causes Ralph to stir to life, and to see a new existence through new eyes for the first time. He raises himself on one arm with his back to Sam.

"I think I'm dead."

Still kneeling next to him, I reach out and touch his new soft, feathered wings.

He has to go.

"Ralph...Say goodbye to Sam."

He sits up quickly and turns to Sam and reveals that their gaze is the same as their thoughts. They won't get to share this life together. The paths they walk intertwined, but now lead in different directions. A cruel Fate, yet a mercy compared to dying and being reborn for a lifetime.

"Joe, wait," Sam starts as he crawls to me, "you saved me. You just saved him. Why does he have to go? Where are you sending him?"

I look at Sam as a mime, sitting silent, while my frown grows from the thought of giving up a brother.

It's the only way.

"He's going to The Realm."

Ralph looks at me with eyes of wonder. Sharp features dress his face as a sharp jaw and sharp almond-shaped eyes are hidden under a mane of thick, Dirty Blonde hair. He appears to be in his early twenties, and much too young to die as a monster.

"Am I really going to The Realm?"

My attention falls to him as I begin, "Yes...I saved Sam, as he said, and I saved you just now. Sam is with me because he was meant to be with me. I took the hate from him that the Necromancer filled his soul with, turning him back into a Human. He was suffering, but he wasn't dying. You were dying just now, Ralph, and the only way to save you was to give you

203

wings...It's the reward I bestow upon souls who've paid for their evil deeds. You're going home now, Ralph, to be with Rebecca again...She's waiting for her Daddy...Don't keep her waiting...I'll give you a moment with Sam to say goodbye."

Motionless, he sits. His eyes move at a frantic pace, rolling in his head as he blinks through hot tears. He was reborn as a Servant, and not as a Human. He begins to move his wings slightly, feeling the feathered instruments soon to be used for his first flight. The path home to The Realm will be his first test run. He shakes his head slightly and turns to Sam, his face reflecting that of his brother who already made his way over. He sits on his knees next to Ralph as they share a frown.

"Tell Rebecca I said hi."

Tears pour down Ralphs face with disregard to his already too-moist cheeks.

"You saved me, Sam...I'll never forget that, and neither will Becky. I'll tell her about you."

Making my way to my feet, I stand a vision of a the very ghosts I filmed in my old life, back when I was alive in the Old World and playing with souls. I feel disconnected from my body, almost drifting instead of standing. I almost fall over when Ralph grabs my leg and holds me in place. I look down to see gratitude greeting me.

"Thank you, Joe."

I muster a small smile and nod my head.

"You're most welcome, Ralph."

204

Returning their attentions to each other, they lock in an embrace and wish each other well while making promises to see each other again. They make their way to their feet and embrace again before Sam steps back a few paces. Ralph turns to me and nods to confirm he's ready. I stand his equal, ready to perform the ritual that defines me. I step forward and place my hands in the pits of his arms and ready myself to send him on his journey.

"Good luck, my Brother...Give Becky a big hug from me and Sam."

He smiles as the tears return.

"I will...Thank you both...May The Creator bless you guys."

"And you as well."

I let the light explode from my hands and my eyes duplicate the feat while the light pours out of me as I lift him up for Sam to behold. He begins laughing and crying, giving the usual reaction when they realize they're on their way to a better place. I lower him slightly, before raising my hands up violently, and send him airborne as a light bursts from the sky and pierces the rafters in the same instant. He catches the light as a bird does wind and flaps his new wings, sending him upwards through the light. He moves quickly into the awaiting false Sun at the end of his path, both vanishing in the blink of an eternal eye. I fall back to my knees the moment Ralph finds The Realm, and the light vanishes from me just as quickly. I lean forward towards the awaiting floor and feel small arms wrap around my chest as Sam does his best to keep me from the face plant I wouldn't mind experiencing if it means I can rest my head for a moment.

205

"I got ya, Joe!...at least...I think I do!"

We fall to the floor together with my body landing hard and my wings breaking his fall. He jumps up the moment he's able and scurries around quickly to find my face in the darkness. It's an easy feat, given away by the small laughter escaping me. He leans in close and examines my face.

"Joe...Are you okay?"

I continue my small mad laughter as I make my way to my knees. I pause and catch my false breath, although unneeded, it's a reminder that I'm still of this world.

"I'm okay, Sam...It feels great to be filled with light...and to give people a second chance."

He kneels in front of me with tears staining his face with the threat of a tidal wave of emotion lying just behind the surface.

"Thank you for helping him. When I was on my way to the Necromancer, I met Ralph. We stood in a line for hours and got to know each other. He told me about his family and how he wished he could see them again. When they overheard us talking about our old lives, they came over. They made it sound so sweet to us, the promise of eternal life, so it was easy for a lot of us to stay in line. I think we all went to survive, but decided in the end that...it was better to die than to be reborn as a monster. Ralph tried to run when we changed our minds...They caught him. I charged at them but, well, what could I really do? Look at me! I'm no match for them! But I tried! I really did! They cast me aside and pinned him to the ground and then..he showed up...and stabbed Ralph...I saw him start to change, but then they pushed me down...and he did it. I remember in my last moment as a person, Ralph was screaming...he was screaming so loud...it's all I could hear...it's the last thing I remember. Thanks to you, he'll never suffer again. To be one of those things...it hurts...I'm glad he's not suffering anymore...so thank you."

I chuckle as I reach out to him and pull him forward into me while a small sob escapes him with his own chuckle mixed in. The happiness he feels for his friend has now overwhelmed him.

"You're welcome...my Brother."

****

Silently, they move. The buildings around them have succumbed to the violent nature of The Days of Ruin as stones and steel create false hills for miles. They make their way from shadow to shadow and follow Roberts lead as the silence of the night stands unscathed from the horrors hundreds of miles away that shake the ground with their voices. They stand miles from certain death, but danger still remains prevalent throughout the New World. The Cursed love a hunt, especially at night. It would only take one scout to bring about a small army capable of overrunning them. They have a Servant at their side and magical steel, yet it's not enough. They would stand a better chance if they stood with the True Ruler of The Abyss. They make their way down the street as silent as corpses and pause long enough to adjust their eyes to the darkness. The street stretches for several city blocks with each block reflecting the next. It's a line of fallen buildings in all directions and offering no shelter. Robert leads them a few more yards before Will draws his attention.

207

"Hey Big Guy," Will sharply whispers, "there's a room still standing in the building next to us."

He points into the dark hole in the wall of the building barely standing beside them.

"Do you see it?"

"I see it," Robert answers quietly.

"Well...should we check it out? We're all tired and honestly, I'm hungry."

Carmen latches onto Wills arm and clings closely to him.

"Will can't skip a meal or he gets dumber," Carmen explains.

They all chuckle quietly as Robert nods his head for them to follow. He leads them into the darkness of the hole to discover an awaiting haven fit for Kings in the New World; A room large enough to comfortably lay everyone in the comforts of the hiding shadows. A single door in the back of the room stands firm. It would keep them hidden as much as serve as shelter, with the view looking out much more revealing than the view looking in. They all gather in their temporary habitat and stand quietly while looking at Robert for answers.

"Let's look around before we get comfortable. Sasha, stay here with the ladies while the rest of us scout the area. We're going to look for food and water for everyone. Keep your swords ready."

Sasha looks at him in the darkness as his eyes find hers

and she nods in agreement.

"We're going to try and contact Joe again, once we know there's no more of those fuckers out there." She barks the command more than makes a request. Robert remembers the fire I warned him about and nods in return.

"Agreed...but, you have to wait until we're all together again. I'm the only Immortal Being between the guys and certain death while we look around. You stand as the same for the ladies."

He walks slowly towards her and continues.

"I love Joe too...Please, just wait for us, Sasha."

Her blue eyes soften in the darkness for no one to see.

"I will, Big...I promise."

His smile returns to him, but like her eyes, it remains invisible in the shadows.

"Thank you. The only thing Joe wanted was for everyone to be safe. He tasked me with the chore...and I can't do it alone."

She curls her lips in the darkness and her brow wrinkles into a soft gesture of understanding.

"We're all family, Robert. We take care of each other...I got your back."

They share another moment of unspoken

understanding before he looks to the guys and nods his head, a gesture to follow his lead. They follow him to the door closed shut in the back of the room, the only other entrance or exit besides the gaping hole in the wall. He draws his finger to his lips to request a hushed moment before placing his hand on the knob. The sounds of the locking mechanism is deafening in the silence, a loud click that sends a wave of sound out in all directions. Motionless they stand, wondering if the sound was heard by anyone other than the people in the room. Only silence greets their loud gesture and reassures them they haven't been discovered. Several long moments pass before Robert turns the knob and pushes the door slowly. The creak of the door reverberates like thunder throughout the remains of the building. Fumbling through his armor, Greg manages to retrieve a lighter from some hidden pocket that no doubt has a stash of survival goodies. He approaches Robert and stands next to him as he flicks his lighter a few times before the flame becomes alive. The darkness disappears slowly as their hearts stop in unison.

So many eyes, of all shapes and sizes, greet them from the back of the room. The glow of the lighter betrays the owners of the flames, reflecting its soft glow back and giving away their presence. The sounds of swords drawing as one shatters the silence as their hearts beat heavy and their lungs draw rapid, shallow breaths. They stand frozen in position to counter attack as they had learned to do so long ago. The eyes shine, unmoving, unwavering...and unblinking. The lighter burns the last of its fuel and flickers a bit before its eternal death.

"Shit! The fucking lighter is empty!"

Robert walks forward a few paces and raises his hand in front of them. Still the eyes stare through the darkness, unwavering, and unblinking. He whispers to himself and commands his palm to bring forth the light inside him. His palm begins to glow as white as snow and the room suddenly becomes alive and vibrant. The perpetrators revealed, are several heads of Deer and Bison and other animals of a similar nature that line the walls, frozen in the light as if still alive and on a highway. Solitary mounts hang from the wall with their silent gazes as the rest of the room comes into vision and reveals racks lined with Jerky of every variety. Pounds of dried meat sit on shelves and hang on racks in the small room, along with a small counter and register sitting to the right of them. It's a small store, but the treasures inside are larger than life. They all fight the urge to charge forward, with the threat of needing a full belly overwhelming the dangers of a horrific death. Robert closes his palms and the world of delicious meat disappears with the light. The darkness is alive with the sounds of rapid, and now very hungry breathing.

"Don't do it guys...Wait until we've looked around."

"Fuck that," Danny barks, "We've gotta eat, man."

"You will, but first let's make sure we're not going to be killed when *you do* stuff your face."

"That's easy for you to say," Amy K. adds, "you don't need to eat, but the rest of us do. I could care less if a Cursed is in here...excuse my language, but...I'll kill a motherfucker right now."

The room is silent, except for Sashas small laughter. She's proud of her shy sister, finally rubbing off on her. It's odd for everyone to hear Amy K. speak in such a manner.

"Then let's move fast."

The light returns to Roberts palm and the room slowly creeps back into their sight, with the delights no doubt screaming at their empty stomachs. He walks forwards slowly as the group falls in behind and they begin to do a sweep of the tiny store. The shelves are barely four feet tall, so keeping everyone in view is no task. They watch each other as much as their steps as they make their way to the far end of the store that stretches barely fifty feet across. The signs of imminent dangers are absent. Robert raises his hands up quickly to signal a halt to their steps. He listens to the silence the way a blind man listens to the world, removed from sight, but still aware of his surroundings. He feels the energy in the air sitting rested, a calmness only associated with a lack of company. They stand truly alone.

Robert begins nodding his head as if agreeing with himself as he reaches up and taps the lightbulb overhead, commanding its lighted presence. The room illuminates a vision of fantasy, a world of food that shouldn't exist. He smiles at them all as they stand wide-eyed and uncertain.

"Well...What the fuck are you guys waiting for?"

The sounds of crinkling bags fills the air as the mad dash of their gluttonous cuisine begins. They scramble about and run into each other as they celebrate quietly. Will stands confused, holding a bag of Beef Jerky and Turkey Jerky, as if the decision is too much for his overwhelmed senses. Carmen grabs the Beef Jerky from his hands and leaves him no choice. Danny and Greg hug the shelves and gather countless bags under each arm while John takes his time to read the labels, as if it matters. The Amys huddle and discuss quietly about which meat they should devour first. Robert looks at Sasha as she smiles at her ravenous family.

212

"We have to watch over them tonight."

She turns her head towards him to acknowledge the receiving of his thoughts.

"I know. I'm just glad they found a little joy tonight...I hope Joe is safe."

He smirks at her and slowly shakes his head.

"When are you gonna learn my Cuz is the Baddest Man on the planet? He's good, Sasha. Don't worry about him."

Her lips tighten to form a small, nervous smile.

"I pray that you're right."

****

In the hum of the silence, nothing moves. I stare at the figure of Sam propped up against the wall while the shadows have become his blanket. The night is as quiet and as still as my heart while silence hangs in the air. I listen to the New World, still absent the sounds of nature, and find it to be an eerie quiet unlike the silence of the Old World. Sams face remains cloaked in darkness, making it difficult to see his eyes.

Is he awake? Is he staring at me?

"Joe."

His small voice splitting the night confirms my

213

suspicions.

"Yes, Sam?"

"You said you were an ordinary guy once...What did you do in your old life?" Here we go again, with a new player in an already old game.

Why the hell is everyone so hellbent on needing to know what I did before I died?

"I was a Ghost Hunter."

No point beating around the bush.

He laughs softly from his spot against the wall as I expected him to.

"Seriously...What did you do?"

It's my turn to laugh softly to myself.

"Sam, I was the best Ghost Hunter the world never got to see."

He sits quietly while taking my words in.

"Don't you mean, 'ever' got to see?"

I sit quietly and take a false breath before I give my life story.

"Nope...I had it right the first time. I worked with souls and documented it. I made documentaries. It was my calling before the Old World ended. I was a gifted man, or cursed, however you want to look at it. I lived my life in the Spirit World. I encountered spirits daily. I would listen to them, talk to them, even see their faces sometimes. I helped them when no one else could. I always felt cursed for never having any true privacy but, in the same instance, I felt blessed because I had never heard of anyone doing the things I was doing and helping them the way I was. I filmed it all and documented my encounters. Unfortunately, I was only out in the public for a few years before the New World was born. I had a small following worldwide, but it was in its infancy."

"Wow...Are you a Medium?"

I never knew what I was.

"If you want to put a label on it, I guess you could say something like that. I read energy. I knew what they felt and sometimes, how they died. I would hear their voices, like I said. I could see them around me as energy. They rarely manifested into apparitions. But...when they did, I filmed it. When the Old World ended and The Creator took everyone, He took all the souls of the world too. My unique self died on that day. The rest of me followed a few months later when...the one you call 'Satan' killed me."

"Son of a bitch! The Devil killed you...*himself*?"

I can see the shock on his face, even in the pitch black.

"He was also known as 'The Serpent'...'The Evil One'...'The Old One'...but yeah, that guy...He defeated me as a mortal man. He tore me in half and threw me into the pit of The Abyss. I remember the flames engulfing me...burning me up as quickly as possible. I thought that I deserved to burn so much, that the flames came to life just to tear me apart...I didn't know The Creator was doing me a favor. He wanted my suffering to end as soon as possible so he commanded the flames to do their job quickly. I was reborn shortly after that. He sent me to the place of my death where I found The Serpent about to slaughter the group. I wasted no time killing him...and I enjoyed it."

I raise my sword from my side and squeeze the handle gently, releasing a small green glow from the blade. The room lights up enough for me to see Sam smiling. I toss the sword over to him and he catches it gracefully.

"This is the sword that cut the horns off of The Serpents' head."

He studies the blade and all of its symbols with the eyes of a scholar.

"You killed The Serpent with this?"

"Technically, no. I ripped his arm off and used it as a Baseball bat to knock his head off."

He laughs loudly, before flinching and calming his voice, and then continues in a more hushed tone.

"Oh my goodness...It sounds like you hit a Home Run."

"With the bases loaded," I reply.

We both laugh together and exchange humorous glances.

"A Grand Slam for the ages, from the sound of it," Sam

concludes.

We both return to the quiet of the night until all I can hear is his steady breathing.

"Sam...when I died...I was scared to go. I know now that it was foolish to be afraid. When your day comes, embrace it. You don't get to choose when and where you will be born, but you can choose when and where and how you will die...Make it a glorious death... when the time comes."

He tosses my blade back to me and stands up before his short legs bring him closer to me. He scurries over quickly finds a seat next to me.

"When I die, I plan on doing it in such a way that my family will be proud to welcome me. I lived as a coward...I won't die as one...I promise I won't."

I lean over and pat him on his back as we exchange smiles between us.

"Get some rest, Sam. We have a long day tomorrow. We'll be leaving the town in the morning to find the others...I'll watch you while you sleep."

"That's funny," he retorts and giggles, "the Devil watching me while I sleep. Back in the day, that would of been a scary thought."

I smirk and giggle to myself.

"I'm *The Fallen One*, Sam...but, I'm still a Servant...Get some rest, brother."

He nods his head and begins his pre-sleep rituals, laying on his side and trying to position himself in a comfortable manner.

"Goodnight, Mr. Fallen One."

We both snicker quietly.

"Goodnight former Cursed, Little Man."

****

"Best Beef Jerky, ever," Will exclaims with a mouthful of the dehydrated meat.

"Hey asshole, that was mine!" Carmen declares and glares at Will as they sit in a familiar circle and smack on their new delights.

"Babe, there's a whole store full of Beef Jerky surrounding us!"

"Exactly! Get your own!"

Everyone laughs as the group sits absent their armor and readies themselves for a comfortable nights sleep.

"That's not fair," he mutters to her.

"Well, I take care of *your* Beef Jerky so I get to have this one," she replies as she snatches the bag from his hands.

218

The girls turn a bright shade of red while Sasha laughs and shoots Carmen a High-five.

"I don't get it," Will confesses.

They all erupt in laughter while Will continues to sit quietly as the gears turn in his head.

"You know what would make this perfect?" Greg asks no one, only hoping to see if anyone else shares in his line of thought.

"A joint?" Danny asks, giving Greg the answer he was looking for.

"Exactly! And guess who happens to have one!..Or six or seven."

They all sit quietly once more as their gazes fall to Sasha. She sits with a blank mask, as the answers they seek are absent her mind. She looks at Robert with the same curious expression they all wear. He sits startled by all the sudden attention.

"What?"

Greg shoots up and walks over to Robert as he sits on the counter next to a small register.

"Robert, Bro, you can answer a question that all of us have asked since the beginning of time...What was The Creators intention when He made weed?"

Robert releases a hearty laugh before leaning back and barking to the sky. Greg stands quietly waiting for an answer, along with every other soul in the room standing just as curious. He finishes his laugh and meets Gregs' widening eyes.

"The Creator created His Earth and everything on it to be used as we see fit, so long as it isn't used in an immoral way."

Greg stands unsatisfied by the mysterious answer and he's not alone in that boat.

"Okay, so you're saying that it's okay for us to use Cannabis...*how* exactly?"

"However you see fit."

"Can we smoke it or is that immoral?"

Robert chuckles to himself before giving a reply.

"The Creator created it to be used for everything that we never used it for. It's for smoking too, to answer your question, because it's a medicine He created. It's the only 'drug' that isn't manmade. It could be used to make our clothes, our paper and our food. When people are killing each other for it is when it becomes immoral."

Greg still stands unsatisfied.

"Okay, well, people HAVE killed each other over Pot in the past, so does that make all Pot immoral?"

"Well, Greg...Have you ever killed anyone over some Pot?"

"No, Bro."

"Have you ever *thought* about killing someone over Pot?"

"Of course not, Bro."

Robert raises his hands palms up and shrugs his shoulders.

"Well...then it's not immoral."

Greg cocks his head and furrows his brow as the uncertainty still runs rampant in his mind.

"Answer me clearly, Bro...*Please*...Is it okay...to smoke Pot? Seriously, if it's wrong, I won't do it."

Robert hops off the counter in front of Greg and adjusts his feathers, ruffling them slightly before letting them fall into their natural resting position.

"Greg...Little Brother...He created that stuff to be used for medicinal reasons, as well as recreational use and everything else. Like all things, don't abuse it. He wants us to live life and enjoy it along the way. There really is nothing wrong with enjoying it...just don't forget to live a little."

"HAHAAA! I knew it!"

He pumps his fist in the air as he spins in place while celebrating to the laughter filling the room. He received the answer he was looking for, as did the rest of the group. They all shared the same fear of offending The Creator above. Gregs dancing comes to a screeching halt as reality sets in.

221

"Shit! I don't have a fucking lighter! It ran out earlier!"

He slaps his head as his eyes bulge from their sockets in disbelief while the laughter rises out of the room and to The Abyss itself.

"Fuck that," Danny begins as he rises, "I'll rub two pieces of wood together if I have to. I need to get high, since I can't seem to find a fucking beer."

Greg meets his gaze and points to the counter behind Robert.

"Let's check the drawers behind the register. Check anywhere we might find a lighter."

They scramble behind the counter and begin a frantic search as the rest of the group settles down and returns to their jerky. The night around them is still quiet and rested and the threat of danger seems absent for the time being. Sasha reaches over from her seat on the ground and grabs a bag of Jerky from the shelf and tosses it to Will. He catches it as his face lights up.

"Thought I'd save you a trip."

He smiles wide as he slowly opens the bag and fishes a piece out.

"Thanks, Sasha...You want a piece?"

"No thanks, Will...I don't eat anymore, remember?"

He pauses in his movement and sits frozen before

slumping a bit.

"Sorry...I forgot."

"It's okay...I miss food though, it fucking sucks not being able to enjoy it anymore."

"So," Amy K. begins, "what would happen if you *did* eat something?"

The thought had not occurred to her and she'd never attempted it. She turns to Robert as he stands in front of the counter while watching over them all.

"Big...What *would* happen if we ate something?"

He crosses his arms across his chest and shakes his head, as the answer is one that he doesn't wish to give his voice to. His suddenly cold demeanor causes her to press for answers.

"Look, if we shouldn't do it, tell me. If you don't...I think I'm gonna give it a shot."

He tilts his head in submission and glares from under his brow. "Sasha...If I took a bite...it would be delicious and I would enjoy it, no doubt. But that's not the case for you," he warns while leaning

slightly in her direction, "it would turn to ashes in your mouth."

The sounds of soft chewing vanishes as they all focus on Roberts' gaze.

"Anyone from The Realm can still enjoy the Earthly pleasures of food. Anyone from The Abyss hasn't earned that privilege yet. The same goes with all of His creations."

He nods his head towards Danny and Greg scavenging through every last drawer and waste basket behind the counter. The joys of the smoke she enjoys so much would not bring her pleasures either.

"I can't smoke Weed either?"

"You can, but you won't enjoy it...that, I can promise you."

"Well...*that* fucking sucks," she scowls while shaking her beautiful red locks. Her hair seems to glow and catches Johns attention.

"Say, Little Lady, let's talk about your hair. When in the world did that happen?"

"Right!" Danny says as he jumps up from under the counter. Greg slaps his arm and fusses, prompting him to return to the search. Sasha laughs quietly at their foolishness as she addresses John.

"I did one of those temporary dyes and Joe liked it. You all were sleeping and we were out having our day. When I washed my hair that day, all the dye washed out. I convinced Joe to try and change it permanently...and he did," she pauses before looking on, almost apologetically, "That reminds me...You'll have to fix the shower wall when we get back home."

She struggles to hold in her laughter and gives away the

224

secret of our lovemaking in the showers. The group catches on immediately and joins in the laughter, while Danny screams "King Salami!" from behind the counter. Wills sits in silence as the hidden meaning is lost to him while John shakes his head and giggles.

"Can I ask you something, Friend?" He asks and greets Sashas eyes with curious eyes.

"Of course, John."

"What's it like...in The Abyss? I know it had to change under Joes leadership. I'm just curious. I think I've been spending too much time around Carmen and Amy K., feeling like I need to know everything all of a sudden."

He barks a sharp laugh and slaps his leg as Carmen shoots him a humourous smile.

"Hey!"

Greg pops up from his spot behind the counter, giving him and Danny the appearance of playing a Human version of Whack-a-Mole.

"It's true, Carmen. John's been gossiping like an old lady in a knitting circle," Greg says before returning to the place of his scavenging.

They all laugh as the attention falls to Sasha once again. She brushes her red hair away from her face and the color reflects off of her porcelain skin and makes her appear as a vision of beauty.

"The Abyss...isn't a bad place. It's our home now, Joes and mine. It's not the perfect picture of the happy ending every

225

girl wants, but...*it's ours*...and I couldn't see myself ever leaving it, as long as Joe's there."

Her blue eyes return to the stormy skies of the past as the pain of my absence dances in her soul.

"The Abyss became a good place when Joe took over. When I got there, he'd already been there for a while and the people there love him. They look at him the way he deserves to be looked at...they give him respect. Not because he's the leader...but, because he has a good heart...They all want to touch it."

She takes a false breath and continues as her eyes begin to betray the tears they hide just underneath.

"The Abyss itself...is just an empty wasteland. There's pillars in all directions holding up the ground above us, stretching for *fucking miles* in all directions...It's so fucking empty. There's nothing...except our home."

She pauses and shifts in her seat on the floor while forcing a smile and fighting the quiver in her voice.

"We live in a huge castle...or, at least, it seems like a castle to me. The people of The Abyss usually sit in front of the doors and wait for Joe to come out and talk to them...They only come inside when they've earned their wings...Joe does this amazing ritual where he accepts their evil and rewards them with their new feathers...He lifts them up," she pauses as the tears begin to flow freely, "and then the light comes from him. He throws them into the air and they take off into a light that leads to The Realm."

The sobs escape her as the pain takes hold from my heart being absent from her and wounding her more than any Cursed ever could.

"And now he's gone! My love is gone! Goddamn it! Please, let Joe be okay!"

She hides her face in her hands as she continues to wail in the anguish she thought she forever left behind. I stand her soul and she stands as mine. The distance between us kills her slowly and her broken heart is forced to revisit an old wound. It doesn't matter if it's a single second or a year; Our souls only know absence and refuse to accept it, no matter how short it may be. Without each other, we are doomed to waste away. The ladies rush to her side and comfort her as their own tears join hers. Danny and Greg, along with John and Will, join the huddle around her and offer the warmth of their embrace. Robert paces over and kneels in front of them while searching for Sashas' eyes in the mix.

"Sasha...he's alive. Believe me, he wouldn't die without seeing you again. You're his soul. I've told him a million times that he's blessed to have you...I never told him what I meant by it."

She raises her drenched blue eyes to his as he continues.

"He can't die...as long as you eternally live. The Creator blessed you to live forever...My Cuz is

still alive...because *you're* alive."

She fights through her soft sobs to address him.

"Can we try again?...Please."

He nods his head slowly in agreement. He removes his Cowboy hat to release a mane that matches my own; Hair that's long and dark and past his shoulders. He closes his eyes for a second and falls away from the world as his soul reaches out to my own. My body lies broken, unable to feel the energy of Roberts desperate plea for me to answer him. He stands the strongest of The Servants and feels my energy, even though he's merely an apparition to me. I don't feel him in the slightest as my true strength has yet to return to me. He opens his eyes to eight matching gazes all falling on him.

"He's alive."

The new energy of panic grips her tightly as she brushes everyone off her, as the need to hear my voice is now overwhelming my loving Queen. Her blue diamonds spit fire as she makes it to her feet.

"Fuck that! I need to talk to him! Don't just tell me he's alive and expect me to be fine with it! I need him, Robert!" She says before turning from him, "I'll do it."

Robert rises quickly to his feet as the tables have turned and it's now him that shows panic on his face.

"Sasha, you could hurt yourself or Joe if you're not careful. You've never tried to do this over so great a distance. Don't do it. I promise you he's okay."

She shoots him the same evil glare I had grown accustomed to as a living man.

"I'm sorry, Robert... but I'll fucking die to know he's

okay."

She closes her now fierce, blue eyes and sends her soul to the only man to ever hold her so close. Shefeels myenergyslightly, but it's enough tomoveher intoaction. Sheturns her head totheceiling above and screams with her withering soul.

"Joe! Baby! I need you! Please hear me! PLEASE ANSWER MEEEEEE!"

* *

My closed eyes shoot open as Sashas voice whispers in my ear and causes my false heart to erupt in my chest. I jump up from my seat on the ground and the sounds of my movement bring Sam to life as well. He jumps up quickly with his sword drawn, not yet fully awake from the slumber that embraced him only moments before.

Sasha!

I turn to Sam and meet his giant and worried eyes and motion for him to cover his ears. He releases his sword and follows my commands quickly as panic becomes his companion. I see his face disappear instantly as the darkness once again returns to me before I shake the world around me with my words.

"SASHAAA! I'LL FIND YOU! I LOVE YOU, MY QUEEN!!!"

* *

The gasps are loud, even forcing Robert to bellow out a false breath. Sasha collapses to the ground in one swift motion as her small sobs turn to joy. They all stand frozen in time as their jaws hang past their belt lines. The sound of my voice filled the room for a beautiful moment, and brought vitality back to the dying soul in their presence. My love, my heart, my very soul, my loving Sasha. She begins to chuckle as her misery subsides.

"I love you too, My King..."

The ladies begin to weep quietly in joy as they fall to Sashas side once more.

"I miss you, My King..."

Greg shoots up from his perch on the floor.

"Holy fucking shit! We all just heard that right?! That was Joe! He's alive Bro! He's alive! Wooo!"

They all begin to laugh quietly as Greg dances and Sasha continues to profess her love for me as the tears falling from her gorgeous face change in their meaning. She heard my voice and once again, it moved her soul to life.

"Unbelievable," John mutters, "that was a lot more than the whisper we heard last time."

He stands in awe of the moment he just witnessed, as

they all do.

"I'm sorry, Sasha," Robert apologizes, "I should of let you try. I should of known that if anyone could give Joe the strength to reach out, it would be you."

He holds his hat to his chest in front of him as he lowers his head.

"It's okay, Big...I'm sorry I snapped a little bit...but, he heard me, Robert. *He heard me.*"

Robert nods his head in agreement, "We all heard him."

Her eyes fall to the floor, along with new tears as she smiles wide and giggles softly.

"I love you too, My King.

****

"Oh my God! What the hell was that?!"

She heard me. I know she did. She had to.

"I was talking to Sasha...I had to give it my all for her to hear me."

The only sound now playing in the silence is my small laughter.

"Do you think she did?" Sam asks quietly.

Yes.

"Without a doubt," I quip back with a smile.

For the smallest of moments I could feel her heart and the very essence of her eternal beauty...I could feel her loving soul.

"I heard her voice whispering in my ear. She needs me as much as I need her...I feel her, Sam...I feel her when she's near...and I just felt her, even though she's so far away. The bond between us will never be broken, no matter how much distance lies between us."

I fall to my knees as the pain of heartache takes over the joy I was lost in. I feel the area where my heart is begin to sink further down into my chest as a wave of heat washes over me. I feel the sorrow I used to live in when I was still alive, when Sasha played the game of Twisting My Soul. I feel lost without her and my immortal body wallows in an immortal pain. She's my soul and living without her, I cannot. I can only survive to hope to feel my arms find her slender body again. I remind myself, that at the very least, I must survive for the sake of Sam. Drawing a deep breath, I gather my senses and return to my feet.

"She's going to be okay, Sam. They all are...Get some rest...I'll wake you in the morning."

He nods slowly and lowers his sword, but the wild energy in him is running erratic. Sleep will not find him easy.

The task of falling into a slumber will be a difficult one after the bone shaking roar that escaped me. He returns to his perch and falls quietly to his seat. He lowers his head into his folded arms and begins to draw shallow breaths and taking a small step towards the quiet comfort of the dream world.

Goodnight Sam.

****

"My Love is okay...He's okay."

She smiles the million dollar smile that constantly lights up my life. They all talk about my voice

filling their halls with a mighty roar as they've all returned to the comforts of their circle. Greg sits pouting from his failed quest for fire, and Danny appears as his Doppelganger. It appears the small joys will be absent tonight.

"That was crazy," Greg says, "I can't believe how loud it was...It was like Joe was in the room with us."

"He was, Greg," Sasha corrects him, "in spirit. Ask Robert, he'll tell you. The whole kingdom of The Abyss got to listen in on me and Joe during...Robert, you want to take this one? "

She giggles as Robert chuckles and begins to explain.

"Joes soul is capable of traveling throughout the entire universe. He can't control it yet, so when he...gets lost in a

233

moment...he may broadcast his energy unintentionally."

"Wait wait wait," Greg spouts as he turns to Sasha, "all of The Abyss heard you guys having sex? Bahahaaa!"

Her blue eyes flash with offence as the rest of her face mimics the same mask.

"Why is *that* so funny?"

"Because," he snickers, "I heard you guys having sex and I thought he was killing you."

Laughter fills the room and for the first time, Sasha has no words. She can only laugh along with them while her face turns as red as her lovely locks.

"Ahhh dammit," John grumbles as he grabs his palm, "too bad you couldn't find a lighter, Friend. My Arthritis is really flaring up in my sword hand."

"No shit, Bro! Every Potheads worst fucking nightmare. Having a stash and no fucking flame!"

"Heck, even I would of smoked tonight. My feet are killing me," Amy J. adds, "Robert, Honey, does this armor really have to be so heavy? It's making my poor feet swell up bigger than they already are."

"Yes Amy J., I'm sorry Ma'am," he says and chuckles deeply as she presents her chubby feet.

"Well guys," Will begins, "I know it's not the same, but I have some matches, if that will work for you?"

Silence falls over the room as eight sets of giant eyes find Wills dumbfounded gaze. Disbelief has grasped them tightly and has seemingly removed their ability to speak. Carmen looks up to Wills face while his giant frame eclipses hers.

"Baby...Did you just say you have some matches?"

The look on her face begs for some sort of reasoning.

"Uh-huh."

They all sit quietly as he observes their strange faces, these phantoms with perfect circles where their mouths should be. Even Robert stands struck by Wills' simpleness.

"Dumbass! Then *why* didn't you say something when they were looking for a lighter?"

He flinches in his seat and appears startled by the question.

"Uhh because you can't use certain things to light a joint...duhhh."

Every set of eyebrows raises in unison as their thoughts come to a grinding halt.

"What?!" Danny shouts.

"You know," Will begins with his attempt at an rational explanation, "you don't use a Zippo lighter to light a bong...or a pipe...you use matches."

The confusion is killing every living and eternal soul in the room.

"Bro! It's a fucking joint!" Greg hollers. "You can light the fucking thing with a Goddamn flamethrower if you want to! Why didn't you tell me you had matches?!"

"Well, you weren't looking for matches, were you?" He continues in a smug tone, "you were looking for a lighter."

"Oh my fucking goodness! Bro!" Greg screams as he throws his hands up, "you're fucking killing me right now!"

Greg fumbles through his shirt pocket to retrieve the stash he managed to stash away with him for his journey. He pulls it out and, with an empty hand, reaches forward towards Will. He smiles at Greg and gives him a "five" and a thumbs up afterwards.

"The matches, Dumbass! He wasn't asking for a High-five!" Carmen informs him.

Laughter overtakes the silence as they all fall over themselves while Will sits motionless and quiet. He doesn't understand why that would be a bad thing, giving someone a High-five, because in his mind, High-fives are cool. He retrieves the matches from his pocket and hands them to Greg.

"Thank you!" Greg shouts before giving Will the true greeting he was looking for.

"You're welcome!" Will says while smiling and accepting a High-five from his little brother.

"Hurry up and light that shit!" Danny commands.

236

"Fuck that, I'm lighting all of them."

Greg lines up four joints along the seam of his lips. He takes the remaining two he has and tosses one to John and one to Danny. He pursues his joy as he lights all four, one by one, with a single match. He tosses the box to John as he inhales deeply while his face appears as a birthday cake, lined with candles as the cherries glow bright from his smoke starved lungs filling their request. He almost spits his prized possessions out of his mouth as the smoke chokes him. Grabbing two joints with each hand, he passes them all to either side of him. It doesn't take long to make its way back, with only seven smokers and six joints among them. Sasha and Robert remove themselves from the circle and relocate next to the counter, observing with curious eyes as they watch each one react to the smoky pleasures in their own way. John and Amy J. appear relieved from their ailments as the rest sit as smiling fools. The energy picks up as the eyelids fall down, and they all begin to laugh and jest.

"Tomorrow," Robert says quietly to Sasha, "we find Joe."

"We better...I'm not going to make it another day without him. He can't leave this world...I can't lose him twice."

He meets her soft, blue eyes with his own dark, stormy clouds.

"Sasha...When Joe tells you that he will never die as long as you live...he means it...*literally*."

His brow arches high as he stresses the last word of his sentence and it causes her blue gems to turn icy cold.

"What are you talking about?"

He leans closer to her and speaks in a softer tone.

"You and Joe are one now. He will never die...*as long as you live*...I must keep you safe and return you to his side again. I was trying to tell you earlier...You are a part of him...so I gotta keep you safe, above all others."

"Are you saying what I think you're saying?"

Her eyes have become deep blue oceans now, with tides breaking along her bottom eyelids.

"Yes...if you die...he dies."

Chapter 5

The sun greets a new day and reveals that the buildings around them appear more dead in the light than in the dark. The city stands as a vacant landfill as mounds of trash litter the streets in all directions. Robert leads the group through the rubble towards the awaiting hills a few miles away, as the soft sounds of their armored bodies have become the only sounds in existence. He feels my energy and follows it as a predator would its' wounded prey. He follows the pull of my soul, from over a thousand miles away.

"Bro...Thank God I saved those roaches for this morning. Nothing like a Wake and Bake, even if *it is* the end of the fucking world."

Greg passes the last remaining roach to John.

"My Arthritis thanks you, Friend."

John takes a long, smooth drag and passes it to Amy J..

"For your feet, Little Lady," he says with a sly smile.

"Thank you, Honey," she responds as she takes the roach and brings it to her lips.

"I can't stand to smoke anymore, not without some fucking food," Danny adds, "I'm not talking about Beef Jerky either. My mouth is too fucking dry for that shit."

"At least you got to burn one," Sasha jabs at him, "I

wish I could of."

"Maybe one day," Amy K. says, "you and Joe can burn together in Hell, um, I mean, *The Abyss*."

Sasha looks at her with comical blue eyes while suppressing her laughter for her sisters sake.

"Oh my goodness, I just heard it. I'm sorry, Sasha, I didn't mean for it to come out like that!"

They all start laughing as one at Amy K.s words. Robert chuckles softly to himself as he remembers all the stories I told him about Amy K. and her often misguided words.

"Thanks, Amy. I hope we burn in Hell for all of eternity."

The laughter continues and travels throughout the deserted world around them.

"Man, I gotta find some more. That was everything I had left," Greg confesses.

"Not happening, Dude," Will says.

"Shit," Carmen quips, "if anyone can find some Weed in this world, it's our Brother Greg."

Greg giggles loudly from the odd compliment and takes a small bow.

"Thanks Carmen," he says and smiles in gratitude.

"Don't make me a liar, Greg. Go make me proud!"

They laugh together as Will looks back and forth between them while shaking his head in disagreement.

"We don't even know where we are. How are you going to find some?"

Greg shoots him his sly look as he relishes the moments of revealing his minds inner workings.

"It's simple, Bro. You just gotta think like a Pothead."

"You are a Pothead," Danny interrupts, "and I'm so glad The Creator left you behind."

"Amen," Amy J. adds.

They laugh amongst themselves as Greg smiles and looks to the sky.

"Really Bro, you just imagine all the places that would be a good hiding place. Somewhere no one would look, without a reason. Also, you can tell by the houses in a neighborhood. When I was in college, I would drive around neighborhoods and look for the shadiest character. Not a bum or addict, but someone who looked like he sold drugs as much as did them. I always looked for the watch. Dealers always need to know the time and would have nice watches. They always had the most decent home in the rundown Hoods too. Those are the houses I plan on hitting along the way. It's how I found that big ass stash back in our hometown."

"Sounds like you have it all figured out, Little Cuz," Robert says as he turns to him.

241

"Yeah...my system hasn't failed me yet...Hey, I kinda have a weird question for you, Robert...Is there Weed in The Realm?"

Robert roars with laughter as he faces the sky and causes his black cowboy hat to almost fall from his crown. He looks at Greg and nods his head in agreement.

"For real, Bro?!"

"The Realm is what you make of it."

Greg continues walking, but now treads in silence as he thinks about all the possibilities of what The Realm would look like. The dreamy eyes he wears causes Robert to begin chuckling again.

"Stop thinking about it, Little Cuz. You've got a lot of work to do down here before you head up to the paradise in the stars. It'll be everything you've ever wanted, including your happy grass."

"Bro...it's gonna be so fucking cool."

They approach the end of the street and enter the heart of the city. Their journey through the city is halfway finished and has gone by without a hint of danger. The day would be full of peril, just not for them. The night would be a different tale.

****

"What am I gonna do for food?"

Sam stands half awake from the rude awakening I had given him. He was sleeping soundly when I stretched my wings and hit him in the head during his deep sleep. It was time to rise for the day, but what a hell of a way to wake up.

"We'll look for food as we go and I'll make it for you once I regain my strength."

We continue to gather the few belongings we have and adjust our swords on our hips. I take a moment to listen to the environment around and detect nothing. I go on with the business of harnessing my weapon and watch as Sam does the same.

"Hey Joe, I gotta take a piss...I'm going to step out for a minute, if that's okay with you."

Don't let him go. Lead him out. Go first.

"Sure thing, Sam. Don't go far...Stay close enough for me to hear you."

"I will," he says as he makes his way to the door. He pauses in front of it long enough to listen to the stillness of the New World before opening it slowly and walking out with the soft steps of an Alley Cat. First one foot, pause, then the other, until the door closes quietly behind him.

The moment is lonely for me, this final glimpse I would be taking inside the Shower Shack that was birthed from Gregs mind and Johns intellect and constructed by many hands,

243

including my own. The beauty of the morning is captured perfectly as the sun shines down through the open rafters and into the quiet corners. My mind wanders to the moments shared by Sasha and me and the tender and vicious lovemaking that knocked over the stall wall, the only casualty from us restraining our passion. The loving screams return to my hearing, as if lost from a time so long ago. I hear her loving voice whispering my name and feel the tears starting to burn hot upon my cheeks. They would feel the burning sorrow time and again before I would see my Loving Soul again. The sounds of her voice begin to blend in with voices I don't recognize.

Whos' voice it that?

The voices belong to men I've yet to meet.

Sam. He's talking to someone.

Turning quickly, I push my steps with haste as the rush of a phantom adrenaline begins haunting my veins. If my heart truly beat, it would be pounding against my chest. The only Humans in the New World, other than my family, made an attempt to kill my Loving Queen. If not for a merciful Creator, they would have succeeded. New Humans in the New World behave exactly how a Human would behave in any crisis; They would kill or be killed. It's a maniacal mentality that I had hoped to avoid. Grabbing the handle, I hesitate as I hear Sams' voice.

"I live here," he whimpers.

"Alone? Or with others? We heard you speaking to someone. Who's with you?"

Tell them The Fallen One walks beside you, Sam. Tell

244

them of me.

"No one. I'm alone, I swear. I talk to myself because I'm lonely, man! I haven't seen anyone in months."

Peeking through the cracks, I see nothing as they stand just out of sight.

"You're a fucking liar, you little asshole. If I find out you're lying, I'm going to fuck you with my pretty new sword."

He has Sams' sword. Sam's unarmed.

Grabbing the handle to the point of breaking it, I feel my strength return as the anger begins to boil. Death will not come quickly to those who harm my family. Sam now stands as my brother in this life. I pull the door open and am greeted by a long, cold steel barrel pointed at my chest while a tall, lean, light-skinned Blonde man is the wielder. He smiles wide with soft features as I look past him and see Sam held against his will with his blade pressed up against his throat by another man, this one having dark hair and a brutish build. They share the same eyes, full of hate and lust. They want only to take what they want in this New World, even at the cost of Human life. I glare past the barrel at the both of them while keeping my wings still hidden inside the Shower Shack. They don't know that Immortals are now roaming the Earth and that offending one could be their biggest mistake.

"I knew he was lying. You there...Pretty Boy...How many more of ya'll are in this little shit hole? And don't lie to me, bitch...or I'll pull this trigger," he says while grinning with teeth that don't look like they've seen toothpaste in many years. Judging by the State-Issued shoes they wear, I'm guessing they were trash before the Old World ended. It's no surprise to

245

me that The Creator left them.

"It's just me and Sam. Put the gun down...you can't kill me."

"Hahaaa! And why's that?"

"Because I'm immortal, you pathetic, little bitch."

He looks back at his partner and sees the same smirk he wears. Turning back to me, he cocks the hammer on his .357 Magnum and glares at me with eyes that have turned wild.

"Immortal huh? My chrome buddy here would disagree."

"Fuck you and your chrome buddy. I *am* immortal, now put the gun down."

"Shut the fuck up with that immortal bullshit."

"If you fire that gun...you're going to meet a Hell you wish to never know. Either it will come from the skies or from my hands...you have a better chance with the death above than the terror in front of you. Put the gun down, you *can't. Fucking. Kill me.*"

"Say you're immortal one more time and I'll put a hole in your chest, you fucking faggot."

"I'm immortal."

The click of the hammer striking the shell is small compared to the blast that escapes the barrel. I feel the bullet enter my chest and stop against my heart as a small prick that barely registers. I look down at the hole in my robes and see my flesh coming back together as the bullet pushes itself out and the seams of my flesh close shut behind it. Glancing up, I see the faces of the two idiots now in disbelief. I step forward from the shower house and let my wings introduce themselves. Their faces turn to panic at the sight of the winged immortal in front of them.

"I warned you...you can't kill me...and now, I'm pissed off."

He staggers back a step as his immoral twin releases Sam and the sword he would claim as his own and begins his own dance of retreat. Their eyes wide, their souls shine through in complete terror.

"Who the fuck are you?"

"I am the True Ruler of The Abyss, as The Creator has tasked me. To you, I would be the Devil, but not like the Devil you've heard about your whole life...I'm far worse than that guy."

He falls to his backside and continues to scurry away. The screams in the distance confirm my beliefs about guns in the New World. It's why I was taken with a bladed vengeance when the Old World ended. Guns are far too noisy. I pause in my words to point to the sky at the flock that has appeared in the distance.

"I warned you about those guys too. Good luck with them. Let's go, Sam."

Sam turns to face his former captor before looking back

to me.

"Let's go, Sam...they can't harm us."

Reluctantly, he leans down and retrieves his sword and walks forward towards me. The screams and hisses of The Cursed grow louder with each second that passes. Their screeches promise the two fools in front of me that the death from above would show them far more mercy than I would. Sam rejoins my side as I step around behind him and wrap my arms around his chest, letting my wings stretch far into the sunlight I missed so much.

Wings, don't fail me now.

I shoot them a small smile and soft eyes as their faces suddenly plea for mercy.

"I'll see you guys in The Abyss."

Thrusting hard, my wings return to me. The ground shoots from our feet as I carry Sam into the sky, as The Cursed appear just above the horizon. They sit below the tree line to the soon-to-be residents of The Abyss, with their flight hidden by The Creators beautiful trees. They would only have seconds to react when the nightmarish eagles make themselves known. They close the distance quickly as I thrust again, making it high enough to view the battle to come from a safe distance, but far enough away for a quick retreat once the show ends. They swoop over the trees and towards the evil men who shoot into the sky, aiming their chrome buddies at the birds of prey that do not fear bullets. The hisses are loud as they aim their claws at the fools who brought about their own doom with the cries of their pistols. They close the distance between them, and then the unthinkable happens.

248

The lights pierce the clouds quickly and shine down upon the two sorry souls who didn't deserve to be spared. The Cursed burn quickly and retreat from the beams from The Realm, while the remaining dozen or so stand in the street next to the Shower House. The screams of victory are loud and boastful, the gloating towards The Cursed as foul as the threats made towards Sam. They rise into the air quickly and graciously, as if invisible hands gently move them. They continue to scream at The Cursed, but only until they catch sight of Sam and the True Ruler of The Abyss hovering just above the clouds.

"Hahaaa! Fuck you, faggots! It looks like I won't be seeing you in The Abyss after all! We'll be fucking bitches while you cocksuckers burn! I'll tell God that the Devil says hello! Good luck in The Abyss, you stupid assholes! I'll think about you when I'm cuddled up with some Angel bitches! Looks like God loves us more than you! Fags! HAHAHAAA!"

Whispering to Sam, I teach him a lesson to carry throughout his new life.

"The Creator loves all his creations, Sam, even the worst of the lot...but he doesn't tolerate ugly souls."

The beam disappears as they reach the entrance to all their wildest dreams and the hands guiding them release their grasp. They scream in horror as they begin to fall to the Earth below with predatory eyes trained upon them, as The Cursed have become revitalized that their hunt will end in blood after all. They leap into the air and flock towards their falling feast as the screams of the fools fade from our ears. We watch as The Cursed meet them midair and grab them with taloned feet, a new deformity no doubt added by the Necromancer. The blond antagonist screams as his shoulders are shredded by hooked talons and his legs ripped from his body by another Cursed. His

249

legs fall to the Earth and he watches in horror as The Cursed below scavenge for scraps. He will be their plaything and the thought lingers in his face, an expression I can see even from so high a perch. He continues screaming as they begin tearing off his arms, the screams traveling up so high before a Cursed sinks his teeth into the mans' throat, while the gurgling blood pouring out is just as loud. His sidekick suffers a different fate, yet equally terrifying. They grab a hold and guide him down to the street by the Shower Shack where two of the overgrown spawn Reapers await with eager stares. His cries are loud as they force him to the ground and tear open his stomach, peeling back his flesh and exposing is organs. They begin to remove them and toss them aside, but not before taking bites of every fleshy treat. He screams in horror again as they pull his intestines out like cats with yarn, leaving his body to become empty, except for his beating heart and accelerated lungs. The taller of the two pushes the other aside before ripping apart the mans rib cage. He plants his terrible face into the empty cavity and with razor teeth, begins chewing on his victims heart, causing the muscle to explode in a shower of blood and spraying the world around. His body jerks and twitches from being eaten from the inside out. I feel Sams energy turning sour and it's my cue to end the show. Turning, I begin a steady beat of my wings and leave my old town behind. It would seem like a lifetime before I would revisit it. My selfish wish is to hold Sasha again in our home before we have to return to The Abyss and pick up where we left off.

There's still a few walls in our old house still standing.

****

"Bingo! There's one!"

Greg strays from the group, now surrounded by the even larger corpses of fallen buildings, and heads into a small abandoned Head Shop, a novelty store that sold his kind of novelties. He draws his machete as he approaches the fallen door and peers in and is greeted by only tobacco pipes of all shapes and varieties. They reflect his gaze back at him, returning his cautious stare. He turns to the group with a smile of victory.

"Keep walking, this won't take long."

They continue their travels as Greg disappears into the broken building while their armor reflects the suns' rays around them.

"What's it like to be a Servant?" Amy K. wonders.

"It's okay. You get to fly, which is really cool," Robert answers.

"Do you ever feel pain? Or misery?"

He chuckles slightly as he replies, "Pain, no. Misery on the other hand, that's a different story. You still have all the emotions that anyone else would, living or eternal."

"Do you get hungry?"

"No Ma'am," he replies with a smile.

"I know you don't sleep, so you don't dream. Can you still daydream?"

He laughs loudly to the air as they walk along in the midday sun.

"Amy K....you are full of questions. All I can tell you is to wait until you have your wings...Then, you'll know what it is to be a Servant...and no, we can't daydream. We often revisit memories from our past lives though."

"Hmmm...that sounds sad. I thought Servants would only have *good* thoughts."

"Well they *are* good thoughts. I think about my family a lot. My wife, who was my best friend, and my children. They're the greatest kids a dad could ask for. It makes me happy to know they're safe in The Realm."

"Guys! I found it! Hahaaa! Ohhh yeaaah! Two for two!"

Greg runs from the half collapsed building holding a large bag of bright green pot, about three ounces in weight, and touts his ultimate prize. He catches up with the group and tosses the bag at John.

"Here Buddy! Your Arthritis can thank me later! HAHAHAAA!"

He screams in victory as he lunges into John and delivers his own John-Bear hug, as only John could do, while their steel clothing clangs together and rings throughout the city.

"Aaahhh! Easy there, Friend! And thank you Sir, I do appreciate it," John says coyly.

"That's a lot of fucking weed," Carmen interrupts, "I hope you plan on sharing."

"Hell, there's plenty for everyone here," John replies as he turns to Greg, "this looks like that high-dollar medical stuff. How did you know where to find it?"

"Head shops are full of my kind of people," he proclaims while smiling wide, "and my kind of people only smoke the good shit. And they never go to work without a supply! Ha!"

He pulls his small Bag pack off of his shoulder and reaches in to retrieve another bag of his prized possession, a smaller bag about an ounce in weight. He smells the bag and places it back into its little hideaway.

"Man, today has been a good day," he exclaims through a grin.

"Hey, Big!" Danny begins, "Where are we man? I'm dying of fucking thirst, Bro. I seriously need a drink."
Robert turns to Danny at the back of the group and points to the delivery truck full of bottled water they are quickly passing by.

"Really, Danny? You can't see that, Brother?"

His eyes light up and grow unnaturally big as he blurts out, "Holy shit!" before running to the back of the truck and grabbing a bottle from the plastic-wrapped pallet sitting closest to the open door. The cap is a small trial for a thirsty man. The rest of the group makes their way over and mimics his actions. They work on having their fill and are mindful to grab another bottle to continue their journey. Sasha and Robert stand as their lookout as they finish indulging in their newly discovered refreshing joys.

"Hey Sasha," Will begins, "have you tried to talk to Joe today?"

She shakes her head in disagreement and it causes her red mane to dance across her shoulders.

"No...but I need to again. I feel completely lost without him. I don't feel like I belong where I am right now...It just doesn't feel right...It's fucking strange knowing he could be so close, yet, he's so fucking far away."

Will nods his head slowly as he continues knocking back his cool water. He lowers the bottle and meets her sad, wounded eyes.

"I remember way back when you were both still alive and you were still crazy..."

"I was never crazy, Will," Sasha sharply interrupts.

"Well...back when you went bonkers..."

"That's just another word for crazy, Babe," Carmen informs him.

"Okay, well, back when she was ...whatever she was! My point is that Joe always talked to us guys about how much

254

he loves you. He said there is nothing in the world you could do to him to make him stop. If I was Joe, I would want to hear from you everyday."

Her blue eyes become clouds of stormy pasts as the tears well up. She shakes her head in agreement.

"You'reright, Will...You're a hundred percent right...I'll try as soon as we're settled for a bit. We'll take a lunch break somewhere for you guys soon and I'll give it a shot then," she says before turning away and shaking her head, "I'm sorry, I just fucking miss him so much and I'm trying so hard not to think about it."

Will glances at her apologetically, "I'm sorry, Sasha, I didn't mean to make you cry...Can I ask you something else?" She returns her angelic face back to his while fighting her heartache.

"Sure."

"Why did you act all weird when we first met you? You would flip out *constantly* on Joe."

The tears pour down her cheeks as she replies, "The only difference in their appearance is Joe has a small mole on his face...Other than that, their faces are identical in *every fucking way*. Joe and my ex-husband, I mean...It was fucking weird, hearing Joes voice telling me these nice things when my exhusband only said cruel things to me...I couldn't stand to look at Joes face, but his words would draw me to him. I thought, maybe, The Creator was making it right, all the fucked up horrors I went through, when he gave me Joe...At the same time, I kept thinking it was all some sort of prank, that Joe was somehow that evil bastard that I had to endure...I know now that The Creator gave me Joe because I had been waiting for him my entire life. He's so wonderful, and I can't stop crying now because I'm so fucking scared I may lose him, which is the worst thing that could happen to me. I'd rather die than live in any world without him."

Stopping in her tracks, she buries her face in the comfort of her palms and releases her agony. Carmen and the Amys come to her side and embrace her for her dark moment as the sad energy radiates out and creates frowns all around. She wails as her soul screams and her heart dreams. She must have her love again, in this life and the next. Robert catches her blue eyes and reminds her of his words.

Joe's fine...as long as you live.

****

The steady beat of my wings moves us further away from the slaughter we just witnessed. The clouds sail past as Sam shields his face as the misty fog stings his eyes. My wings burn from being worked so hard without a break, and I can feel that my true strength has not yet fully recovered. I feel them giving out, yet I push them still and refuse to give any rest to my wicked soul. The tendons begin to pop in my back and my shoulders experience a real mortal pain, and it's a feeling I did not miss. There is no further warning before my body fails me.

"Joe! JOE!!!"

Sam screams while we plummet as gravity has become my newest enemy. My wings will not save us. I assure softly to Sam that we cannot die and that we will not fail. The clouds

256

below are small and grow quickly before their soft bodies are ripped apart by the falling fools who flew too high. He screams loud and long and his heart beats at a rapid pace, and he pleas for The Creator to save us. We can see the ground quickly approaching, so beautiful and spellbinding as it invites our glorious doom. The trees will offer no comfort to Sams mortal body. I will survive, but he wouldn't be so lucky. We approach the last cloud before certain doom as I close my eyes and send my soul into a familiar darkness.

* *

"Creator of All...Are you there?."

The darkness echoes its usual cries as my voice travels throughout the void. There is no one with me in the dark, and I can sense no figure hiding in the shadows. No one stands with me, yet His voice radiates from everywhere.

"You'll be fine. Continue on, and don't give up."

The silence follows the statement while I stand unsatisfied.

"Don't let Sam die...Don't call him home until he's served his true purpose."

"Sam will be fine. You will protect him."

I feel the anxiety return to my soul as I confess my failure.

"We're kind of plummeting to his doom right now. My

257

wings have failed me during an escape from The Cursed...We only have moments left."

Silence and darkness fill my senses. It seems like an eternity before I receive a reply.

"Then your wings have failed you. You can control the world around you, adjust it to fit your needs. Save him...This, you can do."

****

Light. It fills my eyes in an instant as the darkness vanishes. The world is moving slower now, and Sams' screams become muffled and raspy. The green field below the final cloud on our path glows in the sunlight and reflects the beauty of the sun. I watch as our impact with the clouds becomes imminent, and is the final blanket between Sam and doom.

Nothing is beyond me.

The collision with the soft, yet somehow firm, lonely cloud is surprising at first, but only for a moment. It acts as our security net, catching us and pushing us back into the air before we return to its surface and repeat the process. It's our very own trampoline in the sky. After a few small bounces, I hear Sams small laughter overtake his screams. I join him in the joy of his sudden reprieve.

"Oh Creator!...Thank you so much...Thank you too, Joe...thank you."

I chuckle as I lay out facing the sky, "You're welcome, Sam...Sorry for the scare."

258

He laughs loudly as he spins off his back and onto all fours and peers down over the edge of the cloud. We reside on the lowest cloud, yet the ground below still seems so far away.

"How is this possible?"

I roll over onto my stomach and peer over the edge with him. The view of the world below is a spectacular vision, and we watch as the New World spins underneath us.

"All things are possible, Sam...Something I'm just now fucking learning."

"Yeah, but we're riding a cloud right now...How is this possible?...Are you doing it?"

"I believe so...I'm not really sure. I just hoped this last cloud would somehow become solid...and here we are...riding a cloud."

"We could ride this forever, Joe. We wouldn't have to travel by foot and you wouldn't have to fly...think we could stay on it a while?"

Sasha.

"I think that's a good idea, Sam...I need to do something...and I'll need a moment."

I rise up and kneel on the clouded floor under me before closing my eyes.

****

The darkness alive, my soul travels along an invisible trail to the energy of my true heart; My Loving Sasha. I feel her warmth acting as a beacon and see a small, lighted mist pointing the way to my New World Love. Her energy trail appears as loving as the soul in her and her scent fills the air, creating a line of breadcrumbs I'm all too happy to follow. She's close in the darkness, no matter how far away she may be. I whisper to my love and pull her from whatever life she may be living.

"I found you, My Queen."

"JOE!? Is it really you?!"

I feel my face smiling in the darkness while my eyes fight happy tears.

"It's me, My Love. Please tell me you're safe!"

"I'm fine! All our family is fine and Robert is with us. We're safe, Baby...We're sitting in an abandoned Café somewhere in the middle of fucking nowhere and everyone's eating their lunch. Baby, where are you?"

I pause for a brief moment before answering, knowing it'll surprise her.

"Believe it or not, I'm sitting on a cloud with Sam."

"What the fuck?!"

I laugh loudly and hear my laughter echo and pray if fills her ears.

"Yes, we're on a cloud. It turns out, I can do a few

260

things...I miss you, Sasha."

I hear her voice cracking immediately and it tears my soul in half.

"Baby, I miss you so fucking much! I don't want to be without you any longer! Please come find me, Baby! I need you!"

I remember the unstable girl that moved me in dangerous ways and how my words would bring comfort to her. I do my best to remind her that my soul would always stand as her prized possession.

"Easy now, My Loving Soul. The world can grow tenfold and time can stretch into eternity, but no amount of distance will keep me from my Blue-Eyed Queen. You can go to the farthest corner of the Earth and I will find you. I'll wait as long as it takes to be with you again. I won't stop for anything until I feel the soft comfort of your lips, and gaze into the endless oceans that are your eyes. I'll hold you again. I'll love you fiercely when we're one again. I'll remind you that I am no King, but only putty in your hands. I'd give up all the kingdoms in every realm to walk beside you once more...This I promise you, My Love."

The tears fall from the both of us, only in different places in different worlds. I miss her terribly and it tears me in half, as the agony of her absence has become more than I can endure. I thank The Creator I can talk to her again, at the very least. I need her beautiful curses as much as she needs my terribly poetic words. She is the light in my soul, and without her, I will perish. I do my best to hold myself together for the sake of both of our sanity.

"Baby...I love you...I miss you, Baby...I need you..."

"We'll be together again. I'll destroy the whole fucking world to get to you, Sasha. The Creator knows I will. No man or beast can stand in the path of my love for you without being annihilated. I'll destroy the Sun and Moon and pull the stars out of the sky for the sake of My Queen. I love you too, Sasha...Be strong, Love. A man cannot live without a soul...You'll always stand as mine."

"That's right," she giggles, "I'm yours, Baby."

We both chuckle softly together, yet it's barely a phantom sound in the darkness compared to the loving music we make in each others presence.

"Yes you are, and don't you forget it. I'm getting stronger, Sasha. I'll be with you soon, My Love... I promise."

I hear the soft giggle that usually voices itself before one of her dirty comments.

"Get stronger in a hurry and come find me. You're gonna need all the strength you can get because...when I get my hands on you again..."

"I know I know," I playfully interrupt, "you're gonna fuck the fucking shit out of me, fuck fuckity shit. Asshole, titties, big fat boner, blah blah blah!"

We laugh as one and it makes me miss all the moments I laughed with her by her side, both as a Living man and a Dead man. It hurts to hear her beautiful voice in my head and not lay eyes upon her or feel her loving touch. Still, I laugh in the moment with my loving Sasha.

"*Baby! Oh my God! You took the words out of my mouth! I really was gonna say some stupid shit like that!*" She confesses as she laughs again.

The music of her soul fills my ears in the same manner it filled the halls of The Abyss. I feel her reverberate throughout my eternal essence and can only describe it as an Autumn Sun bathing me in the warmth of its rays.

"*I know you all too well, Sasha. I thank The Creator for every moment that I do.*"

I feel my body becoming weak in the darkness and realize I won't have much longer.

"*Sasha...I'm getting stronger but I feel myself becoming... I'm overdoing it a bit. I'm going to have to let you go soon.*"

"*NO! Baby, please, just a moment longer! Don't leave me yet!*"

The energy in the darkness around me changes to a cold draft as the scared Sasha of old returns. I feel the panic in her at the thought of losing me again. I can't blame her for possessing such paranoia when she's seen me die before.

"*Sasha, I'm coming for you. I promise you I am. I'll stay with you as long as you want me to. We can talk to the end of time, My Love. I'm not going anywhere.*"

I hear the soft, comforted laughter she always voiced when I kissed her tears away in dark moments.

"Baby...you can go. I know you need to rest...it's just so hard to let you go. I feel like it's wrong to do, now that I have you again."

"It's okay, My Queen. You're not saying goodbye forever, it's just for now. I look forward to hearing your voice again, My Love...I love you."

I feel the sorrow overtake us both as we live in a moment we wish never existed. How can anyone say goodbye to their own soul, for any amount of time?

"I love you too, Joe. Be safe, My King...and hurry the fuck up and come back!"

Her sweet laughter follows, ensuring me she's okay with letting me go for the moment.

"I will. I fucking promise I'll fucking find you, just be fucking careful until I fucking do so, you fucker."

We pause in the darkness and revisit our silly laughter together. I hear her unable to catch her breath and can see her in my memory, of all the times I made her laugh until she couldn't breathe. I always find her so beautiful in these moments, as I can see only her truest self. I smile in the darkness as tears continuetofall from my eyes as theydrip with sorrow, and can onlyhopethat hercheeks remain dryin the darkness that hides them. She is my love...She is my life...She will forever stand as my conqueror.

"I love you, Joe."

"I love you too, Sasha...and always will."

****

Silence is the new sound of the gathering as all eyes stand fixated on Sasha, with her blue eyes returning from the blackness they were just devoured by. She sees their faces in the blink of an eye and the tears flowing from all, as their bodies line up around the table in front of her. The raw beauty of the moment moves them all to feel our heartache.

The Café has taken on a beautiful look in the early afternoon sun. The New World around them sits just on the outskirts of the city. The remains of buildings rest behind them as they all sit in the open and watch with damp cheeks as Sasha smiles from the high of our encounter. She begins to laugh softly for a few moments from her seat at the end of the table before slamming her fist hard on its surface. The laughter turns to weeps as she finds her heart wounded by me once more. My absence is of my own doing and she will suffer without me. I'm thankful I'm not there in the moment to see the face she wears anytime she was around the monster who made pretty girls cry, as I remember it all too well, so long ago in the Old World. That look alone defeated me anytime I was the cause of it. I'm also thankful her girls are with her as they offer her the comforts I cannot.

"Hey girl, I know you're upset, but at least you got to talk to him," Carmen says, "and you know he loves you more than anything. He'll find you, believe me. Joe has always been fucking crazy about you."

"It's true," Will delicately states, "we couldn't figure out what the Hell was wrong with him when you tried to kill him and he still wanted to be with you. Believe us...The guy is fucking looney."

Carmen glares at Will and gives him the look he should be all too familiar with.

"Crazy about *her*, Will. I'm not saying he's *actually* crazy, you dumbass."

The banter between them causes Sasha to burst into laughter and leaves her red mane hanging from her head as she faces the sky and howls. She laughs until the tears return before looking at Will.

"Thank you, Will...I needed that."

Amy K. jumps up from her seat on the corner beside Sasha and clasps her hands together.

"Sasha! I know what will make you feel better!"

Amy K. pulls on the leather bindings that hold her breastplate to her chest and loosens it from its duty. She reaches in and pulls out the dusty, old Bible she kept in her possession since the day I left them.

"Maybe you'll feel better if you read a little bit from Joes' book. His words always made you feel better."

Sasha imitates Amys movements moments before and rises suddenly to her feet.

"Oh my God! Thank you, Amy! I can't believe you have it with you!"

266

She lunges across the corner of the table and hugs her sister as their voices turn to laughter and joy. Robert stands the most eager and makes his way to Sashas' side. Unbeknownst to all, this is a rare treat for him.

"Sasha...can I hold it? No one in The Realm or The Abyss has ever seen what was written by Joe. We've all heard about it, but there is only one copy in all of existence...and I can't believe I'm looking at it."

The Guard dog in Amy K. begins to bark.

"Hold on there, Big Guy. This book hasn't left my possession since Joe entrusted me with protecting it. You're not going to try and keep it for yourself, are you?"

Robert giggles and holds his large hands up as if he means to repel her.

"Not if it means I have to deal with *you*."

Finding his answer satisfactory, Amy K. looks up at him and smiles as she hands him the book. He turns away and dives into his new read as Danny taps her on the shoulder.

"How in the Hell did we not know you had that with you? You've had it this whole freaking time? Why didn't you tell us?"

She looks at him with Wills simple manner and gives a Will-esque answer.

"We'll...no one has brought it up, or I would have."

Danny shakes his head and laughs at her and his

crooked smile causes her to laugh along.

"Oh wow," Robert begins as he buries his head further in the pages, "this is really beautiful."

"Which part are you reading?" Sasha inquires.

He clears this throat as he begins, "He gave me an Angel...she stands my true heart...He let us find love...and then tore us apart....we loved in secret...in the shadows of our mind...when reunited...eternal love we did find...no one can take that from us."

Hot tears burn the cheeks of the Blue-eyed Queen in the group. She smiles wide as she looks at no one at all in the distance of her mind.

"I've always loved that poem. It's my second favorite part of his book."

"What's your favorite part?" Robert asks.

"The day I carved the crucifixes into his sword, I fell asleep. I woke up and found Joe writing a passage outside my room. I peered over his shoulder and read as quietly as I could. It was so fucking hard not to break down and cry as I was reading. This was back when we weren't speaking to each other. I was so fucking blown away by his words...I knew that day I would love him forever...I memorized every word that day, looking over his shoulder..."

She takes a deep breath as she remembers the words that led to our teasing contest in the house the ladies lived in before she and I died. The memory lingers as if it were created yesterday.

"She's my soul, a lesson, a blessing, sapping life from loving eyes...I'll resent her forever, but protect her till I die...that is the lesson...My love for her will never cease...that is a blessing."

She fights the tears as she faces him while her lips quiver and threaten to release the sobs hiding in her slender throat. Her eyes reflect the troubles in her soul.

"I love every part of his book as much as I love the man himself...Shit, *I have to see him again*," she pleas as she runs a slender hand across her forehead and brushes her hair away, the frustration now showing in her body language. She sighs deeply and fans her glowing blue eyes to keep her cheeks from becoming slick with tears once more.

"I'm sorry Sasha, I was worried this was going to upset you," Amy K. whispers as she approaches her, "I just thought that his words would bring you a little peace is all."

"Thank you Amy, it does, I promise. It just hurts so fucking much to know we're in the same world, and still somehow, so far apart. I miss the fuck out of that man. I just want to be next to him again. I've never felt so loved, unless I'm in his arms," she pauses to gather herself, "I can't lose him again."

"You won't," Robert assures her, "Sasha, I've only seen Joe this happy once before in my existence, and that was when he was..."

"With...her?" She finishes as she looks at him with wounded eyes.

"Yes, Sasha...with his wife," he confesses, "but you're

269

missing the point. You are the woman of Joes new existence. He found happiness in the Afterlife with you. He loves you like a wife because he sees you *as his wife* in this life. Believe me when I say this...you won't lose him again. You're destined for eternity. He loves you so damn much he's going to see to it that it happens."

He hands her the book still open to the world for all to see my words. She peers into the pages and smiles wide, a sign for her to cherish jumping out amongst the words. She reads softly to the group.

"I watch her cry from afar...I will not lose my Angel...the more tears that fall...the more my soul feels strangled...she stands closer than my shadow...but further than the Sun...our souls will be joined yet again...and our love story will be sung."

She drops the book and gazes to the sky above as her sweet laughter returns to her.

"I love you, Joe."

****

"Seriously freaked out right now...That was amazing."

Sam sits in awe on the cloud that has become our raft on an airy ocean, and watches as I recover my senses on the floating Taxi we hitched a ride on. My head spins as the world returns from the darkness and finds a troubled heart as its' companion. I see Sams' face swim in and out of vision as the sun threatens to steal what little sight I yet hold. I lay myself down gently and let my body regenerate. I'm learning that the movement of the soul causes the body to perish. In my case, leaving my body too long threatens to reincarnate me as a ghost. This vessel will die without me in it. Oh the irony, to become the object I used to chase and film in the Old World.

"I'm glad you're entertained, Sam, but I feel like Dog shit."

He laughs merrily and I join him from the comfort of my cloud.

"Sorry, but that was really cool. You closed your eyes and then you opened them and they were black! All black! And then you started talking to Sasha, and well, I'm sorry I heard that part, but it was like the scariest, most beautiful, long distance phone call ever!...Do you know where they are?"

I shake my head in disappointment from the misty ground, "No luck. Sasha doesn't know where they are. A Café, is all I know."

The screams underneath us interrupt our conversation. I turn over and see Sam already lying low, his eyes just barely exposed to the world below. I move in the same manner, as low to the cloud as possible. I tuck my wings tightly to me as I join him in our new surveillance. The screams grow louder as we hover high overhead and watch as new terrors fill our vision.

They fight amongst themselves in a lonely field, Reapers and flying Cursed of all sorts, and mock the doomed people they found. A dozen men or so lay cowered like beaten dogs as The Cursed dance and hiss with talons that are bloody from the others they have already slain. The bodies of the fallen litter the ground around them and remind the rest of the Fate to come. They beg for mercy that will not come from the Creator above.

Today, it would come from The Fallen One that rests in the clouds.

I can't watch and do nothing.

"Sam...wait here. I'll be back."

I feel his gaze fall upon my face.

"I'm coming with you. I'm ready to be a killer...Let me redeem myself."

I look at him as my eyes begin to burn green, while my soul is beginning to anger from the pain and torment being dealt beneath us.

"Stay close to my side. If I move, fall behind me and act as my shadow. Never be more than an arms distance."

He nods his head slowly and I can see the fear in his eyes blend with determination.

He'll be a fine killer.

We rise slowly and I motionhim to grab a hold of mybody. Heembraces meand grasps tightly and his stout arms threaten to bend my breastplate. I scurry to the edge of the clouded ship we've been riding and peer down at the world beneath.

Be on target. I miss...I fail.

"Here goes...something."

The leap of faith is fast as I lean over and begin our plummet. The world spins from clouds and Earth to a cluster of dancing death and balding heads. We see The Cursed taunt them still, unable to look up when all their joys are below them. My aim is to hit just behind them to spare the still living people on the ground. They don't appear as the innocent Cursed that Sam and Ralph once stood. These appear to have been reborn over and over and their deformities have also become their greatest joys. About twenty in all, it's clear that they stood as evil men who went willingly. They enjoy what they do, and have always done so...and it sickens me. I'll relish the moment of the death I will soon deliver.

We approach quickly as I spin my body to plant my feet upon arrival. They grow larger in our view as we draw close, the eyes, the wings and snarled lips, all details coming to life. A hundred yards to go ensures there's only seconds until war. I assure Sam that the time to be a killer is upon him. The Creator is with him, I remind. Twenty yards disappears in barely two seconds. I hold Sam tight as I position my feet to land on the Reaper on the edge of the group as I meet the Earth.

The force of the impact is loud and brief and sends a wave of Earth and Cursed debris shooting away from the Hellish landing I make. The Reaper explodes underneath the force of my angry feet. The world in front of us stands a wall of dirt and dust and Cursed blood, keeping us hidden for a brief moment from the monsters we are about to greet. I draw my sword as Sam follows suit while the figures in the dirty mist appear still and quiet. The Creator moves his winds and clears the world around us. Monstrous, fleshy bat-like creatures, now more Cursed than man, stand before us. They barely resemble the first New World Cursed anymore, but their eyes are the only characteristic unchanged. Still black with a smoldering red coal, still full of hate, and still trained upon killing me. The six, giant

Reapers accompanying them remain how they always looked, with the tallest seeming to lead the pack. The men upon their backs possess the wild eyes of caged animals as they gaze upon The Fallen One and his friend, the two mystical beings whom they watched fall from the sky. The clearing remaining dust cloud reveals a few winged Cursed rising from the ground.

Shit. I only killed one...I better be quick.

"Leave them alone...I'm the True Ruler of The Abyss...and these are *my* people."

The Reaper walks forward a step and examines the vision in front of him. He lifts a finger and points to my sword.

"Liar...that is sssssteel from The Realm," he hisses with a deep and demonic voice. I raise my blade to give him a better inspection.

"Given to The Fallen One by The Creator himself...now, leave them alone."

He charges forward and hops a step before swinging a mighty claw aimed at my throat. I bring my sword up in the same instance and swipe my blade in front of me, meeting his arm at the elbow and severing the limb. He hisses in terror and grasps the wound as I slice his thighs across the front, splitting all the flesh down to the bone. He falls to his knees as I step forward and spin him around for his brothers to see his pain. Holding his head with one hand, I bring my blade in front of him and place it at his throat. I smile wide at The Cursed as I let the blade slide along the rough flesh, the cut releasing a wave of dark blood. He jerks and spits out the tar as I run my blade back and forth and sever his head from his shoulders. It cuts with ease, all the way through the spinal cord. I lift the bleeding head

274

up for all to see as I kick his headless body and send it to the Earth.

"Leave them alone," I warn again and toss the head to the ground.

They all stand frozen, Cursed and men alike, except for one. A young, tattooed fool with a pistol, laying on his back, raises the barrel and aims it at the head of the Reaper closest to him.

Don't do it, you fool. You'll alert the rest and doom us all.

The sound of the hammer falling upon a dead bullet causes them all to turn to The Fool. They glare at him with disgust and vengeance. They show the slightest movement towards the fallen man before I react in kind, as their body language tells the story to unfold.

They know they can't kill me. They know my purpose. They'll kill them all to gain a small victory.

"Kill these motherfuckers Sam!"

We rush forward towards the beasts as they lay their attack on the men. I feel The Creators power overtake me as the world slows to a near standstill. The characters around me seem to move slower now, as I seem to have frozen the sands in the hourglass. I see their slight movements towards the cowering men as they wear menacing faces created to exist in nightmares. They move so slow, yet Sam and I move so fast. We slow in our charge and share a passing glance.

"Not only will this be easy...it's going to be fun. Kill

them, Sam."

He smiles to acknowledge he received the unspoken command before the shouts of war begin.

I swing my blade at the body of the closest Cursed as he stands almost frozen in his attack on the small man beneath him. Its sting is true, severing the Cursed in two. Sam stands a few feet away and swings his blade for the first time and finds he is true to his aim as the edge finds its mark. He beheads the monster in front of him and watches as the head slowly moves from its shoulders. He glances at me again, and his thoughts come through as clear as crystal.

"This IS fun!"

The war cries reborn, we charge from Cursed to Cursed and separate heads from their shoulders. My feet carry me swiftly, appearing to move me more quickly when placed next to the slowed world. Sam, finally comfortable, starts getting creative in his death dealing. He severs the arms of one before beheading him and spins quickly to ram his sword through the back of the head of another. He approaches the last Cursed, a larger winged beast, and swings his sword from overhead, splitting its gruesome crown down the middle. Grabbing the throat of the last Reaper, I speak to myself in my mind.

Time.

The world returns and rains severed heads and limbs around us while the men on the ground scurry backwards from the carnage. They stare on in horror as I pull the face of the last Reaper down close to mine.

"I see he's getting creative...How many more of you has

he created?"

Holding my blade against his throat, he smiles and stands silent. I stretch my wings into the defensive position of a bird of prey.

"How many?!"

He hisses his disgust and growls, refusing to break words with me.

"Okay, bitch...Have it your way."

I shove him back and spin my body in the same motion with my wings screaming for death. My wing catches the slender side of his neck and slices it cleanly in one smooth motion as I spin around to greet his falling head. His face is frozen in a twist of agony and it's a real pleasure for my eyes to behold. It falls to the ground as lifelessly as his body. The men remain frozen upon the ground and gaze at the remaining two left standing. A small, stout man with a deadly passion for killing and a winged man who calls himself a King are the reasons now that they dare not speak or move.

"Rise...You're safe now," I command softly.

They slowly follow the command and rise quietly as one. The young pistol wielding fool, a dirty, blonde man appearing in his mid-twenties, steps forward with the intent to speak, only his voice is absent. He raises the pistol and aims it at my head.

"Hold on there, we just saved you...We're obviously not looking for trouble."

He smiles and aims his pistol at my sword as if it's a yardstick and not a weapon.

"We don't want trouble either, but as you can see, we could use those swords more than you can. There's a lot more of us than you...and I have the only gun. Don't be stupid...Just give us those swords."

"Hey dumbass," Sam begins, "did you not see what we just did to those things? Your little fucking gun couldn't stop them, but we did...*You* don't want to fuck with *us*."

Sam breathes real fire. He's a warrior now.

"Hold on, Sam," I say and glance at him, "I got this." I return my gaze to the barrel pointing at me.

"This sword was given to me by The Creator....Sams' was given to him by me. They hold meaning. Look, I understand you need weapons, and maybe I can help you...but you're not getting these swords. Now put the gun down."

He smirks as he moves the barrel towards my heart.

"I don't know what kind of freak you are, Mister, but I'm telling you now...You're gonna give us those weapons or *I will kill you*," he says as he emphasizes a hollow threat.

"You can't kill me and would be a fool to try. I don't want to harm you...I want to help you."

"Give me the swords," he repeats himself, "I'm not gonna ask again."

278

I don't have time for this shit.

I tense my body hard and bring the green flames to life once more, consuming me from head to toe. I'm grateful it isn't a skill lost to me, as it seems to have just come in handy. They retreat backwards quickly as the young fool holds his gun up as a white flag of surrender. I let the flames consume me for a few more tense moments before smoldering their beauty. They continue their

backwards strides with eyes full of shock.

"Alright, you win...We're going," the fool claims quickly.

"You don't have to go," I assure, "we didn't kill all those Cursed just to kill you too. We saved you. We can help you all."

"We don't need your help, Freak," he insults as he continues his backwards stride. They glare at us with eyes of distrust.

They won't take our help.

"Let's go, Sam."

We turn from them and head in the direction of the tree line in the distance. Before I can fly away with Sam, I have to leave a trail behind leading any passing Cursed away from the new people of the New World who refused our protection. They'll follow my energy. I look at Sam, dripping in black blood, and feel a beaming pride as a father would. I nod my head to him in respect and he follows suit, his small smile forming in the light of his accomplishment. He strides as a young Lion, the machismo growing in him from his first victory over his former colleagues.

"You did good, Sam," I say as we continue placing striding foot after foot, knowing we have a long way to go.

"It felt good, killing those monsters for The Creator. I hope I made Him proud."

I glance his way and smile as I reply, "You did, Sam. There's a few less Cursed in the world because of you...Less evil...That's always something to be proud of."

He returns my affections, "Couldn't have done it without you, Joe. Thanks for..."

The front of Sams chest explodes from the slug that rips through his body after entering his back, the sound of the revolver coming after the carnage. He pitches forward and grasps at his chest as he collapses. I shoot a glance back and see the group of men, now evil men, who we saved only minutes before. They walked behind us, following us silently, awaiting for their moment to strike. I fall to Sams side as he bleeds out in front of me, his gasps spraying hot, red blood all over my face. He trembles in terror as death comes for him while his pupils bounce in his eyes. The small, panicked dots continue their dance and change in size as the life fades from them. I lift his body up and whisper to him as he prepares to leave the New World.

"Sam...You're going to see your family again, My Brother."

"Am I?" He asks through the blood, "Why didn't The Creator spare me?..I'm dying, Joe...why didn't He save me?"

The hurt pours out of his eyes from a wounded soul.

The Creator didn't shine his light and spare him, when he only stood as the kindest of souls. It was a thing expected when he watched The Creator attempt to spare lesser men. I lean closer as I whisper again.

"The Creator didn't save you, Sam...because I'm going to...I took your wings...It's time I gave you new ones."

He's fading fast.

I slam my palm into his chest and send a wave of Crimson in all directions, as the gaping hole was pouring his blood out fiercely. The light comes from my hands in waves, with the energy increasing with every pulse. Sam screams as the wounds seal themselves and his new wings sprout from his back. My eyes shine with His light as I give Sam all I have in the hopes of saving his soul. He pitches forward and back and all around as the wings finish in their birth and his body becomes immortal. He stops his hollers and goes limp on the ground and his sudden motionlessness causes me to feel a slight panic. I grasp his face and call to him and my best attempt to wake him into a new life.

"Sam."

He stirs slightly before opening his eyes to reveal a radiant, amber glow. He smiles at me from his back and I smile back, as the sight of my brother alive in any form is a blessing I can count. I lift him up to sit before his wings cause him to lose his balance, something to be expected from a newly born Servant. I catch him and return him to his seat.

"Easy, Sam, it takes a moment...but don't take too long," I say as I hear the approaching steps.

"I can help you kill them," he mutters and gazes at me with flames in his eyes.

"I'm sorry, Sam...but not this time. It would stain your soul and prevent you from going home."

"I don't want to go yet...*I'm going* to help you," he informs me as the fires in his eyes burn bright.

He's not going to listen...He loves me too much to leave me.

"Sam...I don't even want you to watch...Good luck, My Brother."

I rise quickly and hook his arms with my hands and lift him up.

"Joe! Wait!"

"Tell your family I said hello. You're going home," I command while continuing the motions.

"Joe!"

I thrust as hard as I can as the awaiting light waits no longer and makes itself known. The brilliant beams catch his wings and lifts him as if it was a mighty wind from underneath. He rises and pleas to stay as The Creator welcomes him home. I smile at his face, so full of hurt, and so beautiful as a Servant. I can see his soul, bright and full of love, showing through his eyes. He reaches the top in a swift moment and vanishes along with the light.

The Creator gets to take all the good ones.

"Good luck...My Brother."

The steps pause behind me, confirming that they've reached me. Turning slowly, I'm met by thirteen wily stares and silly grins, the fools believing they can conquer the now most pissed off Fallen One to ever walk His Earth.

This will not be quick. There will be no mercy.

The cowards who claimed my brother will meet the most fearsome end I can imagine. I glare at them in return of their mockery.

"Well, look at what Fatso dropped," the dirty blond fool cracks as he points at Sams fallen sword. I stand silently and hold my hand over it and demand that the blade to come to my hand. It follows command, as it was created by me with a piece of my soul, and rises to my palm quickly. They pause in their steps as they witness my magic trick.

"Take it."

I swing the sword forward in a hasty manner and release the handle. The blade travels quickly and parts the lips of the blonde fool and its' silver death slides through and sprays his brain matter on the next fool in line. Nerves cause him to bite down on the blade, his teeth chipping away as his locked jaw forces itself into the steel. He twitches slightly before falling to the Earth with a final jerk before he lays silent. The fools he led are now having second thoughts. They step back slightly, but it's a retreat that I will not allow.

"Oh no...no no no no no...don't even think about it...*you guys...are fucked.*"

I'm sorry, Sam.

I scream as I throw both hands forward and create the dome I had created once before, the emerald flames alive and encasing the remaining dozen. I focus my energy, all the hate and ill-will I feel, and create a solid structure of flames. There will be no need to reinforce it. I make it strong and sturdy enough to hold itself while I take my time killing the fools it's trapped. They took my brother...They will pay with terrified souls.

I walk forward slowly and watch as they scramble like rats in a garbage can, scurrying away from the monstrous cat that is coming to play. I watch them touch the walls of my hateful flames and pull back scorched fingers, and relish the terror setting in when they realize that escape is nonexistent. I reach the wall and watch as they fall over themselves in fear, so scared and so full of panic...I watch.

I'm sorry, Sam.

I'm seeing red as I enter the dome and rush to the nearest fool; A larger, dark-skinned bald behemoth covered in tattoos. I grab his wrist and tear his arm off at the shoulder as he screams for mercy, which I grant swiftly and club him into submission to mute his pleas. I beat him to death with his own arm, and pause for nothing, until his head is just a smear in the soft grass.

I'm sorry, Sam.

He lunges at me with a small knife, the next fool who thinks he can defeat The Fallen One. I grab his hand and drive it back towards his own face and bury the blade deep into his eye. I push it until only the handle remains and then tear his head off

284

and throw it as a fastball. It smashes into the head of another and decapitates him in the blink of an eye with force alone. The two headless men stagger about as the rest scream in terror.

I'm sorry, Sam.

I charge forward and grab the next one in line and let my angry hands seize his throat. He pleas for forgiveness as I lift him up and smash him into the wall of flames. He detonates as if full of TNT and a display of flaming limbs suddenly litters the air around me. The pieces shower down as I grab the next one and guide his face towards the emerald fires as he screams loud and panicked before I slowly grind him into the green torment. I move slowly and feel his body jerking violently as his life is slowly burned from him. With his face now gone and the smell of seared flesh hanging about, I pull him back and lift his body over my head and roar as I tear him in half, allowing his organs and blood to blanket me.

I'm sorry, Sam.

Another falls upon my back, attempting a piggy back ride for the ages, and tries his best to strangle me. I thrust my wings up and together and smash him in-between. I feel his rib cage break and his body crunch, the bones and cartilage twisting together in a single second. He falls mangled and broken to the ground as I turn to the remaining six that now shout for The Creator to save them. They scream in prayer, begging for the slightest mercy.

"I forgive you, Joe."

The dome disappears as quickly as I conjured it and the sunlight returns to the world around us. They halt their cries and view the world with confusion, wondering why the coming death has now ceased. They huddle together in fear of The Fallen One, a familiar sight that tears my heart as I'm reminded of my family cowering before a Devil from the past; Back on the night he killed me before The Creator gave me a new life. I could never stand in the same light as The Old One, nor do I want to. Mercy is firmly rooted in my heart, and it's a characteristic that was absent my predecessor.

I'll forgive...but I won't forget.

"You are being spared...not because I've had my fill of death...but because I've had my fill of hate...There is good people in the world...and you just murdered one."

"It wasn't us! *WE* didn't do it! Callum did!" The smallest among them shouts and points to the fool who still eats Sams blade a few feet away. "Please, Mister...We didn't want trouble...He would of killed us if we didn't listen to him...*Please*."

"Shut the fuck up...My brother is dead...and killing you won't return him to my side...As I said...You are spared."

They begin their rise slowly and eventually find their feet. I sling my hand forward as my fiery leash returns to me and grasps the Small Fool by his neck.

"But not without conditions," I finish.

He grabs at his throat and falls to his knees as the glowing tether slowly burns him. I release it and let it dissipate. I walk slowly to him and let them all cower in fear.

"The next people you come across...You will help them, in any way they need help. You will also offer them protection,

286

as Sam and I offered it to you, before your friend took his life."

"We will! I swear to God! I promise! Please just let us go!"

"Which one is it? Do you swear to Your God? Or are you making a promise to The Fallen One?"

They all stand confused and trade worried glances amongst themselves, their minds unsure of what words will suffice. I raise my hand to halt their frantic thoughts.

"The answer is neither...You will be good to each other, because it's the right thing to do...and if you don't," I say as I close the distance between us until our faces are only a solitary foot apart, "you will be dealt with accordingly, by either Him," I say and point up, "or the True Ruler of The Abyss," I say and point to myself, "do you understand?"

Panicked tears streak the cheeks of most as the rest ready themselves to join in. They all shake their heads in agreement without further words, as no more will be needed from them.

"More Cursed will come...Get the fuck out of here."

I present my back to them as I begin my stride from the deadly grounds and leave the scene of horror for so many, yet none more so than me. I let the tears fall as silently as the evening sun on my back as I leave them, only pausing to retrieve Sams' sword. I don't really care if they live or die. My beatless heart is too heavy from this new loss that has found me.

Goodbye Sam.

Chapter 6

"Now see...I could get used to this shit."

Greg draws a long breath from the end of the cigar, and invites the thick smoke to invade his lungs. He exhales as he chuckles and passes it to Robert. Dark eyes meet his gaze from just below his dark hat.

"Oh shit, my bad, Bro," he apologetically says as he reaches past Robert and passes it off to Will, "just a bad habit, you know?"

"It's all good, Little Brother," Robert assures with a wide smile, "enjoy yourself, but don't get so stupid that you become useless to us."

"Shit," Greg exclaims as he rises to his feet, "I can kill Cursed and Blunts at the same time, Bro. I'm good...but I gotta take a piss."

He glances around the small building that they now occupy, a small flower shop filled with the corpses of roses inside dusty vases. The world outside is becoming darker by the minute while the dusk arrives with a cool wind. They stand about thirty miles from the outside of the city now, a small trek compared to the distance yet to be traveled. The room stays lit by the small candles Amy J. found and placed upon the counters. The smell of dead flowers creates a potpourri in the store, now amplified by Gregs Happy Grass. It stands the most pleasant environment, but soon to be a memory. After several moments of adjusting to the darkness of the corners, Greg spots his target.

"Boom! Bathroom, Baby!"

He scurries away from the group as they continue to indulge in their smoky wine that threatens to leave them drunk with dull senses. The quiet of the night invades the room, yet the sorrow is never far away, so long as a Queen stands absent her King. Sasha sits off on her own and stares out at the street as her blue oceans break on the tides along her cheeks. She cries quietly for the comfort of my arms, a feeling I can feel from over a thousand miles away. Her soul stands absent a purpose without me, and it's a pain I can't stand to inflict. My words ring throughout her pained thoughts.

I'll destroy the whole fucking world to get to you, Sasha.

"I miss you, Baby," she whispers to the quiet moment.

"I'm here, My Soul...Don't cry anymore."

My words cause her to spring from the comforts of her chair in surprise.

"JOE!"

Every set of eyes turns to her as shock causes them to morph into saucers. The surprise of her holler draws their attentions, along with Gregs from the bathroom.

"Joe's here!?" Greg shouts as he runs from the bathroom. The dim light cloaks the counter and

he crashes into it with full force and sends his body tumbling

289

over, and the sight appears comical to all but him. They laugh and joke before seeing their brother to his feet and setting their sights back on the Blue-eyed Temptress in the room.

"It's Joe, he contacted me," she says as she dries her eyes, "I heard his voice...He could feel me crying for him...I need a minute."

Sitting on the floor, she begins to feel for my soul. Beautiful blue eyes give way to that of a dark night as the darkness overtakes the beauty. She sees nothing with eyes filled with shadows, only a room filled with emptiness. She doesn't need sight for our embrace. Our senses would be filled with the sounds we so loved most in any world: Our own voices.

"Baby...Are you there?"

Her voice sounds soft and frightened so I waste no time in giving a response.

"I'm here, Sasha...I love you...so much," I say, hoping to mask all the pain I feel from missing her.

"Awww Baby, I love you too! And I miss you so fucking much! I pray that you're okay, all the fucking time, I really do...Are you...okay?"

"I'm fine, My Love...It just hurts not being with you, is all."

Her voice begins to crack, *"I'm sorry, Baby...I shouldn't have left you...I'm so fucking sorry."*

"Hey," I say softly, *"stop beating yourself up...It wasn't*

290

your fault. We did what we had to do for the sake of our family. They live now, Sasha...and we live still. All our hearts yet beat, theirs living, and ours eternal...we still stand in this world...all because of you."

Her soft sobs fill my ears as the group sits a thousand miles away watching her talk to the air, as my souls voice is too soft to fill the room. I can only find Sasha, the loving part of my heart that still beats, and it's enough. We only need to hear each other to survive.

"I miss you, Joe," her souls lips voice the agony inside, *"I can't live without you another moment!"* She wails, the flood of tears finally breaking through. Her cries tear my soul in the darkness, the thought of her being so far away beginning to take a toll on my immortal heart. I fight the tears no more and share in the grief. We cry softly together, yearning to embrace and be whole again.

"I miss you so much, Sasha...It's killing me not to stare into the endless depths of your eyes and see my hearts reflection. Your love is the only love to ever move me in this New World. It will always move me closer still, the miles between us a small thing when facing a man of purpose. I'll hold you again, My Love, and I won't dare let you slip from my grasp, ever again."

The tears flow as our souls grow cold and our hearts less bold. We're just weak fools without the company of each other. I feel the withering of my soul inside, and can feel the strain on hers as well.

You have to be with her. Fool, you're going to die without her.

291

"Baby," she begins, *"I'm going to start walking tomorrow and I'm not gonna fucking stop until I find you again. I'm gonna make you keep your promise. Don't you dare fucking stop loving me when I hold you again. We'll all be together again, Baby, all our family, Sam and Robert."*

Oh my God...Sam.

The loss of our new brother slipped my mind. She suffers much in this life, I dare not speak of the other tragedy to befall our hearts. I'll shoulder the burden alone for now, as my lovers heart is too heavy for more heartache.

"Yes, My Queen...We will...I miss your voice, Sasha...Fill my heart with the beauty of your words."

She chuckles softly in the darkness in front of the room full of our crying family. They watch with sad hearts as we bare our souls to one another.

"I would love to, My King."

I smile in the darkness, as my soul is never more alive than when her soul speaks to me.

Her voice fills the air with a song from Nickleback, Far Away, a song we sang together, filling the halls of The Abyss. We took the music of the Old World down to The Abyss with us, and now hear it voiced in the New World. The tears pour fiercely as she sings away and my mind screams for her love.

"I miss yoouuuu...been far away for far too long..."

She sings loudly, her soul pouring through, and my heart melts inside my cold body. She bellows with heartache and I know she sings true words, the words her soul wishes to voice. I cry softly as she pleas through the music to give it all, and don't give up, something I would never do in a thousand lifetimes. Only my patience wears thin, made more so by the music now filling my soul. I need to be with her, and it kills me not to be. I join her in the harmony.

We sing on until our souls finish their spoken heartache and cry together, our eternal essence truly wounded by the distance between us. I can make out the voices of the others as they comfort her in the darkness. We feel the sorrow of separation, every last one of us, and I suspect that somewhere in the clouds a Fair and Just Creator may have been weeping. He rooted for us when the love in our souls showed Him that nothing in any life is truly impossible. I listen to her soft voice and pray that I would never be the cause of her terrible tears ever again. The pain is unlike any other, and I realize in this dark and beautiful moment that we will wither and pass without each others presence, the only drawback of standing as true Soul Mates.

"I'll find you, My Loving Soul...My Loving Queen...my Sasha."

She composes herself quietly as her tears subside, yet the wet emotions still threaten to tear through the surface.

"Hurry up...asshole."

We laugh together softly as the joy brushes away the tears. Our soul shattering moment becomes gentle as the love in my heart, along with her curses, lifts the moment.

"I'll see you soon, Sasha. The Creator Himself would

stand a weak thing against my love for you."

"I'm looking forward to...OH SHIT!!!"

Sashas screams fill my head as the sounds of shattering glass accompanies the horror I'm being forced to witness. My families screams come through loud and threatening, a sound I wished never to hear.

"BABY!...HURRY!!!!"

The darkness becomes silent.

****

My true eyes shoot open as green, smoldering flames blaze through. My screams are loud as I shoot upwards towards the dusky night sky with the flames pouring from my flapping wings. The ground stands scorched with flaming scars as my soul burns brighter than it ever has. I feel the pull of my soul towards the falling sun, knowing My Love is hidden underneath it a thousand miles from the protection of my hands. It draws me, pulls me, tears me and screams at me to make haste, as my Workhorse breathing becomes alive in my bosom.

Hurry Goddamn it! The ground beneath you moves too slow!

Screaming with a destructive voice, I push hard as my adrenaline awakens in me again. I begin to move faster as the ground becomes a blur and the coming stars above streak overhead. Still, I push harder until the sounds of my wings become mute and I leave sonic booms far behind me. I only

294

hear a soft hum, along with revisited memories of my families screams and the screams of my soul, my Loving Queen, my Flawless Sasha...I hear her scream.

Fly faster, you fucking fool!

****

Half-clouded black and half-blue, her eyes stand open to the terrors in front of her. She screams as she rises from the ground with her sword in her hand while the ladies fall to her side. Robert and the men yell cries of war as they charge forward and begin to slaughter the endless winged Cursed that found their safe haven. The monstrosities tear away the windows with hooked claws and expose black, gleaming Obsidian bones that protrude from their fingertips. They evolved, along with the need to kill the fools who follow The Fool of Mercy, and only seek the one who could end the New World. They followed a trail of energy belonging to The Fool, a scent only belonging to the true soul of the True Ruler of The Abyss, as The Damned did so long ago in the birth of the New World. They seek Joe, but found his energy residing in the Queen of his Soul. Sasha, unknowingly, once again led the monsters to the feast with her beautiful scent.

They crash through the windows of the building and force their way in by the dozens. Greg and Danny slash away as they enter, severing heads and impaling rotting bodies as John, Robert and Will pick off the stragglers that make their way past. The ladies retreat to the back wall of the store, the only wall absent windows, and prepare to make their final stand if the men fall before them. Growing in number, Robert becomes desperate to hold them off and does so the only way a warrior

295

Servant can.

His throaty, deep roar shakes the room as he encases himself in his wings, the feathers

wrapping tightly around his giant frame. He releases his wings with a forceful thrust, sending out a wave of white light that sets ablaze every animated corpse that claws through the windows. He reveals a glowing white Longsword that he conjured from thin air, another weapon created under his wings, along with the light of The Realm. He screams commands and continues his assault on the New World demons.

"Don't forget about your swords! Use them as they were meant to be used!"

"Light," sounds throughout the air before the howls of commanded, illuminated blades cut through the nightmares that dare stand against them. They slash the nightmare world with beaming blades of white and yellow, while Sashas' radiant Baby Blue blade stands ready for blood. The burning flesh overtakes the Potpourri, as the smells of unholy war fill the senses. A Reaper shoots through the glass closest to the ladies and rises before them as his long body towers over the warrior damsels. The men don't notice, leaving Sasha to defend their position and keep the Reaper from attacking their exposed backs. She raises her sword and taunts the overgrown Cursed.

"Bring it, you pussy!"

His throaty scream is deep and unforgiving as he rushes forward with giant hands attempting to grab her with his giant fingers. She thrusts forward and sends her blade through his slender body in the same instant that he lashes out. She will take his new dark life, but not before he inflicts a terrible wound of his own. His claw finds her face and rakes across it with blinding speed. She screams as he falls to the floor while the life drains from him as fresh blood pours across her face. She bleeds, and it's something that shouldn't be.

Hurry, Joe.

****

The pain burns as a slash of torn flesh appears across my face. The surprise of the wound is a grand thing, yet I don't even blink. It scares me, the truth of it, as it becomes clear as crystal: She stands a part of my soul. If she feels pain, I feel pain. If she suffers wounds, then I shall suffer them as well.

I can't let her die.

I tremble with unholy power as I voice my screams yet again. I shoot even faster than should be possible and see the miles pass by the second. I tear the sky in half with a fire so bright I illuminate all the world around as my sonic boom tears trees from the Earth. I pray that all under me who stand as innocents survive the terrors of my wings, but I will not stop, as a promise was made and will be kept.

I'll destroy the whole fucking world to get to you, Sasha.

Grunting, I thrust without mercy on my immortal body. The air heats up around me while a blaze of green appears and cloaks me like a comet, complete with a long, fiery green trail

297

streaking behind. Even with the fires of The Abyss burning the night sky, I feel it's not enough as the panicked screams of my Sasha invade my memories again. I cannot fail The Queen of Curses, nor will I allow such a thing to come to pass.

I feel the energy of my soul getting stronger and the only meaning is clear. I'm getting closer and shortening the distance between us. The stronger bond allows me to use Sashas body and listen in on the nightmare world she now occupies. I hear the clash of steel and screams and hisses of death as the sounds of battle are all too familiar. I feel her panic when she feels me invade her head.

"It's me, My Love! I'm coming!"

She continues to battle the spawns of the Necromancer and keeps her attention set where it needs to be.

"Hurry, Baby...Please."

Her voice sounds more fragile than I wish it to be.

Fucking move Goddamn it!

****

They feel weak, one by one, as the thrusts of swords and fists begins slowing down and causes them to fall back. They step backwards towards the wall and rotate positions, the guys fending off the Cursed and then switching with the ladies. They are mortal and still have the need to rest but, must continue on or face the eternal darkness. Robert and Sasha stand firm and never pause in their attempt to fill their lust for black blood. They come in swarms still, and don't plan to stop. Sasha screams and swings with deadly intentions, sending broken bodies and mangled wings to the ground around them. Robert does his best to keep up, his sword a weighted instrument of death, and swings slower but just as deadly, cutting paths through all in his way. The Amys and Carmen switch with Danny, Will, John and Greg, but the energy is fading fast. Greg can barely swing his machete anymore and leaves his flank exposed to the thrusting claws that are soon to find him. A Reaper rushes forwards to his failing body and seizes upon his fortunate opportunity, as his long, slender arm makes its way past the cutting blades and slashes across Gregs chest. He falls back into the ladies as John and Danny squeeze together to fill the void.

"We're fucked, Bro...We're not gonna make it this time," Greg confesses with surrender in his voice, as well as his eyes.

"Faith, Greg! Have faith in yourself!" Robert commands.

"I have Faith...I don't have strength," he retaliates.

"That's what Faith is!"

"I have Faith!...I don't have the fucking strength," he reiterates.

"You can't fall Greg! Rest for a second! Then prepare for battle and come out swinging or your family is going to die!"

Greg forces himself to his feet while the nightmare rages around him. He prepares to join the battle when a deathly roar brings all in the room, Cursed, Servants and people, to a stand still. They all freeze and peer into the darkness outside the Flower shop while The Cursed begin a backwards pace, but never break their gaze from their should-be prey as they carry out their cautious retreat. Their movements are slow until the roar is heard again. They scramble backwards towards the windows and claw their way out in the same fashion they clawed their way in. A few tense moments pass as they retreat before the only ones left in the room are the possessors of lighted blades. They stand surrounded by shadows and listen to the silence as they don't recognize the voice of this newest threat. Roberts' uneasy stance makes the rest of the group fearful. If a Servant is afraid, then it's definitely a good reason to panic.

"Robert," John whispers, "what the hell was that?"

"I have no idea," he answers with a cautiously quiet voice.

"It sounds big," Carmen adds.

"No, not big," Robert informs, "it's powerful, whatever it may be."

The front of the store explodes outward, seemingly being pulled away more than pushed. The fresh moonlight exposes the winged man who makes his way to the newly created entrance. He walks up and pauses just outside the broken wall and peers in at my family with unnaturally black eyes.

"Don't you mean...*whoever*...it may be?"

The Necromancer folds his leathery wings up against his purple robes and gazes into the eyes of The Giant Servant. Robert stands mute while glaring with his own dark eyes as his sword makes its way into a defensive position.

"Hello, Robert...I knew you would be here," he says as he breaks his gaze and sets it upon Sasha, "but I had no idea *you would be*...Hello, Dear."

"Fuck off," Sasha replies in her Sailors' tongue.

Lightning carries Roberts' feet as he moves with a lethal purpose towards the Necromancer with his giant sword in tow. The Cursed Ruler raises his hands even faster and showers a wave a glittering, metal shards across Roberts' face and chest. The huge warrior Servant staggers back and pauses as his hands try to clean away the evil metal while he falls to his knees. He stands weak and getting weaker still as his eyes peer up at the Madman, something they stand unfamiliar with. He lived two lifetimes looking down into peoples eyes, and now is being forced to look up into hollow vessels. The Necromancer smiles down at Robert as he retrieves the staff hidden behind his back. The red rock cresting the bottom finds itself staring directly into Roberts' face.

"Don't worry...I'm not going to kill you, Robert...not yet, anyways," he calmly states, "I was hoping to find The Fallen One here...so fragile and weak...The victim of a similar metal that drains you now. By destroying the armor of The Creator," he begins spilling his truths, "I created a weapon that almost killed your weak, little Fallen One...the armor of the old ruler, The Old One, made the nice little shards that cover you...I didn't have enough for anything else, you see, because all the greedy little shits in The Abyss that followed The Old One stole it for themselves," he pauses to lean in close to Roberts weakening face, "but I have enough...I have something that will kill your True Ruler of The Abyss...and your Creator in The Realm...There is no force that can stop me," he finishes with confidence.

He stands tall once more and hovers over Robert while

his cold, hollow eyes peer down.

"Join me, Robert...and I promise I'll spare them...If you choose not to...you'll all die."

He sways on his knees as his body moves as a Mammoth tree in an unforgiving wind, and stares at the maker of false promises. He meets his cold stare and smiles.

"Sasha...if you don't mind..."

She steps forward and answers for her fallen brother.

"Go fuck yourself."

He stands less than amused while his small mouth tightens across his face. He takes a second to look at everyone and studies their faces, searching for something hidden amongst the crowd. His eyes fall to Gregs weakened state.

"How about you, Boy? Do you want to die? Are you *ready* to die? You will, if you don't convince this big, clumsy Servant to come with me. I don't want to kill you...I only want Robert," he offers as his pitch black eyes fall upon Sasha, "and the girl."

Breathing heavy, blood escapes Gregs lips as fumbles a small step forward.

"Go fuck yourself, Bro."

The anger rises up in the Unholy man, along with his

rising wings.

"Fools! All of you! I'll take great joy in reincarnating you into beasts! One way or another, *YOU WILL* serve me!"

He releases the roar that shook them all minutes before, and it's a large sound coming from such an ordinarily small beast. He swings his staff overhead and spins it violently in a twirling Ballet as the threat of Roberts death gleams on the red end of it. His intention is to create a Cursed of a new sort, and he needs a Servants soul to do so. It's an eager moment he has awaited for. The spinning stops and he swings his red rock of death from overhead.

Faster than lightning, the speed of sound, and The Creator Himself, my immortal blazing body slams into the Necromancer while I scream with the hate of The Abyss. I roar louder than any Creator in any realm as I drive him into the concrete streets and bulldoze him for the length of a City block. The concrete showers the air along with my hateful voice while my hands wrap tightly around his throat. I lift him up and glare with the brightest eyes I've ever possessed and growl like a true beast of The Abyss. With one hand, I toss him as a Rag Doll and swing my other hand forward in the same motion with my burning tether. I catch him in midair and pull him back to me violently for our deadly encounter as my fist catches his small, Goatee covered chin and drives him back into the Earth. I scream for his death as I stomp without mercy with my boots crushing him as painfully as I could of hoped for. He kicks me lightly on my chest...and it stops me dead in my tracks.

The bottoms of his boots...The metal.

Peeking at me from its hiding place, lining the bottom of his boots, is the metal I met before, along with another strange one alongside it. One foot to step on The Realm and one foot to step on The Abyss, to truly make an Evil King to rule them all. I feel drunk and stagger back a few steps as my vision swims before me. I can see through the blur as he regains his footing and smiles, as the true moment he longed for is finally upon him. I shake my head as a wet dog and cast off the effects.

My hateful eyes return and the look on his face shows he was expecting a different outcome. The true hate of The Abyss is more powerful than anything he could conjure, and it courses through my dead veins, along with the wrath of The Creator.

One way or another, I'm fucking you up.

He slings a long hand forward and the glint of the moonlight reflecting from the dark steel warns me of the death to come. I sway back a few inches and feel the cold metal pass me by, as his aim is almost as bad as the ass-whipping he's about to receive. I bring my hand down to my sword and draw it quickly to press my attack before my hands freeze from the sound of Sashas screams from behind me.

His aim was spot on.

I glance quickly to see Robert collapsing, and reset my gaze to the emptiness in front of me and the sound of flapping, leathery wings. He chooses a cowards way out, hurling death at Robert, knowing it would pause me in my pursuit of his death. I glare into the sky and see the small figure in the distance as he retreats as hastily as he possible can. I make damn sure he's gone before I turn and run to the fallen Servant that now fights to cling to his eternal life as the rest of our family surrounds him. I fall to his side and hit my knees and raise him up to gaze into my eyes.

"Cuz! It's Joe! I'm here, Brother!" I plea through hot tears as the thought of losing my cousin a second time in two lifetimes is a burden my heart couldn't bear. He opens his eyes while shaking and twitching as a false plea for breath escapes him.

"It's in my chest...Get it out."

I examine his robes and find the small tears created by the sharpened blade and dig through until his tormenter greets me. The small metal blade protrudes from the wound it created, an unholy wound that already changed the color of his skin around it. I reach down and place my hands on the small handle.

"Don't move, Robert."

I pull hard and he screams loudly as the blade slips out and drips with the blood of a Servant. I toss it aside and place my hand on the fresh wound. I let my palm fill with light and we all watch as Robert slowly returns to the Robert of old, the cheerful guy who wasn't dying his last death. The wound disappearing, he smiles at me from the comfort of the ground.

"Thank The Creator for you, Cuz," he says and chuckles with a soft appreciation in his voice..

"Are you alright?" I ask with hopeful eyes.

"I'm good," he says as he begins to rise, "I can't believe what just happened..."

His voice trails off as he sits for a second before turning to me and looking me dead in the center of my eye.

"Cuz...I was dying...or changing, at the very least...He found a way to kill Servants."

"He also found a way to kill the King of The Abyss," I inform him, "he almost killed me...if not for Sam."

"Hey," Will begins, "where is the little fella?"

They all look to me for answers as they have done so many times before.

"Hold on...first things first."

I lunge at Sasha in the same moment she mirrors my image, as her own pursuit is at an end. We meet fiercely in each others arms and kiss with a passion that only exists in our presence. It's a moment I pray we can conjure at anytime. We shake the foundation of each others world, the long hours apart more than either of us could survive again, and I lift her up and let her kiss the lips she missed so much as they return the affections they so missed giving. We cry for a quiet moment as we stare into each others sad, yet happy eyes, before I set her down.

"I'm here...You fucker," I jest.

"It's about fucking time, asshole," she returns her sweet curses as her frown fights hard to become a smile once more. We both breathe heavy with our false breath while our eyes refuse to part.

"I'll never leave you again...I promise, Sasha...I'll destroy the whole fucking world to stay by your side," I say as I wipe the wounds away from her face, and mine along with it.

The bluest tears from the bluest hurt eyes meet my gaze and it causes my heart to feel heavy with grief. My soul aches, unwilling to believe the vision before me. I almost lost her again, a mistake I won't dare make thrice. She grabs my face and stares hard while our souls recognize each others presence once more. The light of her own soul returns the bright blue to her souls mirrors and allows my own eyes to grow soft.

"Baby...don't let anything ever take you away again...I won't survive without you...I know it."

I grab her and kiss her and give my soul the feeling of relief it needed while my hands become entangled in the red hair I'm beginning to love so much. I let them fall to the small of her back and pull her into me as we both fight through the tears and frowns, as the misery of our time apart is still thick upon us. I feel drunk again, the way I always feel when in the presence of her loving energy, as our faces recapture the lost love. We share the moment and stretch it again as lovers who now manipulate time. It comes to an end as we slowly pull our faces apart and step back a small pace. She sees a new hurt in my eyes and her brow furrows as she shows worry.

"It's Sam...isn't it?"

I nod slowly.

"Yes...I failed him, My Love."

She steps forward and wraps her arms around me and I supplant a soft kiss on the top of her head. I meet their gazes as I begin to deliver the news of Sams fate.

"Sam...went home to The Realm...He was murdered by

a group of men we came across. They found us in our hometown, and shot him in the back, like cowards...I gave him wings to spare him death...and then sent him on his way, as is the law of The Creator. He didn't want to leave us...and by the time he died...He was a true warrior," I confess and chuckle before returning to soft words, "all the way to the end, and even after that."

The soft sobs escape the Amys as they hold their hands to their mouths to keep the sadness in while the rest of the group slowly joins in sorrow or doing their damnedest to fight the tears.

"So many Cursed in the world," John begins, "and our brother was brought down by, of all things, *other people*...Sons of bitches."

"I think some people are The Cursed, just waiting to be born," Danny adds, "I met some real Shitheads in the joint...No way they could go to The Realm," he pauses to shoot me a stern gaze, "I hope you gave them what they deserved."

"I did...and it wasn't pretty...and it was absent any mercy. They met the most horrific end...a Fate born from the anger and hate I felt after they killed Sam...Half of them were innocent and were only following commands to save themselves, so I spared them...but, I made them watch...to make sure they never follow in the footsteps of their predecessors."

They all nod slowly in agreement, except for Robert.

"I know Big, I know...It's a mistake I need to pay for...I shouldn't of killed them."

He meets my hard stare with a soft one of his own.

"That's not it, Cuz...That's not what worries me. You gave them the Fate they deserved, and if it wasn't the end they were supposed to meet, The Creator would have stopped it. It's what you said about the anger and hate that worries me."

I know exactly what he's referring to.

"It's intoxicating, I know this. I see why Fallen Servants prefer it...The energy is like a drug, but it won't overtake me, nor will it become me."

"I hope you make good on your words...that's how The Old One came to be. The story in The Realm says that The Old One was a good guy, chosen to be a ruler in The Realm, and was tasked with ruling a part of the Kingdom. The Creator gave him a little power and he became greedy, wanting all of The Realm for himself. When he was cast out, The Abyss was born as a pit to contain him, along with the souls needing their wings. He couldn't have the Kingdom he wanted, so he built a Kingdom upon the suffering of others, and he took real joy in the punishment."

His gaze hardens as strong as the steel we all carry.

"He was a nice guy...given a Kingdom...does this sound familiar?"

"That's not who I am, Robert. You know this."

"That's not who he was either. People loved him, but the intoxicating energy of hate created the monster the world came to know as The Devil...The same monster that claimed your mortal life, Cuz...Just don't give in, when you channel all

309

the anger and hate...Don't let it define you, as it did him."

"Cuz, I'm telling you, that's not who I am. The thought of becoming The True Fallen One will always keep me from indulging too much. It's hard to control when I get angry, so I do my best not to...but, when they killed Sam...I didn't give a shit...I enjoyed inflicting the punishment, but only because they deserved it."

He shakes his head slowly from his seat upon the ground, "It's okay to enjoy handing out justice...just don't enjoy the act, or feed off of the energy, Cuz. That's when it happens...the change."

I allow my head to slowly agree, "I won't...I promise."

John steps forward as he begins, "Joe doesn't have a mean bone in his body, my Friend, and I can tell you without a doubt that The Creator chose him because of his heart."

Robert meets his gaze with agreement while his eyes becoming wide and playful.

"You won't get an argument here, Sir...this guy," he says as he shoots me a thumb, "once gave his shirt and boots to a homeless man. Made the old guy cry. Joe didn't know it then, but The Creator sent the man as a test, to see if Joes' heart truly stood worthy...He passed with flying colors. The Creator knew then He chose wisely."

He looks at me with the softest eyes he's yet to possess.

"I still remember that story when you wrote about it online...Made me smile so wide, Cuz. I was truly happy to know you."

I chuckle softly and place a hand on his lumbering shoulder while my eyes threaten drops of joy.

"Oh my God! The internet! I can't believe I forgot about all my Food Blogs," Amy J. blurts as the words come shooting from her mouth, "Sheesh Honey, I must have lost a whole Cookbook when the world ended...Oh well, I can't say I miss it, all the hassle and such...I don't miss it at all, actually."

"I do," Greg states flatly with his eyes blank and his mind wandering to a time long ago, "I really do."

"All the video games?" Danny asks him.

"No..." he trails off for a brief moment before he returns to reality and looks at us all with guilt, "...The porn."

Laughter overtakes the tense energy as he shakes his head and faces the ground, but his confession was a needed distraction. I allow us to indulge in the small joy before ruining it with a dose of reality.

"Guys...we're still being hunted," I say, a sense of Deja-vu stemming from a time long ago when I drew real breath, "we need to be careful...I already failed Sam...I can't fail anyone else."

"You won't, Baby," Sasha says as she grips my hand tight. I return it twofold and it's met in kind.

"I promise I'll do my best not to."

Robert retrieves his feet with the help of John and Will

and grunts as he pops his neck and stretches his wings. His eyes tremble with a worry I've never seen.

"Cuz...we need to get moving, but I don't think I can fly right now...something feels...different."

The weakness, the vulnerability, the fear we're not used to anymore.

"It's fine, Big, I promise...He cast a net on me and it drained me until I almost died myself. It rendered me useless and took a while before I felt better. Relax, my Brother. I'll watch over everyone while you rest a bit. We'll move at dawn."

Greg comes over and invites himself into my arms for a Manly Bro hug before stepping back and a wiping his eyes with the back of his skinny hand. I look at him and can see the hurt on his face.

"I didn't think I'd see you again, Bro...I was just waiting for all the serious shit to be over before I did that," he says and smirks with his silly grin that's as boyish as his stoner charm.

"Little brother, I'm already dead. Nothing can kill me, therefore, nothing can keep me from my family. I'm never going to be far away, when you all need me."

He steps forward and delivers another embrace and squeezes harder than his skinny frame should allow with a small laugh just under his breath. I return the laughter and squeeze in return.

I love you, Little Brother.

He steps back again with small tears lining his eyes and

312

his face no longer trying to mask the pain. He really did miss our bond; A brotherhood starting back around a campfire with a food fight and a bag of candy. The quiet talks we shared that night, and on many others, created a collage of memories spanning both my lifetimes. I remember in this moment that I'm the closest thing he has to a true brother in any life.

"So Greg...You got anything to smoke?" I ask, knowing he needs a distraction. It works, and his eyes light up like a New Years sky.

"Of course! You wanna smoke, Bro? Can you do that?" His eyes are hopeful, even though he already knows my coming reply.

"No, I can't...but I want you to smoke one for me tonight. Smoke a whole fucking bunch, go nuts, Little Brother. Let's all live a little tonight, while Robert rests."

He glances back and forth between me and Sasha as his eyes pry for any hints of secrets she and I may share.

"Don't fucking ask me, Greg. I have no idea what the Hell he's up to," she says and chuckles. The suspense is beginning to bug him, along with the rest of the group who stand more than intrigued. Roberts gaze is as wide as it is questioning.

"What do you got in mind, Bro?"

I smile my little, devilish grin.

"Something."

"Hahaa! Asshole, don't start that shit! What do you

want to do?"

"Create."

He rolls his eyes as his eyebrows threaten to rise completely off his forehead.

"Joe! For fuck sake, Bro!"

I laugh to the sky along with My Love and the group joins in the chorus. I still don't voice an answer to his question, but instead watch as the suspense kills him.

"Seriously, what do you want to do? What are we making?"

My devilish grin returns wide and accompanying a soft laugh.

"Memories."

* *

Peering in, I see only still shadows and no movement while the darkness sits as frozen as my beatless heart. The room is large enough to accommodate my plan, as the groups' soul is in need of nourishment. This room will suffice as long as we have no visitors, which should be a given as the building is small and hidden amongst a cluster of larger buildings. I feel them all behind me, peering over my shoulder into the room in search of a clue as to what motives I hide. Looking back over my shoulder confirms my suspicions, as their eyes all stand as one with question marks dancing in them. I nod my head and pull

314

the door closed in front of me. It's not time to enter yet. I stand quiet and motionless in front of the door and wait for the moment.

"Um...Joe?" Will asks, checking if I'm still alive.

"What's up, Will?" I ask quietly while focusing my energy into a reality.

"What are we doing?" He asks as a questioning child, his voice soft and seeming to come up to greet me rather than down from his towering face.

"Just a second, Will...I'm almost finished."

Behind the door, things are in motion. The sliding of wood and steel radiates through it while the screeching of furniture arranging and the clanging and banging of immortal creations fill the night air with electricity. I hear the soft murmurs of my family behind me and Sasha convincing them in her own words that she has no idea what's happening on the other side. So many F-bombs in such a short span of time.

God, how I love her dirty mouth.

The glow of soft lights begins to drift through from inside the windows a few feet away and illuminates the world in a wonderful beauty as the red and blue and white blends of color come together to dance on the lawn. I hear them gasp and meet their awestruck faces with a beaming grin. The moment is here. Now we can enter. I reach out and grab the handle without breaking our stare and twist it. I pause a moment to capture their expected reaction.

"It's all about the little joys."

I push the door open and reveal the depths of my secrets. The room is alive with soft music and loud colors and a dance floor decorated with the lights from above. The dots of color spin and dance around each other, making the floor seemingly move. A fully functioning Bar sits at the back of the room, along with a couple of Black Top pool tables as a treat I thought of just for Danny. The Food Bar on the right side of the room, complete with a Dinner table, steams with fresh bounties while the Pot Café on the left side smolders its mind altering aromas. The sounds of the Old World fill the air, yet it's a place none of us had existed in together. This would be our attempt at a life in a world that once existed, but no longer does, and acts as our own strange trip back in time. They all stand speechless, except for one who needs us to heed his words of caution, and it isn't the one I expect.

"Bro...is this a good idea?" Greg asks as he stands before me, "We were almost killed, literally, forty-five minutes ago. Shouldn't we be more...careful?" His eyes stand wide and frightened.

"You could die forty-five minutes from now, Greg," I say with a deep sigh, "so wouldn't you want to go out on your own terms? Doing what you love?" I ask as I point to the Bong next to assorted buds in the middle of a round table.

"Fuck....me," he exclaims softly as his eyes suddenly become glued to the vision at the end of my fingertip. He only breaks his gaze to give me one showing a deep hurt.

"Asshole...You really are The Devil."

I smirk and giggle to myself before giving my reply, "Yes, I am...but I'm also your brother. I'll protect you all while you have fun. Robert," I say and direct my attention to him,

316

"there's a King-size bed in the corner, next to the Pool tables. You can rest there while I watch everyone."

He walks forward and takes his place next to Greg and peers in at the blank area where a bed should stand. He shakes his head slowly.

"Uh, Cuz...There's no bed in there."

Reaching forward, I grab the handle and pull the door shut while offering an apology. "My mistake," I say before pushing the door open and revealing the prize I promised.

"There you go, My Brother."

"Ha! Right on, Cuz!" He shouts as he moves past me and becomes the first to enter the colored lights and aroma filled room. He takes a few rushed paces and jumps into the large bed as his giant frame threatens to smash it to pieces. The rest of the group follow quickly as everyone rushes to the Food bar and grabs for plates. Sasha falls to my side as we watch them joking and laughing and above all, for the time being, truly living. It's the outcome I had hoped for. My Soul and I pause a moment outside the entrance.

"They look happy, Baby," she says as she wraps an arm around my waist. I allow my arm to fall over her shoulder and pull her close to me. We watch as they all create edible mountains on their dishes.

"They should enjoy themselves for a while...I don't know how long...how much time we have left with them," I confess. She pulls away to look into my troubled eyes.

317

"Don't talk like that."

"I don't mean it like that, My Queen...War is coming for us...It may come sooner then expected...if this is our last night together with them as a family, we all need to enjoy it, before we stand as warriors...probably for the final time."

She brings our souls together for a kiss, but her blue eyes never close.

"Don't worry, Baby...They have a lot of days left up here...before The Creator takes them all home. We should enjoy their company. I gotta feeling we'll be missing them more than they'll miss us," she says as she points to Greg throwing spaghetti at Will and Danny. They side step it as it splats against the back of Carmens' head. We laugh softly together as Sasha squeezes me tightly while the guys explode in laughter on the other side of the room. The Amys try in vein to help Carmen remove her Spaghetti Wig. I pull Sasha into the building and close the door behind us. The music halts from the Jukebox next to the Bar as I raise my hand.

"May I have this dance, My Loving Soul?" I ask as I lead her to the dance floor. Our song, The Last Song, by Theory of a Deadman, rings through the night air, along with our loving energy. Her blue diamonds shine with love and her heart melts before me, but our actions are halted by Wills booming voice.

"JOE! Wait! Before you guys get all mushy...I want to ask you something," he says as he walks forward slowly and balances the food on his plate.

"Oh, okay...What's up, Will?"

"Well, I was thinking," he begins.

"And he actually didn't hurt himself!" Carmen interrupts jokingly from the Food bar.

"Shut up, Babe!"

She turns to him quickly and sends her black hair whipping around and meets his face with her small, burning black eyes.

"Um...I was just kidding...You want my pudding?" He asks and cowers his tall frame from so far away.

"Talk to me like that again," she warns as she lifts a menacing finger, "and *you* won't be getting any pudding, if you know what I mean," she finishes before turning to carefully select her bounty.

He stands lumbering and confused, as usual, when word play is involved.

"But...I already have it on my plate."

We all laugh together as she spins around and nearly drops her food.

"SEX! Dumbass! I meant you won't be having sex tonight!" She screams while doing her best to contain her laughter.

"What about tomorrow?"

"Oh my God! Shut up, Will!"

We all fall over each other laughing until our sides hurt,

as the duo of Will and Carmen are always one to entertain. Will allows us all to quiet down before voicing his request.

"Um...I was wondering if maybe...you could say the Dinner Prayer?" He turns to the now quiet group at the Food Bar, "Remember I asked if we could pray to Joe for thanks? Well, he's here now, so would it be okay if *he* did it? Tell The Creator *thanks* for us, I mean."

They look to each other, unsure of the answer.

"It would be an honor, Will...thank you, Brother."

Quietly, we make our way to the table. Robert rises from the comforts of his bed and follows. I raise my hand and halt the music, the Jukebox falling quiet as we gather around the table with their food and drinks placed before them. They all look at me silently as I smile and hold out my hands for union. They grasp the hands next to them until our praying circle of old is complete. I bow my head and they follow me lead.

"To our Creator...We thank You for the bounty my family is about to receive. We also thank you for the love and joy we've yet to lose, the comforts of our family is a blessing counted many times over. Thank you for Sasha," I pause as I feel her grasp my hand tight, "I would be lost without her, and can't thank you enough for leading her to me, in my last life and in this one. Thank you for Robert, my guardian Servant. Thank you for Sam, our long lost brother. Thank you for all my brothers and sisters who I love so dearly. Most of all, thank you for having the strength to give us the hope to carry on. All praise to you, the true Creator... Amen."

A succession of "amens" follows my voice and they all

shuffle into their seats as the chatter begins to voice itself again. Robert returns to the soft joy he's found and I rise to follow him as Sasha grabs my arm.

"Baby, where are you going?" Her voice echos through my dark mind.

I smile at her, this girl of old, who never wanted me to leave her side.

"I need to talk to Robert about the war to come. Keep them company, my Loving Soul."

She pulls me down and kisses me softly while my hands brush the hair from her face and find her delicate jaw to hold her captive. I kiss her with purpose as I always do and leave her yearning for more.

"Ooooh God! Baby, we need to find a place to snuggle up later...oh wait, no one can hear us. I WANT YOU TO FUCK MY BRAINS OUT!!!"

Her laughter fills my head as she smirks a coy smile and hides it with her hand. I laugh out loud, yet no one notices. They returned to the food fight they began with cornflakes so long ago next to a campfire.

"You're right...no one can hear us. I'm going to fuck you so good," I whisper to her beautiful mind before being cut off lightning fast.

"SHUT UP! Don't talk like that unless you're gonna do it, you hear me?!"

We share a small laugh between us as I lean down and

321

kiss her again.

"I love you, Sasha, and I won't stop making love to you the next time I feel the warm touch of your skin on mine and your hot breath on my neck, as your soul invites me in. I'll take you to complete ecstasy and keep you there as my mouth travels everywhere you love. I'll never let you go, I'll never yield, I'll never stop whispering your name in the quiet moments between your screams. I'll show you what true love is, Sasha, and then I'll dare you to stop me."

Her eyes glow as her face speaks sorrow as my moving words always make her shed tears. She reaches to my face and grasps me tightly, pulling me back into her lips. We share a painful moment of love, for the beauty of our sorrow will always be tied to the terrifying happiness that always swaps places with it. We love each other still, and will continue to do so for the rest of our immortal lives. We allow the magic to cease and stare into the mirrors we can't get enough of.

"*Now*, I want you to fuck my brains out."

The noise in the room comes crashing into silence and all eyes find themselves directed at Sasha.

"Did I say that out loud?"

"Yup, you sure did, Honey," Amy J. informs her with her cheesy smile.

"Well," she says and shrugs, "it's true. I want him to fuck my brains out."

The group laughs loud as I place my hand over her mouth. She smacks it away playfully and directs me towards

322

Robert. I turn to leave and she kisses her palm and smacks my ass hard, making me feel like a Damsel in a Skirt and she a burly Construction Worker. I walk away from her feeling violated in the most wonderful way.

"Hey, Cousin, mind if I grab a corner?"

Robert lays as a bear in hibernation and gestures for me to take a seat.

"Hang on!" Amy K. calls from behind me, "A little reading material for the Big Guy."

She hands me the Bible with my words inside and smiles softly. I pass if off to Robert behind me and his hands are all to eager to snatch it open. He flips to the Book of Joe and begins to skim over it before prying his eyes away long enough to smile in gratitude.

"Thank you, Amy K.!"

"You're welcome! Okay, I have a ton of food waiting on me. Enjoy!" She squeals and turns away to the path of her cuisine.

"Take a seat, Cuz...It looks like you found your grasp on your power...You feel like a Creator

yet?" He asks as I take my seat. I can feel his eyes wanting to tear through the pages.

"Ummm...kind of. I'm not sure what that's supposed to feel like."

He leans a bit closer to me.

323

"Do you feel like you can do anything?"

The simple question stumps me, as I feel it needs a complicated answer.

"Uhh...yeah?"

A sharp breath shoots from between his lips in amusement.

"Nope...not yet, but you're getting there."

"I flew faster than the speed of light and sound...I think I'm almost there," I assure.

He scoots over towards me and talks softly.

"When you get there, you'll be able to close your eyes and open them to anywhere in the world you want to be...that quick," he finishes and snaps his fingers. The thought of teleportation excites my soul.

"Wow, really?"

"Sure. Why not? You *can* do anything," he repeats as a broken record and returns to the comforts of his soft bed. He shifts himself around a bit and smiles wide.

"Man...this is really soft...I feel a bit stronger, Cuz, if you want to take a moment to be with Sasha...I heard what she said at the table," he says and laughs quietly. He leans forward and punches me on the shoulder, "besides, I have some reading material to keep me busy."

324

Sashas' passionate screams fill my memory and I feel the horses beginning to stampede across my chest. "You don't have to tell me twice."**
******

"Baby, what the fuck are you up to now?" She asks as I pull her out of the building into the awaiting darkness. She giggles quietly, secretly hoping she's getting what she asked for.

"You're not the only one with surprises," I say and pull her into me, "and I have one for us both," I pause to look into her soul and whisper, "close your eyes."

She smirks at me with a lovers grin and her blue eyes full of pale blue light. It pains me to ask her to hide something so beautiful.

"What are you up to?"

"Just close your eyes, Sasha...and don't open them until I say so."

She presses herself harder into me and kisses me softly. She leans back and closes her eyes while the permanent smile I adore so much is stamped across her face. She reminds me of the moment The Creator delivered her to me in a lightning bolt from The Realm. I wrap my arms around her and close my eyes and speak to my mind.

Home.

I feel absolutely nothing at all.

I open my eyes and my catching breath causes her to

open hers.

"Oh my God! Baby!" she barks loudly as she looks around in disbelief, "We're back at our house! How the fuck did you do that?" Her awestruck face says it all.

We stand in the wing not yet destroyed as the rest of the house has fallen inside the room we occupy. The staircase is barely visible under the collapsed roof.

"I can do anything," I say as I pull her into me and start to undress her, "anything."

She tears the robes from herself and begins to tear my armor from my body. Fierce blue fires stare me down while she accepts my challenge.

"Fucking prove it."

****

Her screeching voice fills the room in a high pitch as she screams her satisfaction. She shivers and lays on top of me as the ceiling begins to give away above us as the hole upstairs we created and fell through made the wood and steel weak. It comes crashing down a moment after I spin her over and under me and use my wings as an indestructible umbrella against the falling debris. She laughs softly until I motion my hips into her once more, turning the laughter into a sharp gasp.

"Baby! Hold on...I need a second," she says through quick breaths.

"Hell no...I told you I wouldn't stop...and I'll always keep my word to you."

I shift myself up into position and let the destroyed building roll off my back and wings.

"Really baby...I need a second...put it back in the cage," she repeats her request with closed eyes. I don't need to look into her soul to know there's a problem.

"What's wrong, My Soul?" I question, knowing it will only lead to some kind of heartache. She opens her eyes and smiles a sad frown.

"It's just...I want to hold you forever, Baby. I just want to hold you and feel your body against mine, for as long as I can...Your love is all I need right now."

I smile and say the first thing that comes to mind.

"Is this your way of telling me the sex is bad?"

She erupts in laughter and wraps her legs around me as her hands pull my face to hers. She holds me inches from her lovely mask and stares into my eyes with squinty blue ribbons, as her Crescent Moon smile causes her beautiful cheeks to rise. She pecks my lips and continues her giggles.

"You're still King Salami, don't worry, Baby."

I laugh with her in the fleeting moment while the beauty of her face is captured perfectly, even surrounded by the carnage of a dying building. Her soft laughter, I commit it to my memory. The loving sound of it always got me through the dark moments I lived without her. I remember the days of old...and understand completely why she wants to hold me. We can never be apart, to do so is a sin we dare not repeat anymore.

"Her beautiful laugh...I missed it so...the days apart...the love of old...deep blue eyes...steal my soul...it will never die...this love we hold...her perfect face...her perfect heart...the beautiful love...that she did start...I loved her then...I love her still...and I do it all...on my own free will...because she is my Soul Mate."

We lock in a fierce embrace and our souls refuse to release one another. We fall from the world around us and threaten its very existence with our love. The world can burn to ash and dust and even then...I wouldn't let her go. She releases me for the briefest of moments.

"I don't need a second...I need you right now."

We return to the fires that burn hotter than the Sun itself.

* *

"Holy...fucking...shit...that was amazing," she says through a hurried breath. She closes her eyes and breathes falsely in rapid succession. She holds herself up by planting her hands on my chest and letting her lovely legs straddle me. I lay as far back on my back as my wings will allow and stand equally winded.

"You...are...welcome...again," I say before laughing. She opens her lovely blue moons and smiles wide.

"Baby...I don't know what to do with myself when I'm with you," she says as she once again falls on my chest and giggles, "when we make love, it stops my world. You make me feel so special in every way...I still can't believe you're mine."

It's a sentiment that we both share. I wrap my arms around her and feel the bliss of her loving energy. I smile wide, as the tender love she feels for me is all I have ever wished for.

"That's right," I steal her words, "I'm yours, Baby."

"And you always will be," she continues in a whisper.

"Till the end of time...and even after that," I finish.

She shimmies her body up to bring her face to mine as our lips will always find each other to make soulful connections. We kiss slow and steady and relish the soft comfort we provide while my hands move through her bright, red hair. I stroke it and brush it away from her face to expose the Goddess hidden beneath it. She opens her eyes mid-kiss and catches me studying her beauty and pulls back quickly.

"What?"

I smirk and chuckle silently, "I want to look into your eyes for a bit...that's all, nothing else."

In a mocking manner, she makes her eyes unnaturally wide and stares hard, attempting to goad me into humourous actions. It works all too well.

329

"That's the look you had when you first saw my dick at the Shower Shack," I say and chuckle softly. She turns the tide of the jest.

"I was trying to focus and find it."

We both explode with our laughter as I reach down and pinch her perfect backside firmly, a retaliation for the ego-killing insult she just laid upon me. She slaps my arm playfully and assures me she's just kidding. I plan on paying her back tenfold the next time we share an intimate moment. There will be no stopping me the next time around.

"Okay, okay...you win...Bitch."

"As usual," she quips with a smile that only lasts a fading moment as the insult on the end catches her attention a little late. Her jaw quickly hangs as her blue eyes bulge from their sockets.

"*That's* the look you had at the Shower Shack! Aahahaaa!"

Her eyebrows turn sharp and her blazing blue comets come to life as her lips tighten. She tries her best to look like the Sasha of old, but my infectious laughter wins her over as my happy soul calls her bluff. She joins in the laughter and wraps her delicate arms around my neck, bringing us to the distance we prefer.

"You asshole."

I dare to laugh a bit more as I plant a small kiss on her cheek.

"I love you too, Sasha," I joke as I rise up while she moves to straddle me. She wraps her legs around me as I hold her in place from my seat upon the floor.

The moment grows quiet, but the gaze we exchange is louder than any words. We stare at each other and smile like fools before she embraces me tightly with her straightjacket stranglehold. I hold her tightly as if she might slip away and run my fingers through her hair, wearing a smile I've never worn. The sweet scent of her soul reminds my dead heart that it has a reason to eternally beat. I feel her happy tears burning my shoulder and racing quickly down my back and I wonder to myself if she can feel mine, falling now as if they were a warm, Summer rain.

Thank you, My Creator.

****

"They've been gone a while, Bro...maybe we should look for them," Greg says to John as he passes him a bright blue pipe I modeled after Sashas' eyes. They all sit around a coffee table in the Pot Café in the comfort of real clothes. I made sure to conjure jeans and shirts during my magic trick, as wearing armor all day had to be hard on a mortal body. I still have no clue as to where the armor came from, a question Robert promised to answer another time.

"Good idea, Friend," he says and takes Gregs pungent treasure.

"Nah, fuck that," Danny joins, "they're the baddest motherfuckers on the planet. They're good, wherever they are," he finishes and swigs down his beer.

Will leans forward to join the discussion, passing a joint to the love of his life.

"What if something happened to them? I know Joe and Sasha can kick ass, but...they didn't even tell us they were leaving...I think they would of if they knew they'd be gone for a while."

"Will, don't worry," Amy K. begins as she rises from the circle and stumbles with a stoned mind, "they're probably just fucking like wild animals. It's all they do anymore."

They laugh hard and Roberts booming voice comes from half a room away. Amy K. looks at them all in surprise.

"Seriously! You all heard Sasha say he was gonna fuck her brains out. That's most likely what he's doing, or did, I don't know. No ones ever fucked my brains out before. I would think it wouldn't take *too* long, would it?"

The bellows and howls of laughter stretch to the ceiling as the proper Amy K. voices the language of Sasha. They scream in laughter until their breath escapes them altogether.

"Amy K...please...just stop," Carmen begs through the laughter, "girl, you're killing me."

"What? I'm just saying that fucking peoples brains out sounds like it would be *quick* work. It wouldn't have the same effect if it was slow work, if *that* would even work...What the Hell am I talking about?...I think I may have smoked too much."

Sides splitting, breath eludes them as they fall over

themselves. Robert laughs from his bed, most likely glad he was already laying down. She floors everyone with the expression she wears.

"I'm going to look for some water...it's so dry in here," she says and begins her quest. She walks away softly as she stares at her stepping feet.

"Honey, be careful now," Amy J. calls after her, "watch out for marshmallows."

"S'mores! Let's make some fucking S'mores again!" Danny screams as he jumps up from his seat.

"Guys!" Greg interrupts, "you guys remember the Peanut Butter and Jelly Quesadillas? Man! Those were fucking good, Bro! Let's make some more of those!"

Roberts laughter continues from the soft comforts he will enjoy for as long as he can. He closes the Book of Joe and joins in on the conversation.

"You guys crack me up. I see what Joe was talking about now. He said you could be the craziest bunch of people under the right circumstances...and holy shit, was he right."

"Hell yeah, Bro! We're a dysfunctional bunch, but give us some weed and a little alcohol and we're good," Greg confesses.

"I'd have to agree with my Cousin," Robert admits, "speaking of which...They *have* been gone awhile."

****

Pausing outside of our shattered Earthly home, I stare at the night sky before Sasha grabs my arm and spins me to face her.

"So...next time....I was thinking...," she says as she looks at me with playful eyes, "about wearing something nice for you, like that one time."

"Oh yeah?" I ask, revisiting the memory of her slipping out of her Trench Coat and revealing her lingerie.

"Yep...Would you like to know what it is?" She asks while running her hand down my chest and settling on my waist, just below my belly button.

"Why don't you describe it...and I'll take a guess," I reply as I let my hand run through her hair before allowing it to fall to her slender shoulder.

"Okay," she says as she removes my hand from her shoulder and kisses it, "it has little, leather straps."

She pauses and places one of my fingers in her mouth and draws on it succulently while letting her eyes seduce me as much as her mouth does now.

"Holy shit," I mutter while restraining myself, "I'm liking what I'm hearing...go on."

She giggles and removes my finger and places my hand on her warm, inviting breast.

"It has...little buckles on it," she says bashfully while directing her face down but keeping her eyes fixed on mine. Her gaze appears fierce and causes me to shudder, along with the images of her in a leather Teddy.

"Go on....*Please*, go on," I plead and cause her to giggle again. She nods and continues.

"And it's about twelve inches long and if you tap on the end of it, it goes boing! Boing! Boing!"

She holds her gaze on mine as I feel my face twist in shock as I realize she's talking about a Strap-on.

"Sasha, what the fuck!?"

Unable to contain herself any longer, she explodes in the sweet laughter I live for. I keep myself composed to keep her joke alive and breathe more life into it, just to keep her serenading me with her lovely voice.

"Sasha, I mean it! What the fuck? I said go on! I'm listening!"

Throwing her head back, she loses her voice and can only snort between her fits of laughter. I laugh along with her and fill the silence of the New World with our happiness.

"Didn't expect me to say that shit, did you?" I ask as she falls forward into me while trying to catch her breath.

"No, I really didn't, Baby," she answers before looking up at my face.

"Our love story would be a very different story if that was the case," I say before continuing, "The Story of Joe and Sash...oh? Sasho?"

"Sasho?" she questions with wide eyes, causing me to blurt out an explanation.

"Well I don't know the male variation of Sasha off the top of my head!" I exclaim.

"The male variation of Sasha," she begins slowly while holding her laughter again, "is Sasha. It's unisex."

"Oh yeah...I don't know how I forgot that," I admit, not knowing how I could of forgotten such a simple trivia.

"Oh Baby," she says while taking my face into her hands, "At least you're pretty, My Love."

"Oh fuuuuck you, Lady," I say before bursting out in a new fit of laughter. She clings onto me and squeezes me tightly as we both laugh like fools.

"See...This is what I love most about us....*This*, right here," she confesses before looking into my eyes, "I love that we're friends, as much as lovers."

"Well, apparently I'm too stupid to know the difference, so there's that," I exclaim while crossing my eyes.

She giggles again and slaps my face playfully before putting the conversation back on topic.

"I mean it...You're the best friend I've ever had."

"I'm definitely your dumbest friend, I know that much," I joke " but I learned how to count to eleven-teen so I'm getting more genius-er."

"Shut up," she says before laughing again, "we should get back to them. We've been gone awhile already."

Wrapping one arm around her, I bring my free hand to her face and slowly close her eyes by sliding two fingers down her face and over her eyelids.

"As you wish, My Queen."

****

The flash is quiet and brilliant, just outside the door. It shines bright enough to appear as headlights through the window as the light pierces the dimmer room they occupy. They retrieve their weapons from their sides, the only apparel never to be unworn, and burn a hole though the door with their stare. It opens quickly to expose the bringer of the light.

"Take it easy, Fellas," I begin as I lead Sasha into the room, "it's just us."

Greg marches forward with a glazed look in his eyes, leaving no doubt he had been indulging for awhile.

Which means we were gone too long.

"Bro! Where the fuck have you been?! We didn't know what the Hell was going on!...What were you doing?"

I exchange a wily smile with Sasha before I answer.

"You can figure it out, Bro," I say and playfully punch his arm.

"Ha!" Amy K. screams from the Bar, "I called it! I told you all! I said they were fucking like wild animals, didn't I? Didn't I say it?"

Sasha turns to her with a witty gaze that matches my own.

"What? Amy...what?"

"Well it's true, right? You guys were doing it?"

"Amy, what the fuck?" Sasha exclaims as she chuckles at her sisters new take on her language, "*when* did you find this side of you? Don't get me wrong, I'm loving it and hell yeah, you know we did!"

Amy K. shoots her a thumbs up and swishes down a bottle of water in the same motion while leaving Sasha and I standing dumbfounded. Amy K., surprisingly out of character, is the last one we would ever think to speak in such a manner. I find it as endearing as Sashas' filthy mouth. I turn to Greg and point at her with a stunned and questioning gaze.

"She smoked a lot...like a lot, Bro! I don't know why, but...when she gets high with me," he says and peeks in her direction, "she's like the coolest chick ever."

I crack a tiny half smile and begin shaking my head in agreement.

He likes her.

"Amy K. is a good woman, Greg...You two actually make a lot of sense."

He looks at me and Sasha for a few seconds before he realizes I'm playing matchmaker. With his eyes wide, he raises his hand and tries to brush it off.

"What? Nah, Bro...I don't think so. I just think she's a really cool smoke buddy and kinda pretty and funny and she's really smart too! She has a cute laugh and it makes me laugh when she gets to rambling on. She says the most random shit," he says with a smile, "she's just a cool chick."

Sasha catches his gaze with soft eyes.

"Greg...I can talk to her if you want...I can tell you like her. You looked at her a moment ago the way Joe looks at me."

He tries his best to hide the smile that threatens to show itself as he makes an attempt to dissuade us once more.

"No...it's okay."

I glare at him and probe his mind for his true intent.

"Greg...Brother," I voice softly as I let my eyes speak for me.

"I'll talk to her when I'm ready," he finally admits. I let out a forceful laugh and grab a hold of him, squeezing him in a relieved happiness. I remember the days he proclaimed he would never love a woman over his grass. He just took the first step towards making the statement a false one.

"Good luck with her, Bro," I say quickly as I point at Amy

339

K.. She now stands covered in water and fumbles with another bottle. It slips from her hands and she swipes it away in an attempt to grab a hold of it. It rolls to the floor in front of us and comes to its' final resting place at Gregs feet. He peers down at it and then back at me.

"Follow the signs, Bro," he cracks and swats my arm. He reaches down and retrieves her water and begins his slow walk towards her while the gears spin in his mind and work on what he would say. I laugh as he walks a few inches taller with his chest a little bigger, and his soul terrified beyond belief. Sasha leans into me with her soft laughter approaching my ear.

"I remember being nervous like that around you," she whispers sweetly, "it was sooo intimidating when I first started catching your attention, Baby. I thought...this guy, who's so perfect, couldn't possibly be mine...and now you are...but I was scared shitless like a little girl until then."

I wrap my arm around her slender shoulders and pull her close as her arm finds its home around my waist. I share in the confessions of when I was a mortal man.

"You are the most beautiful woman I've ever laid eyes upon, Sasha. When you first tried to make a move, that night at the campfire, I thought I was going to have a fucking heart attack."

She laughs softly and turns her slender frame into my chest and squeezes me affectionately.

"But, after you kissed me," I continue softly, "I felt true fear, because my heart loved you in that moment...It loved you immediately...and my soul always follows my heart."

We stand quiet as we reminisce about that night, when she pulled me into her and forcefully tasted my lips for the first time. I feel her nuzzling her face into my chest and can tell she's smiling wide. I want more than anything to make her smile wider still.

"Sasha," I whisper.

"Yes, Baby?" She asks while keeping her face resting on my chest.

"May I have this dance?"

Releasing me suddenly, her delicate blue eyes find mine full of love. She stares into my face and smiles her beautiful grin for all the world to see, but only my eyes find it, as it is meant to be. I lead her to the dance floor and strike up our song as I turn to meet my Sweet Angel. She wears the most loving expression, with her soft, flaming red hair hanging perfectly around her face, and I feel the false breath seize in my throat. This woman, this beauty in front of me, can't possibly be real. She stands a true Goddess and possessor of my soul. We let our arms find the bodies they love to hold and grasp each other as if it's the only thing we know how to do. She looks up at me with a shine in her loving, blue stars while the green glow in my eyes dies down, as her shining light will always eclipse mine. She finds them loving, and she finds my hands equally loving. I let my hand glide across her slender cheek while her eyes make love to my soul, and feel the burning fire in my chest as my very essence is ignited. I feel the need to laugh and cry and rejoice and curse all in the same moment. Such is the true definition of true love.

"You make me happy...like I never thought possible, Sasha. I'll always hold your hand, My Queen...I'll always make you smile," my voice ends, unable to voice any more confessions of love. My soul now stands in awe of her angelic face, illuminated by the soft lights overhanging the dance floor. Her smile threatens to turn to a joyous frown and call forth the happy tears, as the connection we share has become stronger than ever. It stuns us both as we continue to gaze upon our true wishes in the flesh, the vibe between us alive and taking an energy of its own. Never in time has there stood two people more perfect for each other.

"And you do, Baby, you really fucking do," she exclaims softly with her voice shaking. "My soul feels alive in me when I think of you, even if I'm standing beside you, I still think of you," she says as we sway slowly to the music, "there were so many days in The Abyss when you were helping lost people, giving them their wings, and I would watch you and think to myself...How did I get so lucky? Then...I would smile away and laugh to myself...The Creator really blessed me."

"And me, My Loving Soul," I reply and find her lips with my own, "and we're blessed with an eternity together," I whisper as I take her lips with mine. She runs her loving hands through my long hair and rests them on my shoulders as we kiss the dance away. We stop time once more and let our love engulf us. Our dance has never been sweeter and it kills me harshly when the song ends.

We pull back in the same moment the song ends, only to lock faces tenderly again and continue our passion as the cheers of the Amys are loud and screeching. We release each other to meet our own dreamy eyes and laughing smiles before we greet the rest of the amused faces in the room. Neither of us have ever felt so euphoric.

"You two are like a Fairy Tale!" Amy K. screams to the

air, "just like in the Book of Joe! You wrote your love so beautifully," she says as she gives me a long, loving stare, "and to see it come to life in front of me is like...a miracle!"

We chuckle and squeeze the afterlife out of each other. I find her exhilarated blue oceans swimming with love.

"This is one Fairy Tale destined to have a happy ending," my tongue professes. Her blue eyes squint as she suppresses a small laugh while her joyous tears roll down quickly.

"Girls get the Prince in the Fairy Tales...I got a King...King Salami," she jokes.

The laughter is loud as I pull her into me and squeeze her tight while begging her to drop the joke before my eyes find Danny next to the bar. I shoot him a happy glare along with my middle finger for naming me so. He erupts in laughter, knowing its meaning, while the bright lights on his bald head hide his crooked smile in shadows, and presents two thumbs up in return. We laugh hard together as a family, and do so, as if it would be our final time. True living starts with true loving, and laughter is a fine path for the soul to get there. We all live in the moment...and the night will remain ours.

Chapter 7

"HAHAHAAAA! No fucking way, Bro!"

Greg falls back in disbelief as I levitate the pipe from his fingers with only my gaze and glide it over to Johns' awaiting hand. The pipe lands softly as the cheers shake the smoky room. I raise my hands in victory as we sit around the table with Robert the only one absent. He refuses to leave the comforts of his bed and keeps his face buried in the pages as my words shake his soul in their horror and beauty. He tuned all of us out hours ago.

"I can do anything, Little Brother...What else you want me to do?" I ask, the request more for my benefit than his. I enjoy entertaining my family and it makes us all feel like the Old World never ended, which is a rare thing in the New World. I wonder quietly to myself if we would of ever known each other if the Old World had never died. It would be a shame to never know their hearts.

"Fuck...do something hard," his says before his eyes light up, "make Will smart!"

We explode in laughter as Will leans over from two seats away and pops the back of his head softly, yet Greg offers no apology. They playfully fight with Carmen being the punching bag between them, their playful banter filling the room and making it feel like a College Dorm and not a secret hideaway.

"Guys! Stop!" Carmen orders sharply as she gets

344

slapped from both directions, "seriously, you fucking idiots! You already fucked my hair up with your dumbass Spaghetti fight and I don't need to get bruised up too! Dumbassess!"

We laugh hard at their predicament as I meet Carmens eager eyes. I can hear the request in her unspoken voice. She wants something, but chooses not to ask. I study her face and read her like a book, making sure my aim is true before I make the offer.

"Carmen...did you see Sashas' hair? Don't tell anyone, but, I became quite the hair dresser in The Abyss," I joke, "and I could maybe do something with your hair? It looks like you still have some Spaghetti in there, by the way."

The guys laugh as Will pulls a hidden strand out of her hair.

"Babe, you have Spaghetti in your hair...This is gross," he says and flings it aside.

"No fucking shit, Will! Did you forget you put it there? Dumbass!"

"Nuh-uh, Babe! It was Greg that threw it!"

"Yeah, but you moved and let it get all over me, so it's *your* fault."

Will eyes stand as wide as the dinner plate he was overloading earlier and plea with me to intervene. He knows all too well he'll never win an argument with his smarter half.

"Anyway, as I was saying," I direct my gaze at Carmens' small, dark eyes, "I can change your hair if you want," I assure

345

as she ponders a change and instinctively reaches for her hair.

"Change it...how?" The cautious woman in her asks.

"However you want."

"Make her bald," Will states plainly.

She glares at him with a look of horror and shock, "What? You wanna see me bald? What kind of weirdo dumbass did I marry?"

She never breaks her gaze from his face. He never meets it, instead looking around at all of us. He feels the small hole she's burning in his head before succumbing and finding her eyes.

"Babe...I think you're so hot...You could be bald and you would still be hot...but, please don't ask Joe to cut off all your hair, I was just joking."

Laughter makes its way around the table as Carmen embraces her simpleton husband and coos from his flattery. He hugs her tight and kisses the top of her head as she squeezes him in the manner Sasha strangles me. I smile at their love, a love that began in the Old World and survived the new one. Their bond is one of the most beautiful relics from the Old World.

"You know what, Joe?" Carmen pauses and looks at Will, "make me a blonde so I can match my hubby. I wanna be a stupid-ass blonde too."

The joyous shouts of laughter are heard around our table again as I stand up and reach over to Carmen with my hands gesturing for her to stand. She rises slowly and takes a deep breath and shakes off the nerves that now seize her. It's a panic that comes from any woman who's about to enter the Salon chair. I know all too well that she will demand perfection and anything less would invite tears.

"Just how blonde exactly do you want to go? Dirty blonde? Platinum? Any shade in-between, just be as specific as possible...I want to make sure I get it right."

She stares off at the ceiling while she contemplates, trading the view of the ceiling for Wills hair, a bright, Sunny yellow that screams that he belongs on a beach. I see her go back and forth in her mind before finally coming to a compromise with the other woman inside her.

"You think you can do...Blonde highlights? I like my dark hair, but I think it would look so cool with the streaks and shit everywhere. I always wanted to do it but *someone*," she says as she shoots Will with imaginary bullets from her small, dark barrels, "said that, because I'm dark complected, I would look like a sunburned Barbie doll."

Screaming laughter again all around, my immortal sides begin to ache and my face feels permanently stamped with a Jokers grin. I shake it off and focus my energy to my hands, as my fingers feel the heat of eternal power again. I bring my face to Carmens and whisper for her to close her dark eyes. I bring forth my magical hands and the light begins to form in the center of my palms. I wait for her to follow my command before I begin. She closes her eyes with a final, deep breath and I waste no time in my task, letting my hands glide over her hair and creating a beautiful blend of gold and yellow tendrils of all varieties, while keeping her dark hair intertwined. I make my way to the tips and pull away as she starts laughing.

347

"I can feel that! Haha! It feels so strange!"

"Open your eyes, Carmen," I instruct softly. She opens her eyes with a lovely grin and pulls forth a lock of her hair.

"Oh my God! OOOOHHH MYYYY GOOODDDD! Joe this is fucking awesome! I love it! Oh shit, I need a mirror," she says as she scurries away in search of anything shiny with the bellows of our laughter behind her. Will rises up and follows his heart as John makes a request of his own.

"Friend...that was really amazing what you did with that gals hair...Can you do something for me?" He asks while standing as curious as I do.

What could he possibly ask me for?

"Of course, Sir. You name it. What do you need?"

He leans forward and speaks quickly, "I don't ever want to shave again. Can you do that?"

I laugh to myself as I reply, "if that's what you want...I guess I can do it. I've never tried to make hair...stop growing. Actually, now that I think about it," I say and reach up to my face, "I've had a five o'clock shadow since I became the True Ruler. My hair stopped growing...maybe I can do it for you...I'm not sure."

"If it's any trouble, Friend," he says bashfully before I cut his words short.

"None at all. I can do it, Sir," I assure.

I reach over without further argument and wipe both

348

hands across his jaw line from ear to chin, and his small beard falls off as if my hands were razors. I trace every line where stubble resides, careful to hit every base. I don't need a moment to focus this time around, and it's a welcomed change. I'm finding my rhythm in the loud messy waves of eternal power. I clean my hands of his beard as he searches his face, carefully inspecting with his fingers. He smiles wider with every smooth glide of his fingertips and chuckles quietly as thoughts of razor blades forever absent from his life dance in his head. I see the gratitude pouring from his eyes as he stops his inspection and slams his hands quickly on the table with a booming laugh.

"Hot damn, Friend...Bravo, good Sir," he manages through the giggles.

Praise comes at me in all directions and I see Amy J. lean forward with a bashful soul to voice her request as I take my seat. I know her all too well, my food loving friend, and have seen the way she peered at Sasha, Amy K. and Carmen, and hid her envy of their youthful good looks. I speak to her in her mind before she can beat me with audible words.

"I can't make you younger, Amy J., but I can help you a little bit...with your weight...That's what you want, isn't it?"

Stunned at the words entering her mind, she freezes in place and meets my eyes to find them full of understanding. A lifetime of being plagued by her weight, her love for cuisine and creating delicacies forbade her from being the thin girl in the crowd. Such things never mattered to her. She loved every aspect of the kitchen, from creating to consuming, to feeding people to the compliments it brought about, and the kitchen loved her as well, as the energy of a good meal was a positive one. Even through all the love it brought, she secretly screamed

349

inside to be recognized for the beautiful woman that she alone saw in the mirror. I see the tears well as she realizes that I'm speaking to her with my mind and soul.

"Joe...You just spoke to me in my head...didn't you, Honey?"

"Yes Ma'am...I hope I didn't come across as mean, but I know your weight bothers you. I may be able to help you with it and give you a new start."

We both jump up startled as Carmens screams race from across the room as she finds her reflection in the window, and her joy causes Robert to almost jump out of his wings. He stumbles off the edge of his bed and looks at her with comical eyes while we share a small laugh. I reset my undivided attention back on the sad eyes of Amy J..

"I have a medical condition that keeps me heavy...It's my Thyroid, it's all out of whack...I would love to be thin, if that's something you can do...and Thank you, Joe, for offering at the very least."

"You're most welcome," I voice out loud, causing everyone to turn to me with looks of confusion. I rise from my seat once again and she mirrors my actions as the groups eyes and ears all lock onto us.

"Are you ready?"

She takes a deep breath before giving her reply.

"As ready as I'll ever be, Honey," she says as she reaches for her glass of wine, the red fluid now resembling a token of victory as she raises it up in salutation, "to a new beginning."

I chuckle softly as I reply, "yes Ma'am...A new beginning."

"What the Hell is going on?" Danny voices everyone thoughts.

I raise my hand to him for a gesture of pause as I walk around the table and grasp her hand to lead her to the Dance floor. I take her a few steps away from everyone and display my wings, readying them for the minor miracle I need them to participate in creating. I pause a moment to give her instructions.

"However you want to look...Whatever size you want to be...Whatever you see as the real beautiful you...That's who I need you to imagine when I wrap you in my wings...Are you ready?"

She wipes the tears from her face as she nods quickly.

"Close your eyes."

We share the last embrace she would share with anyone as a Plus-size girl. It's a girl she loves, but secretly wants to starve. I stretch my wings around her and let them fall gently around her body. I ruffle my feathers to create a soft blanket and peer down to see the top of her head pressed against my chest.

"Your own beautiful self," I remind. She nods quickly once again.

The glow of the light is brighter than any sun anywhere

351

in His universe. It pours out from the cocoon I wove around Amy J. as the sounds of everyone in the room becomes panicked before Robert assures them all is well. I feel the change, my wings coming closer to me as the woman inside shrinks away. The flow of light subsides a bit and begins to calm in waves as the light show lasts a grand total of ten seconds. In such a short span of time, a new life is crafted. I open my wings slightly and take a peek inside in the deafening silence that now fills the room. The sight in front of me is one to behold.

The eyes, so brown and full of blazing light, remain unchanged, along with her curly blonde hair. The woman in front of me stands half the woman she was as the full-figured gal is now a lean and athletic lady. Her clothes hang from her now thinner body as she stares down at her feet in disbelief.

"My God, Honey, are those my feet?"

I laugh loudly as I place my hands on her now much slimmer shoulders.

"Yes Ma'am...those are your feet."

She lifts them one at a time for closer inspection and laughs softly to herself.

"Big people always talk about seeing their feet for the first time," she says before looking up to meet my gaze, "not that big a deal...they're just feet, Honey," she finishes with the largest smile she's ever conjured.

"You're so beautiful Amy K., but you've always been beautiful...I'm glad you finally feel like it."

She allows her hands to travel over the new vessel her

soul will now occupy while her smile fights to remain a smile against the threat of a happy frown. She begins to cry softly and it's the only sound in the room as she jumps into my arms.

"Thank you, Honey! Thank you so much! Thank you and may The Creator bless you, Joe! Thank you...thank you..." she trails off as the sobs take full hold. I let her cry in joy and hold her as I release my own happy tears, as the overwhelming joy she feels radiates throughout the whole room. We cry in happiness, everyone in the room, for what seems like a short lifetime before she composes herself enough to meet the group as her new self.

"Go ahead...show it off, Amy," I say and chuckle. She releases me and steps out from the privacy of my wings for all to see.

"Take a good look at this girl!"

She shouts as she begins a sensual twirl across the floor towards the sounds of screams of surprise. The group shouts and hollers approval while her laughter is loud and pleasing. They all rush to embrace her and bounce around while rejoicing and the energy overwhelms my soul. I feel the burning love inside me, an energy that always attracted Sasha as it does now. She makes her way over to me with tears burning hot upon her cheeks.

"Baby, that was so sweet. She feels alive again. Thank you so much for doing it."

I wrap my arms around her as I always seem to be doing.

"She needed a change. She wanted to be a thin girl her

353

whole life...and now she is."

"Because of *you*...I love you, Joe...Everyone loves you so much because you always do things for them without asking...and not because it's the right thing to do...you do it because...*it's you*...it's who you are."

"It's how The Creator wanted all of us to treat each other before the Old World ended. There's no reason why we can't treat each other with love now in the New World."

She releases me for a moment and points at Amy J. receiving a new kind of attention as John approaches her and offers flattery.

"I think John wants to treat her with some love," she informs me and laughs.

"And it looks like my little brother is following his lead," I reply as I point out Greg taking Amy K. by the hand and whispering sweet nothings into her ear. She giggles and walks with him to the Pot Café.

"Yep..." Sasha trails off and looks at me, biting her bottom lip with mischief, "there's gonna be a whole lotta people fucking like wild animals tonight."

We laugh together and embrace for a happy moment, with her observation on its way to becoming a reality. In a world of Cursed and death and Fallen Servants, it stands as a miracle that love could be found in such a place of misery. It may as well be the Old World, as they all live as if their old lives never ended.

354

"Let's help them bring out their inner animal," I say as I release her and clap my hands twice in a rapid fire pace. The jukebox begins to blare an oldie but goodie, Lynyrd Skynyrds 'That smell', changing the vibe in the room from joyous to adventurous. Hands raise in unison as they cheer and head to the dance floor. Greg dances with Amy K. all the way from the café with their laughter accompanying them along the way. Will and Carmen join the group as everyone laughs and dances up a storm, except for the three immortals in the room. Robert and Sasha laugh and watch as I stand with the worst feeling of impending doom. It's a blessing when the new Amy J. waves Sasha to join her on the dance floor. She looks at me as if to ask for permission.

"Go dance with your sisters. I'll keep an eye on things, my Beautiful Queen."

She jumps up into me for a quick peck and returns my loving words before she turns from me and races screaming to her girls while they scream in welcome. They dance and drink on the dance floor while they spin the world. I stand quiet and meet Roberts gaze, nodding my head for him to join me. I dare not send a thought and have Sasha pick up on it. He makes his way over to me as I turn and lead him out of the party. We make it a few feet from the closed door behind us before his voice comes booming from behind me.

"This has got to stop, Cuz. I know you feel it, as I do. We need to be cautious," he warns through clenched teeth. I feel the hate less than a mile away now, making his words true. They're coming fast and bring terrible intentions.

"You said I could do anything...Just sit back and watch...I got this, Cuz," I say without ever presenting my face, "they're almost here...Look over to the East."

355

I point at the painted nightmare in the sky just above the moon and see the dark cluster moving quickly overhead. They move closer to us, feeling the trail of energy I emit, and ready their talons for the flesh of The Fallen One. I hear the hisses born into the night air and the screeching of evil laughter blending into the nightmarish mix. I wait for them patiently to be close enough before I unleash my anger.

Just a little more...You won't ruin my families last good night on His Earth.

I suppress my roar to spare my family, yet a loud grunt forces itself out as I throw my hands forward with terrible force and send a wave of emerald fire streaking through the night air. I cover the entire sky, making my aim more than true. It travels fast and deadly and sets ablaze every last winged soul of death that had come to claim our lives. Their screams of excitement turn to bellows of horror as they cook in mid-air and flail about. They try to pull the fires off their flesh with no success as their wicked skin melts away. They stood no chance against the newly harnessed power I tapped into, nor will their master when we meet again. I pray they tell him of my airborne sea of fire. No doubt he remembers the wave I sent him in the grocery store not so long ago. Robert approaches my side, but my eyes never leave the sky as I watch dead Cursed crows fall from the air while scanning for new threats.

"That was pretty cool, Cuz...You're almost there."

"Almost? Really?" I exclaim as I raise a hand and bring fire forth.

He laughs and pretends to blow my hand out like a

birthday candle. I extinguish my flames and laugh with him.

"When you get there, Cuz, you'll know. Doing tricks and mastering fire is one thing, but you need to learn that you can have control over all things. You're not there yet," he says as he shakes his head in disagreement and I meet his eyes from under the brim of his hat, "but you're getting there, and judging by the light show, you're getting there fast."

I smile as I nod my head, "let's keep this quiet...The light show. I don't want them to think about fighting tonight. They need to enjoy themselves as much as possible...I don't believe we'll have another night together...this is it."

"Nah, Cuz, this can't be it. They're going to be here together for a long time, you wait and see."

The screams inside are loud and joyous and I recognize the banter going on between Will and Carmen, as Will is no doubt getting himself in the trouble he lives in. We both chuckle softly.

"I hope you're right, My Brother."

"I am. You'll see," he shoots back quickly, "and they won't know what happened out here. If more come..." he pauses and finishes the statement with his widening eyes.

"We'll worry about it if the time comes."

"Not if, Cuz...*when*," he corrects me.

We stand quietly for a few moments and search the stars.

357

"Cuz," he begins, "The Book of Joe...It's going to change the way the people left behind see the world. I'm not supposed to tell you everything I know, but...I think it's important you know a couple things."

"Such as?" I ask, suddenly burning with curiosity and meeting his now confessing eyes.

Nodding slowly, he continues, "The book isn't just a book...it's a tool He created through you. He carved a path from the very beginning of your life to lead you to the Bookstore where you found the journal. When we were still living, the path you were on then was to prepare you."

"I know that, Robert...I think. I was a Ghost Hunter in the Old World."

"No, you were a magnet for lost and hurt souls...You know this, it's what made you special your whole life...*you know this*...don't you?"

I feel the rush of old emotions flood through me, of all the times wandering in the darkness and feeling completely at home with the dead. Suddenly, all the touching moments with the lost make more and more sense to me.

"When I came across a spirit in the Old World...I could always feel them, the emotions they had when they died...I could feel their fear...their misery...the hopelessness before they stopped breathing...I could see their faces sometimes...beautiful faces...and always hear their voices...they talked to me all the fucking time...they would beg me to help because they knew I could hear them...I didn't need the equipment to see and hear the dead that walked among us. That was for the benefit of the families I was helping or the

358

investigators I was teaching...it was also the mask that allowed me to *be me* without people thinking I was insane...the lost souls...they knew I could see them...and I would always put the fucking equipment down and pray with them in the end...I couldn't film them when they needed me."

"And now you help the souls in The Abyss...You pray with the lost and give them their wings...You've been sending lost souls to The Realm since you were living...you know, I actually met a couple of them when I got to The Realm...they wouldn't stop going on and on about how you saved them."

I laugh quietly to myself as the tears flow. The attempts were successful, as I always prayed they would be.

"Then *I was* preparing for the afterlife...it makes sense."

"And you always had a talent for the pen too, Cuz. You write from the soul, and that's exactly what the people of this New World need. They need to be able to hear things from the soul, and you captured it perfectly. The book you wrote will either save them all, showing them how to lead their new lives, or none at all...it's up to people to receive it for what it is; A book of lessons on love and Humanity...You wrote this book without knowing it would be the most important weapon in the war to come."

"How can the book be a weapon? There's only one copy, in the whole fucking world."

I stand stunned and saddened at once.

"This war will last years, Cousin. Killing the Necromancer and every Cursed in the world won't matter if people don't be good to each other on their own free will. A new threat will always rise up. That's where the book comes in...a book written by The Fallen One himself...People should see it as simple as it is...just like I said...a book of lessons on love and Humanity...even as The Fallen One, you never lost either quality."

Quietly, I view the darkened sky above while absorbing his reply, as only the eternally Fallen One can, and wish for clouds under my feet someday.

"And I never will...all praise to The Creator, the true and only Creator."

He chuckles softly.

"You got that right," he replies as he places a caring hand on my shoulder and turns me to greet him, "there is one other thing you should know about."

His demeanor becomes serious and gives me a fit of worry. He reaches inside his robes and retrieves a piece of paper and I can see the written words visible through the backside of it. He passes it to me and I unfold it quickly to the sight of familiar handwriting. I gasp as I read phantom words.

We love you, Babe. We're proud of you.

"Oh God..."

My world is spinning from the sight in front of me, my fingers tracing the small letters and knowing all to well the hand that created them. I feel sick as guilt washes over me.

"Am I a bad person, Robert? I haven't thought about her in so long...Does that make me a terrible Husband? I've been concentrating on Sasha...our new happiness...that I haven't had a single thought about my wife...Where did you get this?"

The armor. He went to The Realm.

"When we left you fighting The Cursed...I took them to The Realm."

"You saw my wife?" I inquire while gripping his shoulders with new energy. "What did she say? Is she okay?...Did she talk to Sasha?"

My heart stands frozen at the thought of them sharing a conversation.

"She's fine, Cuz, and so is your son. We didn't get the chance to talk. She left us a chest full of the armor that everyone's wearing, with the help of a few Servants. We caught a glimpse of them from a distance, but never got to speak...We were in a hurry, so to speak."

"Why?" I ask. My mind can't conjure any other words.

"We weren't invited...We snuck in to get the armor...I thought we would need it to rescue you."

"My wife..." my voice trails off. Her green eyes invade my memory. I can't seem to remove the blanket of Hellfire that now sits across my back and shoulders. I feel lost tears falling from my eyes. I bring the note back up to my face and clear my vision to stare at her words once again.

"Did Sasha see this note?"

"No. I took it and placed it in my robes immediately. They were all fixated on the armor so they didn't really pay attention."

"What do I do with it?" I ask as I fumble with it in my hand. My nerves have me shaking as in my old life.

"Whatever you want to do with it," Robert replies.

"It's going to sound strange," I begin, "but I want to keep it...but I know I shouldn't...Sasha would never understand...She would see it as a betrayal."

"Then get rid of it. No point in upsetting her, Cuz. Burn it into your memory and then get rid of it...if that's how you think she'll feel."

I look at the note in my hands and read my wives' words silently as her handwriting is unmistakable. I feel her touch on the page, a soft, caring energy that she radiated with anytime we shared an embrace. It feels like a long lost drug re-entering my veins. I shudder as I realize I have to let go of my mortal life and embrace my new wife in my afterlife, as Sasha was given to me when my wife was taken. The note I hold gives me a glimpse of a past that I would of killed for at one time, but no longer. I need to focus on Sasha and keep from hurting her in any way. It wouldn't be fair to keep this letter, no matter how much my heart tells me to do so. I allow my green fire to return to my hand and remove all lingering doubt with the caress of my flames. The note burns to ash in my fingers.

"I'll always love my wife, you know that, Robert...but I don't ever want to upset Sasha, ever again. It almost killed her, to not be at my side...She's my soul now...I know she is...When she was scratched by the Cursed when I was on my way to you guys...the cuts opened up on my flesh...We stand as one in this life...She really is my soul."

He nods his head slowly in agreement, "don't feel guilty, Cuz. You're a good man and were a good husband to her...in a life you no longer live. You're right about you and Sasha. If she suffers a wound in battle...you will feel it. Same as with her heart. You stand as one...that's all that should matter anymore. Love your wife...but don't forget who stands a part of your eternal soul now."

I blow the ashes from my fingertips.

"I know who holds my heart in this life...it's okay for me to let go of my past life...I'll always love my wife and son...but I need to focus on my eternity with Sasha...I hope the Creator forgives me if that's wrong."

I bow my head and take a shaky breath. I cast off the sadness that was pasted on and return myself to the lively Fallen One that everyone was expecting to see return. I must push it from mind, the thoughts of my lovely wife, and remember my new wife, the lovely Sasha. She earned her place at my side. I can't cling to the ghost of an Angel from another time. She doesn't exist anymore, only in my memory. To hold on to the apparition of her would only invite madness.

"You're not wrong for loving Sasha *and* loving your wife. You're blessed, Cuz, to know true love in two lifetimes. Cheer up," he says as he smacks my arm, "now let's go inside and finish the party. Gregs probably smashed right now," he confesses as his eyes become wide, "that kid can smoke!"

We both laugh quietly in agreement as I nod my head and stand a bit surprised at his sudden dropping of the guard.

"And before the night's over he'll probably have Amy K. just as smashed as he is," I reply and sigh deeply, "they're all gonna live like wild animals tonight...They won't have the strength to get through tomorrow."

I meet his eyes quickly with the fear-streaked eyes only a family man can possess.

"Maybe this wasn't such a good idea."

"No, Cuz," he begins with a smile and places his hand on my shoulder, "it was a great idea."

Laughter cuts the night air once more as we exchange a playful gesture, me slapping his hand away and him retaliating with a swat of his own.

"They're gonna drag their assess tomorrow...I'll just have to fight twice as hard," I conclude. It would be the only way to ensure their safety.

"I got something for them, Cuz," he assures, "so don't worry...just think of it as a Supercharged cup of coffee...I'll take care of them before we begin our journey."

I smile wide, showing all my toothy grin.

"The journeys already begun...let's go inside and continue walking the path. It just so happens to cut through a dance floor and I want to dance the night away with Sasha, as she wanted to do on our wedding night. I don't want to keep her waiting...and the night won't last forever."

"Right on, Cuz."

I stop our steps as quickly as they begin and place my hand out for him to freeze. He stands as a mannequin.

"One last thing...What do you think of my family?"

He chuckles softly, "Well...as strange as it sounds...you fit right in. You all fit together, even the Stoner kid."

We both share a loud laugh before he continues.

"They're all good people, Cousin. The Creator must have thought so too if he left them here to continue the fight. He chose wisely, as He always does. They're good people...they're worth fighting for," he says and places his giant hand on my shoulder again.

"You got that right, Robert."

****

"Joe! Let's fucking party, Bro!"

Stumbling forward, he almost burns me with his lighted delight, a pungent blend of fruit and Pine trees. Robert and I barely make it past the door as Greg and Amy K. cut us short from rejoining the group, now lively and full of energy and dancing as if it's their last night among the living.

It might be.

Greg reaches forward and tries to place the cigar in my mouth.

"Greg, Little Brother, I'd like to, but it's not for me. Sorry, Bro."

His face crinkles as he pretends to look annoyed and his eyes disappear even further into his face.

"Nah, shit, don't stress. More for me! Haahaaa!"

He drags on the end of the cigar before passing to Amy K. and placing his arm around her waist. She giggles bashfully and returns the gesture as we lock eyes.

"Amy K....something you and Greg want to talk about?" I allow my small, mischievous smile to magically appear as hers grows along with it.

"Well, we decided that we're going to be a couple now...We're together," she finishes as her eyes brighten up like the sun. I step forward into both of them and embrace them softly.

"Find whatever love you can in this world, while you can," I whisper just over the music, "and don't let it go...at any cost."

Greg laughs loudly to the air as he pushes me back a step and meets my gaze with a Jesters mask.

"Bro, we're not getting married. We're just gonna hang out and see how it goes."

My eyes fall from my face as my jaw tries to win the race against them.

"You really telling me you have no love for this

woman?"

He looks at me and then at Amy K., before repeating the process. It's as if his mind is trying to figure out who I'm speaking of.

"Well...of course I love her...she's my friend, and more...okay, you know what?" He questions as he turns to Amy K., "you know how I feel. Let's not take advice from the worst example of a couple we've ever met. HAHAAA!"

He turns to me in time to see Sasha walking past me to swat his skinny arm in a joking fashion, while his giggle is an admission of his jest.

"I'm just kidding, Sasha. If Amy and I find half the love you guys found, we'll consider ourselves lucky."

"And if you don't" Sasha begins as she smiles at Amy K., "I'll let you borrow my sword when you're ready to flip out and kill him."

We all laugh pleasantly as Sasha takes a shot at herself, something she'd never done before. She's always so dismissive of the subject of her trying to end my life so long ago. If she can joke about it, it must not bother her as much anymore and is a needed change. I've grown tired of forgiving her suffering over a past that cannot be altered.

"I may take you up on that, Sasha," Amy K. admits. Greg allows his bulging eyes to fall to hers.

"What? Bro! I mean, Babe! What the Hell did I do?"

"Ummm....she's my friend *and more*? You can't call me

your girlfriend?"

I bark a sharp laugh as I look at Gregs confused face. He meets my eyes as I laugh and nod my head.

"Good luck, Greg."

Sasha retrieves her sword and holds it out to Amy.

"Here you go, Amy."

We laugh together as Sasha sheathes her sword and we walk away from the about-to-be dueling duo. I squeeze her hand tight as we make our way over to John and Amy J., now engaged in a deep conversation while they dance the night away.

"We're not even going to bother you guys...Just need a piece of the dance floor, Sir."

John nods his head to me and continues looking into Amy J.s eyes, while their slow dance is about to be imitated by The Fallen One and his Eternal Love. I take Sashas' hand in mine and place it on my shoulder. I place my hands on her waist and pull her close and we begin to sway to the music. Her eyes shine brighter than the sky, the blue in them seemingly alive and moving. She appears as a true Angel, one that would forever stand at my side. She reminds me in this moment that The Creator gave her to me.

She's really mine.

"That's right," she agrees, hearing my thoughts, "I'm yours, Baby."

"You are, My Love...and I want you to always be...Marry me. Right now."

I feel her shudder from surprise as she pushes me back to look deeper into my eyes. She sees a fierce beast born from her heart that yearns to devour her love.

"What's gotten into you?"

I place my hands on her slender face as her eyes threaten to burst with tears.

"*Your love* has gotten into me. Sasha...I was married to the only woman I loved in my old life. She was my everything...in another life. I share this life with you...I want to marry you...I want you to be my wife...Will you do me the honor?...Will you marry me?"

"Oh my God," she begins, her voice visibly shaken, "of course I'll fucking marry you. It's all I ever wanted...but not tonight. Tonight is about them...Let it be about them...Tomorrow, after we win our war...I'll marry you, Baby...Oh God, I love you so fucking much."

She lunges into my arms and is forever now My Loving Queen. My dead heart bursts with happiness as we begin to cry together. I feel truly happy in this life, as I stood in my old one with my wife beside me. The Creator blessed me with her when I was yet living. He blesses me now with Sasha. We find each others face and begin to lock lips for the first time as an engaged couple. This New World can't stand a completely terrible place when even The Fallen One can find love.

The world goes on around us, and without us, as our loving feet never pausing from the dance we sway to for the

369

rest of the night. We whisper to each other about the next part of our lives as husband and wife and plan for the eternal life ahead. The hours pass as the stars spin overhead, with time stopping for us to indulge in our gifts of each others hearts. We dance until the morning. Not once do we break our loving embrace...as it should be for a future husband and wife who want nothing else but to love each other.

****

"What time is it?"

Danny asks no one in particular as he pulls himself up from behind the Bar. Everyone lies motionless at random spots throughout our Dance Hall, the result of falling where they may. Greg and Amy K. sleep in a reclining sofa at the Pot Café while John and Amy J. share the floor beside them. Carmen and Will found use of the bed I created for Robert, which left Robert on a chair at the Dining room table, nose deep into my book. He never put it down, only taking breaks to wipe imaginary sweat from his brow. The sunlight cascades through the window onto the dance floor as Sasha and I finally pause our dancing feet.

"It's morning time...so sayeth King Salami," I inform him and chuckle. He smirks and then grabs his head, the result of his attempt to drink an endless supply of beer. Groaning like an old tree in a storm, he finishes rising to his seat and tries to cast off the hangover by grabbing his beer. He takes a long swig before addressing me.

"Damn...I feel like shit...I hope we don't have to fight today...I'll just choose to lay down and fucking die."

370

Sasha and I burst out laughing, causing everyone to stir from their slumber. A series of moans and groans litter the air before snoring overtakes the silence yet again. Danny continues to drink like a fish as we take a seat at the bar.

"You'll be fine, Danny...How have you been, Brother? We haven't had a chance to really catch up yet."

He stirs a bit and squints his eyes as he addresses me.

"I've been okay, man," he clears his throat, "I'm not gonna lie to you. I've been stressed over all this end-of-time bullshit...I know you have work for us to do."

"There *is* work to be done, but right now...We have to focus on the war coming for us all."

"Shit," he begins, "that sounds like a lot of fucking work *before* the work...I'm tired, Joe...I'm

tired of this life."

"Danny," Sasha joins in, "your life hasn't even begun yet. When the war is over, people are going to need to know what went down here...You're a big part of it...You're a part of the *worlds history*."

"Again...that sounds like work," he says and chuckles through his crooked smile. He pauses to grasp his throbbing head once again. I seize the moment to speak.

"Danny, when it's all said and done, everyone on Earth will know your name. They'll know you stood with The Fallen One in both lives...When I was a man...and when I became The Fallen One. You are my brother and I love you. I wouldn't count

371

on anyone else to handle the workload to come, Bro. You guys," I say and point around the room, "are the ones who will spread the word and save Mankind. I'll save the world from being destroyed...You guys will save it by rebuilding it."

"So...much...work..."

We all share a quiet laugh as he continues his bitching. He pauses in his nagging to extend his hand to me, and I accept it.

"I'll be ready, Joe. I know I complain a lot...but, the truth is that I'm ready for something new. But...I already miss our home, man. When it's all said and done, I think I want to go home. I'll put in my work...but, after that, I'm going home and putting on my sweats and drinking some fucking beer."

"I won't argue with that, Danny," I say and release his hand, "and you will have earned it by then...like you said...so...much...work...but you'll have an army beside you, helping in the war."

His eyes shoot open as my words catch his attention.

"An army?"

"Yes...an army. I have Servants in The Abyss training a small army to help defeat the Necromancer and his new...creations."

He sits most intrigued at the thought of standing alongside me at the head of an army.

"How many?"

"The final tally was two hundred and fifty thousand. It's not as many as we'll need...but it's a damned good start."

"Son of a bitch! Fuck yeah...that's good news," he says and returns to his brew. He sets it down and continues on with a renewed energy.

"Are they the ones who reached from the fires and grabbed The Cursed in the store?" He asks with his eyes wide and full of questions.

"Yes Sir, the same. I can summon them anytime I need to...but I didn't know I was allowed to call upon them."

"Are they people?...Or something else?" He asks. I don't know why, but it feels insulting to hear

the lost souls to be thought of as anything less than people.

"They're people, Danny, just like you and me. Most of them were there when I took over. They suffered under the old ruler, so when I came aboard, they didn't know what it was to be treated with compassion. They're just people, but they fight for The Creator, and for me."

"Man, that must be so awesome, commanding people to do what you want."

"Not once," Sasha rejoins the conversation, "have I ever heard Joe command someone to do something. They do it because *they want* to do it. Joe made a big fucking difference. The people there love him."

"Done!" Roberts screams from the table as he shuts the book and stands wiping tears from his face. He does his best to compose himself before turning to us.

"Cuz...absolutely amazing...You should of did this in your old life, write books."

I meet his soft eyes from across the room.

"I always wanted to write a book in the Old World. It just wasn't in His plans...I guess I didn't have anything to write about, until now."

"True," he says nodding his head.

"It's a shame," Sasha begins, "that so many people in the Old World never got to experience your words, Baby."

Robert sets his smiling eyes upon her.

"The Creator saved them for the New World...to save the world."

"My book alone isn't going to be enough," I add as I draw my sword, "and we've got a long ass day ahead of us...we need to get started," I set my hardened gaze on his, "today's the day?"

He nods slowly, "Today is the day...The army of The Abyss will walk the Earth."

****

"Holy fuck...Got anymore of this shit?"

We stand laughing as Danny and Robert stand with hands joined and Robert passes the light from his palms to Dannys. Robert made his rounds, filling everyone with light and delivering the Supercharged cup of coffee he promised. The dance floor is now sleeping in the comforts of the sunlight as we all dress in our attire for war.

"Wow, I feel amazing!" Amy K. squeals, "I mean really, I feel like I could run a marathon right now. If *only* there was a marathon open somewhere...I'd find it and run in it. I bet I could win. I don't think anyone could beat me in anything right now. Does anyone want to Arm Wrestle?"

We all begin laughing at her and her newfound energy. She hops in place as a Prize Fighter would and pops a couple of jabs at Gregs' face. He leans back to avoid the tiny fists now directed at his face.

"Bro! Babe, I mean. Calm down!"

She giggles before jumping forward and planting a kiss on his lips. He catches her and shares a moment with his new girl, kissing her bashfully and pausing only to smile. Will stands up fully dressed in his golden armor and it matches his golden mane. He appears as a Greek god of Mythology.

"I feel...like...Superman."

We laugh again as he stands taller than usual with his eyes and face firm and ready to deal justice. Carmen approaches him while chuckling at her giant lover.

"Well, you look like a Superman, Babe. Today you're

gonna fight like a Superman and tonight you're gonna...you know...the other "F" word, like a Superman."

His blue eyes become giant saucers as the excitement shoots from them.

"FLY?!"

She slaps her head as we all begin laughing.

"Yes, Will, you're going to fly...Un-fucking-believable."

"I'm kidding, Babe, I'm not *that* stupid," he says as we all laugh at him. Robert finishes up with Danny and shrugs his shoulders and flexes his wings. He turns to me, now completely clad in my dark armor, as my Black Steel shines against the white Moon on my breastplate.

"Now," Robert says with conviction, "we're ready for war. Let's find a suitable place for you to summon your army."

I feel the adrenaline of the afterlife course through me as I grab Sashas hand and flex my own wings. I shoot out a sharp breath to match my ever sharpening green eyes. My soul begins to burn inside me and sends a rising sensation racing throughout my body. I'm ready for the flesh of The Cursed, but still have worry in my heart for the Innocent.

"Before we do...how do we spare the ones that stood as Sam? When I summoned the lost souls from The Abyss in the store, I instructed them to take some captive. Not all of them wanted to be Cursed. There has to be some way that we can spare the Innocents he's forcing to fight for him."

His lips become a tight line of disappointment as he

shakes his head in disagreement.

"There's no one way, other than to ask every one of them before you kill them...I'm sorry, Cuz."

The memory of Ralphs' cries won't allow me to accept the answer.

"There has to be a way...I killed a Cursed that attacked me and Sam back in the Shower Shack. Sam knew him before they were changed. Sam talked to him before he attacked us and he remembered his old life. He remembered his family. He didn't want to die as a soulless monster. I changed him into a Servant the moment he passed from this life...His name was Ralph."

"Honestly...I don't have a simple answer for you, Cousin. There is no way of knowing who was willing and who was forced...If we take their lives, they are reborn as Cursed again. The only way you could ever truly help them is to kill the monster that gives birth to them...When he falls, the cycle is over. The remaining we can capture and interrogate to find out who was forced against their will...It's the only way I can think of."

"Sam told me that, to be a Cursed born from the Necromancer is to live in agony. He said it hurts to be a Cursed....a hundred thousand souls are suffering under him right now...Not all of them chose that misery...I just want to end their suffering."

Sasha wraps her arms around me to offer a measure of comfort while my saddened soul accepts the truth for what it is.

Innocents will die, as they have in every war since the beginning of time.

"Sorry, Cuz...The battle should be over quickly. We outnumber them two and a half to one, with your army alone. The Creator is sending his own army to fight alongside us. We should outnumber them about five to one when the time comes...We can take as many alive as possible when we begin our assault."

Nodding my head, I accept the gravity of the situation and address everyone with caution in my voice.

"When the battle begins, you all stay together and keep each other safe...I'm going after the Necromancer...The quicker I kill him, the faster the war will end," I say and meet Sashas lovely blue eyes, "you stay by my side, no matter what, My Love."

"To the fucking end," she finishes as he eyes morph into sharpened blue almonds. Her brow turns to the Sasha of old as her hate forces her lovely mask into a frightening war paint. She stands, once again, as the Most Beautiful Psycho ever; A creature now born only when she feels her loving, eternal husband is threatened.

I gaze upon her and feel the love through all the hate. Her eyes become soft at the sight of mine and the war paint washes off for a tender moment for me to savor the beauty I fell in love with so long ago. We smile at each other as she unsheathes her sword in the instant I release mine, bringing it up to meet my blade with a clash of steel that rings as loud as our love. We both giggle as I set my eyes upon the group.

"Today...don't forget about your weapons...Don't forget about the light."

378

Nodding slowly, they all agree as their hands trace the phantom track to their blades. They feel them in their palms without thinking, as doing so has become a reflex as involuntary as blinking. I turn and lead them to the door and hear their soft steps at my back. It's the only sound that breaks the silence as I silently pray that I'm not leading them to their doom.

If there's real luck in the world, please let it be with us today.

* *

"This is it? This is where you're going to summon the most terrifying army to ever walk the Earth? C'mon Joe! Have some imagination, man," Danny says and laughs to himself as we all stand on the large corpse of an old cornfield.

"This will have to do...There isn't a lot of time left...I can feel the hate just a few miles over those hills," I say and point off to the giant mounds of soil lining the horizon a mile away.

"Fucking Children of the Corn, man," Danny jokes and laughs again. We chuckle along with him.

"Let's meet my people...Let's meet the army of The Abyss."

I take a few steps away from the group and stare out into the field while the wind catches my hair and flings it wildly about. It reminds me of a time so long ago, before The Days of Ruin, when I would dance and sing in the streets and be as

379

carefree as the wind itself. I feel the stirring of an old energy that feels like the adrenaline that only comes from stepping into a Boxing ring.

It's time to come out fighting...or go down swinging. My Creator, if you can hear me...send whatever help you can this way. We're ready...We won't fail you.

Raising my hands to the sky, I present the fires of The Abyss. My emerald flames dance from my palms as the wind begins to increase its stride while the clouds forming overhead become as dark and cruel in nature as The Evil One who preceded me. I see the path from The Realm beginning to reveal itself while the ground becomes alive underneath me. The two Realms are about to meet for the first time in any existence, and will do so for the sake of the New World.

The sky tears open and reveals a brilliant beam of eternal light as the Earth quakes from within. Servants fall from the sky like beautiful Spring Rain and float along the lighted paths. The Servants of The Abyss sprout from the Earth in the same manner as fresh, green grass while wearing a dark armor that matches my own. The sight of two hundred and fifty thousand Lost Souls of The Abyss rising up and standing alongside two hundred and fifty thousand Servants falling in place is a miracle witnessed by only seven mortals. They meet in the middle, a common ground, and unite for one purpose; The greater good. Servant feathers line our sight as Servant and Fallen Souls stand as a mixture of united terror, and it's the first army to consist of souls from both Realms. We all watch as the last remaining souls sprout and the last flocks of wings touch the ground. I let them gather themselves for a moment while I listen to the whispers of my family behind me.

"Baby...," her voice whispers softly in my head.

"Yes, My Love?"

"You look so fucking hot right now."

I laugh loudly as I turn and meet her smiling face and find her laughing along with me while giving me an approving thumbs-up. My family stands as confused as the New World army that mirrors their minds, watching these two smiling fools forgetting that Armageddon has come for them.

"Thank you, Sasha...but not now, My Love."

"I know I know," her mind speaks as she rolls her eyes, *"I'm Joe and I always have to be serious, blah blah blah..."*

The laughter shoots from me as I walk over to her slowly while her body sways from the anticipation of meeting my loving hands once again. I meet her blue gaze with my loving eyes and place my hands on her waist and lift her slowly to the Heavens while our smiles seem to be engraved upon our faces. She laughs loudly as I bring her face to mine and pause to whisper to her with the loving confessions she years for upon my breath.

"Here we stand...The end of the world...A loving Dead Man...His loving Girl...The world around...so dead and cruel...but I only see you...My Shining Jewel...If tomorrows Sun...never arrives...it'll be because...I destroyed the skies...and I did it for you...and for our beautiful life...my loving Sasha," I chuckle softly and kiss her lips quickly, "soon to be my wife."

Slowly, we fall into each other as I hold her against me and enjoy her lips. We forget about the end of Mankind, the army , our family, and our lives. We only exist in this moment to enjoy the lips we starve for with endless cravings. I hear her

381

beautiful voice sigh softly and feel her body relax in my arms. She could stay with me in this moment forever and I stand as one with her in such regards. I wish I could conjure some magic and somehow pause this moment and live in it for an eternity. Our smiling faces greet one another as we pull away from our bliss.

"Tonight, Sasha...Marry me, tonight."

Her blue eyes become crescents moons as the love bursts from her.

"Baby...I'll marry you tonight...and every night after that, for all of eternity...After all, Sasho loves you."

Laughing to ourselves, I place a hand on her backside and deliver a firm, yet teasing pat.

"You're never gonna let me forget about that, are you?" I ask before she smiles and shakes her head.

"Well, don't start with that shit right now," I say while giggling, "and I love you too, Sasha," I remind her as I set her to her feet. I hold my closed hand out to her and let my fist ignite in my flames for a brief moment. It ends quickly, yet I pause in opening my hand. Through my little show, her gaze never leaves my eyes. She knows full well what it is I'm doing in this moment. I open my hand to reveal a golden ring, confirming what she was hoping for. The blue diamond matches her eyes but glows only half as bright as her Angelic eyes now stand. She gazes at it for several long seconds before retrieving it from my palm and her eyes threaten to burst with tears as she slowly places it on her finger. She rips her gaze away, but only to find my face and kiss me with the passion that keeps me alive. I feel myself falling from the world of horror and into the world of her love, and it's a place I wish I could remain forever. I really could have, if not for the now five hundred thousand sets of eyes watching in confusion. I pull myself away from her and smile wide.

"It's time."

She strokes my face with her silky palm.

"Get this over with so we can get fucking married already."

I laugh quietly under my breath.

"As you wish, My Queen."

We break our gaze as we're met by two sets of new eyes, but only one stands familiar. A paleskinned Servant with golden hair and fierce, golden eyes approaches and is accompanied by a general from The Abyss. It's my own personal General who stood by Sasha so many times as I gave lost souls their wings. I meet the eyes of the Servant.

"You lead the forces of The Realm in this battle?" I ask with my eyes as much as my words.

"I do, but I lead under you."

"And I follow The Creator, as I know my General does," I reply and turn to the steel clad warrior beside him.

"It's good to see you again, Gage."

"Likewise, Sir. The Abyss has missed you...We're ready,

Sir."

"Good...I'll need you both to lead your forces...I'll take care of the Necromancer." Turning to the army in front of me, I take a slow bow and watch as a sea of faces all do the same, Servants and Fallen souls alike. My family mimics our actions behind me.

"MAY THE WRATH OF THE CREATOR BE WITH YOU TODAY!!!" My voice thunders.

"AND ALSO WITH YOU!!!"

Their voices echo my praises to the one and only Creator.

"Today...The Realm has fallen to the Earth...The Abyss has risen from the ashes...for a single purpose...to honor and protect all that was created!"

The cheers are deafening while the sounds of war drums begin to beat in the distance and warn of the approaching death and destruction. I won't have a lot of time to address the souls I now command. I raise my hands and demand their silence.

"The fool, know only as the Necromancer, has raised an army...We've met these Cursed...They are faster than you...More deadly than you...He crafted his monsters well...but the one thing he could never teach them...We have in abundance...And that is the strength of The Creator...it's through His grace that we will be victorious today...it's through Him, we become his vengeful hands...AND WE WILL SHOW THESE UNHOLY MOTHERFUCKERS THAT YOU CAN'T STAND AGAINST ALL THAT WE HAVE BECOME!!!"

****

The crowd screams around him as he does his best to look over the shoulders of so many of The Abyss' Lost Souls and The Realms Servants. He does his best to remain hidden, as his face stands just a little too familiar. He watches as Joe preaches on about the end of Mankind and how we all stand now to save it. He watches in awe as the sight of Joe commanding the army inspires him, making him ready to carve the flesh of The Cursed. He would share this battle with Joe...and do everything he can to make sure that Joe doesn't see his face. The consequences of his actions could influence the outcome of the war. The Creator, along with his mother, would never forgive him for sneaking out the backdoor of The Realm. He cannot let anyone see him...as he shares the face of The Fallen One. The screams around him become deafening and the sight of his father upon the hill with his sword in his hand is a sight he won't soon forget. He'll carry it for a thousand years, this image of his father standing as a Warrior Chief and commanding an army for The Creator. He's truly proud of his father in this moment...and does his best to hide his smile.

****

Thunder shakes the ground and fills the air all at once as hands raise with bladed weapons in a sea of wings and steel as far as my eternal eyes can see. They scream for the war to begin as Servants and Fallen Souls unite in the chants of victory. It stands a sight that not even The Creator could behold as so many of his warriors are ready to conquer evil in His name.

I turn to my family and find them equally starved for blood and death. I open my arms to them and invite them for our final embrace as a family before we all charge off to war. They come forward and we share the embrace we created when I first returned to the New World with my new wings. We murmur softly to each other our well wishes and Danny makes sure to add a few blessing for King Salami, reminding me I still have a score to settle with him for the awful name he conjured so long ago. We share a quiet laugh and a fleeting moment of love. I'm sure to address each one and remind them that I stand as a loving, Fallen one who would forever love his family. The sentiments are shared all around. I release them all and turn to find the nightmares now in view.

The hills swarm with The Cursed and appear as a massive army of Ants on an Anthill. The mile between us would shorten soon enough when they take flight. They march and beat their drums while hissing a song of sinister lyrics as the chants of eating Fallen flesh and Fallen Souls travel across the plain to our Cornfield. I set my attention back on my new army as they wait for my commands.

"Servants!...Tame the skies! They prefer to deliver death from above! Souls of The Abyss!...The ground is yours! Be aware of them raining death upon you!"

I draw my sword and raise it to the darkened skies and command its fire forth.

"Keep them busy while I find the Necromancer...I promised him a long time ago...THAT I WAS COMING TO FUCK HIM UP!!!"

Screams of approval meet my promise. I begin walking towards our enemy and feel my family close behind as Sasha falls to my side and the army follows on cue. The vision in front of me dares to scare The Fallen One himself, and would, if not for the seven souls who march behind me. They make their way quickly beside me as the army of New World Cursed begin their screams of war.

They're not afraid...They're ready.

I glance to my right and see Greg on the end of the line shuffling headphones into his ears. It stops me in my tracks and the entire army pauses behind us.

"Greg, what the Hell are you doing?" He glances at me as he pops the ear pieces out of his ears.

"Music, Bro. When I would train when you were gone, I always played my jams to pump me up. I'd get fucking high and beat some shit up. Hahaa!"

I smirk at my Little Brother doing the very thing I would do in the Old World. Sasha and I carried over the music of a lost time into the New World, down into the very depths of The Abyss. She sang so many songs from the Old World and her voice was always filling the halls of our unholy home. Music always soothed my soul, as it does Gregs now, because he still stands as I used to stand; A living man.

Even Dead men love a good tune.

"What are you listening to?" I ask.

"I found this Ipod a while back," he begins as he makes his way to me, "and it's loaded with rock and roll. Good shit, Bro, every track. I'm a little nervous, so I thought I'd pump myself up a bit...Is that alright?"

387

"Yeah, that's fine," I say and pause while my eyes betray my mind as I daydream of another time.

"Are you sure?" He questions, snapping me back to reality.

"Yeah, it's all good, Little Brother...Mind if I join you?"

He stands with questioning eyes, as do the rest of my family. I glance down the line in both directions and see their faces resting on tilting heads. Sasha smiles at me and winks one of her radiant blue gems.

"How?...You have an Ipod?"

"I'll make one," I inform him and snatch away his little music box.

"I'll take one," Danny requests.

"Me too. I think it would make it easier if I didn't have to hear all those monsters screaming on the end of my sword," Amy K. adds.

I look at everyone else and see they wish to make the same request. Even Robert looks intrigued.

"Let's all listen to some music while we work," I reply to all as I step back and wrap my wings around me.

I let the energy surge quickly, as time is running out, and open my wings while nine replicas of Gregs' portable Jukebox drop all around me. I raise my hands and levitate them all as everyone comes forward to take their pick. I hand Greg back his with a smile on my face as the Ipods are rounded up.

"They're all exactly alike...Pick a track...It's your call."

He smiles slowly and thinks about his choice for the briefest of moments.

"Track thirteen...That's my jam."

Thirteen was my lucky number in the Old World.

"When the time comes, I'll cue the music on everyones...Track thirteen."

"Hell yeah, Bro," he says as he returns the ear pieces to their rightful place, "track thirteen."

They all mimic their brother as my family readies their ear pieces and conceal the tiny electronics underneath their armor. Sasha and I do the same before sharing a small kiss. She returns to my side, as do the rest of them before Robert approaches me while placing his own buds in place.

"This is it, Cuz...The day we talked about when we were living...finally becoming Gothic Super Heroes."

We chuckle to ourselves and embrace for a hug as his giant hands pat the top of my shoulders while I do the same.

"I'm ready, Cuz," I answer him, "and I've been waiting for this day...Let's kick some ass."

We smile at each other as we shake hands while his dark Cowboy hat, the only relic from his old life, is now hiding his kind eyes underneath it. We nod to each other as he releases my hand and retakes his position. I look forward to an ocean of horror that's ready to break upon our shores.

The Cursed are shortening their distance with every step and causing the ground to shake with the march they make towards their awaiting doom. Drawing my sword once again, I raise it into the air and begin our own march.

The sounds of feet marching in unison on both fronts is maddening, while the air is alive with only its' song and filled with electricity. We march towards the sea of a hundred thousand balding heads and leathery wings, with their hissing curses becoming audible as they taunt us with our deaths. I feel my legs begin to speed up into a slow jog towards the awaiting fate that not even The Creator knows.

This one's for the World.

Chapter 8

Like Warhorses, we pick up our stride. The wave of death ahead of us stands ready to greet us as their own feet begin to quicken. They cover the entire mile between us and the hill which they still pour over, a legion of angry ants coming to devour an unholy Fallen and his tribe of Servants and Lost Souls. I begin to push my steps harder and the rumble behind us reminds me we're not alone. The threats of The Creators' vengeance rises up behind me as they ready their voices and souls for war.

Less than a quarter mile to go, the need for dying Cursed overwhelms us. We push forward to the chaos. I feel them all next to me doing the same, now every sword we possess raised to the sky in a toast to Cursed flesh. Quietly, my family and I charge forward. The distance shrinks with the tides of the armies about to crash into their destiny.

Almost there.

The Cursed scream as they charge in full sprint with only a hundred yards left between us as a horde of them take to the skies while a legion of the unnaturally tall Reapers lead the rest. They hold their banners high with the vision of a man in the stars, representing the new king they wish could rule. We break out into our own charge, running forward with our blades beginning to come to life and shining the Holy light upon the unholy. Our Servants begin to fill the sky above us as there's only feet left between us.

Cue the music.

Electric guitars scream through my world as Mudvaynes "Not Falling" track illuminates the world around me. We push hard now, all of us on cue, as the lead singer begins to scream as we begin our own cries of war. The music fits accordingly as I growl and spin my body full circle, bringing my sword up and slashing the first Reaper to greet us and sending his long, slender body into the air in two pieces.

The war is on.

The cries of all paint the day as the sounds of clashing steel and cleaved flesh become alive in an instant. Throwing my free hand before me, I send my green wave of fiery death forward and set ablaze the first fifty in front of me. They claw their skin as my family presses forward and slashes with light bearing blades and ends their suffering with Sasha leading their charge. The singer screams about seeing demons, as we all do now in the New World.

Greg picked a good song.

Charging forward with a new lust for blood, I scream as I swing my blade at the monster in front of me. He reaches up to shield himself from my steel, only to find his hands severed along with his head. I deliver a straight kick and send his body as a bowling ball, the force creating a line of fallen Cursed into the heart of their army. I hear a familiar voice in my head, next to the blaring music.

"Cuz! Find him! I'll protect your family!"

Glancing around, I spot Robert ahead of my family and now standing as a shield with his wings spread to funnel the death away from them, giving them a chance to deal with the monsters already holding their attention. He swings his sword from left to right and demolishes the flesh before him. He glances back and nods his head.

"Go Cuz! I got this!"

"Not without Sasha!"

"I hear you, Baby! I'm coming!"

I see her breaking away from my family and slashing the Cursed between us. I raise my hand and lift all in her path, as if they're merely stringed puppets, before swinging my arm and sending them crashing into their own air support. She runs to me quickly as I begin to dismantle the next monster to dare attack me. He swings his claw as I swing my sword, parting it from his wrist. He screams and grabs his wound with his free hand as I grab the forearm of his severed limb and drive it through his face. I turn in time for Sasha to jump into my awaiting arms.

"HOLD ON!"

Violently, my wings spread and send a wave of Abysmal emerald fire out to scorch those around us. Thrusting hard, we rocket into the air as I slash through the river of Cursed that fly above us while cutting them down with a fiery blade. The ground under us shrinks as I make my way into the clouds and above the air battle to see the skies under us alive with the battle between The Realms' Hawks and the Vultures of the New World. Sasha squeezes me harder as she finds my eyes lost in the clouds.

"What are we doing up here?!"

"Learning from my mistakes. His actions in the past have taught me well. He's not on the ground, Sasha. He's being a fucking coward and hiding in the clouds. I'm sure of it."

393

Removing my headphones, I continue searching the clouds for as far as I can see. I need all my senses, as I caution myself not to underestimate him.

"Baby, they follow our energy. Isn't there some way you can follow his?" She asks as she removes her own.

I glance at her and see her eyes pleading for drastic measures. I nod to her and close my eyes for a brief moment and remember the energy he emitted the night he leapt from the sky with his Fishnet of Death. I open my eyes to a world full of vibrant colors as streaks of blues and reds litter the New World underneath us. Only one energy doesn't blend in with the rest.

The dark one. The black trail...The one leading to the clouds.
"Gotcha bitch."

"Get him, Baby."

She draws my attention and my eyes greet a brilliant, white glow around her face, and I realize I'm looking at the very scent of her soul that the Old World Damned would follow. For the first time in my new existence, I can see her sweet soul, as well as smell it. If only I could savor the moment. Instead, I burn it into my memory. "Hold on, Sasha." Turning my body to the trail, I push madly with the wings of a War Eagle. My breath shoots from me as I cling to Sasha and begin a race through the clouds. The trail is spotty and resides in the clouds behind the advancing Cursed, a perfect hiding place for a coward. I beat the air with my wings and move ever closer to the trail that leads from the back of their army upwards towards the clouds. He knew I would find him as I figured he would, proving me correct as we greet the sight of twenty or more balding heads sitting on a small, overhanging cloud hidden amongst the tail

394

end of the darkened skies. The trail of dark energy ends within the small crowd.

"There he is, Baby!"

Long purple robes flutter behind the winged warriors he created as the figure wearing them paces quickly. He turns his eyes to the sky above and sees the harbinger of his doom. Shouting commands, he points to the Heavens where we now hover, and I feel my heart beating once again as a hammer against my ribs. I grasp Sasha tight and whisper to her.

"Stay close."

"Be safe, My Love," she replies, borrowing my words, "and let's go fuck him up," she concludes with her own.

The path is direct, and my wings begin screaming as we plunge towards the small cloud holding the coward who rules no one. I growl as a beast and hear Sasha screaming loud as we meet the few that took flight to meet us. I release my hold with one arm and throw my hand forward and watch as they all explode before us and send a shower of black blood and broken bones to the Earth. I drive myself down to the cloud and slam my feet hard upon its misty floor. I release Sasha as she spins from me and draws her sword. I join her deadly Ballet and unsheathe my own while releasing screams that are only half as sharp as our blades. She lunges forward and decapitates the first Cursed to greet us as I take the next one, driving my sword through his terrible face. Pulling my sword back, she finishes the job by taking her second crown in as many seconds. They charge forward and begin their maddening swipes as we meet them with calm slashes of our blades moving quickly and spilling the guts of the Reborn. I tear through them with ease as the figure in the back of the crowd paces even faster while the dark energy around him spikes and calms, along with his irrational thoughts. Sashas' voice cuts the air as she cuts limbs from our enemies while her petite frame becomes the largest presence among us, or so it seems as they all begin to turn from her. They're wise not to piss her off, instead choosing to fall back to protect the man in the purple robes who wishes to be a Ruler. Charging forward, a half dozen meet us in the middle with shrieks of horror, yet their voices are soon to be cut short. I charge ahead of Sasha and tear the closest three in half with a single swipe of my blade before I fall to one knee. She runs up the center of my back and leaps from my shoulders to bring her blade to rest on the crown of the next one. Her blade cuts through, all the way to the jaw, as I reach forward with both hands and seize the remaining two Cursed. I levitate them to the air above us and bring my hands together as they mimic my motions and collide with a sickening thud. They explode and send a wave of dark rain upon us as the remaining six huddle around their master. They pose and hiss as we stand covered in the blood of their brothers.

"I told you I would be coming to fuck you up."

Leaping from the edge of the cloud, he takes flight, yet it's the response I figured I would receive. His purple robes become a streak as he pushes his wings hard to escape from the doom I promised him. The remaining Cursed charge forward to slow our pursuit, but it's a task that they fail in miserably. I scream and unleash my flaming wave towards them and bathe them in the fire they fear so much. They scream and fall to their knees as I take Sasha in my arms.

"Hold on, My Love."

The pursuit continues as I lift off once again and chase after the dark energy trail left behind. I feel the urgency, a warning in my dead heart, to be wary of my foe. This doesn't seem right. It doesn't seem like something he would do.

He's never been...obvious.

"There! Baby! He's heading to the ground!"

He needs reinforcements.

I fall into a nosedive and press Sasha into me as our eternal hearts race as one while we speed to the Earth below. The dark trail fades even though he's in sight, as my senses begin failing me the slightest. It becomes a thing of little importance as I shorten the distance dramatically with a few hard pushes of my wings. He meets the ground, but he's only alone for the smallest of moments as I collide with the Earth behind him. The dust hangs in the air, creating a false cloud made of Earth. We quickly make our way through it to be greeted by the sight of the Necromancer taking flight once again with The Staff of Evil clutched in his hand.

"He was picking up his staff. He's leading us to a trap," I say and turn to her, "stay here. I have to go alone."

Her eyes become wide with disbelief.

"Fuck that! I told you I would be with you to the fucking end...I meant it...even if it's our eternal end."

"Sasha...*Please*."

She takes a hold of my waist and stares into my panicked eyes.

"You're fixing to be my husband...I love you, Joe. I don't want to live in any world without you...if you die...I want to die with you."

"I'll never die as long as you live, My Queen."

Roberts words haunt her as fresh as the day she heard him speak them.

"Protect me...and we'll both live."

"I will," I reply and accompany it with a kiss, "to the fucking end."

Wrapping my arms around her waist, I secure my hold and take flight once more. The ground rushes away from us as we move after our target again and find that the head start given to him is just a small, meaningless consolation prize. I can see remnants of the dark trail leading to another cloud, this one a great deal higher than all those around it. We sail upwards as a kite lost to the wind, as my wings thrust us higher still until we meet the cloud holding the purple robes. With his staff in hand, he directs it at Sashas loving heart.

"NOOOOO!"

Screaming wildly, I force the distance between us to become nonexistent. I spin my body at the moment of impact to shield My Love, crashing into him wings-first with the force of a meteor. I thrust Sasha to the clouded floor in the same instant to protect her from the Hell I'm fixing to unleash. Quickly, I flip my body over on his and pin his arms to the misty ground with a colossal force.

"Take a shot at me, bitch!"

I scream as I raise my right hand and slam it into his hooded face.

"But don't you *ever* take a shot at My Love!"

The ground and pound begins as my fists slam into his face with the force of Atom Bombs, driven by pure hate. I grab his robes with my left hand and bring his face up to meet my right fist, as the crunch of bones screams in the air. He falls to his back with the energy of a dead man, and his life begins fading fast. I will have answers from this cowardly pretender before I destroy his soul for all of eternity. Raspy and filled with blood, a small laughter escapes the coward I now sit upon.

Standing up, I grab the robes and lift him up with me, bringing his hooded face to mine. Sasha takes her place at my side and grabs the hood and slides it off the balding head to reveal the decoy we'd just spent valuable moments chasing after.

"Hissstory taught you well....Fool...but it didn't teach you everything...," he begins to giggle, "he knew you'd follow him...or his energy, to be more ssspecific...sssuch a Fool, indeed."

The energy trail was his residual energy...That's why it was fading.

Grunting madly, I slam him back into the clouds and hover over him as he chokes on the broken bones of his jaw.

"He spared himself, only for a moment. I will hold his severed fucking head before this war is over," I lean down close to his destroyed face as my voice becomes a stern whisper, "he lives for only a moment...Tell him that."

Reaching down, I grab his face and begin to squeeze. I feel his cheekbones begin to crack as he does his best to scream through the blood and pain. I growl loudly and allow my fingers to finish the job, his cheekbones imploding into the mess that is his face, as his body jerks and twitches while his dead nerves fire off for the final time. I release my hold and rise slowly before turning to Sasha with shame in my eyes.

"Son of a bitch," I say and meet her sad, blue eyes, "how could I be so blind?"

"It's okay, Baby...Look at the ground."

Taking her hand, I make my way over to the edge of the cloud and peer down at a war for the ages. The armies are one now, a mixture of Cursed and Fallen Souls and Servants all screaming for death. The hundred thousand we met in battle are little more than a few hundred as they crumbled in the face of a half a million of The Creators' warriors. I feel relief for a brief moment, cut short by words I wished never to hear.

"Cuz."

I turn to Sasha with panic in my voice.

"It's Robert."

She can see the doom I feel. She places her hands over her heart and shakes her head softly as my eyes blacken.

"Robert! What happened?"

Silence greets me for a short lifetime.

"Cuz...There's a problem...Wherever you are...come find us."

The world returns to me as I reach forward and take Sasha in my arms. She clings to me as I plunge off the cloud and head straight for the war about to conclude. We cut through the air quickly.

"Baby...what happened?"

I feel the tennis ball in my throat and swallow it hard as I voice our biggest fears.

"Someone from our family...has fallen."

****

Slamming with the force of a comet, the Earth takes to the air. The rubble flies in all directions as the thunderclap of my feet impacting the ground reverberates across the battlefield. Walking with Sasha from the dust, I'm greeted by a line of The Cursed on their knees and my army their captors. Two rows of them stretch forward for two hundred yards or more, held hostage by The Servants and Fallen Souls holding blood-streaked blades to their backs. They tie them up with strings of light that burn the flesh of the monsters. Peering all the way down, I see Robert and my family at the end of the columns. They stand with their backs to us, staring at the ground before them. We begin our long march to them.

Black eyes containing red coals greet us as we walk, as the captured Cursed stare at us as we pass. They see the Conquering King and hiss accordingly, seeing that it is not their own. They whisper to themselves as some even call to us, begging for a moment. There is no time for the words of a Cursed. Not until I know my family is safe.

"Mercccyyy...," he pleas to Sasha from his knees while flexing the broken bones protruding from his back, where his wings used to be.

"We'll think about it," she says without pausing as we continue walking.

I feel my stride picking up as they become more visible. I see the heads of everyone in my family but two. I turn to Sasha and find her staring at the ground.

"I can't look, Baby...I don't want to know."

The sadness stings my heart to see her wounded so. I see her soul calming within her, as the misery of loss comes back to haunt her yet again. I feel her emptiness, and it haunts me as well.

"I need you, Sasha...by my side...I won't survive without you...It doesn't matter who it is...I'm not ready...I need you."

She takes a deep breath and raises her soggy blue eyes to me while forcing a false smile on her face while the tears rush past.

"I'm here for you, Joe...I've got you, Baby."

My face mirrors hers as the tears fall and grieve a loss we've yet to know. I squeeze her hand and continue to lead us forward. The distance shortens as our feet move us quickly.

Our family is now in full view as Roberts wings sit idle and allow me to see past him at the sight of Amy K. on her knees. She hides her face as she cries for the second love she must give up in her life.

Greg...no.

Screaming wildly as my soul tears to pieces, I run forward and shove past everyone to find Gregs face covered in blood and his eyes wild and fading from the world, yet he clings to a small measure of life nonetheless.

He's alive! It's not too late!

"Greg! Brother! I'm here, Bro," I plea through hot tears as I raise his head to gaze into his eyes. His eyes find me and he flashes a wide smile, now streaked with blood.

"Joe...hey, Bro...," his eyes turn soft as he fights to remain in this world, "I'm sorry."

"You have nothing to be sorry about...I failed you, Greg...I'm the one who's sorry, Little Brother."

He gasps and sends a wave of red blood pouring out of his mouth. I lift him up and hold him against me while my eyes find Roberts' saddened face.

"What happened, Robert?"

He looks at the ground in front of him as he replies.

"I'm sorry, Cousin...I didn't see it coming."

"Robert! What happened?!"

He reaches forward with an opened hand and reveals a small, red stone no bigger than a splinter of wood. It's red gleam is glowing, more so now that it's streaked with Gregs blood.

"I got it out...and pulled the hate from him...but this is something different, Cuz...He's still dying."

"No!" Amy K. screams, "not Greg...I love you...Please don't leave me alone in this world," she begs through the tears.

He turns his head and greets her crying face while his devilish grin appears as he confesses his heart with his dying breaths.

"I love you, Amy...I've always liked you since the day I saw you...I'm sorry I didn't say something sooner...I wish I did...but I know that I can leave this world, now that I know what love is...I'm not leaving you alone...I'm leaving you with a love...I never thought....was real."

She wails as she throws herself onto him and cradles his body against hers. I release him and rise up from the horror my heart is witnessing.

"He'sssss....changing," a voice says from behind us. I turn to see the red coals beaming at me from the face of the captured Cursed while he smiles wide. I approach him quickly as I begin my interrogation.

"What are you talking about? Robert took the hate from him, along with the stone...How is he still changing?"

"He's going to change...after he dies...and be reborn from my master," he glances at the stone in Roberts hand, "his ssssoul is marked."

I reach forward and take his throat in my hand before lifting him off the ground and bringing his face to mine.

"So...When he dies, he goes to your master?"

His eyes squint as he smiles.

"Yesss."

No.

"I don't think so," I reply and drop him to his back. I turn quickly and return to Gregs side. Amy lies him on his back as he assures her he doesn't mind the pain, doing his best to comfort his love, even in death.

"I heard him, Joe...I heard what he said, Bro...The Creator will save me, won't He?"

"Of course He will, Little Brother...Your next stop is The Realm."

He grunts loudly as the change begins to make itself known.

"Damn!...I wish I would of picked a different track, hahaa! The irony, Bro...listening to a song about seeing demons...and now I'll become one...Death feels...silent...I should of picked track two."

"What's track two?" I ask as the tears fall from my face and the faces of everyone else. He smiles through the pain with kind eyes.

"Listen to it and see...The Creator won't save me, Bro...I love you, Joe."

The sobs escape me while my brother dies before me, and I stand feeling helpless to it all.

"No, Greg...The Creator's not gonna save you, Bro...This time, your brother's going to save you."

Lifting him back up, I hug him tightly as he does his best to return his happy Bro-hug. The tears escape us all, as well as the moans and wails of loss.

"I learned a long time ago," I say as I hold him through the misery, "The Creator always gets the good ones...give my family my love...and tell The Creator he owes me for this one...there's no way in Hell you're not going to The Realm."

I turn my crying face to the skies above and scream with all the hate and love I can muster from an eternal soul. The ground shakes and the winds scream past us as my hands and eyes explode with light. I slam my right palm into his chest and create a brilliant shower of sparks as I destroy the evil which was left inside him. He gasps and thrashes in my arms as his new feathers sprout from his back, and is accompanied by everyone sobbing in a mixture of sorrow and happiness by the moment of Gregs mortal life coming to an end. He falls lifelessly as Ralph did, his eternal eyes closed and his breathing ceased. I lift him up and I cradle him in my arms and whisper his soul to life.

"Open your eyes...and see the world again," I whisper. His eyes stir briefly before opening to reveal a brilliant green that matches my own. He gazes upon my face as we sit in the silence.

"Joe...Am I dead?"

I chuckle softly, "yes...You died, Greg."

His eyes roam over my shoulder to the sky above.

"Am I in The Realm?"

"No, Little Brother, you're not."

His shocked eyes find mine.

"I went to The Abyss?! After all that?! I really went to The Abyss?!"

I laugh to the sky before finding his wide eyes again.

"What's wrong with The Abyss, Little Brother? I live there, asshole! You make it sound like it's a bad place!"

I roar with laughter as everyone falls to their knees around us and says hello to the new Servant known as Greg, who was once our brother, but has now passed and been reborn eternal. Amy K. crashes into him and squeezes the

407

afterlife from him as Sasha did to me when I returned, and her happy cries make us all cry happy tears. He holds her close as he talks to her.

"I'm here, Amy! I love you, I really do! I should of said it long ago," he says before they embrace for their first kiss as a Servant and a mortal.

"I'm so happy you're alive, Greg...I already felt lost without you."

It pains me once again to have to break the bad news to her.

"He's alive Amy K....but he can't stay. He really is destined for The Realm."

His horrified eyes find mine quickly.

"I can't stay?"

"No, Little Brother...I'm sorry."

"Why not?" Amy K. asks.

"He's a Servant now, Amy. Servants belong in The Realm. I hate to say it, but...I'm The Fallen One. I don't have the authority to keep the ones I create. I can only reward a soul with eternal wings...they have to go to The Realm when they're born...It's their reward."

"Can we at least say goodbye and shit?" Danny interrupts as his bald head now shines black with dried Cursed blood.

"Of course we can…We have a little time," I finish as I rise to my feet. I pull him to his and steady him as he feels his wings for the first time.

"Dammit this is weird hahaa!" he laughs as he holds his balance and stretches his wings as the new feathers ruffle in the soft wind. Amy K. falls to his side and places herself under his arm.

"I got you!" She shrieks and wraps him tight in her stranglehold.

"Whoa, Babe! Trying to get used to this over here," he jokes as she tiptoes up to him and pecks his lips.

Everyone gathers around and jokes with their brother for the final time before he begins his sudden, new journey. He makes his way over to Amy J. and John and reminds them to love each other in their new romance, to remind each other of their love as much as possible and how he wishes he confessed to Amy K. sooner. He points to me and Sasha as an example of how we never stop breathing life into the words. They agree to love as much as they live. He finds Danny next and they embrace for a quiet moment as the tears flow, as Danny had become his closest brother in my absence. They share a soft word about the party they'll have on their next encounter. He turns to Will and Carmen next as they all embrace as one. He tells Will to keep an eye on Carmen, to take care of her at all costs. They share the bond of marriage, he explains, a blessing he wishes to have had with his love. All of a sudden, he's not the kid I'd grown to love. He stands a wiser man, but will always stand as my little brother. He takes a few minutes with Amy K. and kisses her farewell while we watch the sad moment of lost love come to fruition. They embrace for a small eternity before he leaves her with moist cheeks and turns to me and my loving

Sasha.

"Bro...I know it's my time, but I'm still sad to have to go...Thanks for everything, Bro. I gotta say, I don't know if I would of wanted to experience the end of the world with anyone else. You saved my ass, Joe...I wouldn't of survived without you, Bro."

He steps forward and we share the Bro hug he was always happy to give, as well as a silent moment of understanding. I needed my little brother as much as he needed a mentor. I remember all the nights he kept me from losing my sanity over Sasha in exchange for wisdom on life and love. The memories flood back, so many memories of our one liner arguments and late night hangouts. The laughter shared and the memories created would echo through my eternal mind for eternity. I release him and look into the only other eyes like mine on the entire planet.

"I love you, Little Brother," I say as hot tears burn both of our cheeks.

"I love you too, Bro," he says through a smile before looking at Sasha, "I love you too, Sasha. You're always going to be my psycho-bitch-sister-in-law though. Hahaa!"

She laughs loudly and smacks his arm as he returns the laughter.

"I'm just kidding...Take care of him."

"I will, *BRO*!" She jokes and tags his arm again while we laugh together as a family for the final time. He kisses Amy K. once more before turning to me.

"I'm ready."

I place my hands under his arms and let the light begin to seep from me. I lean forward and whisper to him.

"Good luck, My Brother."

The light explodes from me, along with his laughter, as I raise him up and allow The Realms staircase to reveal itself. The light cuts through the sky to the very spot I stand holding my little brother, with its beam illuminating us in its glory. I throw my hands upwards to the sky and send him on his way, his wings flapping for the first time and doing their job. He screams his trademark "whooo!" as the light pulls him away from us and up into the clouds that camouflage the entrance to The Realm. We watch as he disappears into the misty sky and takes the light along with him. It's in this moment I feel the sting of the loss and feel my heart beyond heavy as we lose Greg. The wails of anguish surround us, along with a serpents voice.

"One down," he hisses from the Earth I dropped him on, "the rest of you will ssswiftly follow."

I look at him long and with evil intentions, studying his features. He's completely bald, a sure sign that he had been reborn several times over. There is no good left in him.

No reason to hold back.

"No...not one down. Your master didn't claim his soul. The true Creator did...It's not one down...It's one up."

I walk slowly and let him feel the hate coming from me. He stares up at me from the ground as I approach.

"Greg is a Servant now...He'll never be a Cursed for your pathetic, little coward of a King."

I reach down and grab a hold of his shoulder and bring him to a sitting position. I stand before him and kneel down to meet his eyes.

"Answer a few questions and I'll make your ending swift...Answer honestly."

I reach down and place my hand on his knee while grabbing his ankle on the same leg. I pull up slowly and feel the bones creaking and the tendons popping as I bend his leg in a way it wasn't meant to. He begins to grunt and grind his teeth, but the pain is unpleasant enough to make him honest.

"I'll answer you...Stop now..."

I release the tension and pause in my attempt to snap his leg.

"Where is he? How was he able to attack Greg?"

He hisses through clenched teeth making him appear more sinister that before.

"He was in the hillsss...watching...waiting for his chance to ssstrike...He wasn't aiming for the boy...He was aiming for the big one," he finishes and gestures his eyes in Roberts direction.

"Why Robert?"

"Because the loss would of hurt you more...He wants to make you suffer for what you do."

I stand baffled by his words.

"What is it he thinks I'm doing?"

He hisses and stares at me as he leans forward.

"You...ssstand in the way...of a perfect world."

"I'm a thorn in his side, in other words?"

"You're a fool who will meet his end at the end of his staff...just like the boy."

Gregs face flashes through my mind as his laughter and jests ring in my ears. I feel the anger take hold.

"Greg went home...as you will soon find yourself," my hands shoot forward and grasp the neck of The Cursed, "tell him I'm going to keep my promise...I'll have his head before the end of it...as I take yours now."

Growling, I yank as hard as I unhumanly can and tear his head from his neck and invite the spray of dark blood that covers my face. I see another in line a few feet away growling and hissing with hate. The anger grips tight as I once again hear Gregs' laughter in my wounded mind.

Hahaaaa!

"What? You want to try me, you little bitch?! Here, get some!"

I leap to my feet and send the severed head in his direction with lightning speed. It smashes into his face and

413

collapses it completely. He falls back and begins jerking from the death blow that removed his face from his head. The Cursed next to him curses me for killing him, but all I hear is Gregs voice while the anger takes over.

Joe! Let's fucking party, Bro!

Charging madly, I run to him and pull him to his feet. I smash my forehead into his face before tearing him as a sheet of paper, the grotesque tear starting between his neck and shoulder. The blood sprays as the rest of The Cursed on their knees become lively and spit venom, yet their curses are lost to my hearing. My mind is elsewhere.

HAHAAHAA!!! No fucking way, Bro!

A roundhouse kick straight out of The Abyss separates the next one from his head as they all scream and taunt while the Servants and Fallen Souls who hold them hostage begin to worry. Their leader shouldn't be acting as the former ruler of The Abyss did.

Bro...what...the hell...is going on with you two?

I scream loud and as a beast while my hands burst with green flames. I throw my hand forward at the one closest to me and burn him with a blaze that now acts as an incinerator. The flames shoot from my palm with unholy hate and blazing speed and the fires cook him within seconds. He falls burnt to a crisp as I feel a hand grace my shoulder. Spinning wildly, I almost knock her down with my wings. Amy K. stands before me with tears streaking down her sad face, causing me to drop my hands to my side and the flames to die immediately.

"I'm gonna miss him too, Joe."

The sobs cause my chest to heave rapidly while the tears begin to stain my cheeks.

"I'm gonna miss him too, Joe," she repeats as she walks forward.

I wail in agony as I take her in my arms and squeeze her tight and am reminded that she's the only one to stand as wounded as I. She cries with me as we sink to our knees while our family comes to our side. I feel Sasha stroking my hair as I cry with Amy K., her small hands bringing comfort to me in the smallest ways. I feel like a child who lost his first pet, and the stubborn pride screaming that no other could replace him that comes along with it.

I lost my brother...and someone is going to pay.

Chapter 9

"I'm sorry Amy K....I should of protected him."

I sit with sad eyes as I voice my guilt and shame to the woman who had to say goodbye to the man she loved...because I failed. We all sit in the makeshift camp as Robert interrogates the captured enemies in a tent nearby.

"It wasn't your fault, Joe...It was all written in the stars."

I meet her eyes and find them full of understanding, even though they still pour out the sad showers.

"Still though...I should of been with you all...How did it happen?"

"We were winning the war...The Cursed were dying all around us. We were kicking the shit out of them, as Greg would say," she says and giggles, "they fell so quickly...We were celebrating, all of us, when Greg screamed and collapsed. He started clawing at his chest and Robert jumped on the ground next to him and pulled the shard out...Then he took the hate out...but Greg...He kept dying...We never even saw where it came from...It happened so fast."

"He was hiding in the hills...He knew I would chase him, Amy, so he dressed a Cursed in his robes and left his residual energy on it...I chased a phantom through the clouds while the war was going on...He was never in the sky...He just wanted me to think he was."

"Clever little bitch," Danny says softly.

"I should of known," I say to him, "he was never predictable...I was a fool to think he slipped for once."

"Nah Joe, don't feel like that," he offers comfort, "like Amy K. said...It was all in the stars."

"I'm not so sure it was," I inform him, "this Necromancer has a way of screwing up... everything...He always knows how to stay a step ahead, somehow."

"Informants?" John chimes in.

"Possibly. But in what world? The Realm? The Abyss?"

"He's getting his information from somewhere," Carmen adds quickly.

"I don't know where he's getting his info from, Honey, but I don't give a damn. He took Greg from us...I want his head," Amy J. says with a fierceness in her eyes I've never seen. Maybe it's her new body that makes her soul appear so different. She sits brewing with evil thoughts.

"Me too," Will adds as he turns to me, "say Joe...what's next? We hunt him down, right?"

"The war's not over," I reply.

"Huh?" Danny asks confused, "look around you, Joe. Look over there!" He points off to the battlefield not far from where we sit, "what do you see?"

I look over and scan the field of dead Cursed for as far as the eye can see, the ants now slaughtered upon the hill they raced over only an hour ago. I turn back to meet his crooked frown.

"Nothing."

"Exactly! We wiped out his entire army. There's no one left. This war is fucking *over*. We just track him down now and kill the son of a bitch."

"The war's not over, Friend," John tells him, "as long as he lives...The war is always going to be upon us."

"Hell no," Danny quips back, "it's a manhunt now."

"John's right, Danny," Sasha informs him softly, "as long as the pussy lives, he's not going to stop creating Cursed...He'll never stop. All The Cursed you killed today have more than likely already been resurrected in other people...There's almost a hundred thousand dead Cursed out there...which means there will be a hundred thousand reborn soon, if they haven't been reborn already."

"Son of a bitch!" he yells while throwing his hands up and turning from us, "so much fucking work!"

I chuckle to myself as he turns back to face me and I greet his eyes.

"The war's not over."

The voices from a few yards over draw all of our attention as Robert walks forward with a Cursed who appears frightened. He turns his head in jerky movements as he scans us

418

all. He appears as a scared cat.

"Cuz! This one is an Innocent. He was forced. He has some information."

I look him over and find his skin absent scars and his head almost completely covered in hair. He had only been changed, but never reborn. His soul stands closer to Human than Cursed.

"Tell me what you know."

"Yes, Sire."

I pause and stare into his blackened eyes.

"Don't call me that. I'm no King, but I fight for one...My name is Joe...Do you remember your name?"

"Yesss. It's Diego."

"What did you hear, Diego? What information do you have?"

He looks around nervously and leans closer to me. The Servants accompanying Robert direct their blades at his throat in the same moment. I raise my hand to stop them as I step close to him.

"You can speak freely, Diego."

He nods quickly.

"He's coming for you, for everyone, very ssssoon."

"Now? So quickly? We just destroyed his army."

He looks around nervously again, as the words he's about to voice terrify him.

"You destroyed a sssmall piece of his army...I heard him sssay it was much bigger."

"How big?"

"A million...or more."

I look at Robert with a worried gaze. He must be disguised as a mirror because his face reflects my own.

"Where can we find them? Do you have any idea?"

He shakes his frightening head quickly.

"I'm sssorry, I don't."

"What else do you know?"

"He's making a new kind of Cursssed. He was waiting for the battle. They never intended to win the battle...It was a roundup of Sssservants, he was after," he pauses to do his dry heave and regurgitate imaginary vomit, as his nervous tick is the same as the rest, "as I was sssaying, he's making new warriors, nightmaresss...that only he can control."

I feel the lump in my throat return. I glance at Robert and see he must of also swallowed the imaginary watermelon that I did.

"Has he successfully made any yet?"

Please say no.

"Yesss...A small unit. There's not very many...three, I think."

"What makes them so special?"

"They can travel freely between any world He created. They have no boundaries, as Ssservants don't...he wants to use them to invade The Realm."

This news troubles my soul as much as losing Greg.

"So he's making his move then...to join everything."

His head shakes and his arms seize up around his chest.

"Yesss...I heard him sssay he has one foot in The Realm already...and one in The Abyss."

"Informants," John states vindicated. He looks at John as he nods his head in agreement.

"Yesss...informants...a Ssservant has betrayed The Realm...and a Lost Sssoul has betrayed you, Joe."

"Coward! You pathetic coward!"

We all turn to The Cursed sitting alone a dozen feet away and completely bound in lighted chains. He screams and hisses as he stares at his Cursed brother who betrays their kind. I walk over and greet him with burning eyes.

"Don't listen to him...he liesss."

"And let me guess...*You* tell the truth...Tell me something true then, Buttercup."

He hisses at my insult towards him and leans forward as much as his chains allow.

"You can't kill him."

I lean closer to him as I whisper.

"I can kill *you*."

I bring my hands together suddenly before me and collapse his skull as if a melon. His headless body falls to the ground and begins a slow dance with no one. He writhes for a few more seconds before finally resting as Robert quickly approaches.

"Cuz, you shouldn't have done that...He's going to tell the Necromancer that you know everything."

I look at him with a sly smile.

"Exactly."

"Ohhh...pretty smooth, Cousin. Beat him at his own game."

"He assumes I'm some dumbass that's always going to use force to get what I want. He thinks I'm just a mindless idiot without an original thought in my head."

"Ha! He doesn't realize he's screwing with a real smooth criminal. Show him who he's fucking with, Cuz!"

"Exactly."

My eyes fall back on the New World Cursed, Diego, as he meets my gaze with frightened eyes.

"Thank you, Diego...Was there anything else you can remember?"

He shakes his head slowly, "that's all...I'm sssorry."

"Don't be sorry...Thank you...Do you remember your old life?"

He nods quickly in agreement but holds his voice hostage.

"What did you do for a living?"

His head jerks as his soul travels back in time.

"I was a Carpenter...I used to...build houssses."

I smirk and reply, "I did that for a while in the Old World. The feeling you get when you build a house that will become someones home is indescribable...The brother I just lost was pretty handy...the New World will need people to rebuild it, Diego," I lean in close to him once more, "would you like to be a part of the New World again?"

Slowly, he nods in agreement while his terrifying eyes becoming beacons of sadness.

423

"Good...Close your eyes."

He obeys my command and shivers uncontrollably as his nerves find him and plague his body. I slam my hand forward into his chest with my lighted palm and feel the heat burning me immediately. Holding him firmly, I draw the hate from him as he screams and thrashes from the disintegration of his wings, the fleshy bones sticking out of his back and oozing a dark blood. The fires envelope him in an instant while my wings become a cocoon, wrapping him tightly. I feel his body shaking against me as the flames subside. Opening my wings, I let a dark-haired, middle-aged man fall out to the New World. The force of the gentle fall causes him to jump to life and scurry backwards in a panicked haste as his brown, human eyes return to him along with his body. He stares at me while breathing rapidly.

"Welcome to the New World, Brother."

He feels his face before gazing at his hands while his rough features turn soft upon realizing he's no longer a nightmare. His shocked face finds my smiling one.

"I'm a man again?"

"Yes."

"Did you just kill me?"

"No."

"But you did...*something*?"

"Yes."

I smile at him as we play the game I used to play with my long, lost brother.

He looks at the world around him, all the faces, and all the death in the distance. He takes in the world as if he's seeing it for the very first time. He glances at me again before making his way to his feet.

"What happens now?"

"What do you want to do, more than anything, now that you have your life back?"

He looks at the ground for a moment and whispers to himself.

"Find my family."

"Diego...I can think of no better reason to live for...Go find them...You've earned it."

I look at the two Servants with Robert and nod my head in his direction. They walk forward to assume the mantle of escorts.

"These guys will give you a lift, wherever you need to go. They'll see you to your families side...Good luck, My Brother."

His eyes meet mine with gratitude exuding from them.

"Thank you, Joe...I'll tell stories about you...The kindest Fallen One to ever walk the Earth."

I laugh as I reach forward and shake his hand.

"Thank you...I've been called worse today."

We share a small laugh as they turn away and head off to find Diego a path to his home. I turn to Robert as Sasha approaches and finds my waist with her slender arms. He makes his way to me upon seeing that I'm trapped in the web of Sashas embrace.

"Cuz...What *does* happen now? Are we going after him?"

I think about his words for a silent moment before finding my tongue.

"Keep interrogating the remaining. Everyone that you can prove innocent, bring them to me. I'll change them back into people and then they can decide their own Fate."

"And the ones that aren't so innocent?"

I look at him quietly as I shake my head in disappointment.

"Killing them only gives him back his army, as does setting them free...Send them to The Abyss."

His wide, brown eyes bulge from his head as he stares without voicing a reply.

"I've dealt with worse, Big. I'll handle their asses until they realize *my path* is the *only path*."

426

He smirks and gently slaps my shoulder.

"Right on, Cuz."

Turning back to his duties, I turn my attention to the apple of my eye.

"Hello, my Sweet Wife."

She laughs loudly as she squeezes me with a renewed purpose. She ends her embrace and reaches up to slowly stroke my hair.

"I'm not your wife, yet...but...I guess we should get used to saying it, right?...Hello, my Handsome Husband."

We giggle together and embrace softly as I kiss her lips slowly and steadily. I always find the ecstasy of her mouth so invigorating. I kiss her lips just a little bit harder, for a little longer. She pulls back and stares at my face with the most angelic eyes she's ever possessed. Her soul feels complete, and it shows through the mirrors.

"I love you."

It's all I can muster as her beauty strikes my mind senseless, like it always does.

"I love you too, Baby."

We return to the lips we love...but only to be pulled away by the screeching of my name in the sky.

The Servant flies to us quickly with his face appearing as

a blur of panic and fear. His giant, blue eyes burn a path from the sky to my face as his mouth screams my name for all the New World to hear. Instinct takes hold as I nudge Sasha aside and shield her with my wings as my hand moves to rest on my sword. He finds us and lands clumsily, falling and tumbling a few feet from us. He jumps to his feet and meets my eyes full of anxiety.

"Joe! I've found you! We need to leave!"

I reach forward and grab him by his shoulders and attempt to snap him back into reality.

"Calm down. What's wrong?"

"The army is coming! They're on their way! We need to retreat to safety!"

His eyes shoot around us as I call for another Servant to fetch Robert. The rest of my family gathers and stands with fear in their eyes. This new development is definitely screwing up my plans, if not The Creators.

"What army?"

His eyes scream at me along with his tongue.

"THE NECROMANCERS!"

"Alright...just take it easy," my words harden just a bit, "we have an army too."

"No," he begins as a frightened child, "we don't...I've seen it...We're barely a small fraction of what he brings."

My dead heart begins to freeze as loud steps enter my hearing. Robert approaches with worry in his eyes as he joins the group.

"How many?" I ask softly.

His eyes shoot in all directions as if he sees phantom numbers in front of him.

"I counted and counted, as much as I could. They kept coming and I would count them, as fast as I could and before I knew it I couldn't keep up. They just kept coming and covering the world, so I counted..."

I squeeze his shoulders and stare him dead in his panicked eyes.

"How...many?"

His face turns to horror once more.

"I lost count at around seven million."

"Holy shit!" Danny exclaims as his eyes find mine, "*that's* work."

"Impossible, Cuz," Robert says as he looks back and forth between me and the harbinger of bad news, "there's no way he could of amassed that kind of army."

"I watched them cover the world," he informs Robert, "and they kept coming...so many Cursed...and a few creatures I didn't recognize. He made more monsters, he must have...but make no mistake, they stand in the millions...and they're less than two miles from here."

The murmurs make their way around the group as the sudden news of impending doom sends our hopes of victory crashing into the nonexistent. I look at Robert and find him in shock while his dark eyes burn a hole in the ground in front of him.

"Robert...Ready the army."

He stands taller upon receiving my words as his eyes grow darker and as sharp as his blade.

"Right on, Cuz."

Turning to Sasha, I feel her fear cutting through me. She looks at me with a look I've seen only once before in my life; The day my mortal life ended. She gazes upon me as if I'm about to stand as a dead man, just not the eternal type. The rest of my family stands silently wearing the same doomed expression.

"Guys," I say softly, causing all of them to look at me in the same moment.

"We're going to be fine...I'll walk beside you, in everything we do."

"I hope you're right about that," Danny voices in a soft whimper as he returns his gaze to the ground, "because, if you're not..."

"You die," I finish. Their eyes glue themselves to me.

"You all stand as my family...and I love you...I'll be damned if I let you slip from this world...I already failed Greg and Sam...I won't fail you too...I swear it on my eternal life."

"Same with me guys," Sasha adds, "I swear on my eternal life I'll protect you...Nobody fucks with our family."

"Amen," John adds.

We all exchange glances and smiles, but leave words absent our final huddle. We all embrace one by one and speak with our eyes about loving one another. Taking my sword in my hand, I draw it out to the sounds of its steel brethren echoing the same. We stand as a warrior family, and we're ready to march to the end of the world.

****

The sounds of the wind are whispers of kindness compared to the hiss of the seven million Cursed that now stand less than a half-mile away, frozen in their steps and waiting for commands to kill. The soft sunset hangs behind them and illuminates their bodies as atrocious mannequins while a flock of dead buzzards circles them overhead. They stand and watch as we watch, all half million of us ready to meet their attempt on our lives. The wind whips my hair behind me and graces the army at my back. The sunlight pours over my face and the faces of my army. I stand quietly, with my family beside me...and we watch.

"Baby," she whispers, cutting the quiet air.

"Yes, My Love?"

The silence greets me long enough for me to turn my head and meet her gaze.

"Nothing...Just wanted to hear you call me 'your Love' is all."

I smile softly as she reflects my image.

"You'll always be My Love, Sasha."

I take her face in my hands and kiss her softly before we pull back and return to our small smiles.

"You'll always be mine, Joe."

I smile and kiss her softly on her cheek before whispering into her ear.

"I wouldn't have it any other way, My Love."

Releasing her, I walk out a dozen feet from my family and turn to greet them, along with the army of Servants and Fallen Souls. I bring my hands together in front of me in a show of respect and bow as the crowd mimics my movements a second later.

"MAY THE CREATORS WRATH BE IN YOU TODAY!!!" My voice echos across the world in front of me.

"AND ALSO IN YOU!!!"

The silence returns, with only the wind to accompany it.

"Today...the worlds of The Realm and The Abyss and Man may suffer...but it won't be because we didn't try. It won't be because the enemy won. It won't be because we didn't have it in us to overcome such a beast of an army. It won't bebecause we gave up faith in the face of our enemy. IT! WON'T! BE!...because we will not lose today."

I turn my body and point out to the abominations waiting to claim our lives.

"They outnumber us...but it is *THEM...WHO WILL FALL!!!*" Grabbing my sword, I raise it to the air and allow its fire to burst from the steel.

"WE ARE THE VENGEFUL HAND OF A MIGHTY CREATOR!!! LET'S GO OUT THERE AND REMIND THESE MOTHERFUCKERS JUST WHO WE FUCKING ARE!!!"

The cheers reach the sky as we all shout fromour souls and raise our weapons in a gesture of ill will to The Cursed. They scream loudly and call for the death of the New World animals, and praise The Creator for giving them the odds to kill more than one. I greet Sashas smiling face as her words invade my mind.

"So...fucking...hot."

I laugh for a brief moment before beginning my stride back to her side. She watches every step I take and makes her own blade ready for combat. I reach her in time to deliver a small kiss as the world begins to shake.

What now?

The sky tears itself open as the sounds of The Realms Trumpets trample the sounds of the world. A path of light cuts through the sky to the ground in front of me, causing us to all take a few small steps back and ready our weapons. The trumpets grow maddeningly loud and cause us all to wince from the noise. The flying Cursed fall from the sky and onto

433

their brothers as the sounds of The Realm is too much for unholy souls. The light becomes filled with Servants drifting down the lighted path to the Earth in front of us. Six in all touch their feet to the ground while the light dissipates slowly and their path home becomes lost to them. The tallest one, a blonde standing as broad as a barn door and appearing as more of a Drill Sergeant, steps forward and gazes at me as if I'm merely a troubled teen. I meet his eyes with the look of a King.

"Joe."

I step forward and present myself.

"And you are?"

He shoots a sharp breath from his nose as a Workhorse and not a holy warrior.

"My name is Hugh, and I was sent here by The Creator."

"For what purpose?" I ask. He stares at me as he swallows the lump in his throat.

"The Necromancer...He's been busy."

"I see that," I say and point at the millions of awaiting Cursed, "and that's probably not the half of it, I'm assuming...since you're here."

"You know of his treachery then?" He questions me.

"I do...His plan of a perfect world."

"It's already in motion...He's attacking The Realm as we

434

speak."

"Whoa, wait. How the fuck is that possible?"

He shakes his head while a look of disappointment overtakes his face. John answers the question for him as he has already done twice today.

"Informants."

He nods in agreement.

"Someone from The Realm betrayed us all, allowing him access to the path to The Creators Sanctuary."

"How many attack The Gates?"

He shakes his head as he answers, "too many...around fifteen million strong, is our lowest estimate...It could be as much as fifty million."

"Son of a bitch," John mutters in disbelief. I look at Hugh and voice the elephant on the battlefield.

"So...What does that have to do with you standing here?"

He meets my gaze as his eyes become apologetic.

"The Creator needs your army."

"All of them?" Sasha interrupts. He meets her wide eyes with sorrow.

"Yes...I'm sorry."

"If I give up my army," I say as I grab his attention with louder words, "then that means my family will fall today. I swore I wouldn't let that happen."

He steps forward and glances back and forth at us all.

"The time will come when The Falling Realm will meet The Rising Abyss, to determine the fate of the world," he continues as he pauses in his steps, "but right now, if you don't do this...We're all fucked...The choice is yours alone."

"So that's our options?" Die now or later?" Danny asks as he looks around at us, "what kind of shit is that?"

"Can we go to The Realm with you? All of us?" Amy K. asks quietly.

"No Ma'am...Just the army."

"Well," she continues, "if I have to die, I guess it'll be for the best reason of all time...Because we helped The Creator...I can live with that."

I meet her smiling eyes and find that she's truly not afraid of death. I look around at everyone else as they await my reply.

"Guys...The choice is yours."

They all stand quietly and contemplate the end.

"Ahhh fuck it. I say we all die today," Danny says and

chuckles.

"I'm fine with dying for The Creator, Friend," John adds.

"I agree...I'm ready," Will states as he grasps Carmens hand. He makes me proud in this moment, once terrified to hold a sword and now ready to die on the end of it. He now towers a braver man in any world.

"Let's do it, Honey...Let's get ready to meet out maker!" Amy J. yells. They all agree with her and ready themselves for their final battle on Earth and plan for their next stop to be in The Realm. Turning to Hugh, I see the relief on his face, as well as the bewilderment. "Truly warriors of The Creator, this group," he exclaims.

"The best bunch of misfits I've ever had the pleasure of knowing, Hugh...The army is yours...Take them."

He bows his head to me in respect and waits for me to address them all. I turn to the army and raise both my hands to the air to draw their attention.

"The Realm...has come under attack by a much bigger force than the one that greets you here...They need you...The Creator, needs you...You've already made me proud to be your leader...Make The Creator proud and defend The Realm...May good fortune find you."

"And you as well," they answer as one. Turning back to him, he greets me with kind eyes.

"The Creator sends you His blessings...He's sending you a few gifts...Rewards for your loyalty."

"We'll see if I'm around to enjoy these gifts, now that I stand alone."

"You've never been alone, Joe...He was always with you...He thanks you."

I bow my head to him, returning respect as Robert approaches me quickly.

"Cuz, if The Realm is under attack..."

"I know, Robert...It's all good, Cuz."

"My family is there. *Our* family is there. My wife, Linda...she's my best friend, you know that. And my kids..."

"Go to them, Robert. I wouldn't have it any other way, Cousin...Watch out for all of them."

I step forward as we hug and grasp with all our strength.

"I'm gonna miss you, Cuz."

"Same here, Big. Love you, Brother."

We release as he turns to my family and tips his hat to them.

"Gonna be weird with you being gone, Big Guy," Danny says, "kinda got used to sitting in your big-ass shadow when we couldn't find shade."

We all chuckle at Dannys joke as Robert reaches out and accepts a group hug from his adopted family. John locks eyes with him and voices one last request.

"Any words of wisdom, Friend, to leave behind?"

He smiles wide and steps back as he draws his sword. He traces the end of the blade into the Earth and carves out three letters.

J. K. L.

"J. K. L. ?" Danny asks, "what does that mean?"

He smiles as he explains the words he lived by in his mortal life.

"Just keep laughing...Just keep loving...Just keep living...It's all you need in life...and you guys have all the life in the world ahead of you."

I smile as the tears streak down my cheeks as my cousin in my mortal life reminds me why we stood as one. We were always different to others, but for all the right reasons. I don't fight the tears, such a thing is pointless when saying goodbye to a part of yourself. The tears will always prevail. I give him one last hug as he prepares to make his departure.

"Just keep living, Cuz."

I laugh to myself to hide the sobs.

"You too, Robert."

We release as he steps back and tips his hat one final time with his smile shining true. He turns away and walks out of my eternal life forever with the sun shining on his shoulders, as it will always find itself there when basking a Servant in its warm glory. He disappears into the army that's about to return to The Realm, and a step closer to the family he left behind and loves so much.

Hugh walks forward to the army and raises his hands above his head as I did only moments before. The skies tear open once again as a giant light washes over the army in a solid, golden beam and lands firmly on the soul of every Servant and Lost Soul from The Abyss. They drift slowly as one, a giant creature of steel and feathers and good intentions, and their rise to The Realm is a sight for everyone to behold. Even The Cursed watch from so far away, licking their sickening lips with anticipation. Their biggest threat just became their biggest dessert. We watch as they make it into the clouds with the light swallowing them whole. It fades as quickly as it graced our presence. I stand now looking at seven mortals and my blue-eyed soul in the flesh. The moment has come to meet our maker.

"Well, this blows," Danny says.

The lightning is quick and surprising, hitting only a few yards from us. It's brilliant light illuminates the entire New World for a split second, blinding all the mortal eyes that stand with me. They cover their heads from the shock, but my gaze never wavers. Two figures stand in the impact crater amongst the dusty air with their faces hidden, but the outline of their bodies are visible. A shorter man accompanies a taller one, with the shape of their wings becoming more clear as the wind clears the brown mist. I feel the energy of the short one and smile wide as they begin their walk forward.

440

"Sam."

"Sam?" John asks as he pulls himself off of Amy J..

"Our brother has returned," I say softly.

Making his way forward, I'm greeted by the face I thought lost to us forever.

"Joe! I'm back!" He says as he rushes to my arms. We hug tightly and laugh for a small moment before he releases me to another familiar face.

"You remember Ralph?"

"Of course. How are you, Ralph?"

Standing taller than I remember, he flings his golden hair to the side.

"I'm okay," he says as he looks at the army waiting for us to finish our reunion, "but what a time to stop by!"

Everyone approaches Sam and greets him back to the New World, but our visit is rushed by the hissing of The Cursed growing louder. They all take a moment to meet Ralph and make small jests about the force we're about to lead into battle. He seems at home, as does Sam. We pause our reunion when Sasha taps my shoulder and points off to a single Cursed flying in our direction.

He reaches the midway point between us, the dusty ground between the dark army and my lonely band of brothers and sisters, and lands with a thump. Even from a quarter of a mile away, the difference between him and his brothers is apparent. He stands a true monster.

"What's he doing?" John asks as we watch him pace slowly.

"Terms...He's coming to offer false terms of surrender," I inform him quietly. "He's going to promise mercy, thinking we'll accept, now that we're outnumbered completely...but I know better. Wait here, all of you...This won't take long."

I sprint towards the nightmare and thrust my wings once to catch the air, and once more to send me propelling in his direction. I sail effortlessly and glide quickly to my intended target. He watches as he walks slowly, and is a giant of a Reaper, but with a few very noticeable changes. He waits as I land a few feet from his new monstrous body.

"Fool," he begins as he crosses both of his sets of long, grotesque arms. He stands with the appendages he was born with, along with another set growing from his hips, and his body has become unnaturally long and slender.

"Do not speak..Only listen," he instructs as he folds his new set of leathery wings.

He falls to his arms as if attempting a push-up while his knees break and he bends his legs to walk in an unnatural stance, while his new arms at his waist become a new set of legs. He begins walking around me as a terrifying insect while I stand frozen in place. He begins his false promises.

"Surrender...and your people will be ssspared."

"Bullshit," I cut him off, "don't take me for a fool, you fucking idiot," I reply.

"Very well...give us the Servants with you...and every lassst one of you will die quickly."

He continues his frightening crawl around me while his head spins on a pivot and never breaks his piercing gaze.

"Like I said...Don't take me for a fool...you fucking idiot."

He makes his way in front of me and rises up, his body creaking and cracking from the addition of so many new bones. He towers above me as he peers down and continues in a more honest breath.

"You will die. Every last one of you is going to sssuffer before the true end...and then you'll be reborn and stand as I do...Do not think you will survive this, Fool. You cannot win the war we bring to your doorstep. A Tsunami of Death comes to wash over you all. You cannot sssurvive the Hell that threatens to remove you from the world forever."

I look up into his burning red coals and smile as I breathe life into my own reply.

"We *are* the True Hell."

I reach forward quickly with no warning and grasp the new arms protruding from his hips. I pull my arms apart and separate his from his waist with a crunching pop. He screams as I drive one of his torn arms into his chest with a maddening force and break his ribs. His screams are muffled when I shove the other arm through his face in the very next instant and watch as he trembles before me. I see the light fading from his eyes before he stumbles back and falls to his knees. I walk forward and meet the dimming bulbs to give him a message to

443

deliver to my nemesis.

"Surrender...and we'll *still* kill every last one of you...*We will* fuck you up."

His eyes blink, acknowledging he heard my words, before he falls lifelessly to the Earth. I spit on him as I turn to my family and begin a slow jog back. I launch myself into the sky to quicken my arrival to their side. It only takes moments to reach them and land before them with new instructions.

"This is it...When I charge the field...I want you all to turn and run. Sam and Ralph can lift you and carry you all to safety...This is *my* fight...This is not *your* death."

"No, Sir," John states flatly, "we're with you, Joe."

"To the fucking end, Baby," Sasha reminds me.

Looking around, I see everyone else nodding slowly as they steady their nerves for combat.

"Okay then...Let's do it."

I barely have time to finish my words as the ground begins to rumble from deeply within. I turn quickly to Sam and Ralph.

"What's going on? Is this something else from The Creator?"

"No!" Sam begins, "this isn't us! I don't know what's going on!"

444

The ground begins to buck and heave under us and deliver an earthquake of epic magnitude. The Earth shifts under us and sends us all to our backs as the ground behind us, where the army stood, falls away into the giant sinkhole that now grows before our eyes. The rocks scream and bust to pieces as giant slabs of ground begin to protrude up in random directions. My family scrambles to their feet and place themselves behind me and Sasha as we stand ready for war. The ground continues in it's thundering recreation with familiar sounds starting to accompany it. We feel the rumble deep from within as the creators of our panic begin to make themselves known.

From the crater, a monster rises and walks forward. Misshapen pupils return from our past and fall upon me as he exits the dusty world behind him. His eight foot stature seems small compared to the destruction he marches in front of. He walks on two legs as is his choice, with his body built like a nightmarish, albino turtle. He walks towards me as his brothers begin to fall in place behind him. The Damned have returned from the dead. The giggles that haunted us all in the New World begin to fill the air as the domino effect of broken ground continues to play along, tearing the Earth behind them and so forth. It continues on in the distance and His beautiful Earth is once again being destroyed by The Evil Ones' children.

I set a fiery gaze upon the sky above me.

"Really? *Really*? In-between two armies now, that's great! What else you got for me?!"

I pause and listen to the silence for an answer that never comes. Turning slowly, I meet the terrified faces of everyone I love in the New World.

"I guess the Necromancer had one more trick up his sleeve...That's why they haven't charged."

A sickening, gurgling voice escapes from my memory and voices itself to the air.

"Fool of Mercy!"

Turning around with all the courage I can muster, I meet the face of The Damned, only a dozen feet from us.

"My name is Joe."

"I know your name," he shoots back quickly, "and I know who you are...My King."

We all look around at each other with shock and awe while our faces reflect the same image.

What?

"Your King?"

He kneels before us and the rest of his brothers do the same, creating a sea of large heads and milky white, pulsing backs stretching to the darkness of the approaching night. The dusking sun falls lovingly and blankets them. He rests motionless as he speaks.

"If you would have us."

Standing confused, I ask the only thought dancing through my mind.

"What is this?"

He rises and approaches me slowly, aware that I still stand as his enemy in this moment.

"We pledge our lives to you, King of Mercy, and will follow you into battle, if we can stand once again in the good graces of The Creator....We've been in hiding...and waiting...for *you* to emerge...We'll stand with you...*if* we can go to The Realm, when this is done...and finally be our true selves."

"That's not my decision, whether or not you make it to His Home."

"But it is, My King. You can forgive our past...and give us wings...You have that power. The decision rests with you."

I stare hard at him with soft eyes as his misshapen pupils twitch in his head.

"Kneel before me."

He takes his place on his knees again and looks at me with a hopeful gaze.

"Do you vow to protect my family, who will stand as your family when we accept you?"

He bows his head as he replies.

"I do, My King."

"Do you accept the light of The Creator into your heart?"

"I do, My King."

"That's all I'll ever ask of you...Rise, and greet us as your family." He rises up and smiles a horrid portrait that shines with a dark beauty.

"Welcome to the army of The Realm, My Brother."

He bows his head in a deep respect before turning to the army that now stands as ours. He raises his massive arm and screams a blood curdling howl. The cheers meet him in kind as The Damned begin howling and giggling and shaking the remaining ground with their large hoofs. They scream to The Realm and praise The Creator with terrifying voices of love. He turns back to me and bows his head again.

"How many of you are there?" I ask.

"We are a force of three million...and that's not all."

He turns back to the screaming sea of monstrous faces and screeches in his own language. He raises his arms and, in the distance, a nightmare reincarnates itself; a fleet of large Hellships rises to the skies above. The Damned pour forth in the same moment to greet their new mortal family who they will now protect with their dark lives.

"No fucking way! We have an Air Force too?!" Danny screams as much as asks.

He giggles his sickening sounds and turns to Danny and his razor teeth actually appear pleasing.

448

"Yes, you do...Danny."

"Shit," Sasha barks as she climbs up the back of a Damned and rests herself on his bodies natural saddle, the area just on top of his pulsing back, "we have a Calvary too."

The Damned stands tall and allows her to rise above the world as the Warrior Queen who stole my heart. I set my attention back to the leader.

"Is that alright with you?" I ask as I point at Sasha getting a feel for her new Warhorse.

"We stand as you see fit...It would be my honor to carry you into battle, My King...if you would do me that honor?"

I slowly agree with a small nod of my head.

"The honor is mine, Brother."

"Hell yeah! We got this now!" Danny yells as he climbs aboard his own beast of mayhem. He finds the saddle and holds on to the shoulders of The Damned as he stands tall and brings him eye-toeye with Sasha. They laugh as one as they peer down at the rest of us.

I walk past The Damned leading them and approach the remaining three million still standing in wait. They fall silent as I approach and their bodies become still once more. The lumbering statues appear as a true army of The Abyss, as if their faces were chiseled out of some sort of nightmare stone. They stand and watch with eager, misshapen eyes.

I raise my hands to the sky with green flames sprouting

from my palms.

"MAY THE CREATOR BE AT YOUR SIDES TODAY!!!"

"AND BY YOURS, KING OF MERCY!!!"

The silence returns to the world as I lower my hands while they stand motionless and hold their collective breath.

"Today you take the first step to becoming *true Servants*...Stand with me in this war...and it will be so...The Necromancer has vowed to destroy The Realm you now fight to protect. He wants to join all of time and space and rule it in his own vision. He stands far worse than the coward you *used* to follow. He will not show you any mercy...Do not show him any kindness...We will win this war...and you will stand as Servants...PREPARE TO SHAPE YOUR OWN DESTINIES!!!"

Drawing my sword, I hold it high above my burning eyes.

"ALL PRAISE TO THE CREATOR IN THE REALM!!!"

"THE TRUE AND ONLY CREATOR!!!" They thunder back.

We all roar as one, my family, The Damned, and my very soul. I make my way back to the line of Damned who position themselves to be our war chariots. We all climb aboard The Damned of our choice as I take to the shoulders of The Damned who spoke as their collective voice.

"Damned Soul...Do you have a name?" I ask as I take my place upon his back. He stands on all fours, as they all do, and form a defensive line in front of the army while each holds a member of my family. He snorts and begins to scrape his foot

450

on the ground as a Demonic Bull.

"My name is Tuu."

Follow the signs.

"Like, the number two?" Amy K. asks from the top of The Damned next to us.

He giggles softly and looks at her with his monstrous eyes..

"Yes."

Like a soft wind on a still day, Gregs' voice rings throughout my suddenly sad mind.

Death feels...silent...I should of picked track two.

Reaching inside my breastplate, I retrieve the Ipod I cloned from Gregs.

Track two.

I stare at the little device and smile to myself. Looking up, I see everyone in formation on their steeds of war; John, Danny and the Amys to my left and Sasha, Will, Carmen, Sam and Ralph to my right. They look at me with sad eyes as they retrieve their own devices. I allow my lovers eyes to fall upon Sasha before they turn to the miserable eyes I hate to possess.

"I love you, Sasha."

She smiles softly, understanding the hurt in my soul as I

miss Greg.

"I love you too, Joe...Track two, huh?"

She knows my sad mind. I smile at her as I nod.

"Track two...for Greg."

I look down the line in both directions as they all nod in agreement and place the silent headphones in their ears.

"For Greg," I declare to the New World.

"For Greg," Sasha echoes.

"For Greg!" Danny yells.

Amy K. sits taller as she voices her turn.

"For Greeeeg!"

We join in her tribute with our voices thundering as one.

"FOR GREEEEEEEG!!!!"

The roars escape us with the pain of loss as our fuel while our brothers memory drives our steps. We spur The Damned as they roar along and begin their race to the destiny of all. They begin pounding the ground to shorten the distance between us and the unholy army that now stands hissing with hate while cloaking a touch of fear. This was one development the Necromancer couldn't see coming, when even The Creator of all was blind to it.

452

Like riding a horse, my legs move with every step of the beast underneath me. I hold on tight and lean forward as a Jockey and see my family taking the same approach. The muffled sounds of their unholy hooves pounding the ground are accompanied by the vibrations of every step. I see the ground moving fast before me as the sharp breathing of The Damned mixes with the small thunderclaps. The sun bathes us as we charge towards the New World nightmares waiting in the brilliant sunset.

For you Greg.

A piano fills our ears as our pocket jukeboxes come to life, a song I know all too well, The Sound of Silence, covered by Disturbed. Its soft melody fills the world around until I hear nothing but its beauty. I feel the sadness, knowing this was Gregs last request. The piano plays as the world slows, while the thundering of The Damned steps are no longer audible, but felt nonetheless, as three million stampede across the Earth behind us. The storms of dust clouds erupt behind us all as we charge forward without pause while the music plays on.

Hello darkness my ollld friieennnd.

Burning with our mad souls, we draw our blades as one and hold them high as we release the agony of our anger. Loudly, we roar.

I look around me and find their faces frozen in loud cries of war, yet I only hear the music. Their jaws hang in an angry shout, but the tears upon their cheeks speak of sorrow. I roar loudly and feel my own cheeks hot and moist. Observing my family, I see their torment in the soft sunlight as the music plays. Dannys bottom lip betrays his crooked smile and curls as the tears fall from him. I see Carmen screaming through her

453

own tears as Will does the same. John and Amy J. roar on while the sad rains pour from their faces. Amy K. screams through the painful showers released by her sad eyes, with her mouth wording her lost lovers name as she holds her sword high. Their faces appear so beautiful in a mixture of sadness and sunlight and soft music. I see Sashas face, as her blue eyes burn with a hate and vengeance, as she roars thunderously for her lost brother. The music plays on with the piano as soft as the lyrics and completes an alternate universe to the sounds going on around us, as our Demonic Rhinos continue pounding the Earth while our enemy grows larger by the second.

The sun bathes us as we rush towards our destiny. Our line takes on the formation of Seagulls in the wind, a sharp point spearheading the army and leading them to the heart of our enemy. The music plays softly, the only sound we hear, and our swords remain held high as we approach the awaiting doom.

We close in on our enemy with only a few hundred yards to go. Our blades burn in a quiet New World where only piano keys and thundering feet exist.

Silently...we roar.

Epilogue

"I'm really nervous...What's going to happen?" A womans soft voice asks from the small room where they watch the battle unfold. A large transparent cloud sits under their feet as they watch the last family of Earth ride The Damned from The Old Abyss.

"Don't worry, Bro, I mean Ma'am. My Bro's got this! He's a bad motherffff...I mean...bad ass dude," he pauses and points at the large figure behind them in the misty shadows, "forgot The Creator is here," he tells her. He turns to the figure hidden in the mist.

"Sorry, Sir...Creator, Sir...Honestly, I don't know what to call you."

He chuckles softly to himself, revealing a large, warm voice with a pleasing tone.

"It's okay, Greg...I have to agree...I picked a fierce warrior."

"He's the best, Bro! No one can mess with Joe! You saw how he kicked ass before he was even The Fallen One! I mean, damn! Bro was killing 'em before he even had wings."

"He's always been a fierce person," the woman adds, "he was the nicest guy in the world...until you pissed him off...but his heart is the best."

Underneath them, Joe and the army close the distance. They have only a small stretch between themselves and the clash of swords and claws. Even from so high up, their voices thunder to The Realm.

"MAN! I wish I could be there!" Greg hollers as he jumps in place with excitement. "Joe's gonna fuck them up!" He cowers slightly after his words and glances back, "sorry...I just wish I was beside my brother."

"You will be again," The Creator assures, "after he wins the battle. The both of you shall return to the New World."

"I'm not so sure this is a good idea," she warns softly as she turns to Greg, "I don't want to mess anything up."

He reaches over and places a hand on her petite shoulder as her fierce, natural green eyes meet his new, angelic green ones.

"You won't," Greg tells her as he turns to the misty wall behind him, "right?...I mean...am I right?"

"Joe has proven to me that, some endings, I don't even know...but he's also shown us all that love prevails over every obstacle."

"She's not an obstacle...She's his true heart now," she says softly, "and *I'm happy* for him."

"Trust me," Greg tells her, "when the world ended, you were the only one he thought about. He loves you and always will."

"I know he does...but he's in love with *her* now...and I'm fine with that. I'm just so worried I'm going to screw everything up...I only want him to be happy."

They continue watching the coming battle underneath them as Greg closes his eyes and allows his hearing to travel down to the New World. He whispers soft lyrics as they drift through his eternal mind.

"Track two...track two! Haahaaa! Joe got it! He figured it out!" He turns to The Creator behind them.

"He saw the sign...Was he always this good at reading the world?"

"Sometimes, I wasn't even finished laying out my groundwork and he would pick up on it...He was an eager student and he picked it up quickly."

"I bet it was cool seeing the Old World the way he did," Greg says in wonder.

"No," she begins, "it wasn't. It was scary for him...but, he constantly said he knew he was right...and when he was, it terrified him."

They watch as the encounter is only moments away while the sun bathes both armies as they prepare to begin their war. She sighs deeply and turns away from the battle with her nerves setting her on edge. Greg follows her and walks up behind her in time to hear her soft whimpers.

"Hey...don't worry."

"I'm fine," she falsely states. He places his hand on her shoulder and turns her crying eyes to his.

"We know how things work up here...They will one day too...Believe me when I say it...Joe's going to be happy to hold his wife again."

Afterword

The journey is about to take a maddening twist in so many directions and I want to thank all of you who have continued on to this point. The Book of Joe: Ghost of an Angel, is the next installment of the story and promises to be every bit of a thrill as The Fall of The Realm. Follow on as Joe faces new challenges of the heart while desperately trying to save the world...and himself.

I want to thank my wife, family and friends for all of the support they've given me throughout the process of writing this story. I want to thank my cousin, Linda Garcia, for allowing me to honor her husband in writing, my brother from another mother, Robert Garcia, who we all love and miss so dearly. We love you, Cuz. I hope my words do you justice. I want to give a huge thanks to Maria Linnikova, my dear friend(and gorgeous model)who helped bring the character of Sasha to life and portrayed her on the cover. Thank you for giving Sasha an identity. You truly captured her. Another huge thanks to Devin May, who portrays Joes' long, lost wife, also on the covers. I'm humbled by your lovely presence on my work. You and Maria complete the package that is this story. I also want to thank the readers who reached out and contacted me about the first book to tell me how much you enjoyed it. I'm humbled by your words and hope I can live up to all your expectations with this novel. Another big thanks to Jose Martinez for all your continued support and constantly finding ways to contribute. Thanks, Bro. A huge thank you to my sisters, Jo Ann Gallegos Pardo and Leann Tyler for constantly being so supportive. A very huge thanks to Amanda Barrera and Toni Hernandez for being some of my biggest fans. There's still a lot of you I need to mention and will do so in time. If you didn't see your name here, don't worry. I still have a lot of books to write, continuing with the next volume of the story. I hope you enjoy the ride.

Gothic Super Heroes

"Damn, Cuz, you're getting big! You look good, Brother."

It was the beginning of the last encounter with my cousin Robert. We ran into each other in Victoria at the Walmart. We traded stories for a few minutes, it was all I had to spare. I had a shopping cart full of extension cords and various equipment, preparing for a hunt. People were waiting on me. I should of let them wait all day. If only I knew.

"We'd be a crazy team, Cuz, like Gothic Super Heroes."

He was referring to our unique looks, as well as our shared heart. We didn't give a damn if people stared at us for being different. We like black, we like crosses, and we could care less if you had a problem with it. Of course, we would care for you, and help you if you had a problem. Such is our heart, and how we connected so much. Scary and dark on the outside, full of light and love within.

Over a long period of months, Robert and I would exchange messages often. We talked quite a bit about life and the afterlife, the paranormal and everything else under the stars. Almost everything. He never mentioned being sick in any way. He wouldn't burden those he loved.

When we talked about family is when he truly burned with passion. He loved all his kids and his best friend, who he happened to marry. They were the light inside his tall nightmarish frame, a dark polarizing figure, but not nearly as intimidating as the Angel full of life that the exterior served to mask. Only an Angel could love so much.

You always wanted to team up and hang out, Cuz. Gothic Superheroes, fighting crime and scaring the shit out of people all at once. It didn't happen...yet. My final tribute to you will not be these words. Those words are being written on another canvas, a book coming to life. I've wrote you in, alongside myself, for what will be our final encounter. We'll finally be the team we talked about, Gods Gothic Superheroes. I'll honor your spirit, immortalizing it in the written word. I'll never forget you, Cuz. How could I? We're the only two in the family like us. I know your heart. I'll give everyone your message here and now, the one you no doubt want us all to remember:...J. K. L.

We finally had our adventure...Rest in peace, Cuz.

Credits
Author-Joe Gallegos
Cover Models-Maria Linnikova, Devin May
Photography by Dean Kibler